THE
WISH
GRANTER

A Ravenspire Novel

C. J. REDWINE

Balzer + Bray
An *Imprint of* HarperCollins*Publishers*

Also by C. J. Redwine

Defiance

Deception

Deliverance

Outcast: A Defiance Novella

The Shadow Queen

Balzer + Bray is an imprint of HarperCollins Publishers.

Library of Congress Control Number: 2016949521
ISBN 978-0-06-236027-4

Typography by Sarah Nichole Kaufman
17 18 19 20 21   PC/LSCH   10 9 8 7 6 5 4 3 2 1
❖
First Edition

For Isabella, my sweet little girl who underwent heart surgery while I was writing this book. I'm so glad your heart can now keep up with your joyful energy!

And for Melinda, because we both know this book wouldn't have happened without your steadfast encouragement and belief.

ONCE UPON A TIME . . .

HUMANS WERE PATHETICALLY predictable. Always longing for more. Always desperate to get their way. Shamelessly grasping for what remained out of reach, even when it cost them dearly.

He despised them.

Alistair Teague rubbed his fingers absently over the smooth surface of his carved ivory pipe—an unwilling gift from the human who'd betrayed him—and raised his nose to sniff the air. A midnight breeze blew in from the nearby Chrysós Sea, sweeping through the leaves of the olive grove with a faint hiss and carrying with it the sharp scent of a human's terrible desperation.

The magic in Teague's blood responded, surging through his chest, cold and insistent, and he drew in another deep breath as he pocketed the unlit pipe and straightened his immaculately tailored dress coat.

The salty tang of the sea and the wild sweetness of the trees tugged at the part of him that missed living on the fae isle of Llorenyae, but the scent of a human ready to stake everything he had on a chance at gaining the deepest desire of his heart was the true intoxicant.

Teague had lived in exile among the humans in the kingdom of Súndraille for nearly two hundred years, and it never got old.

Their desires. Their greed.

Their weaknesses.

Weaknesses that had kept his business thriving and his pockets full of coin but had failed to silence the fear that one day another human might get the best of him, and this time, instead of being exiled, he might be killed.

He shivered as he turned south toward the scent of the desperate human. The thought of losing the centuries he still had left to live—of sinking into the dark abyss of the unknown where he would no longer be the Wish Granter of legend—haunted him.

It was the gnawing terror of what came after he'd breathed his last that had given him an idea that was going to guarantee no human ever had power over him again.

He moved through the trees, his steps a whisper against the loamy soil, his magic drawn unerringly toward the human in need.

Toward the young man who was the key to Teague's plan.

Passing by the boy's sister, huddled asleep at the base of a tree, dirt smudging her tear-streaked face, he made his way to the edge of the grove where the land fell away and the sea hurled itself against the shore below. The boy stood facing the water, his hands fisted at his sides while he stared at the night sky as if hoping the answer to his troubles could be found among the stars.

Teague smiled, his magic unfurling from his chest to flood his veins. The boy's fear was heavy in the air. His shoulders bowed beneath the weight of it. He was out of options, out of hiding places, and out of allies.

He was exactly where Teague wanted him to be.

"You won't find answers in the stars, Prince Thaddeus," Teague said.

The boy whirled, his dark eyes wild. "Who are you?"

"My name is Alistair Teague"—he leaned closer, his gaze locked on the boy's—"but some call me the Wish Granter."

"The Wish Granter?" The prince's voice shook. "That's a bedtime story to frighten children."

"Oh, I do more than frighten children." Teague smiled coldly as his magic begged for release. "I give people the deepest desires of their hearts. What do you want, dear boy?"

As if he didn't already know that the bastard prince and his twin sister had been exiled from their father's palace upon the birth of the queen's son—her womb miraculously opened after seventeen years of barrenness thanks to the bargain she'd made with Teague. He'd tried to make an additional bargain—a seat as the king's adviser in exchange for getting rid of the bastards so that the queen's son had no competition for the throne—but she'd refused and sent her own hunters after the twins and their servant mother instead.

Maybe she'd suspected that Teague had no plans to remain a mere adviser to the throne. Maybe she'd wanted the satisfaction of killing her son's rivals without magical help. Either way, Teague had been forced to change tactics. A simple word in the ear of one of the queen's hunters had sent the man straight to the family's hiding place with instructions to kill the mother and the sister and bring the prince to Teague for double what the queen was offering as reward. The man had succeeded only in killing the mother before the princess had taken him down with a hay rake, but it didn't matter. The prince understood the terrible danger he and his sister were in. He knew more hunters would track them down. He knew they wouldn't survive without help.

Help Teague was happy to offer.

For a price.

If the queen wouldn't give him access to the throne, then he'd put Súndraille's crown on one who would.

"If you really are the Wish Granter, then prove it." The prince raised his chin in challenge, but hope flickered in his eyes.

Teague's smile widened, and he clapped his hands. The sound reverberated through the ground like thunder. The crash of the waves against the cliff became a deafening roar as the water surged upward toward them. The prince shook as the enormous wave crested the cliff, curving toward the fragile human who trembled beneath it.

"*Athrú*," Alistair said, and, as the water fell, it became showers of golden coins that spilled across the boy's shoulders to pile around his feet. With another clap of his hands, Alistair sent the sea back to its rightful place and bent toward the prince. "Tell me your wish."

The boy swallowed hard as the coins slid across his boots. "I can wish for anything?"

"I can't bring back the dead, and I can't force people to love you, but anything else is well within my powers."

"Can you protect my sister and me from the queen?"

Teague's eyes narrowed. Trust a human to think of something

yment Receipt

thany Library (CMLB)
3 617-7323
w.library.cedarmill.org
ednesday, August 28, 2019 1:36:30 PM

itle   : Legendary : a Caraval novel
eason   : Overdue item
harge   : $2.25

otal charges : $2.25
aid   : $2.25

Account balance: $0.00

Payment Receipt

Bethany Library (CMLB)
503 617-7323
www.library.cedarmill.org
Wednesday, August 28, 2019 1:35:54 PM

Title   : Glass sword
Reason   : Overdue item
Charge   : $0.75

Total charges : $0.75
Paid   : $0.75

Account balance: $0.00

so *small* when the world was laid at his feet. He needed the prince to wish for more, or his plan was never going to work. "Is that really all you want?"

"That's all that matters. We've lost our home. Our mother." The prince's voice caught, and he swallowed hard. "All we have left is each other. The queen's hunters won't stop chasing us until they kill us. I just want to keep my sister, Arianna, safe."

The boy held Teague's gaze, and Teague swore silently. The stupid prince was telling the truth, and that kind of wish wasn't worth the price Teague needed him to pay. It wouldn't put Teague anywhere near the throne, and it wouldn't give him the power he needed to protect himself from the fickle betrayal of humans.

He had to get the prince to wish for more.

"Your sister would be safe if you were the ruler of Súndraille." Teague kept his voice soft and compelling, but anger flared as the prince shook his head.

"My father is the rightful ruler of—"

"Your father betrayed you and sent you into exile." Teague's voice sharpened. "The queen won't rest until your family is dead. And there's only one way to change that. You have to take the throne."

The boy recoiled. "I can't do that. I just want my sister to be safe."

Teague's smile stretched wide and feral. "The hunters are closing in. It's only a matter of time before she's dead, just like your mother. I can keep her safe, but I will only do so if you make the right wish."

The wish that would put Teague one heartbeat from the throne and set his plan into motion.

The prince considered Teague in silence, his eyes haunted. Finally, he said, "And if I don't wish to be the king? If I wish for my sister's safety instead?"

Teague's smile winked out. "Then I will decline to grant your wish, and will leave you to the mercy of the queen's hunters." He leaned forward. "All you have to do is wish to be the king of Súndraille. No one would have power to hurt you or Princess Arianna again."

No one but Teague.

"In the stories, wishes always come with a price." The prince squared his shoulders as if braced for a blow.

"Everything comes with a price." Teague stepped closer. "But I'm all that stands between your sister and death. Is there a price you wouldn't pay for her life?"

The prince closed his eyes as if something pained him, and then said quietly, "No, there isn't."

Magic burned beneath Teague's skin, as cold and absolute as the triumph that filled his chest. Removing a scroll of parchment from his inner pocket, he unfurled the wish contract and quickly pricked Thaddeus's finger with the tip of his dagger. Pressing the boy's bloody finger to the debtor's signature line, he whispered, "Go ahead, dear boy. Make the wish."

ONE

THIS CORSET WAS going to be the death of her.

Arianna Glavan, (suddenly official) princess of Súndraille, leaned against the long wooden table in the center of the busy palace kitchen and threw chunks of butter into her bowl of flour, remembering at the last second not to wipe her fingers on her fancy silk dress.

How any girl with her rib cage cinched in a vise was supposed to dance her feet off, much less eat from the buffet table, was a mystery Ari had no desire to solve. It was bad enough that she was going to have to stand in the receiving line with Thad and greet the nobility who, up until the royal family's unexpected death three weeks ago, had treated her brother with thinly veiled contempt. To smile at them with bones cutting into her waist while her lungs labored to take a full breath was more than she could bear.

Especially when she planned to eat at least one of every item on the buffet table. Stars knew, it was the only thing she was looking forward to tonight.

Quickly cutting the butter into the flour with her fork until a pastry dough formed, Ari passed the bowl to one of the kitchen maids, who'd just finished whipping up a sauce to go with the basted lamb shanks, and turned to her best friend, Cleo. "Help me out of this." She gestured vaguely toward her dress.

Cleo tugged at the blue scarf that held her curly dark hair out of her eyes and returned to pitting the bowl of dates in front of her. "I can't," she whispered. "Thad already knows I lied about you being sick last week for Lord Mitro's banquet, and attending your brother's coronation ball is far more important than that. You have to go. You're supposed to be a real princess now."

"I meant help me out of this corset." Ari motioned her friend toward the enormous walk-in pantry that was nestled on the far side of the kitchen, opposite the hearth ovens whose heat flooded the room, leaving everyone who was working with flushed cheeks and glistening brows. "Please, Cleo. I'll probably die if I have to dance while wearing this."

"Fine. But if you get me in trouble again, you'd better buy me a year's worth of art supplies." With a quick glance to make sure Mama Eleni—head cook, undisputed boss of anyone who set foot inside the kitchens, and Cleo's mother—was distracted by the crepes, Cleo wiped her fingers clean on her apron, ducked past a trio of maids carrying trays of thinly sliced apples baked into cinnamon-dusted florets, and followed Ari into the pantry.

When the door was firmly shut behind them, Ari swept her hair into a messy knot at the top of her head and turned her back to Cleo. "Unbutton me, but make it quick. Mama Eleni will have heart failure if she finds me undressing in her pantry."

"She won't have heart failure." Cleo's fingers flew down the row of tiny pearl buttons along the back of the dress, and golden silk, several shades lighter than Ari's skin, sagged away from her bosom, revealing the bone-ribbed torture device her new lady's maid had sworn Ari couldn't do without. "Mama will make sure *we* have heart failure."

Ari wiggled her shoulders, and the gown's tiny scalloped sleeves edged down her arms. "You have to unbutton it further. The corset is tied at my waist."

"Cleo? Ari? Where are those girls?" Mama Eleni's voice cut through the air.

"No time to unbutton. Give me the scissors," Cleo said as someone answered Mama Eleni. "If Mama finds us and gives me hearth-scrubbing duties again, you're helping me. I don't care if you're supposed to act like a princess now."

"Maybe as princess I can order Mama Eleni not to punish you." Then at least there'd be a benefit for having traded her comfortable anonymity as the bastard daughter the king was happy to forget existed for the trappings of a royal life.

Ari reached for the scissors that hung from a ribbon beside the door and handed them to Cleo, who paused for a second. "This looks expensive. Are you sure you want me to—"

"I can't breathe, my ribs feel like they're touching my spine, and my stomach is being squished so tight, it's leaking out over the top of this thing." Ari turned to let Cleo see the situation.

"Stars help us, you look like you're growing another set of breasts. Here." She whirled Ari around and tugged hard on the laces holding the princess in place.

Ari choked. "Can't. Breathe."

"I can't get any leverage. It's laced too tight. How did Franci get you into this in the first place?" Cleo jerked the laces, and Ari began worrying that the raisin bread she'd eaten earlier was going to make a reappearance.

"There was . . . a lot . . . of pulling and . . . swearing."

"I didn't know Franci swore." With a sharp snip, Cleo cut through the laces. Ari drew a deep breath as the corset loosened.

"She didn't." Ari tugged at the corset until she could pull it over her head. "I did."

Cleo laughed. "You aren't supposed to do that anymore, Ari. You're a proper princess now."

"Hardly." Ari dropped the offending corset to the pantry floor, adjusted the straps of the regular undergarment she'd had the foresight to wear under it, and pulled her gown back into place. The silk was surprisingly comfortable now that she wasn't fighting to breathe. She rubbed it between her fingers as Cleo quickly redid her buttons.

Ari *wasn't* a proper princess. She was a girl who'd slept in the servants' quarters with her mother, who'd been almost entirely ignored by her father, and who'd only been allowed to attend lessons with her brother when the king realized that Thad, his chosen heir despite the boy's bastard status, was serious about refusing to perform to expectations unless his sister received an education too. She'd scrubbed floors, cooked feasts, bargained with merchants, translated ancient texts, and memorized the history of her kingdom—but nothing she'd done had prepared her to be acknowledged as Súndraille's true princess and to have the eyes of the nobility watching her every move.

If the corset was any indication, she was going to be a disaster.

An ache blossomed in her chest, spreading through her veins

with every heartbeat. Tears pricked her eyes, and she blinked rapidly.

"There." Cleo turned Ari to face her, and her dark eyes filled with sympathy. "Don't cry. You'll ruin the mysterious golden-girl look you've achieved with this gown."

Ari gave her a wobbly smile. "I'm the least mysterious girl anyone has ever met."

Cleo smiled. "The nobility doesn't know that. To them, you're the princess the king kept mostly hidden from them all these years. And now you're going out there in this gorgeous gown with your big brown eyes and your Ari attitude, and they'll be enthralled."

"I miss my old life." Ari's voice trembled, and a tear spilled down her cheek as she whispered, "I miss Mama."

Cleo wrapped her in a tight hug. "I do too. She'd be so proud to see you like this. Now get out there before Thad starts looking for you and—"

The pantry door flew open, and Mama Eleni stood glaring at them with Thad peering over her shoulder. "What are you two doing in here?" she asked.

Ari aimed a swift kick at the corset and sent it sliding beneath the shelves of preserved cherries beside her. "Last-minute ward-robe consultation."

"You have flour on your hands," Thad said.

"That happens when you make pastry dough." Ari quickly dusted her palms together and blinked the last of her tears away. Thad needed someone to stand with him tonight, and she was all he had left. It didn't matter that she kept forgetting to behave like a real princess. It only mattered that when he faced his new subjects she was at his side.

"Princesses don't make pastry dough," Thad said, his dark eyes on hers.

Ari snorted. "This one does."

"Princesses also don't snort." Thad's voice was strained, but he didn't sound angry. He hadn't sounded angry since the night they'd fled from the bounty hunter who'd killed their mother and awakened to the news that the entire royal family had taken sick and died, leaving Thad, in the absence of any other blood relation to the king, with an uncontested claim to the throne. Instead, Thad sounded tense. Worried. And grieved in way that even Ari, with her shared heartbreak over their mother's death, couldn't seem to touch.

"I did not approve of her helping," Mama Eleni declared as Ari straightened her shoulders and walked out of the pantry with Cleo at her heels.

"You specifically told me not to use so much butter," Ari said.

"Lies! The king was very clear that you are only to do the things a true princess would do, and I would never disobey him. Even when I am understaffed, and he has yet to fill my requests for more help." Mama Eleni reached out with her rough hands to tug Ari's hair out of its knot and smooth it behind her ears. "Look at our princess in a gown. Ready to dance! Maybe you'll find a nice young man tonight and be swept off your feet. Now, no kissing behind the ballroom pillars, and no—"

"*Stop*, Mama," Cleo said as Thad tugged on his collar as if it were choking him, and the princess's cheeks heated. This wasn't a fairy tale. She was in more danger of losing her footing while dancing than of being swept away by a handsome nobleman's kisses.

Ari's stomach fluttered as Thad took her arm and turned toward the hallway that led to the ballroom. Casting a desperate look at Cleo, she asked, "You'll be there?"

"Of course. I'll be the girl with the tray of fizzy wine." Lowering her voice, she cast a quick glance at Mama Eleni, who'd turned away to supervise the assembling of the fruit platters, and then gave Ari a reassuring smile. "If you need me to accidentally dump wine on anyone, just give me the signal. You'll be fine. This will be over before you know it."

"No dumping wine on anyone." Thad pulled Ari out of the kitchen. "No sending signals of any kind."

"Cleo was kidding." Ari pushed her nervousness and her longing for her mother into a corner of her heart and tried to pretend she felt up to the task ahead as she matched Thad's pace down the white stone hallway that connected the kitchen to the ballroom. Arched windows lined the passage, and long, sheer curtains fluttered in the sea breeze that swept in through the open windows and chased the lingering heat of the summer's day out of the palace. Bells rang from the palace's tower, sonorous and deep, announcing the beginning of the coronation ceremony.

The same bells had announced the royal family's funeral three weeks earlier, and black bunting still fluttered from the tower in honor of their deaths.

"I know Cleo better than that," Thad said. "She may be the accomplice instead of the instigator when it comes to the two of you, but dumping beverages on unsuspecting people is a habit of hers. Remember what happened when we were twelve?"

Ari snorted. "You deserved it."

"Maybe I did." He slowed his pace as the door to the ballroom came into view, spilling a cacophony of voices and music into the hallway. "Ari, I'm serious about you acting like a proper princess tonight. It's important."

"Why? You're the king. You're the one everyone is here to see."

Thad glanced at the doorway and spoke rapidly. "We can't hold a kingdom without alliances, both from within and without. Tonight there will be a host of potential allies in that room. Members of Súndraille's Assembly, royalty and nobility from seven of the ten kingdoms—"

"Including Eldr?"

"Yes." He gave her an exasperated look.

Ari brightened. "I'll be in charge of courting a relationship with the Eldrians. Draconi make excellent allies." And if she was really lucky, maybe she could convince one of the Eldrians to step outside and shift into a dragon for her. She'd always wanted to see a dragon in real life. Maybe the dragon would even give her a ride. Thank the stars she'd had Cleo cut her out of that corset. The night was starting to look interesting.

"I'm being serious, Ari."

"So am I."

He looked at the ceiling and drew a deep breath. "You have to be a proper princess. No snorting in scorn."

"Even if someone richly deserves it. Understood."

"You dance with everyone who asks."

"Wait . . . *everyone*? Even if they're old?"

"Yes. And you make polite conversation. No wayward opinions about how boring you think small talk is."

"It's not just boring, it's entirely useless." Ari twitched her skirt to the side as the first trio of maids from the kitchen, carrying trays of food for the buffet table, hurried past.

Thad lowered his voice. "It's not useless. Think of it as an interview to see if you both understand how to be diplomatic."

Ari sighed. "So to be clear, I'm not supposed to show my true opinion—"

"If your true opinion is something other than polite, diplomatic interest."

"I can't express myself with inarticulate noises—"

"Not under any circumstance."

"I have to dance with everyone who asks, even if my feet hurt or I want to go eat some snacks in peace—"

"And that's another thing. Don't get caught stealing snacks." He gave her a stern look.

Stars, not this again. "It was only the one time. Besides, technically you can't steal something that is offered to you for free."

"It was still difficult to explain to Lady Barlis why the newly acknowledged princess of Súndraille would stuff one of every appetizer in her handbag and try to smuggle them out of the ballroom." Thad held her gaze. "Just be a proper princess tonight. Please. We need allies, and these people need to believe wholeheartedly that you are next in line for the throne in case . . ."

"In case you die? You're seventeen, in perfect health, and nearly always surrounded by guards. Why are you talking like this?" Her voice was sharper than she'd intended, but his words had ignited a spark of fear she didn't know how to extinguish. The loss of her mother was a dark pit of grief inside her. She couldn't bear the thought of losing her brother too.

He cast a quick glance at the open doorway fifty paces to their left and leaned closer to her. "There are only two of us left, and it's my job to make sure Súndraille stays safely in the hands of a competent leader. Someone the people will follow. When—*if* I'm not here to rule, then you have to be ready to take my place. That means you need powerful allies. And you don't get powerful allies unless people view you as a real princess. A true heir to the throne."

There was an edge of desperation in his voice, and she studied him for a moment. He'd lost weight in the three weeks since the rest of their family had died. She'd baked obsessively—it was the only thing that kept her grounded in the chaotic upheaval of her new life—but even Thad's favorite dessert hadn't tempted his appetite. His formal coat hung a little loose across his shoulders, and his high cheekbones were sharp slashes in a face that otherwise looked remarkably like her own—golden-brown skin, full lips, and the wide dark eyes they'd both inherited from their father.

Whatever burden of grief Ari was bearing, his was twice as heavy. The weight of the kingdom had fallen across his shoulders, and if he needed her to pretend she was comfortable acting like nobility, she could do it. They only had each other now.

Before that thought could worm its way into her heart and send another piercing ache through her veins, she forced herself to give him a little smile. "Fine. No scorning dumb ideas, no turning down dances with potential allies, no complaining about small talk, and no sneaking a Draconi into the garden for a little midnight dragon ride. You really know how to take the fun out of things."

Thad laughed—a quick burst of merriment that seemed to surprise him as much as it did her. Tucking her arm in his, he said quietly, "Thank you. You and me against the world, right?"

She pressed her free hand against her fluttering stomach and took a deep breath. "Always."

TWO

THE CORONATION SPED by in a blur of droning words from the head of the noblemen's Assembly, the unfamiliar weight of the crown on Ari's head, and the stomach-churning knowledge that the eyes of Súndraillian nobility and the invited representatives from seven other kingdoms were focused on her. It was a relief when the ceremony concluded and the dancing began. At least now she had to deal only with the scrutiny of one dance partner at a time.

Also there were the delights of the buffet table to consider.

Three hours later, Ari was busy wishing a pox upon the ballroom and everyone in it. She'd danced with every person who asked (oh joy). She'd made small talk until she was in danger of losing her mind (more joy). And she hadn't put a single snack into the beaded bag that hung from her wrist (one giant stinking heap of joy).

She'd been the most proper princess who ever set foot in a ballroom, if you didn't count the times she'd accidentally stepped on the hem of her gown and been forced to clutch her dance partner to keep from tripping. Three hours of behaving like royalty and all she had to show for it was a headache and a list of dance partners who'd wanted to talk only about Thad and the sudden death of the royal family as if she might spill a tidbit of gossip for them to devour.

Lord Hamish from Ravenspire had speculated that someone from the Assembly had poisoned the king, queen, and baby prince in the hope that Thad would make a more malleable ruler. Sir Jabin of Balavata had talked for *ages* about the economic ramifications of having a seventeen-year-old king whom half of Súndraille seemed to distrust. Lord Kadar of Akram had winked and assured her that many a throne had been taken with bloodshed and there was no shame in it.

But none of the foreign guests was as bad as her partners from Súndraille itself. Each wore a black cravat in honor of the mourning period that would continue for another three weeks. And each asked razor-sharp questions that both grieved and infuriated Ari. She had her answers memorized by now.

Yes, their father had asked them to leave the palace after the baby prince's birth, but he hadn't done so out of anger, and he'd given them a generous stipend to help them build a new life somewhere else.

No, she hadn't realized the queen had placed a bounty on their heads and ordered their deaths so that there would be no competition for the throne.

No, Thad hadn't killed the royal family. They'd all died in their sleep from some sort of blood disease while Thad and Ari had been several cities to the west of Súndraille's capital, Kosim Thalas.

Yes, Thad was capable of ruling. He'd been raised to assume the crown, and she'd yet to meet anyone who took the responsibility of his position more seriously than her brother.

Her current partner, Lord Pachis, hailed from the eastern coast of Súndraille and was old enough to be her father. Her cheeks ached from smiling up at him while he lectured her on the rigors of ruling a kingdom where crime was growing and the economy was shaky. When he launched into speculation that Thad might not be up to the task, Ari stopped listening.

Over his shoulder, she caught sight of the beautiful queen of Ravenspire, who was dancing gracefully with her new husband, the king of Eldr, despite the length of her bloodred gown.

Beautiful, graceful, *and* married to a dragon. Sometimes life was so unfair.

Lord Pachis paused and looked at her expectantly. Ari cursed silently and ordered herself to remember what he'd just said. Asked. Whatever.

She came up blank. She'd been too busy being jealous of Queen Lorelai to pay attention to anything else.

He frowned. "I meant no offense, Your Highness, but it *is* a pressing question on the minds of many in the noble class."

"What question?"

His frown deepened. "The issue of parentage and bloodlines. How do you and the king propose to deal with those who say a bastard shouldn't be given the throne? Especially when the royal family died under mysterious circumstances and the new ruler is of such a tender age—"

Ari barely managed to keep a pleasant expression on her face as she said, "I propose that those who have an issue with the coronation take it up with their representatives from the Assembly. Thad was declared the lawful king because he and I are the only remaining blood relatives of King Waldemar, and Thad is the elder twin. The royal family's death was determined to be caused by a blood-borne disease. Unless you're suggesting that the entire body of the Assembly is somehow involved in covering up murder with the intention of putting a seventeen-year-old on the throne, I would like to stop having this discussion."

He blinked and drew back.

Her stomach dropped, and her cheeks heated. She'd been too blunt. Too outspoken for a princess who'd only been invited to the coronation because Thad had refused to cooperate with what was expected of him unless she was given equal consideration. She'd offended Lord Pachis, and she couldn't afford to give anyone more reason to distrust Thad and speak ill of him behind his back.

"Forgive me, my lord. I am not myself." She tried a wide smile, though it felt like her lips were stretched too thin across her teeth. "I'm afraid that after three hours of dancing, I've become quite famished and am feeling a bit light-headed."

He glanced once at the generous curve of her hips and then stepped back and bowed. "I can see that you are not accustomed to going a few hours without food. Allow me to procure some refreshment, Your Highness. Perhaps a bit of fruit and some lemon water."

Ari caught herself midsnort and tried to swallow the noise. The terrible, half-choked gurgle that caught in the back of her throat sounded for all the world as if she intended to vomit.

Lord Pachis's eyes widened. "Are you quite well?"

"Thank you for the dance, my lord." Ari turned on her heel and hurried away before the duke could insult her again or renew his offer. Who danced their feet off for three hours and then pretended to be refreshed by a bit of fruit?

Not this girl. She needed meat and at least three pastries. Lord Pachis could think what he wanted.

Ducking away from the dance floor, she limped to the massive tables set up along the northern wall, grabbed a plate, and filled it. Popping a stuffed date in her mouth, she turned and scanned the ballroom, skimming over the busy dance floor and the clusters of people conversing over full plates of food until she met Cleo's gaze. Her friend was standing near a clump of ladies in bright, frothy gowns, her face expressionless as she held a tray half full of wineglasses.

Just past Cleo, another middle-aged nobleman caught Ari's gaze and began moving toward her. Panic tied her stomach in knots at the thought of having to endure one more round of diplomatically answering another set of questions while dancing on the packed ballroom floor. The room was too warm, too close, and the clash of voices and music surrounding her felt like it was closing in.

Ari met Cleo's eyes once more, glanced around the room, and then jerked her chin toward an open door that led out to the palace gardens. Cleo instantly began weaving her way through the guests as Ari hurried along the edges of the room and out the door.

The moment she was outside, she drew in a shaky breath and willed herself to be calm. Lanterns with tiny bells hanging beneath them swayed from the branches of the trees closest to the ballroom. A path of crushed stone cut through lush flowering bushes, whose waxy blooms filled the night air with a honey-sweet scent. The distant thunder of waves against the palace cliffs and the chirrup of crickets in the trees eased the panic that had driven her from the ballroom.

A breeze drifted through the garden and cooled the heat from her skin. She slipped her shoes off to let her feet sink into the luxurious carpet of grass that edged the bushes. Taking a bite of a crepe stuffed with beef and sweet cheese, she tipped her head back to gaze at the stars that dusted the heavens like silver sugar.

Maybe somewhere in the night sky, her mother was looking down on her. Maybe she already knew the kind of trouble Thad was facing with his subjects. The kind of trouble Ari was having adjusting to being a real princess.

Ari closed her eyes and remembered her mother's soft voice. Telling Ari not to scrub the floors because she'd chap her hands. Consoling Ari when the king refused to acknowledge her by weaving stories of poverty-stricken princesses who did heroic deeds and saved kingdoms. Urging her to take care of her brother, who lived beneath the weight of his father's expectations without the benefit of his love.

"I'm trying," she whispered, hoping her words would somehow find their way to her mother's ears.

"What are we doing out here?" Cleo asked as she came to stand beside Ari, the tray of wineglasses still in her hands.

"Escaping." Ari opened her eyes.

"If I escape for too long, Mama will hear of it," Cleo warned, though she made no move to go back inside.

"I'll cover for you. I can't go back inside yet. If I have to suffer through one more conversation about how Father and his family died or why Thad is too young to take the throne, I'm going to forget how to be diplomatic." Ari took another bite of crepe.

"I doubt Thad would like that very much," Cleo said as she set her tray of wine down and stretched her back.

"What wouldn't I like?" Thad had left the ballroom and joined them. His black cravat was still perfectly tied, his dress coat impeccably smooth, but he looked haggard. As though a bone-deep weariness was consuming him. Maybe this was what being king did to a person.

Or maybe, like Ari, his night had been filled with people speculating about his ability to rule Súndraille and the possibility that the royal family's death had been a convenient way for Thad to come into power.

"I was saying that you wouldn't like Ari to forget how to be diplomatic, Your Highness." Cleo lifted her hair from the back of her neck and turned toward the sea breeze.

"You don't have to start calling me Your Highness simply because I'm king now." Thad pressed his fingers to his forehead as if he had a headache and then looked at his sister. "And we really do need you to keep being diplomatic, though I'd love a front-row seat to you putting a few people in their place."

"Point me in the right direction," Ari said, and was rewarded with a weary smile.

"Things will settle." Thad sounded cautious. "Once people see that I can work with the Assembly and that I can take a strong stand against the violence and crime that seem to be spreading out of the slums and into the city proper."

"I'm afraid I can't let you do that." A short, immaculately dressed man with pale skin, auburn hair, and unnerving golden eyes stepped out of the garden and into the light of the lanterns.

Thad sucked in a sharp breath. His voice shook as he asked, "What are you doing here? You weren't invited."

The man smiled, slow and cruel, and Ari shivered.

In a voice like polished marble, he said, "Come now, dear boy. Did you really think something as inconsequential as a guest list could keep me away?"

Ari stared at the man, and then looked up at Thad's face.

Her brother's lips were set in a thin line, and anger—for the first time since the night their mother had been killed by the queen's hunter—lit his eyes. Without looking at her, he said quietly, "Ari, Cleo, go back to the ballroom."

"I don't think I should." Ari moved to stand by Thad while Cleo took a tiny step back toward the ballroom door, torn between obeying her king and staying with her best friend.

The princess faced the man in front of them. He barely came up to her shoulder, and his clothing suggested nobility of some kind; but the cold, calculating look in his eyes reminded Ari of the man she'd once seen the palace guards haul into her father's throne room on charges of attempting to assassinate the queen.

"*Go.*" Thad spoke through gritted teeth.

Right. Because ordering his sister to do something she didn't want to do had worked *so well* for him in the past. Besides, she was done with Thad's subjects questioning his abilities and his right to the throne.

She met the man's gaze. "You aren't on the guest list. Leave at once, or I will call the guards to deal with you."

The man cocked his head to stare at her, and Ari clenched her fists to control the tremble that shuddered through her. She felt like a helpless mouse pinned beneath the claws of a ravenous cat.

"She's of no interest to you," Thad said sharply. "And you have no reason to be here."

"Ah, but I do like to check in on my debtors." The man turned his gaze back to Thad. "Especially when he owes me so much."

Thad was the king of Súndraille. He didn't owe anyone, and Ari had had enough of this man with his cold eyes and his creepy smile.

"Guards!" she called sharply.

Two uniformed guards who were standing just inside the ballroom door pivoted toward her voice. The man in front of her snapped his fingers, and the door separating the garden from the ballroom slammed shut. The guards pounded on the door, but it refused to open.

"What have you done?" She meant her words to sound commanding, but there was a tremor in her voice. Cleo mumbled prayers to the stars and hugged her arms across her body as Thad stepped in front of the girls, his broad shoulders nearly eclipsing Ari's view of the man.

What kind of man could shut a door with the snap of his fingers? He couldn't be from Morcant, because only the females of royal lineage had magic there. He couldn't be from Vallé de Lumé, because it was a sorceress, not a wizard, who controlled the land.

That meant he had to be fae.

And that meant Thad was in way over his head.

Thad took another step toward the man. "Open that door and leave us be. We've settled our terms. I owe you nothing for the next nine years and eleven months."

Ari stared at Thad, her mind racing to make sense of his words and coming up empty. The panic she'd felt in the ballroom earlier snaked through her veins again, sending her heart racing. What was going on?

The man smiled. "Didn't read the fine print, did you?"

Thad froze.

"Why do you think I wanted a king in my debt?"

Thad glanced at Ari, his gaze haunted.

The man closed the distance between them. "The fine print, my boy, says that you are to do nothing to impede my business in your kingdom. You cannot interfere with my activities. This is simply a courtesy visit to let you know that there will be a little trouble at the docks tomorrow morning, and that you are to order the city guard to stand down. In fact, stand them down in the merchant district as well. Not just tomorrow, but for the foreseeable future."

Ari glared at the man while her heart pounded. She didn't know what kind of business he had in Súndraille, but if he didn't want Thad's interference, it was likely he was part of the growing wave of crime and violence Thad's new subjects desperately wanted him to end.

"And if I don't?" Thad's voice was full of the kind of bravado he used when he knew he'd been beaten but was refusing to admit it.

The man's smile winked out. "Then you will pay your debt in full. Immediately. And nobody survives that."

Thad's shoulders bowed, and the man snapped his fingers again. The door flew open, and the guards tumbled out, but the man turned and disappeared into the darkness.

"We should go back inside," Thad said quietly. "People must be looking for us by now."

Ari dug in her heels and pulled him to a stop when he tried to move toward the ballroom. "That's it? No explanation for the creepy little man with the debt he's holding over your head?"

"No."

"Oh, I don't think so." She glared at him. "Did you see what he did with the door? He has to be fae. Why are you mixed up with someone who can do magic? And what did he mean when he said that when you pay your debt in full, you won't survive?"

Thad met her gaze, his expression fierce. "I was backed into a corner, and I had to make a bargain with him. It's my problem, and I'll deal with it. But *you* are going to stay out of this, and whatever you do, you are going to stay far away from Alistair Teague. Promise me."

"Fine. I'll stay away from Teague." It was an easy promise to make. Teague made her feel like she was dangling by a thread over a deep, black hole. But if Thad thought she was going to stay out of this and ignore the threat to her brother, he was a fool. It was the two of them against the world; and the last thing Thad needed to deal with on top of questions about the legitimacy of his kingship and an economy shaken by a spike in crime was a fae threatening him over a bargain.

She couldn't stop the nobility from questioning Thad's ability to rule. She couldn't stop criminals from targeting Súndraille's cities. But she could figure out what kind of fae creature Alistair Teague was, and maybe that would help Thad figure out how to get free of him.

As a group of Draconi who appeared to be close friends of the Eldrian king spilled out into the garden, laughing and dancing, Thad straightened his shoulders, nodded to Cleo as she snatched up her tray of fizzy wine, and then took Ari's arm and gently steered her toward the ballroom.

Ari stayed by his side, smiling until her face felt like it would never resume a normal expression and gritting her teeth at the barbed questions and insinuations many Súndraillians tossed at her brother.

Thad was going to have to make time in his busy schedule to have a heart-to-heart with her about whatever bargain he'd struck. In the meantime, she'd start asking questions about Teague. If a fae creature with magical power was in Súndraille, someone would've heard of it.

If Teague thought he was going to use the bargain he'd made with Thad to take her brother's life, he was going to have to go through Ari first.

THREE

ALISTAIR TEAGUE SURVEYED the docks with cold satisfaction.

Deckhands hauled boxes of freight up the long ramps that led from the dock to the ships rocking gently in their berths along the inner harbor. Merchants scurried around piles of goods, issuing orders, while the ships' captains called out commands to check rigging and move lively. At the mouth of the dock, where the weather-beaten planks met the crushed seashell road that edged Kosim Thalas, the harbormaster stood with a schedule of departures and arrivals in his hands.

Not a single city guard in sight.

The sun crept higher, tearing through the early morning mist with pale fingers. Flocks of seabirds cawed as they swooped over the golden waves of the Chrysós, diving to snatch fish with their sharp beaks. Alistair allowed himself a small smile. Like a seabird, he was prepared to descend on his prey without warning.

Without mercy.

And now he no longer had to account for interference from the crown. With the new king of Súndraille firmly in Alistair's debt, he could conduct his business out in the open.

His would be the name whispered in secret by a kingdom too terrified to speak of him in broad daylight. He would be the cautionary tale parents told their children at night and the clarion call of hope for those desperate enough to bargain their lives away. He would do as he pleased with relentless force; and by the time he made a move for the throne, there would be no one left to dream of opposing him.

Once upon a time, he'd served a crown with no desire to wear one himself.

But that was before the betrayal. Before his exile.

Before the fear of another human uncovering his secrets turned his dreams into nightmares.

When he was in power, when the kingdom was cowering at his feet, he would force every subject to sign a contract in blood. A promise that if they ever asked questions about him—his present or his past—they would immediately pay for it with their lives. He'd finally be untouchable.

He glanced around once more, meeting the eyes of Daan, his debt collector, and the handful of enforcers who were scattered about, blending into the busy rhythm of the dock until the time came to spring the trap.

A flurry of activity at the mouth of the dock caught his attention, and Teague's eyes narrowed as a woman carrying a small child on one hip and a worn satchel over her shoulder shoved a piece of parchment into the harbormaster's hands and gathered her other four children close while he read the document.

A shipping order. Confirmation that she'd scraped together her meager coin and purchased a berth for herself and her miserable brood aboard a large Eldrian cargo ship bound for the remote port of Ailvansky.

She'd been careful. Secretive. She'd trusted no one.

It didn't matter. Teague had spies everywhere, including the dock. Cold rage filled him as she took the parchment from the harbormaster with shaking hands and urged her children onto the dock and toward the ramps.

Humans. Greedy, easily manipulated, and unfaithful to their last breath.

He eased behind a merchant who was loudly ticking off the items on his cargo list and waited while she rushed her children past his hiding place. She was muttering desperate pleas for them to move faster. Be quieter. *Hurry.*

As the last child, a boy who looked maybe ten years old, moved past Teague, pushing a younger girl ahead of him and glancing around the dock with worried eyes, Teague left his place of concealment. Lunging forward, he grabbed the boy's arm and spun him around.

The boy's eyes grew big, and he pulled back, but he was no match for Teague.

"Oh, Sela, I believe you're forgetting someone," he called, his voice cutting through the dockside clamor and bringing the woman to a halt.

She spun, and terror flooded her face at the sight of her son caught in Teague's grip.

"Please." She dropped the satchel and raised a trembling hand toward Teague as her other children clustered around her, their eyes fixed on their older brother. "Not my boy. Not him."

Teague stepped toward her, dragging the boy with him. "It wouldn't have been your boy at all, Sela, but you tried to cheat me."

"I didn't . . . I wasn't . . ." Her voice faded, and tears gathered in her eyes. "Please."

"Your collection day isn't for another three months, but trying to break your contract with me makes the debt come due immediately." Teague reached a free hand into his vest pocket and pulled out a glittering diamond flask with a gold stopper.

"No!" Her voice broke.

He shoved the boy toward his siblings and unstoppered the flask as Sela pulled her son close. "Nine years, eight months, three weeks, and two days ago, you made a wish that I would save your dying husband. You promised me your soul if I would take away the disease that was killing him." His eyes snapped to hers, and rage burned in his chest while his magic spread through his veins like ice. "I kept my end of our bargain. And how do you repay me? You try to run!"

"Because my children need me!"

"They have your husband." His gaze was pitiless.

"He died. Two years ago this fall. Hit by a horse and carriage while we were at the market." She threw the words at him, desperate and fierce. "When I made the deal, I thought he would be alive to take care of any children we might have. To provide for them. But he *died*."

"That's what people do," Teague said viciously. "And that changes nothing about our arrangement."

"But my children! They'll be left with no one to take care

of them." Tears streamed down her cheeks and fell to the dusty wooden planks beneath her feet.

Teague smiled. "They'll have me. At least until I sell them to a slaver in Balavata." He met the gaze of his collector and motioned sharply for his men to move in.

Sela looked wildly around the dock as the enforcers stepped forward. "Run!" she yelled to her children, but it was too late. Teague's men had them surrounded.

"Please, I'm begging you!" She fell to her knees and clutched for her children as the enforcers dragged them away from her.

"Beg all you want." His voice was soft as he stepped toward her. "Plead. Grovel. Promise me anything if only I won't take what you already agreed to give."

She reached for his boots with trembling hands. "Not my children. They aren't part of this. Please. Take me, but spare them."

He crouched beside her.

"And if I do that, what will my other debtors think? Why would they not also try to defy me?"

She choked out her children's names between sobs.

Teague raised his voice to be heard above her cries. "*Ghlacadh anam de* Sela Argyris *agus mianach a dhéanamh.*"

Strands of brilliant white streaked through her veins to gather in her chest. Somewhere behind him, a child wailed. Sela's eyes rolled back in her head, and Teague stood, holding out the flask as the light slowly separated from her body and hung in the air before gently winding its way into the mouth of the bottle. Sela's body hit the dock with a thud, and her children screamed.

Teague pushed the stopper back into the flask and returned it to his pocket.

Another soul captured and ready to join the hundreds that had come before it and be turned into apodrasi, a new drug of his own creation that was lining Teague's pocket with enough coin to make a lesser man happy.

Teague, though, wasn't happy. Coin didn't protect you. It didn't save you from your secrets.

Only absolute power did that.

He looked around the docks, smiling grimly at the shocked, terrified faces of those who were close enough to have seen Sela's soul exit her body.

Still not a single city guard in sight.

Power was telling the king to leave the docks unprotected and having him obey.

Power was knowing when his debtor was going to betray him.

Power was the fear he saw on the faces of those who dared to meet his gaze as he stood over Sela's body.

Leaving her corpse crumpled on the dock, Teague turned on his heel and walked away.

FOUR

IT HAD BEEN two days since the coronation ball, and Ari still hadn't found a minute alone with Thad. Instead, she'd been trapped into sessions with the palace seamstress, who was measuring her for her fall wardrobe, afternoon tea with the nobility who'd stayed on at the palace for a few days after the ball before returning to their distant cities, and long discussions with the palace steward about managing the things usually delegated to the queen.

She didn't know which was worse—the nonstop burden of princessy expectations that were (almost) ruining her appetite or the bright flare of panic that stole her breath and sent her pulse thundering in her ears when she thought about Thad being indebted to the strange man who'd crashed the ball. If she could just do something about it—get to the bottom of whatever was going on and make a plan to deal with it—she'd feel better.

Instead, on the morning of the third day after the ball, Ari found herself seated beside Thad on the royal platform in the palace's Assembly hall, surrounded by a crowd of royally appointed nobles whose job was to bring their city's needs to the king.

Judging by the lengthy list of discussion topics the Assembly had submitted to Thad, there was a lot that needed his attention.

Ari could think of something that needed his attention too, and since this was the first time her brother had slowed down long enough to be in the same room with her for more than a few seconds, she was going to make the most of it.

As pages drew the sea-gold curtains to let the morning sun in, and members of the Assembly broke away from their clustered conversational groups and headed toward their assigned seats at the enormous U-shaped table that lined the room, Ari leaned toward Thad.

"Put me on your schedule."

A frown puckered his brow, and he looked up from the list of discussion topics. "What for?"

Oh please. As if he didn't know.

"For the talk we need to have." She gave him a look that dared him to pretend ignorance.

He pretended anyway.

"What talk?"

"Don't play dumb." She lowered her voice when she realized that Ajax, the head of Thad's personal security detail, was standing in earshot just to her brother's right. "You know exactly what I'm talking about."

"We don't need to have a talk right now." He looked down at the topics on the parchment in front of him. "We have bigger problems."

"Bigger problems than your debt to a fae who threatened to kill you if you don't do what he says?" Her voice was bright panic laced with anger. "I don't think so."

"Keep your voice down," he whispered as he pushed the Assembly's list toward her. "Look at these."

She glanced at the parchment and then looked back at him. "What does that have to do with anything?"

"Did you read any of it?"

"In the half a second I took to look at the thing my brother is trying to use to distract me from the discussion we need to have? No." She glared at him.

He took a deep breath as if reaching for patience and said quietly, "All right. We'll have that talk. Soon. But right now I need you to see that our kingdom has bigger problems it needs us to deal with." He pointed to an item on the list. "The western cities are being raided by bands of what they assume are refugees fleeing the unrest in Akram. They need extra protection."

She followed his finger as he tapped another item. "Export sales of food remain strong, but our own people are buying less of everything our merchants offer. That means either their coin is going to something else, or they lack confidence in me as a leader and feel the need to save their coin in case I send our economy into ruin."

"Or the nobility who distrust how the royal family died and who don't think you're old enough to make a good king are fabricating these reports in order to spread rumors of instability that doesn't exist," Ari said.

He gave her an approving nod. "Right. So our job today is to listen carefully, to take action where we're sure it's needed, and to send reliable people to research the reports we can't verify. And we have to do it all without giving anyone in the Assembly more cause to worry about our leadership."

She drew back as the last of the crowd found their seats and whispered, "*Your* leadership. I'm just a reluctantly official princess who'd rather be baking."

The head of the Assembly stood and called for the room to come to order as Thad leaned close and said, "They need to see you as capable of ruling too. Just in case. We're in this together, right?"

She nodded, though the slash of panic in her chest was stealing her breath.

Just in case.

Just in case Thad got on Alistair Teague's bad side.

Just in case he didn't survive.

The head of the Assembly gave Thad the floor, and he began moving down the items on the list, calling on each representative to explain in detail what his or her city needed from the king. Roads to the south had been nearly washed away by spring storms and needed to be repaired. Merchants from the north were concerned that the prices of merchants in the south—with their easy access to ships and tourists—were fixed low enough to drive the northern merchants out of business. Slums were growing. Jobs were declining. And everyone agreed that the introduction of apodrasi some months ago was to blame for much of the poverty and crime that was spreading across Súndraille.

Ari wondered how long it would be before the king's decision to pull the city guard from Kosim Thalas's merchant district made its way onto an Assembly discussion list. It had only been three days since Teague's demand and already representatives from the capital were murmuring about a spike in violent crime.

The meeting went on for hours. Ari tried to pay attention. She nodded at the appropriate times and jotted notes on blank parchment, but between speakers, her thoughts returned to Thad's debt to Teague and the danger he posed to her brother.

All she really knew was that Teague was fae, Thad had made a deal with him, Teague had threatened Thad's life if the king didn't order the city guard to stand down in Kosim Thalas, and Thad had been scared enough to obey.

And if Thad—responsible, always-serious-about-his-royal-duties Thad—was scared enough to leave parts of Kosim Thalas unprotected, then she was scared too.

She needed a plan. She needed to *do* something to keep her brother safe, but until she learned the truth of his dealings with Teague, she didn't have much to go on.

As the Assembly broke for lunch and the representatives moved toward a side room where a buffet had been laid out for them, Ari turned toward Thad, a question already on her lips, only to find that he was already striding away, his head bent toward Ajax's as they discussed something.

She hoped he was discussing how to keep a creepy fae from coming onto the palace grounds and not just running away from the conversation he needed to have with his sister. This was beginning to feel like that time he'd broken her vintage vase from Loch Talam—a gift from the visiting king who didn't realize Ari wasn't usually treated like royalty—and then tried his best to avoid her for over a week before finally confessing to the deed.

Ari turned and surveyed the room as it slowly emptied. If Thad wouldn't give her information, then she'd just have to find someone who would. Maybe she couldn't get the details of Thad's connection to Teague, but she could figure out how to deal with the fae. She scanned the representatives who still lingered until she caught sight of a tall woman with a sturdy build, graying black hair, and dimples in her cheeks. Lady Tassi was one of two representatives from the city of Efesnero, which had the port closest to the fae isle of Llorenyae. If anyone in the crowd knew how to keep a dangerous fae from entering the palace grounds, she would.

"Lady Tassi," she called as she stood and made her way off the platform.

"Yes, Your Highness?" Lady Tassi's voice was soft and soothing, and for a bittersweet moment it reminded Ari of her mother's.

Quickly swallowing against the sudden ache in her throat, Ari approached the noblewoman. "I wondered if you might eat lunch with me today."

Lady Tassi covered the quick flash of surprise on her face with a formal curtsy. "Of course, Your Highness. Shall I get us both a plate of food? The buffet room is a bit crowded, and I'm afraid some of the Assembly members are more interested in questioning you on recent events than in letting you have the time to eat."

Ari gave the buffet room a side glance and conceded the point. She'd never work her way through that crowd in time to question Lady Tassi about the fae. "Thank you. I'll wait for you on the platform. You can use Thad's chair."

If Lady Tassi thought it was strange to be offered the king's seat at the royal table, she gave no indication. Instead, she disappeared into the buffet room and returned within moments bearing two full plates of food.

Ari smiled as Lady Tassi set the plates down and sat. "It looks delicious. Thank you."

"May I ask why you honored me with this invitation?" The noblewoman raised a bit of braised beef to her lips.

Ari searched her face, but there was no animosity. No calculation. Just curiosity, a trait Ari could appreciate. Lady Tassi had impressed Ari as someone who'd remained above the speculation and unrest regarding Thad's kingship. She hoped that meant the woman would be willing to speak frankly with Ari. Deciding honesty would be the quickest way to the answers she sought, she said, "I invited you to lunch with me because I have questions about the fae, and I figured since you live close to them, you might have answers."

Lady Tassi dabbed her lips with a napkin. "We live close enough to have a few dealings with them each year. Is the king interested in developing a trade treaty with the fae courts in Llorenyae?"

"Possibly," Ari said as she brushed extra sugar off a persimmon cookie. "Our concern is the fae who can do dangerous magic. Not little magic, like the stories of the fae who can grow flowers or change the weather, but powerful fae. The creatures in children's myths, such as the Wish Granter or the Warrior of the Winter Court."

"All of them can do magic." Lady Tassi reached for her glass of cherry cider. "But of course the older ones or those born with special abilities have much more power."

How much power did Teague have? Could every fae shut a door with the snap of its fingers?

"Well, then how do we keep the palace safe in case a member of the fae courts decides to use magic against us?" Ari leaned forward, eager for the answer, but when Lady Tassi gave her a quizzical look, the princess grabbed a skewer of honey-roasted peaches as if that had been her goal all along.

Until she figured out the exact details of Thad's dealings with Teague, she couldn't let anyone suspect the king was tangled up with one of the fae. Especially if someone connected the rise in crime in Kosim Thalas to the king's strange reluctance to send the city guard to patrol its busiest streets.

"For safety measures, we put iron fences around our estates and keep iron weapons handy, and we keep some bloodflower poison handy. The combination is enough to weaken or even kill most fae, though of course we aren't trying to kill anyone we're in business with." Lady Tassi nodded a greeting at a passing nobleman while Ari's mind latched onto these new pieces of information.

She couldn't put up an iron fence without attracting attention, both from Teague and from the citizens of Kosim Thalas, and she didn't want to advertise the fact that they were trying to keep out a member of the fae. Iron weapons and bloodflower poison, however, she could manage.

Thad was hiring a slew of new employees that afternoon to replace those who'd decided they no longer wished to work at the palace in the service of their new king. Most of the staff who'd left had been old enough to retire anyway, and Thad had settled a decent pension on all of them, no questions asked.

Once Thad had a new weapons master in charge of maintaining the armory, she could gather some iron scraps from the smithy and commission some weapons. And she could make some sort of excuse for going to the merchant district in Kosim Thalas without Mama Eleni—that woman's watchful eye would make asking her favorite spice merchant about poison absolutely impossible unless Ari wanted to explain herself to the woman who now saw her as a girl in need of a mother's guiding hand.

As Lady Tassi and the other representatives returned to their seats and Thad entered the room to finish the last nine items on the docket, Ari turned to a fresh sheet of parchment and began making a short list of things she needed.

Iron.

Bloodflower poison.

An excuse that Mama Eleni would accept.

Maybe a book or two on the fae so that she could learn more about how they worked and how to deal with them.

And, of course, a new weapons master capable of turning her iron into dangerous weapons.

Ari stared at her list, thoughts racing, and let the rest of the discussion slip past her. She had a starting point now. And by the time she cornered Thad and made him tell her the whole truth, she'd be well on her way to being able to protect her brother.

FIVE

THE SUN WAS just beginning to set when Sebastian Vaughn finished delivering freight to the shipyard for the merchant who'd hired him for the day. The thick, metal-studded cudgel he'd strapped inside his coat rested heavily against his chest, a reassuring weight as he faced east and began his weekly trip back to the home he'd left behind once his father had been transferred to the kingdom of Balavata and his brother Parrish's body had been laid to rest.

When Sebastian reached the city proper with its narrow streets and its canals snaking through the busiest sections, he stopped at the first dock he saw and paid a ferryman to row him to the market closest to east Kosim Thalas. It was an indulgence he rarely wasted coin on, but it was nearly dark, and he didn't want to be on the streets any longer than he had to.

Besides, he had some thinking to do.

He leaned against the side of the faded green boat, relishing the quiet swoosh of the water as the ferryman's oars dipped and pulled, and considered what he'd learned at the waterfront. The new king was hiring—some said as many as forty-nine positions were available at the palace—and one of those positions was that of weapons master. Sebastian didn't have much in the way of credentials. He'd been working any job he could find, but he'd had no steady employer. No one would hire a boy from east Kosim Thalas on a permanent basis.

But with quite a few members of the palace staff refusing to work for the new king out of loyalty to the recently deceased royal family, and with plenty of workers uneasy about casting their lot in with the king when rumor had it many in the upper class didn't support him, Sebastian figured maybe the king was desperate enough to overlook Sebastian's upbringing and youth.

Maybe desperate enough to not ask too many questions about why Sebastian, an eighteen-year-old boy living in poverty and filth, knew how to use every weapon in the king's arsenal and then some.

It was the best hope Sebastian had of finding steady income and a roof over his head.

The best hope he had of finally saving up enough to leave Kosim Thalas, escape his father's reach, and never look back.

The ferryman slowed his rowing as they bumped their way past a handful of boats leaving the dock the led into the eastern market. Once they'd docked, Sebastian tipped the ferryman and leaped from the boat.

Moments later, he'd picked up his weekly food order from a local merchant and was facing the entrance to east Kosim Thalas, his stomach sour at the thought of what lay ahead.

His mother didn't deserve his weekly visits to fill her cupboards with food and to make sure she wasn't lying passed out or dead, unnoticed and unmissed by anyone. He knew that. She deserved the anger and hatred she seemed to constantly expect from him, no matter how many times he refused to give it. But Sebastian wasn't doing this because he felt obligated to the woman who'd given birth to him and his brother and then ignored their screams while her husband whipped them whenever he felt like it.

He was doing this because hatred and rage were the hallmarks of his father's life. Making a different choice was the only way he knew to exert control over the kind of man he hoped to become.

Dusk clung to the streets in pockets of gloom that stretched hazy gray fingers toward the darkening sky. Sebastian strode toward the gate leading into east Kosim Thalas, shutting down all reflections about his parents until nothing remained but one burning thought: survive.

His steps lengthened, and he flexed his shoulders as he pushed past the last of the market's shoppers and walked through the cracked, decrepit archway that served as an entrance to the corner of the city that only the desperately poor and those who hoped to prey on them dared to enter.

He reached for his cudgel and pulled it free as he left the gate behind. Tension hummed through his muscles. The scars on his back tingled and burned as he focused on every movement, every sound that whispered toward him.

He walked rapidly, passing buildings of faded pastel clay with weeds growing out of cracks in the walls and the bitter stench of cheap pipe weed hanging heavy in the air. The four-story buildings were depressingly uniform in their decay. Inside, tiny apartments were rented out for coin or pipe weed or the kind of favors that the nobility in their fancy estates had no idea existed.

People sat on front stoops watching the street with careful attention. Sebastian met the gaze of a few of the runners—children responsible for quickly informing the right people about the arrival of the city's guard or an unsuspecting member of the upper class—and gave them a look that promised consequences if they interfered with him.

He didn't want trouble with those who ran the streets.

And he'd made sure to earn a reputation for seriously injuring those who brought trouble his way.

Sebastian turned a corner and faced the hill leading toward his mother's house. Keeping his face expressionless in the face of the crumbling, filthy buildings took effort.

East Kosim Thalas had never been pretty, but before the recent introduction of Teague's newest business venture, a drug called apodrasi, it had at least made a passable attempt at being clean. Now, addicts huddled on doorsteps or on broken blocks of stone, pulling at their hair and gnashing their yellowed teeth while they tried to sell their labor or their bodies for enough coin to get another vial. Now, the street bosses weren't content to commit crimes against the merchant and noble classes. They had sellers moving through their own streets, giving free samples to those too young or too beaten down to refuse an escape from the life they led.

Apodrasi and Alistair Teague, the undisputed crime lord of all Súndraille, were east Kosim Thalas's curse, and no one knew that better than Sebastian.

Making his way into his mother's building, he climbed the rickety stairs to the third-floor apartment where he and Parrish had survived her neglect and his father's whip.

He stood outside her door, scars aching, the tang of pipe weed resting on the back of his tongue, and listened while he fought to stay calm.

It had been six months since his father had left for his new job collecting payments for Teague in the neighboring kingdom of Balavata, but still Sebastian's hands shook and his chest ached at the thought that the man who'd raised him might be on the other side of the door.

Dragging in a deep breath of dusty, smoke-scented air, Sebastian unlocked the door and entered. As the door clicked shut behind him, he rolled to the balls of his feet and raised his cudgel while he swept the room with his gaze.

His mother lay on the threadbare sofa, a filthy blanket pulled haphazardly over her legs while she slept, her fingers still curled around a pipe that reeked of the cloyingly sweet scent of apodrasi. The candle on the table beside her had guttered out, and a small puddle of wax had spilled across the surface, hardening around a layer of dust and bits of pipe weed leaf.

He walked past the couch and checked the tiny room that doubled as a makeshift kitchen and bedroom. It was empty.

The ache in his chest eased. His father was still in Balavata. If there was any justice in the world, he'd never return.

"Who's there?" his mother asked, her voice husky with sleep and the lingering effects of apodrasi.

He moved into her line of sight, and she pulled herself up to a sitting position.

"Come to rob me?"

He sighed, a headache beginning to spike. "I never come to rob you."

"Ungrateful boy, leaving me just like your father."

It was ridiculous that even after years of shoring up his defenses against her, she could still find a way to hurt him.

He held up the sack. "I brought food for the week."

"Did you bring coin too?"

He turned to unpack the sack's contents into the single cupboard that hung over the slab of wood that served as a countertop.

"I asked you a question."

A question he was sick of answering. "No."

He ignored her string of curses and put the bread, figs, lamb strips, and potatoes into the cupboard. The oranges went into a cracked bowl on the countertop. Then he turned and interrupted her tirade.

"If you didn't buy apodrasi with any coin you got your hands on, I might bring you some."

"You know nothing." She gave him a smug little smile and shoved her tangled gray-black hair out of her eyes. "Your father makes sure I get what I need."

His hands clenched into fists, and his heartbeat roared in his ears.

"Does he?" Sebastian snapped. "Is that why your cupboard has nothing in it until I bring you food each week?"

She recoiled from him and bent to fumble along the floor for the pipe she'd dropped. When she sat up, she was holding her pipe and a tiny glass vial with a few iridescent drops of apodrasi left inside.

Mumbling something under her breath, she upended the apodrasi into the pipe and reached for the candle. When she discovered that there was no flame left to light her pipe, she turned beseeching eyes toward her son.

Sickness crawled up the back of his throat at the need on her face, and the answer to the question she'd always refused to answer was suddenly clear.

"Teague takes some of Father's pay and gives it to you in apodrasi, doesn't he?"

She lifted a shaking hand toward him. "Candle?"

He worked to unclench his fists. To draw a breath past the band of tension that felt like it was crushing his chest. When he was sure he'd erased all outward signs of anger, he approached her, blinking against the stench of her unwashed body mixed with bitter pipe weed and the sickly sweetness of apodrasi.

"You need help," he said quietly. "A new place, far from here. Some time to come down off the drug and start over fresh. Hiding from your life in the bowl of a pipe isn't the same as making a true escape."

Her lips quivered, and her voice lashed out bitterly. "Like you did? Like Parrish? Leaving me here. Never coming back. Just like your father."

He closed his eyes and crushed the fleeting longing that once—just *once*—she would speak to him like he mattered.

"I'll be back next week. Don't forget to eat."

"What about a candle?" She lunged off the couch as he strode toward the door, her voice rising. "Sebastian! A candle? Please?"

He closed the door behind him and closed out the sound of the vicious words she hurled at him as he hurried down the stairs and out of the building. His hands were fists again, his stomach jittery as he walked toward the gate. Why was it that even after eighteen years of learning to expect nothing better, he was still disappointed every time he saw her? What was wrong with him that a tiny piece of his heart clung to the devastating need for her to see him as someone worth loving?

It was useless to think about. Useless to let it burrow under his skin and slice him raw. Instead, he had to focus on getting through east Kosim Thalas in one piece so that he could show up at the palace in the morning, apply for a job, and hope the king gave him a chance.

Picking up his pace, he moved through the city and tried to convince himself that by the time he reached the stables where he'd been sleeping, the memory of this visit with his mother would no longer ache.

SIX

IT HAD BEEN nearly five days since Sebastian had been hired as the palace's new weapons master, and the job was nothing like he'd thought it would be. All he wanted was to manage the king's arsenal of weapons in peace and quiet, saving his coin until he could afford a solitary cottage somewhere far from Kosim Thalas on a cliff overlooking the Chrysós Sea. Somewhere his father would never find him.

Instead, he was trapped inside the training arena on the palace grounds, polishing swords and listening to a cluster of nobles in fancy clothing speculate about which jewel-encrusted dagger would match their summer wardrobe best.

Not trapped, he reminded himself before his lungs tightened and desperation to fight his way out of the crowded space pushed every other thought from his head.

He wasn't trapped. He wasn't caught between the monster who'd raised him and the viciousness of the streets outside his front door. He was performing the duties of his new job—a job a boy like him was lucky to have—and he could walk away whenever he wanted to.

Not that he would. Not until he'd saved enough coin to buy his cottage and his solitude. Enough to lift his mother from the filth and poverty of her life and set her up somewhere else.

Maybe a fresh start would be enough to save her from herself. Sebastian had long since given up believing it would be enough for him. He wore his grief, his shame, and the imprint of his father's rage deep beneath his skin, where all the coin in the world couldn't scrub it clean.

He leaned over the whetstone that rested on a wooden crate and patted it with an oiled cloth.

A hand descended onto his shoulder. "Are these all the daggers in the king's collection?" one of the noblemen asked.

Sebastian jerked upright and took a quick step back, breaking the man's hold on him.

The nobleman, a tall, lanky man wearing a fitted linen suit that would restrict his range of motion in a fight, stood loose and relaxed in front of Sebastian, his brows climbing toward his hairline as he waited for the weapon master's response.

Not a threat. Just another in a long line of young nobles flocking to the palace to curry favor with Súndraille's king. Or, based on a few conversations he'd overheard inside the arena, to keep an eye on the king and report any failures to their fathers.

The man broke eye contact with Sebastian and looked at the other members of his group. "Did Thad hire a mute for a weapons master?" He laughed, and several others joined in.

Sebastian forced his hands to relax instead of forming fists, and took another small step back so that the entire group was in his line of sight while the wall that lined the arena was to his back.

"All the weapons available for visitors' use are there," Sebastian said quietly, nodding toward the display of jeweled daggers and ornately handled swords that lined the table to his right.

"He speaks!" The nobleman threw his arms wide, and Sebastian clenched his jaw as he held himself still.

Not a threat. Not trapped.

"Leave him alone, Makario," said a young woman with friendly eyes and the impossibly small corseted waist that seemed to be popular among the nobility for reasons Sebastian couldn't fathom.

Who would agree to cinch themselves too tight to be able to draw a full breath? How would they run or fight if necessary?

Of course, nobles didn't have to run and fight. They didn't look over their shoulders for threats in every shadow or worry that if they were caught in the wrong place at the wrong time, the city's guard would beat them and throw them into prison to rot.

Makario shrugged and wandered toward the display table. "Just making sure the king put out enough weapons for us to enjoy our practice today. And making sure that in his haste to replace the previous weapons master he didn't hire an imbecile to be in charge of sharp objects."

"Makario!" the woman snapped. "He can hear you!" She gave an apologetic little shrug in Sebastian's direction. He wanted to tell her that words meant little when they came from a man who wouldn't follow them up with action, but it didn't matter. She pitied Sebastian because she saw him as a victim.

He would never be anyone's victim again.

Sebastian waited, watchful and still, as the group bickered good-naturedly over which of them would throw daggers and which of them would parry with swords whose tips were capped with cork to prevent injury to their opponents. When teams had been chosen and weapons assigned, Sebastian skirted the arena to check the targets and arrange the sparring areas to the group's liking.

He had just finished securing a new sheet of canvas with a bull's-eye painted in the center to the enormous stack of hay bales at the south end when the woman who'd pitied him approached.

"Here." She fished a silver coin out of the little pouch that hung from the glittering woven metal belt that wrapped around her waist. "For your troubles." She pressed the coin into his palm and squeezed his hand with hers. He jerked back as if she'd burned him.

The coin landed in the sawdust at his feet, and a delicate frown etched itself between the woman's brows. "It's okay. Thad won't mind if we reward you for good service."

His scars ached. It took everything he had to calmly bend down and scoop up the coin as if the unwelcome touch from another person hadn't set off a reaction inside him that felt like the entire Chrysós Sea was trapped within, tearing at his skin as it sought release.

He nodded to her as he pocketed the coin and hurried back to his corner of the arena where he could sit with his back to the wall and polish swords in peace.

Not trapped. No threats in sight. Just doing his job until he could buy his freedom.

He repeated the words to himself over and over again as he oiled the whetstone and slowly passed the sword over its surface, back and forth until the blade gleamed in the sunlight that filtered in through the windows that surrounded the upper deck of the arena.

The laughter and shouts of the nobility faded into background noise, their movements flashes of color he tracked with his peripheral vision while he focused on the task in front of him. He was finishing the third of five blades when the arena suddenly fell silent.

He lifted his head, his hand gripping the sword's hilt while he scanned the arena for the cause.

A girl who looked about his age stood at the entrance taking in the scene with avid curiosity, a partially full burlap sack hanging from one shoulder. Her sun-streaked brown hair was pulled back in a braid, and a simple silver armband gleamed against the golden skin of her right arm. Unlike the others in the room, her clothing was plain, her sandals sensible. If Sebastian had to guess based solely on the lack of corset and the simple linen sheath she wore, he'd say she was a member of the merchant class. Nobility didn't fall silent for merchants, though, and there was a familiarity to the line of her jaw and the shape of her dark eyes.

"Your Highness." Makario bowed low, and the rest of the group followed suit.

Sebastian came to his feet in one fluid motion, and the girl's gaze instantly landed on him.

He bowed quickly, though she was already waving her hand in the air as though she was shooing a cloud of gnats.

"No bowing. Just . . . as you were. Go back to throwing shiny things, or whatever it is you're doing."

"Would you care to join us, Princess Arianna?" someone asked.

"Trust me. You don't want to hand me a dagger and tell me to throw it. Somebody will need medical attention." She aimed a smile at the crowd in the arena, but her eyes were still on Sebastian.

He watched as she approached and remembered at the last minute to loosen his grip on the sword he held, though the air of confidence surrounding the princess said she was the one person in the arena who would follow her words with decisive action.

"I hope I'm not disturbing your work," she said as she reached him.

He blinked and glanced at the whetstone beside him. Since when did nobility care if they interrupted anything?

"You're my brother's new weapons master, aren't you?" she asked.

He nodded cautiously and waited for her to tell him to fetch a jeweled dagger to match her dress.

"I assume that means you're an expert at both using and creating various weapons?"

He nodded again and began praying inwardly that she wouldn't ask for something awful like a weapons demonstration in front of the gathered crowd. He'd do it—he didn't dare turn down the princess—but the thought of being on display in front of dozens of people wrapped a fist of panic around his lungs.

The people in the arena had yet to continue their games, and the princess lowered her voice as she asked, "Would you happen to have some free time to make me a few weapons and then teach me how to use them?"

He stared at her. Weapons for a princess? She'd want pretty daggers or finely wrought swords—both of which were beyond his skill level. What would she do to him when she found out he wasn't fully qualified for the job he'd taken? The silver coin in his pocket felt like fire against his thigh as he drew in a deep breath.

He had to earn enough coin to pay for the freedom he so desperately wanted. If that meant he needed to figure out how to make a set of jewel-crusted daggers for the princess, then that's what he'd do.

Somehow.

"Is it . . . Did I ask for the wrong thing?" the princess said quietly, and Sebastian was hit with the terrible certainty that she was paying attention to him. Not to his role as a servant of the king but to the stillness of his body, the watchfulness of his gaze, and the muscles that bunched in his shoulders.

"We're operating under the assumption that he's an imbecile," Makario said. "He barely speaks. Of course, you can't always assume the same intelligence in the servant class as you can in the nobility."

The princess's spine snapped straight, and fire lit her eyes as she whirled to face the rest of the arena. "You forget that until my brother was crowned king, I was a member of the servant class. Are you questioning my intelligence as well? Or are you simply confusing idiocy with his choice to not spew every thought that crosses his mind? Because, I can assure you, you would do well to keep a few of your own thoughts private, Makario."

The fist around Sebastian's lungs unclenched.

"I can help you," he said softly, and hoped it was true.

The princess stared at the crowd. Several of them glared back. "Games are over for the morning. There are peach tarts, biscuits with fig butter, and freshly squeezed juice set out in the dining hall. Feel free to help yourselves."

Her tone was a clear dismissal, and no one hesitated to return their weapons and file out of the arena, though there were murmurs of discontent to go with the sharp looks aimed at her. When there was no one left but Sebastian and the princess, she turned back to him and held out her hand.

He stared at it. Did she want to try one of the weapons he'd set out? Which one? Was he just supposed to read her mind?

"I'm Ari," she said, and his cheeks heated as he realized she was simply offering him the customary hand-clasp greeting used between those of equal class.

It would be a terrible insult to refuse to touch her. He didn't think she was the type to dismiss him from his post over it, but it wasn't worth the risk.

Quickly he pressed his palm to hers, surprised to feel calluses on her fingertips, and then pulled his hand away.

He curled his fingers into a fist, and then flexed them again in an effort to look unthreatening.

"What kind of weapons do you want?" he asked, his voice louder than it should have been because she was watching his fingers curl and flex, and he couldn't shake the sense that she was seeing far more of him than he wanted her to.

She tossed the burlap sack to the floor between them. It landed with the sharp clink of metal striking metal.

Her voice was firm. "There are large pieces of iron in this bag. I need them turned into weapons. Something for the king, and something for me. Something I can keep with me at all times. Nothing that's too hard to carry. I don't want it to kill me when I trip on the stairs."

"*When* you trip?" He raised a brow.

"It happens with alarming frequency."

"You might be better off with a metal that's lighter than iron."

She went still, her eyes boring into his. "I want iron."

He inclined his head. "As you wish. Just know that the weapons will be heavy, and that can have a detrimental effect on your ability to use them. If you incorporate silver—"

"Silver doesn't work. They must be completely made of iron."

He held her gaze and said slowly, "There's only one use for weapons made of iron." And stars only knew what the princess of Súndraille was doing arming herself against the fae.

She locked eyes with him, and silence stretched between them for a moment. He had the clear impression that she was assessing his character and deciding if she could trust him. He did a quick inventory: sword held loosely, blade pointed down, free hand uncurled and relaxed, boots solidly on the floor, no fighting stance visible. Keeping his eyes on hers, he waited.

Finally, she said, "How long until you can have my weapon ready and begin training me to use it?"

"Two days. Three at the most." If he gave up sleep and pushed himself.

She nodded. "I'll see you in two days."

"Or three." Panic was a quick skitter of nerves up his spine. He had to figure out how to balance the weapons. How to make them both deadly and light enough to carry comfortably.

Scraping the iron into shape was going to be the easy part.

She smiled. "I have confidence in you. I'll see you in two."

He was already pulling iron out of the sack before she finished walking to the door.

SEVEN

MORNING MIST ROLLED off the sea and crawled along the merchant district's canals as Ari and Cleo disembarked from the palace's long, sleek narrowboat and stepped onto the dock. Two of Thad's newly hired royal guards followed them. It had been over a week since Thad's coronation and the unsettling appearance of the little man with the cold smile and magic in his fingertips.

Or in his blood. Or wherever fae magic was kept.

Ari hadn't yet found an opportunity to question Thad privately about his bargain with Teague. Her brother had been beleaguered with responsibilities from early morning until long into the night. Closed-door meetings with high-ranking nobles, visits with dignitaries from neighboring kingdoms, heated discussions with the Kosim Thalas steward over the rise in crime, and Assembly sessions that he'd required her to attend as part of his push to get her ready to rule in his place. She'd protested because, after her lunch with Lady Tassi, Ari had her own list of things she needed to do, none of which included dying of boredom in an Assembly meeting, but Thad refused to budge.

When she wasn't busy enduring the meetings, Ari had spent the last few days reading up on the fae and the isle of Llorenyae. She hadn't learned anything from the palace library that she hadn't already heard from Lady Tassi.

The one useful thing she'd done was to gather iron from the palace smithy and charge the (very intriguing) weapons master with making something deadly and not too heavy. With the creation of the weapons under way, Ari had turned her attention to getting some bloodflower poison. The palace physician didn't keep any on hand and had looked at her strangely when she'd asked for it. That left a trip to the market and her favorite spice shop. Preferably not on Mama Eleni's regular market day—nobody killed a perfectly good plan faster than Mama Eleni.

"It's odd coming into the city without your mother," Ari said, trying to ignore the throb of pain that ached in her heart at the thought that she'd never come to the city again with her own mother. Missing Mama was a wound that refused to close. It was a dark hole in the corner of her heart that hurt every time she brushed up against it, and she knew that no matter where she went or what became of her, that pain would belong to her for the rest of her days.

"Just pray Mama keeps believing you had an early lunch with Lady Zabat. If she finds out we came to the markets on one of her non-market-going days, she's going to kill us." Cleo paused for effect. "Actually, she can't kill you because you're the princess, so I'll take the fall for us both."

"She'll never know." Ari linked her arm through Cleo's as

they left the dock and entered the merchant district.

Crowds were already starting to move along sidewalks paved in white stone. Merchants stood outside their shops, splashing buckets of water on the pastel walls or briskly sweeping dust from their stoops. Friendly poppies in riotous colors peeped out of window boxes and lent their sweet scent to the smell of baking bread and spiced tea as the girls passed a café and turned west.

"Spice merchant first and then lunch?" Cleo asked, sniffing appreciatively at a display of sweet cheese pastries. "Oh, and can we stop at the glassblower's? I want to see if he has any broken bits he'll part with."

"What are you making this time?"

Cleo's voice brightened. "I got scraps of leather from the tanner's last week, and I'm going to dye them in the prettiest colors. I might have to use a lot of dye . . . Maybe don't mention this project to Mama."

"My lips are sealed. What does broken glass have to do with leather scraps?"

"I want to create a portrait that marries the delicate beauty of glass with the tough resilience of leather. I'm going to call it *Girl*."

"Sounds perfect. I need to stop at the bookstore first to do more research. The spice shop is north of there, and the glassblower's is closer to the docks, so can we do that last?" Ari steered Cleo to the opposite side of the street.

"I didn't hear you mention stopping for pastries. I didn't sneak behind Mama's back only to skip our usual pastry break."

Ari laughed. "Never let it be said that I skipped our pastry break. We'll do that after the spice shop."

The Open Page was a blue rectangle at the end of a narrow street, just past a milliner's. Rahel, the owner, was a thin, bird-like woman with narrow features and a soft, pleasant voice.

There was another customer in the shop when Cleo and Ari entered, leaving their pair of guards outside the door. Both Rahel and the customer quickly bowed when they recognized Ari. She waved at them to rise and continue with their transaction as she turned to peruse the shelves of leather-bound books and scrolls of parchment.

"You have to stop doing that," Cleo whisper-hissed in her ear as she took a book of her own off the shelf.

"Doing what?" Ari stared at her friend.

"Acting uncomfortable when people bow to you."

"Well, I *am* uncomfortable."

"But they have no choice. If they don't bow and their disrespect is reported to the city guard, they'll be fined. You can't wave it off when failure to show you deference could cost them more than they make in a month." Cleo flipped a few pages of her book and then set it back on the shelf.

Ari was silent for a moment as she considered Cleo's words. "You're right. I hate that it's so awkward. I'm just me. If they spent any significant amount of time with me at all, they'd realize how ridiculous it is to bow to me all the time."

"You'll get no argument from me there." Cleo grinned at Ari, and then turned as Rahel ushered her previous customer out of the shop and approached the girls.

"Your Highness, Cleo, what a delight to have you in my shop this morning." Her eyes darted toward the store's entrance. "But . . . this isn't your usual market day. Where is Mama Eleni?

Does she know you're here?"

"We have guards with us, and Ari is the princess now, so she can do what she wants, and Mama Eleni doesn't need to hear about this. Ever." Cleo's words tumbled from her mouth in a rush.

Rahel twisted her fingers together and glanced at the entrance again. "Quickly, then. What can I help you with?"

Ari couldn't exactly say "Good morning. I want to know how to stop a powerful fae who happens to live in Kosim Thalas. Can you help?" Not without starting rumors that she couldn't afford Teague to hear. Not until she really *did* have the ability to stop him from hurting her brother.

Pasting a smile on her face, Ari said, "I'm researching Llorenyae, specifically the fae and any lore surrounding them. I have storybooks of fae myths, but I'm more interested in the actual history of the fae."

Rahel frowned as she examined her shelves. "*Thirty-nine Summer Nights*?"

"I have that one."

"*Magic in the Moonlight: A Nursery Primer*?"

"I have that one too. I don't want a storybook. I want a history book. Something that will separate fact from fiction when it comes to the fae," Ari said.

Rahel ran her hands down the spines of the books in front of her. "There is one book, *Leabhar na Fae*. Have you heard of it?"

Ari shook her head.

"I'm not surprised." Rahel left the shelves and walked to her desk, casting another glance at the doorway. Ari followed her gaze but saw nothing unusual in the street beyond. "*Leabhar na Fae* means 'Book of the Fae.' There are only three copies in existence, and two of those are in Llorenyae. One in the Summer Court and one in the Winter Court. The third copy is owned by a collector of rare antiquities in Balavata. He won't sell the original to you, but his daughter has transcribed a copy that can be borrowed for a fee. Would you like me to order it for you?"

"And it isn't a story? It's factual?" Ari asked.

"It's the history of the fae since time began. Of course, the language in the first quarter or more of the book is so archaic, it's nearly impossible to understand unless you are a scholar of all things fae, but the latter part of the book is quite informative, I'm told. It contains the usual lore—fae substituting their changeling babies for human babies, humans killing younger fae with iron, the great war between the Summer and Winter courts—"

"Anything about using bloodflower against them?" Ari asked. "Bloodflower and iron together?"

Rahel's pleasant expression dimmed into something alert and watchful. "May I ask why you're looking into bloodflower and iron, Your Highness?"

Ari shrugged and tried to sound casual. "Just taking precautions. I've heard there's a powerful fae living in Súndraille. He makes deals with people and I thought . . . Are you all right?"

Rahel's face had gone clammy, and she looked faintly sick.

"Rahel? Did I say something wrong?" Ari asked.

"Why are you asking these questions, Your Highness?" Rahel sounded shaken.

Ari tried to sound casual. "I've heard rumors, and I just wanted to see if they were true." When Rahel didn't look convinced,

Ari rushed on. "The king needs to know if we have a fae living among us, making deals with his subjects. I've heard the name Teague—"

"Don't make a wish, Your Highness. It's not worth it. It never is." Rahel leaned across her desk, her voice trembling. "There isn't anything you want that could be worth the pain of dealing with the Wish Granter."

Ari blinked. "Um . . . I'm not talking about the Wish Granter. I'm not interested in children's stories. I was talking about a creepy little man named Teague."

Rahel drew back, straightening parchment on her desk with fingers that shook so much she knocked the parchment to the floor. Her voice was a whisper. "All fae myths are based in fact, Your Highness. Teague *is* the Wish Granter, and you would do well to stay far away from him."

Ari frowned. It was difficult to accept that the horrible stories Thad's nanny, Babette, had told the twins about the Wish Granter were real, but it was clear Rahel believed she was telling the truth. And it was equally clear that Teague had powerful magic and had come to an agreement with Thad.

Maybe that meant Thad had made a wish, though she couldn't imagine what he'd want badly enough to get involved with a creature like Teague.

Rahel was still waiting for Ari's reply.

"I'll stay away from Teague," Ari said. At least until she was prepared to force him to release her brother from his debt. "Please do order the book for me. When will it be in?"

"Four or five weeks." Rahel looked past them to the city street outside her door. "You should leave now. Go back to the palace.

This isn't a day for marketing."

Ari examined the street as she and Cleo left the bookshop and turned right to walk the three blocks to the spice merchant. It was still somewhat crowded, though there were more men than women entering the shops, which was different from their usual market day. Still, Ari saw nothing to explain Rahel's nervousness.

"She was acting strangely today," Cleo said, shoving an errant curl out of her eyes as their guards fell in step behind them.

"She obviously knows enough about Teague to be afraid of him." And she'd unwittingly given Ari a new piece of information—the name Wish Granter. Ari had never actually believed a powerful fae had been exiled to Súndraille and went around granting your deepest desires at a terrible price. But Rahel wasn't a liar, and Ari had seen Teague's magic with her own eyes, right after he discussed the bargain he'd made with her brother.

What had Thad wished for? And what was the price he'd agreed to? Dread curled in her belly, heavy and cold.

"Rahel was acting strangely even before you brought Teague up," Cleo said, interrupting Ari's thoughts.

Pushing her questions to the back of her mind, Ari looped her arm through Cleo's as they turned north and picked up their pace. "Maybe because if Mama Eleni finds out Rahel helped us while we were at the market without permission, Rahel will need to go into hiding in Balavata to survive."

"I concede the point. Now slow down. Not all of us are blessed with legs up to our chins."

Ari shortened her stride and reviewed the assets she had in her secret battle against Teague. Iron being fashioned into weapons by the new weapons master. A book on order that contained the entire history of the fae and hopefully their weaknesses. Or at least the weaknesses of the Wish Granter. And soon, if her luck held, she'd have some ground bloodflower.

Teague had crossed the wrong family this time.

"There really are a lot of men on the street today," Cleo said as they turned onto the road that ran by the spice shop. "And they don't seem to be shopping."

Ari glanced around. Young men around her age moved in pairs from shop to shop on the street they'd just left behind. They were dressed in a ragtag assortment of patched clothing, and there was a hardness to their expressions that sent a whisper of unease down Ari's spine. The buzz of customers moving with purpose from one item on their list to the next had fallen silent, though there were still plenty of people on their current street.

"Your Highness!" A man rushed from his spice shop to bow deeply as the girls came abreast of his doorway.

"Edwin, how nice to see you." Ari beamed at the merchant.

His gaze darted along the street before returning to her. "What are you doing in the market today? Where is Mama Eleni?"

"It's just us, but we—"

"Come in! No lingering in the streets today." Edwin all but pulled the girls into the shop. The guards took up their post outside the entrance as Edwin flipped the wooden sign that hung above his display window to Closed and faced the princess.

"What's wrong?" Ari asked as Cleo made a show of rubbing her wrist as if Edwin's grasp had hurt her.

"Forgive me, Your Highness." He glanced at the street again. "But it's Thursday."

"That's what generally happens after you have a Wednesday," Cleo muttered.

"We'll only be a minute," Ari said, despite the chill that was spreading over her skin at the strange way Edwin was acting. She'd gotten away with lying to Mama Eleni and sneaking out to the market once. Princess or not, the chances of that happening again any time in the next decade were slim to none. And she needed the bloodflower poison. She especially needed it without having to explain why to Cleo's mother, who would undoubtedly try to take on Teague herself for daring to upset her king and her princess.

The inside of the spice shop was cozy and warm. The dark red floor and pale yellow walls glowed in the light of small candelabras spaced throughout, and racks of jars were filled with colorful ground spices and herbs.

"We should do this quickly. What would you like, Your Highness?" Edwin asked, his tone urgent.

Ari frowned. "Why is everyone in such a rush today?"

Edwin shook his head sharply. "Now is not the time to discuss it. Please, Your Highness, tell me what you need."

Ari met his gaze. "Bloodflower poison."

He frowned. "If you have rats in your stable, may I suggest monkshood or elderberry?"

"We don't have rats."

"But then why . . . whatever animal you need poisoned can be killed with monkshood or—"

"I need bloodflower." She looked him in the eye. "Nothing else will do."

He glanced at the window behind her and then motioned sharply for her to come farther into the shop. Cleo and Ari followed as Edwin led them to a small, dusty cabinet in the back. Fishing a key out of his pocket, he fit it into the lock with hands that shook.

"What's wrong?" Ari asked quietly as the cabinet door swung open with a creak.

"We aren't supposed to carry bloodflower," Edwin whispered as he reached into the cabin and pulled out a small red jar sealed with wax. "If anyone finds out I gave this to you . . . Please don't tell anyone, Your Highness."

Ari took the jar and slid it into the little satchel hanging from her wrist before pressing a generous amount of coin into Edwin's hands. "I don't know who told you that, but bloodflower isn't against the law. You won't get in any trouble."

His smile was a wretched parody of itself. "It isn't the law I'm worried about."

The handle on the shop's front door rattled, and a man called out, "Time to pay your fee, Edwin. Open up."

"What fee?" Ari looked from the door to Edwin's stricken face.

The merchant sprang into action. Wrapping a hand around each girl's arm, he pulled them toward the back exit.

"Your Highness, it isn't safe on the streets today. You must take your guards and get back to the dock quickly." He reached for the door. "And, please, don't tell anyone you were here."

A dull thud hit the back door, and it flew open with a bang. Edwin stumbled backward, dragging the girls with him, as two of the young men Ari had noticed earlier strode into the shop.

"Why don't you want anyone to know these pretty little coin purses were here, Edwin?" the taller one asked, his dark eyes boring into the shopkeeper's face.

The shorter one grinned at Ari, putting what was left of his yellowed teeth on full display. "Looks like nobility to me. Bet someone would pay handsomely to rescue you from where you're going."

"No!" Edwin lunged forward as the man reached for Ari, and suddenly there was a wicked-looking knife in the tall one's hands.

"Step outside, ladies, or I'll gut Edwin where he stands." His voice was hard.

The fear that had been slithering over Ari's skin became a wild rush of panic that shook her knees and turned her fingers cold.

"Please." Edwin raised his hands in supplication. "Just take my weekly fee. I have it ready for you. Take it and go. These girls mean nothing to you."

The shorter one sidled up to Cleo and ran his hand up her arm. She flinched and pulled away. Faster than a blink, he whipped his hand into the air and slapped her.

Anger blazed through Ari's fear, leaving her with nothing but a terrible need to hurt the one who'd laid his hands on her friend. Without a second thought, she balled up her fist and plowed it straight into the middle of his face.

Blood spurted from his nose, and he reached for her, but she'd already grabbed Cleo's hand and started moving. Together they ran out of the shop and straight into the chest of a thick barrel of a man with graying black hair and close-set eyes.

He grunted and shoved them back into the hands of the two men who'd exited the shop on their heels. "They look like someone would pay their ransom. Teague will be pleased with this catch. Tie them up, put them in the wagon, and then finish collecting the protection fees. We don't have all day, boys."

"Teague?" The name left the bitter residue of fear on Ari's tongue as the young man who held her dragged her away from the spice shop.

"You're in it now, miss." The shorter one spat blood on the ground and dug his nails into her arms.

No, she wasn't. She was the princess and somewhere at the front of the shop, she had a pair of trained guards waiting for her. She just had to make them hear her.

Dragging in a deep breath, she screamed, "Guards!"

Cleo joined her efforts, but the men laughed. The shorter one leaned close enough that Ari choked on the fetid stench of his breath and said, "Haven't you heard? The city guard has to stand down where Teague's business is concerned. King's orders. No one is coming to rescue you, miss."

She hadn't been screaming for the city guard, but it didn't matter. Her guards were too far away to hear her. She'd been a fool to make them stand outside the shop so that they wouldn't overhear her conversation.

Ari met Cleo's wild gaze and tried to come up with a plan, but panic clawed at her.

No one was coming to save them.

They were on their own.

EIGHT

A HUSH HUNG over the steep hill that held the pauper's cemetery in Kosim Thalas. Somewhere below, merchants hawked their wares and ferrymen dipped oars into the city's canals and bumped their narrowboats against the landing platforms scattered throughout the market, but high on the windswept, grassy hillside, there was only the occasional caw of a seabird and the profound silence of the dead.

Sebastian climbed the narrow stairs that were carved into the ground between row upon row of small, plain stones and glanced over his shoulder to make sure he was still alone.

Not that he worried his mother would drag herself out of her drug-induced stupor to visit her eldest son's resting place. Or that his father would return from Balavata and take it upon himself to examine the results of his handiwork. Still, Sebastian felt exposed on the open hillside with his back to the road, and he quickened his pace.

Thirteen stairs between each flattened terrace that wrapped

around the hillside. Five hundred fifty-nine stairs to reach the forty-fourth terrace. Ninety-eight gravestones to the right, just beyond the gnarled trunk of an olive tree that had long since stopped producing fruit.

Grief was a dull blade pressing relentlessly against an old wound. Sebastian rubbed his hand against his heart as if he could somehow ease the ache.

Crouching beside his brother's grave, he traced his fingers lightly over the name he'd clumsily carved into the stone six months ago in the days between his brother's death and the graveside memorial that only Sebastian had attended.

Parrish Vaughn, Beloved Brother

He'd left off the words "and son." His brother deserved to be buried without the taint of their father touching his final resting place.

"I got a job," he said quietly while the wind whispered through branches of the olive tree and the sun baked its heat into the gravestones. "I know it sounds crazy, but I'm working for the king now. I live at the palace—well, actually, I live in a little room attached to the king's arena. I'm the weapons master."

If he concentrated, he could almost remember what his brother's laugh had sounded like. What it had felt like to have Parrish loop an arm around Sebastian's neck and ruffle his hair while he teased him about being smarter than the other kids on the street. *So smart, Sebastian. So stubborn. If anyone makes it out of these slums without first working for Teague, it will be my little brother.*

It was cold comfort to prove his brother right.

Another glance over his shoulder confirmed that he was still alone, and he brushed loose grass from Parrish's stone. "I'm earning a decent wage now. I have to deal with the nobility to get it, but they aren't all bad. I met the princess, and she's nice."

Nice wasn't the right word for Princess Arianna, but he wasn't sure what would fit better. How did you describe someone who dressed like she didn't want to be noticed but looked everyone in the eye? Someone who treated a servant like an equal but commanded the nobility with the confidence of someone who hadn't spent a second's time worrying about the consequences of displeasing them?

It didn't matter. He had more important things to discuss with his brother.

A faint sound reached him, and he twisted to see a pair of women in faded blue shawls slowly climbing the stairs.

Turning back to Parrish's stone, he said, "I can't stay long today. The princess has me making weapons, and she didn't give me much time to do it. I just wanted you to know that I've found a good place to settle for now. I'm safe. I'm still bringing food to Mother each week, though I don't stay long. You know what she's like."

His voice faded as his heartbeat thrummed in his ears. Parrish would care about Sebastian's safety and Mother having food to eat, but he knew what his brother would really want to hear.

Taking a deep breath, he said, "Father is still in Balavata collecting for Teague. I don't know when he'll return. And I don't know if I'll still be here when he does. My new job pays me triple what I was making working odd jobs for merchants, and within a year I'll have enough saved up to buy a cottage far from here."

It was hard to force the next words past his lips. Hard to keep the rage that bubbled within him locked away when he thought of his father's role in Parrish's death, but he had to. It was the only way to save himself from becoming what he feared most. "I know I said I'd punish him for killing you, but . . ."

The scars on his back tingled and ached.

But—one little word that held the balance between who Sebastian had been raised to be and who he was trying to become.

But he didn't want to be in Kosim Thalas when Father returned.

He didn't want to stare into Father's eyes and throw the truth of Parrish's death into his face.

Not because he was afraid of his father's fury, though he was.

Not because he knew there was no speaking the truth to him without suffering the consequences, because that lesson had been absorbed with every lash of his father's whip.

He didn't want to confront his father because deep inside him, beneath the scars and the shame, a vicious pit of rage bubbled silently, waiting for a crack in his defenses so it could pour out of him and lay waste to anyone in his way.

What if he was no better than his father?

What if once the crack split him open, there was no pulling back? No shoving his fury back into its cage?

His heart thundered at the thought, and his throat closed around a breath of warm, grass-scented air, but he fought the panic before it could take hold.

He wasn't his father. He refused to be.

He was safe for now, and he had a plan.

Parrish would understand. He'd wanted nothing more than

for Sebastian get away from east Kosim Thalas, their father, and the long arm of Alistair Teague.

Pressing his hand against the gritty headstone, Sebastian said, "I'll visit again as soon as I can. Rest well."

There were a few others climbing the steps as Sebastian made his way down the hill, but none of them spared him a second glance. In moments, he'd left the cemetery behind and was hurrying along the edges of the merchant district toward the distant palace.

It would be faster to cut through the market and pay a few kepas to take a narrowboat to the landing platform closest to the palace, but it was Thursday. Collection day. The market would be crawling with Teague's people, and Sebastian wanted nothing to do with them.

He could make it back to the palace on foot quickly enough, and he could use the time to plan his approach to the rest of the iron weapons the princess wanted from him. She'd ordered one for herself and one for the king, but she'd given him enough iron to make at least three weapons, maybe four. He'd already fashioned a throwing star, but it still needed to be balanced. He'd drawn a model of a simple dagger, but he'd need to use the smithy's fire for that. What else could he make out of iron that wouldn't be too heavy to easily carry?

"You're making a big mistake!" A girl's voice cut through the air, and Sebastian stopped with a jerk. "Let us go this instant, or suffer the wrath of the king."

He pivoted toward the merchant district and scanned the streets. The voice sounded like the princess, but that didn't make sense. What would the princess be doing in the market on a Thursday? Even if she remained unaware of the true owner of Kosim Thalas's streets, her guards knew it was unsafe. He'd seen the pair she'd recently been assigned—two men fresh from the streets themselves, though they'd cleaned up well. If they were truly committed to protecting the princess, they should've stopped her from leaving the palace.

He caught movement to his left and whirled to find the princess being dragged out of the merchant district toward one of Teague's wagons by a thug who worked for a street boss in east Kosim Thalas. Another of Teague's men pulled a shorter girl with curly hair behind the princess. Both girls shook with terror.

Sebastian's jaw clenched, and he leaped over the low stone wall that separated him from the merchant district and headed straight for the princess.

"Get off me!" The princess's friend clawed at the man who held her, and he shoved her to the ground. She landed in an ungainly sprawl with a sharp cry of pain.

Sebastian's pulse thundered, and he broke into a run as the princess swore like a servant and twisted toward her friend.

The man holding the princess raised a fist and sent it flying toward her face.

Sebastian launched himself forward and slammed into the man, breaking his grip on the princess and sending him crashing into the side of the wagon.

"Daka!" The man swore as viciously as the princess had and reached for his dagger, but Sebastian was already there. Pinning the man's wrist beneath one boot, he snapped his other foot into the man's face.

Blood gushed from the man's nose, and his eyes rolled into the back of his head.

With one man down, Sebastian pivoted, expecting an attack from the second. Instead, he found the shorter man fending off the princess.

Her form was amateurish—she had no idea how to harness the power of her height—but her determination was a thing of beauty. She kicked, scratched, and dove at him with her fists flying.

The man, momentarily taken aback, had gone on the defensive, but he was recovering quickly. Sebastian leaped to the princess's side as the thug yanked a blade from his hip sheath.

"Left!" Sebastian barked, and the princess dodged the man's blow.

Sebastian pulled his cudgel from his vest as he lunged for the man. He absorbed one solid blow to the face before swinging his weapon into the man's stomach. The man folded, air rushing from him in a painful burst. Sebastian reached for his knife hand, but the princess was already there, applying painful pressure to the small bones of his wrist until the weapon clattered onto the road.

"You . . . fool." The man gasped as Sebastian scooped up the knife and then shoved the man to his knees. "Do you have . . . any . . . idea who . . ."

"You're the fool," Sebastian snarled. "How dare you lay your hands on the princess?"

"He works for Teague." The princess's voice was flat. "Don't say your name. Don't say anything. No one is going to suffer for helping us."

She reached for her friend and gently helped the girl to her feet.

The need to punish the man was fire in Sebastian's blood. He stood over him, flexing his fists.

A warm hand brushed lightly over his arm, and he jerked away from the touch. Turning, he found the princess, her hair disheveled, her dress torn, looking at him with steady eyes.

"Leave him," she said quietly. "I need help getting Cleo home."

Sebastian drew in a deep breath and felt the fire inside him flicker and die. Quickly, he offered his arm for Cleo to lean on and joined the princess on the long walk back to the palace.

NINE

ARI GRABBED A plate, took one of everything from the breakfast laid out on the serving bar, and sank into a seat at the (blessedly empty) dining room table, her body aching from fighting Teague's men at the market the day before. She took a bite of coddled egg and considered the results of the previous day.

She had a tiny jar of bloodflower poison. She had the rare *Book of the Fae* on order. She'd learned that Teague had a system of street bosses and runners collecting fees from the merchants—coin they paid to have Teague's disgusting henchmen leave them alone for another week. She had the bruises to prove that Teague's employees meant business. Cleo did too, which had required an elaborate story to satisfy Mama Eleni, who had spent the morning muttering dire threats against Lady Zabat's maids for daring to spill milk and cause her daughter to slip.

But most important, she'd learned that the terrifying nursery tales of the Wish Granter were based in truth—a thought that still made her heart race and her hands go cold. Nanny Babette had always started each story about the Wish Granter with the adage "He'll grant you the deepest desire of your heart, but in ten years he'll return for your soul." Ari had always thought the adage had to be an exaggeration meant to frighten children away from the belief that they could use the powerful fae without enormous cost. Now her stomach sank as she remembered Thad telling Teague he had nine years and eleven months left. If he'd made a wish, he was in more trouble than she'd thought. Whatever price he'd agreed to—and surely it wasn't his soul; her brother was far too smart for that—the stories always made it clear that the wish was never worth the price. The Wish Granter always won.

She was determined that this time he would lose.

Ari spread a generous dollop of creamy butter over her slice of raisin bread. She'd also learned that the new weapons master was more than a match for Teague's men. He was as strong as a smith but as quick as a stableboy. It was an interesting combination.

And it was a stupid thing to think about when Ari had real problems in front of her.

Thad didn't owe Teague for another nine years and eleven months. That was plenty of time for Ari to learn how to use an iron weapon or, better yet, find a secret weakness hidden in the *Book of the Fae*. Something that wouldn't depend on her (questionable) coordination. Something that would intimidate Teague into letting her brother out of his contract without killing him.

It would help if they knew where Teague lived so that when they were ready to renegotiate the bargain, they could find him, rather than waiting for him to show up unannounced. Maybe the location of his home was something she could uncover.

She licked a crumb from her finger, drank some orange juice, and made a plan for the day. She'd go to the arena to practice with her new iron weapons and thank the weapons master again for his courage yesterday. Also, she was going to take his advice (she'd been too upset by her confrontation with Teague's men to get the weapons master's name) and tell her pair of guards to look for other employment.

She raised a fork full of lamb sausage and froze at the sound of voices rapidly approaching the dining room.

Stars, the nobility, who'd come from the outskirts of Súnd-raille for the coronation and were still in residence, were coming to eat their breakfasts and here she was sitting in her stained, almost-too-small kitchen dress looking absolutely nothing like a proper princess.

Ari's pulse kicked up, and she hastily put her fork back onto plate while she scrambled to catalog her options.

She could remain where she was, but the thought of trying to finish her breakfast under anyone's prying eyes was nearly enough to ruin her appetite.

She could race out of the dining room using the servants' entrance, but it was at least two hundred paces in the opposite direction, and there was a decent chance she wouldn't make it before they came into the room. Then she'd be stuck explaining why she'd been fleeing, and, stars knew, she had no desire to do that.

Plus, running away meant abandoning her breakfast, and Ari had a full day ahead of her. She needed her strength.

That left her with only one remaining choice. As someone

pulled open the wide double doors that led into the room, Ari grabbed her plate and dove under the table.

The tablecloth settled in her wake. Ari scooted toward the middle of the table and prayed no one would sit close enough to her to accidentally kick her. Having to justify why she was hiding beneath the table would be mortifying.

Also she was pretty sure "diving under tables with plates full of food" was another item on Thad's ever-growing list of things proper princesses didn't do.

She held still, balancing her plate in her lap, and listened as at least two people filled their plates from the serving bar. They spoke quietly, and Ari recognized the voices of Thad and Ajax, Thad's head of security. Strange that Thad would invite Ajax to dine with him, but they'd been inseparable lately. Maybe keeping a man with Ajax's skills close was Thad's way of dealing with the threat of Teague returning to the palace.

Unless Ajax had an iron weapon and some bloodflower poison, his skills weren't going to be much help.

They were nearly to the chairs when Ari realized she'd left her cup of juice on the table.

It was an obvious sign that someone had been there, but hopefully it wasn't like seeing a nearly full glass of juice would make Thad suspicious that his less-than-proper sister had decided to finish the rest of her breakfast beneath the table. Besides, it could've been any one of the three dozen nobility still in residence.

Not that any of them ever showed their faces before mid-morning on a non-Assembly meeting day, but still.

"It looks like Ari has already eaten," Thad said as he and Ajax took seats five paces down from Ari's (seriously uncomfortable) seat on the floor. "None of the others would get up this early on purpose. She left most of her juice untouched. I hope she's feeling well. It's not like her to leave her food behind."

"That much is obvious." Ajax sounded amused.

Ari glared at Ajax's shins and defiantly stuffed two bites of sausage into her mouth instead of one. So what if she was curvier than was fashionable? She was also smart, confident, pretty, funny, loyal, and a lot of other excellent things that she couldn't remember while she was busy wishing she could throw her fork at his unprotected legs.

"You will speak of my sister respectfully, or you will be out of a job." Thad's voice was sharp, and a rush of warmth flooded Ari's chest. "The princess is worth more than the rest of the nobility put together."

"My apologies, Your Highness. I never meant to question the princess's worth or her appearance," Ajax said. "I like a girl who can fill out a dress."

"One more word about my sister, and you won't be able to find work anywhere in Kosim Thalas. I don't care if I need your specialized skills. I will not tolerate disrespect toward Ari. Understood?"

Ari mentally cheered for Thad and popped a grape into her mouth, only to nearly choke as she heard Ajax's next words.

"Understood. And since we're meeting this morning to discuss my skills, I wanted you to know that I've considered your request, and I will take on the entrapment and destruction of the Wish Granter, but for twice the price you named. He's a very powerful fae."

"Done."

Ari sat frozen, her fork halfway up to her mouth. Entrapment and destruction?

Thad was sending the head of his security to assassinate Teague. What if Ajax failed? Was avoiding the price Thad had agreed to pay really worth going to war with Teague?

It was definitely time for a heart-to-heart with her brother.

"When will you do it?" Thad asked.

"Within the month. It takes time to prepare and come up with a plan."

"You told me you'd killed fae before." Thad's foot tapped the floor impatiently.

"I have. In Balavata. Helped some bounty hunters from Llorenyae stalk and kill a pair of rogue fae who angered the Winter King. But we're talking about the Wish Granter. I'm going to need an iron cage, poison-tipped iron arrows, and time to figure out his routine so I know when to strike. Might also be helpful to have a few trained monsters from Llorenyae to help."

Ari started shaking her head even as Thad said, "Do it."

Do it? Bring fae monsters into Súndraille in the hope that this guard knew how to control them? What if they got loose and turned against innocent people? What if they refused to attack Teague? Súndraille wasn't equipped for the kind of beasts that roamed Llorenyae. This could be a disaster. Ari's stomach sank, and she slowly lowered her fork to her plate.

Thad must be truly desperate to even consider such an option.

"I'll need a barn made out of stone and stalls made from iron cages," Ajax said.

Thad was silent for a moment. Finally, he said, "And if they overpower you? If they get free?"

"They come trained with specific commands. We'll be able to control them. The bounty hunters I worked with are very professional."

"Fine. I'll task every servant I can spare with building a barn to your specifications, and I'll hire more if necessary so that we can finish it quickly. I'd prefer if you waited to attack Teague until after the ball we're hosting in the princess's honor three weeks from now. If something goes wrong . . . she deserves to be launched properly without the taint of her brother's death hanging over her head."

Ari's heart thudded against her chest, and she clutched her plate with shaking hands.

If he was so certain that failure meant his death, then why risk it in the first place? He had nine years and eleven months left. Surely an assassination attempt should be the final, desperate gamble they played just before time ran out.

"I'll wait until after the ball unless Teague appears to be escalating against you. We have to keep you safe, Your Highness. Once the Wish Granter is destroyed and your soul is no longer in danger, you can—"

Ari's blood ran cold, and her plate hit the floor with a thud, spilling her muffin onto the rug.

"What was that?" Ajax demanded, bending down to peer beneath the tablecloth.

Ari ignored him as she crawled out from under the table beside Thad's chair. Remaining on her knees, she crossed her arms over her chest and glared at Thad through eyes already swimming with tears.

"You bargained away your *soul*? How could you?" Her voice shook, and a tear spilled over, chasing a trail of heat down her cheek.

He closed his eyes as if in pain, and then said quietly, "Give us the room."

"Your Highnesses." Ajax stood, bowed stiffly, and left.

"What happened?" Ari wiped tears from her face and tried to go back to glaring at Thad, but icy fear had blossomed like a pit within her, and she couldn't tear her mind away from the image of Teague coming for Thad. Tearing her brother from her and leaving another sharp ache of pain burrowing into her heart for a lifetime.

Her brother's eyes met hers, and desperate regret filled his face. "Mother had just been killed. The queen was hunting us. I left you asleep in the date grove and considered throwing myself into the sea—"

"Oh, Thad."

"—but that wouldn't have solved anything. She would've hunted you down next. Teague found me there."

"What was he doing wandering around a date grove so far from Kosim Thalas?"

Thad shook his head. "I don't know. Maybe his magic senses when someone is truly desperate."

"Desperate enough to wish to be king in exchange for his soul?" She tried to keep the disappointment from her voice, but he looked wounded anyway.

"I didn't want to do that, Ari. I just wanted to protect you the way I wasn't able to protect Mother." He pressed his fingers to his forehead as if it pained him. "I wished for you to be safe from the queen's hunters."

Ari trembled. "That's not worth your soul plus ten years of looking the other way while Teague does whatever he pleases to the people of Kosim Thalas."

"I didn't know about the clause that said I couldn't interfere with Teague's activities, but, yes, saving you would've been worth my soul."

Now she glared again, though her tears were falling harder. "We could've figured out another way, Thad. You and I. Made a plan. We're good at that."

"No, *you're* good at that." He smiled, though his eyes were sad. "I'm good at realizing when your mad schemes are about to cause disaster."

"Well, look who's causing a disaster now." Her voice was sharp.

"I know." His shoulders slumped. "He wouldn't grant my wish."

"But you said you owed your soul and—"

"He wouldn't grant my wish to spare you from the hunters. He would only grant a wish to make me king." He stared at his hands, his fingers laced together so tightly his golden skin was turning pale at the knuckles.

"Because he wanted no interference from the throne as he took over the city with his nasty henchmen."

Thad frowned and met her gaze. "What do you know about that?"

Ari found something very interesting to study on the carpet. "One hears rumors. All right, so the only way to save us from the hunters was to wish to be king. Obviously it was dark outside so you couldn't read the contract very well and see the bit about letting him get away with whatever he wants, but I think it would help us to read it now. Maybe there's a loophole. I have the *Book of the Fae* on order. There might be something in there that will help. Where's the contract?"

"He kept it."

"He kept— Honestly, Thad. Why would you let him do that?" Ari snapped.

"You've met him!" His voice rose. "No one *lets* him do anything! I made the wish so I could keep you safe. I thought once I was king I could exile Father, the queen, and his son and then spend the time I had left preparing you to be Súndraille's queen. I didn't know the royal family would die, or that I would have to stand by and watch as Teague hurts the people I've sworn to protect."

"Thad—"

"I can't even look at myself in the mirror." His voice shook. "I wear a crown gained by trickery, and I can't make it right. All I can do is keep you safe and train you to be the kind of ruler I can't be."

She wrapped her arms around him and swallowed her tears as he leaned against her.

Maybe Thad couldn't make this right, but she could. She had to.

TEN

STEP ONE IN Ari's plan to take on Teague was to learn how to use a weapon without accidentally putting out her eye.

She stood in the arena, looking over the small collection of iron daggers, arrowheads, and throwing stars the weapons master had fashioned while also discreetly looking over him as well. He really was young for the job. He had maybe a year on her, though something in his eyes looked much older. And he was tall. Even with Ari's height, she had to look up to meet his gaze. There was a stillness, an *awareness* to him that told her he missed very little—something she was grateful for after yesterday.

Everything about him—from his close-cut black hair to his ruthlessly neat uniform to the muscles that filled out his (very intriguing) shoulders—said that he was a person of incredible discipline.

Ari could appreciate that, even if it did make her want to check her own clothing for the stain that her midmorning snack had probably left behind.

"Have you ever used a weapon?" he asked. His voice was as quiet and controlled as his body. Very different from the dangerous snarl he'd used against Teague's men the day before.

"Besides my brain and my fist? No."

The corners of his eyes crinkled. She decided to take that as a smile.

"Do you want to practice something for close combat or distance?" he asked, his eyes grazing over the bruises Teague's men had left on her upper arms.

"Both," she said. "And you never told me your name. If we're going to be friends, I need to know what to call you."

"Friends?" He stared at her as though she'd suddenly sprouted another head.

"Well, of course. We're going to be spending hours together each day until I master some weapons. And while I'm very smart and capable, I will admit that coordination is sometimes a problem for me, which means it might take more than a few sessions to feel like I can carry a weapon without cutting off my own arm by accident. And if I'm going to be spending hours every day with you, then we're going to be friends, because the alternative is too exhausting to contemplate."

Especially when she already had enough on her plate. She had a brother to worry about, a best friend with a black eye, and a fae monster who needed killing. She wasn't going to add "awkward daily sessions with the weapons master" to the list.

"Do you always talk this much?" he asked, a trace of amusement in his voice.

"Do you always talk this little?"

His eyes crinkled again.

Yes. Definitely a smile.

"I'm Sebastian," he said.

She gave him a wide, generous smile. "It's nice to make your acquaintance, Sebastian. Now, where do we begin?"

They turned to the long table full of weapons that had been placed for the nobility to use. The iron weapons were set off by themselves, but Ari couldn't resist running her hand over the shiny surface of a thin, curved blade with a delicately woven handle in silver and gold. Her fingers slid against the edge, and a quick bite of pain hit as the blade nicked her skin.

"Ouch." She pulled her hand away, and blood welled on her fingertip. "The blade is sharp."

He gave her a look that clearly said, "Were you expecting a sword to be dull?"

"This proves my point, you know." She looked around for a cloth to dab against her finger, and he fished a clean rag from his pocket and handed it to her, careful not to let their fingers touch. She'd seen his discomfort when he'd briefly taken her hand at their first meeting. Was he unwilling to touch anyone, or was his reluctance specific to her?

She bent her neck and did a surreptitious sniff test.

She smelled like peaches and pastry dough. If he had issues with that, there was nothing she could do for him.

"What point?" he asked.

"I will need a lot of training before I'll be ready to carry a weapon. Which would you suggest I learn to use?"

He ran his eyes over her body as though cataloging her center of balance.

"For long range, I made an iron throwing star. It's thin and as light as I could get it." Sebastian said. "For close combat, you can keep a dagger strapped to your hip or your ankle, but you're going to have to learn to *be* the weapon in case you're disarmed at short range."

"Oh stars, we're in trouble."

"You already said you use your brain and your fists."

"I also said that coordination is often a problem for me."

"If you train hard enough, your muscles will remember what to do. It will be second nature." He sounded resolute. "Besides, I saw you yesterday. You're fierce and determined. Once I show you how to put some power behind your punches, you're going to be formidable."

"You're serious about this?" She glanced down at herself and then back up at him. "You're going to teach me how to win a fistfight against a grown man?"

He met her gaze, his eyes glowing with purpose. "I'm going to teach you how to stop him before it ever gets to that. But first, let's start with the throwing star."

He picked up the iron star and handed it to her. It was heavier than she'd expected, but the weight felt evenly balanced.

"You can carry this with you in one of those wrist bags girls like to wear."

Ari twisted the star so that the light from the row of windows surrounding the upper deck of the arena gleamed dully against its surface. "If you'd told me last week that I'd be willing to smuggle a weapon in my handbag instead of snacks, I'd have called you crazy."

He blinked. "You smuggle snacks in your handbag?"

"Sometimes the situation calls for it."

His eyes crinkled again, and Ari grinned as she hefted the star. "So you want me to throw this?"

"I'll teach you how."

"I might put out your eye."

"I'll take the risk."

She closed her fingers over the star and turned to look him in the face. "Thank you. Not just for this, but for yesterday too."

"You're welcome." He gestured toward the center of the arena. "Now let's go see if you really can put out my eye."

Forty minutes later, Ari had yet to hit the target. She stood in the center of the arena facing both a bale of hay and Sebastian, who'd given up trying to demonstrate proper throwing technique in favor of standing to the side so he could evaluate her stance or her grip or whatever it was she was doing wrong.

"Again," he said.

She held one of the star's five points between her index finger and her thumb, brought her arm up over her head, lunged forward with her left leg, and threw.

The star plowed into the sawdust ten paces from her feet.

Ari glared at the (stupid, probably defective) thing and muttered something very un-princess-like.

"Are you flicking your wrist?" Sebastian asked.

Was she? "Probably."

He raised a brow. "I don't think you are."

She blew a stray piece of hair out of her eyes and went to collect the star. "Fine. I'll flick my wrist."

She scooped the star off the ground and resumed her stance. This time when she released the star, she flicked her wrist.

The star drove into the ground at her feet, narrowly missing her little toe. Sebastian started toward her.

"Daka!" she swore like a stableboy, then glanced over her shoulder at the open doorway, but they were alone. If any of the nobility had overheard her use of servants' slang and told Thad, he'd add it the long list of things Ari was no longer supposed to do now that she was a proper princess.

"Are you hurt?" Sebastian knelt and collected the star, running his gaze over her foot.

She sighed. "The only thing I've managed to hurt is the floor."

"And the post behind you." His voice was still carefully controlled, but Ari could swear she heard a trace of humor in it.

"Basically the only thing in this entire room that is safe from me is the target."

"You're close to hitting it." He delivered this piece of nonsense with absolute sincerity as he rose to his feet, the star in his hands. "With a few adjustments to your technique, you'll hit the bull's-eye."

"I *have* been adjusting my technique."

"You're flicking your wrist too late. You want to cock it back and release it just as you straighten your arm. Watch me."

He lifted his arm, wrist cocked, and then brought it down. Flicking his wrist just as his arm straightened at shoulder height, he sent the star flying directly into the center of the target.

Or at least she assumed the star went into the center of the target. Frankly, she was too busy admiring the way his shoulders bunched beneath his tunic to pay much attention to anything else.

"See?" He turned to her.

"No, I wasn't . . . yes! Yes, I see the star"—she glanced quickly at the target—"right in the center. Well done."

He raised a brow. "Thank you. Your turn."

"Where did you learn how to use all the weapons in our arsenal?" she asked as he went to collect the star. The sudden stiffness in his (unfairly distracting!) shoulders sent her scrambling for a different question. "I mean, you're about my age, right? Kind of young to be a master of so many weapons unless you had training. I know there's an academy in . . ."

He'd turned to face her, and the look on his face told her she'd stumbled into something he didn't want to discuss. "I picked up things here and there. If you have questions about my ability to perform my job—"

"Oh please." She stopped herself from rolling her eyes. Barely. Score one for proper princess behavior. "You just impaled a hand-sized star into the dead center of a target fifty paces away. And you destroyed those men who were trying to take Cleo and me yesterday. Your abilities are not in question. I was making conversation. It's what friends do."

He frowned as he approached to give her the weapon, careful to keep from touching her.

"This will be a lot easier for both of us if you tell me what topics are off-limits for conversation with your friends."

He stood, silent and still.

Fine. She could outwait him. She crossed her arms over her chest so she could look vaguely intimidating and accidentally poked one of the star's edges into her rib cage.

"Ouch," she muttered, and then gave Sebastian a look that dared him to remind her that the star was sharp. "Are you going to answer my question, or am I going to have to continue to injure myself while I wait you out?"

Stiffly, he said, "I don't have off-limit topics—"

"I beg to differ."

"—because I don't have friends. I don't need them."

Ari's chest ached at the carefully blank expression on his face. At the way he said the words as if they didn't matter. She smiled—not a gentle, pitying smile because, stars knew, she hated being on the receiving end of those, but a genuine, wide, all-teeth-on-display smile—and bumped his shoulder with hers. "Well, you have a friend now."

He stiffened as she touched him, and then slowly relaxed, though she could see that he was forcing himself to look like the touch hadn't mattered.

She turned toward the target. This time, she was going to hit something other than the floor. Apparently it was all in the wrist. Her arm whispered against Sebastian's as she raised it over her head, and he immediately took several steps forward and to the right so that he could watch her form.

Drawing in a deep breath, she focused on the target and tried to remember every step of the process. Grip one edge of the star between her index finger and her thumb. Step forward with the opposite leg. Cock her wrist. Drop her arm and straighten it at shoulder height and then flick her wrist. Or was it flick her wrist just before she straightened her arm?

She hesitated a split second as her arm fell past her shoulder, and then quickly snapped her wrist forward and threw the star with all the strength she had. It flew to the right, and Sebastian gasped as it grazed his side.

"Oh no!" Ari rushed to him as blood soaked his tunic. "Please tell me I didn't just kill you."

"You didn't just kill me." He peeled up the stained fabric to reveal a long, narrow slash of open skin.

"I'm so sorry." Her hands hovered uncertainly in the air as he let the tunic fall, covering the wound as it kept seeping blood.

"It's just a flesh wound," he said. "I've had worse."

She stepped closer to him, trying to gauge how much blood was on his tunic.

"At least it wasn't my eye." The corners of his mouth twitched slightly.

Seriously? *Now* he was going to (kind of) smile?

"I can't believe you're making a joke. I could've impaled you in the stomach. Or the heart." Her eyes widened as the sickening possibilities hit her.

"This is nothing." Blood dripped off the edge of his tunic. He grasped it and began pulling it over his head.

"I'll get the medical supplies. Where are they?"

"In the chest beside the stairs that lead to the upper deck."

The tunic slid over his head, and Ari stared at the muscles that defined his stomach. At the wickedly raised scar that slashed across his chest. At the, stars help her, way his shoulders moved as he rolled the tunic into a ball and pressed it against his wound.

She needed to focus. Preferably on something other than Sebastian. She was turning to fetch the medical supplies when Sebastian twisted at the waist to throw the bloodstained tunic toward the edge of the arena. The sight of his back stopped her. His skin was a mess of crisscrossed scars, some faded to a faint shining white, others still a raised purple-red line that said they'd been inflicted within the last year.

The ache that had started in her chest when he'd said that he didn't have friends ignited into something that seared her heart and pricked tears against her lashes.

He was her age. Yet some of those scars looked like they'd been there for at least a decade. She'd like to meet the person who could lash the skin from a child's back, and then she'd like to strap that person to a bale of hay and keep practicing until her throwing star landed dead center.

"Do you have the medical supplies?" he asked as he turned and caught her staring (mortifyingly) openmouthed at him. His body went still, and an expressionless mask slid over his face. His eyes were guarded, as if bracing himself for her unwelcome pity.

Which meant Ari had to talk about something else—*anything else*—to cover up the awful ache she felt when she looked at him. She took a breath, hoped inspiration would hit, and said the first thing that came to mind.

"You must lift a lot of heavy things. Hay bales maybe? Swords? Multiple swords at once? I don't know how else you'd get muscles like these. Not that I'm looking at your muscles. I mean, I *am*, but only because there's really nothing else but sawdust to look at, and so . . ." Stars above, *why* was she still talking? "I'm just going to get the medical supplies now, and both of us are going to pretend this entire conversation never happened."

She hurried to get a bandage and cleansing ointment, and prayed that she wouldn't say another unbelievably awkward word about muscles or lifting things or basically anything that didn't have to do with bandaging his wound. When she returned, the guarded look in his eyes had faded, though he was watching her like she was a puzzle he couldn't quite figure out. She dropped her gaze to the cut on his side, and his body tensed.

She'd have to touch him to put the bandage on, and that would be upsetting to him. It was bad enough that she'd sliced him open with a throwing star. She couldn't force him to endure her touch as well—and he would choose to endure it because she was the princess. A member of the servant class wouldn't risk arguing with royalty.

"Here's the thing," she said as she moved to his side. "I want to bandage your wound because I can reach it better than you can, and because I feel terrible for hurting you. But we're friends, remember?"

"So you keep telling me." His voice was a shade warmer than neutral.

She'd call that a small victory.

"Friends are equals."

He made a sound in the back of his throat.

"That means friends don't tell each other what to do and expect obedience," she said.

"Which is why a weapons master and a princess don't get to be friends," he said gently.

It was a setback, and it stung more than Ari thought it should, but she hadn't survived life as a bastard daughter ignored by her father the king—unable to fit in with either the nobility or the servants until Thad took the throne—without learning how to handle disappointment.

She handed him the ointment. "You're going to change your mind. I can be pretty relentless. Obviously today's session is over. I'll give you a few days to recover before I come back for another one."

"I don't need a few days."

"All right, I'll be back tomorrow morning," she said.

"Princess Arianna, if you need help tonight, for any reason, I sleep in a cot in the office attached to the arena," Sebastian said with quiet intensity, his gaze brushing over her bruised arms. "I'd be surprised if Teague's men would visit the palace and try anything, but just in case. I'm here."

She smiled at him. "Thank you."

Now that she'd made progress on learning to use a weapon—if she could count the fact that she'd hit something other than the floor as progress—she needed to make a solid backup plan to protect her brother and stop the Wish Granter. Leaving the throwing star on the table, she slipped the iron dagger into her purse and left the arena.

Before she made any more plans or asked more questions, she was going to dip this blade into bloodflower poison and strap it to her hip.

Just in case.

ELEVEN

TEAGUE WATCHED AS the princess strode out of the arena and headed toward the palace.

He hadn't counted on her resourcefulness or on how quickly she would figure out a way to hurt him. In fact, one look at her ungainly height and abundant curves, and he'd figured she was the least of his worries.

He wasn't afraid to admit when he was wrong.

Young Thaddeus wasn't a threat. Not anymore. His blood bound him to the contract they'd signed. He couldn't lift a finger against Teague.

His sister was another story.

He glared at her, though she couldn't yet see him. His plans were in place. Ten years of doing as he pleased throughout Súndraille, and when Thad gave up his soul, no one would think to challenge Teague for the throne.

He'd finally have power that had nothing to do with owing someone a wish.

The boy's sister would either get in line with his plans or he'd find a way to force her to cooperate.

Cold determination filled him while he watched the princess. She moved with purpose, walking quickly past the line of trees that framed the palace road as she approached the garden that hugged the western side of the palace.

He waited until she'd passed, and then fast as a thought, he was behind her.

"Arianna Glavan, we need to come to an understanding."

She gasped and spun to face him, and he had his hand wrapped around her throat before she could do more than stagger back a step.

He ran the back of his other hand over her cheek and cocked his head to study her eyes.

Terrified.

Angry.

Defiant.

It was the defiance that sparked his interest.

And his fear.

The defiant ones didn't break when you threatened them. They didn't cave to bribes or bargain for their own safety.

But every human had a breaking point. He just had to find hers.

She jerked her head, but he held her fast. She was tall, but he could reach her throat, and that was all that mattered.

"Get off our property," she rasped.

He smiled as he imagined peeling the skin from her bones. It was hard to be defiant when you were in too much pain to do anything but scream. He couldn't kill her, though, unless he had no other choice. She was Thaddeus's weakness, and the boy would instantly break the terms of his contract if his sister was harmed. Teague needed to lay the groundwork for his own ascension to the throne before that happened.

Which meant he had to find the key to controlling the princess.

"You've been asking questions about me. Do you know what I do to people who pry into my business?" He held her gaze, but she didn't flinch.

He tried again. "Do you really think that's the best way to keep your brother safe?"

Her eyes narrowed. "You can't touch him for nine years and eleven months unless he breaks the terms of your contract. Your magic has rules."

The bravado in her voice was thin, but there was no mistaking the furious courage in her eyes.

His smile widened. Not herself. Not her brother. Where was the princess's weakness?

His voice dropped to a whisper filled with every considerable ounce of malice he possessed. "Perhaps I can't touch young Thaddeus, but he wasn't the one asking questions with you yesterday, was he?"

Her eyes widened, and the pulse beneath his fingers fluttered.

The friend, then.

Perfect.

"I will only say this once, Princess. Stay out of my affairs. That includes my contract with your brother. Tell your friend—Cleo, isn't it?—to stay out of them too. If either of you disobeys, I will tear her apart, piece by piece. Do we have an understanding?"

Her lips trembled as she nodded, and he slowly released his grip on her throat.

"A pleasure seeing you again, Princess. Let's hope for Cleo's sake that our paths don't cross for the next nine years and eleven months."

She rubbed her hands as if they were chilled, and at the last second, he realized she was reaching for something in her wrist bag. Snatching her wrist, he plunged his hand into her bag and pulled out an iron dagger.

The dagger stung his palm, and he dropped it as a welter of blisters rose on his skin. Foolish girl. Did she really think she could stop him with a small bit of iron? Fury ignited cold tendrils of his magic as he glared at her. Slowly he raised his palm to show her the blisters as they bubbled up, hardened, and then sank down to become smooth, unlined skin once more.

"If you want to kill me, my dear, you have to bring something far stronger than a dagger." He bared his teeth, and she took a step back. "You thought you were dealing with a regular fae, but you were wrong. I am beyond your comprehension. I was alive when this kingdom was founded, and I will be alive to see it fall."

She opened her mouth, but nothing came out.

He straightened his jacket and stooped to put the dagger in his pocket. Then, inclining his head to her, he said, "Watch yourself, Princess. Cleo's life depends on it."

TWELVE

SEBASTIAN WAS GETTING used to being around the princess. Instinctive panic still hit when she accidentally touched him, but he'd stopped gauging the distance between them as if it might bite him. Stopped bracing himself for her disapproval and anger.

She walked into the arena one evening nearly a week after her first lesson wearing a simple green dress and carrying a small cloth-wrapped bundle. Waving away the instant bowing of the nobility, who were playing a rousing game of pin the dagger on the outlaw, she came straight for Sebastian.

"You have a bruise on your jaw and a cut on your mouth. What happened?" She stood directly in front of him and studied him openly, apparently unaware that her social status was supposed to make him invisible and that the nobility were watching.

He shrugged.

She stepped closer, and he tensed.

"Someone hit you."

"Sparring session with one of the noblemen. Makario likes to make sure he lands a few punches. It's easier to let him win than to deal with his temper if he loses. I'm just grateful it was a fist and not a throwing star," he said, and then snapped his mouth shut. What was he *doing*? Making a stupid joke about the princess crossed a line he couldn't uncross.

She laughed, and he watched her for signs that she didn't mean it.

Her eyes were lit with mischief, and her body language was relaxed and open. She meant it.

"That cut on your lip will open again if you aren't careful. Guess it's lucky for you that you smile with everything but your mouth." She winked at him.

Winked at him.

And stars help him, he felt the corners of his lips twitch in response.

She grinned, though there was a shadow of something serious behind it.

This was not how a princess was supposed to treat a servant. He should be invisible. Expendable. She shouldn't care about him beyond the job he was supposed to perform. She shouldn't; but if there was one thing he could say about the princess with absolute confidence, it was that she did as she pleased without worrying about what others thought of her.

As if to prove her point, she turned to the assembled crowd, most of whom were only halfheartedly practicing with their weapons as they watched the princess and the weapons master. "There are games and refreshments set up in the front parlor. Perhaps you'd like to reconvene there."

As it had before, her tone left no room for debate. The nobility filed past them, and Sebastian kept his back to the arena's wall, working hard to keep from rolling to the balls of his feet as his scars tingled and his heart raced.

This wasn't the kind of crowd he had to worry about. He wasn't trapped. He was just doing his job until he could buy true safety.

And speaking of doing his job, he'd volunteered to be available to help the princess after dark if she felt threatened. He'd spent the last week sleeping restlessly, his cudgel beside his bed, but she hadn't knocked on his door. Either she hadn't needed help, or she hadn't been able to get to him to ask for it.

He was betting on the latter, though all he had for evidence was the shadow that had haunted her face since the afternoon of their first sparring session. She'd returned the next day visibly shaken, the faint smudge of a bruise around her neck, but she hadn't volunteered any information, and it wasn't his place to ask.

He studied her while she watched the last of the nobility leave the arena. The bruises on her arms were nearly gone, as was the one on her neck. There were no other visible injuries. He couldn't assess the areas of skin that were covered by her dress, but she hadn't walked like she'd been injured. He checked the angle of her hips and was satisfied that she wasn't favoring one leg over another.

"Looking for something?" she asked, and there was an unfriendly note in her voice for the first time since he'd met her.

He snapped his gaze up to her face, and realized with absolute mortification that she'd caught him staring at her hips. A girl of her beauty and confidence was probably weary of having men notice her curves and her skin and her— Had he lost his mind? He had no right to notice anything about the princess except that she had the power to take his job from him with a single word.

Taking a step back, he schooled his expression into a blank mask. "My apologies, Princess Arianna."

She huffed out a little breath and shifted the cloth-wrapped bundle she held. "I don't want apologies, Sebastian, unless I know what you're apologizing for."

He tried to find words that wouldn't be offensive, but there really wasn't an acceptable way to tell royalty he'd been running his eyes over her body because somehow he'd foolishly thought it was his job to make sure she hadn't been hurt.

"Well?" She looked at him expectantly. "I promise you, this is the wrong moment to choose to be silent. I've had my fill of being treated like the way I look matters more than who I really am."

He opened his mouth to assure her that he hadn't been noticing the way she looked, but he couldn't lie. He'd paid attention to the glow of her skin. The way her eyes danced with her every emotion. The curves that filled out her dress in a way that he found far more intriguing than a boy in his position had any right to.

Shoving those thoughts aside, he said, "I was checking to make sure you were all right."

She raised a brow, and her voice was flat. "You were staring at my waist because you were concerned for my well-being. Really? That's the best explanation you can come up with?"

"Yes. No! Not your waist. Your hips. I was staring at your

hips." Stars help him, he didn't realize how terrible that would sound until it left his mouth.

"Well, I hope you liked what you saw, because I'm leaving." She turned on her heel and started for the exit.

He was going to lose his job. His chance at freedom from Kosim Thalas. And he was going to lose the respect of the princess, which shouldn't bother him but somehow did.

"Wait!" He took a step forward, and then stopped as she slowly turned to face him. His pulse was thunder in his ears at the sight of her angry expression. "After your run-in with Teague's men, I promised to help you if you felt threatened in the palace. You haven't come, but something is clearly wrong and has been for a while, and I worried that it meant . . . that you'd been hurt. I was looking at the way you were standing. If you'd been hit someplace where it wouldn't show, you'd be compensating for the pain by putting your weight on the side of your body that hurt the least."

Stars knew, he had experience in trying to find a way to absorb the red-hot agony of a beating while still moving about his everyday life.

Her expression softened.

"I meant no offense." He realized his hands were fists and made himself unfurl them.

"I believe you," she said simply, and he could see that it was true. "And as proof that our friendship can weather the occasional argument, I'll even share my snack with you."

She held up the wrapped bundle.

"You don't need to do that."

She blew a stray piece of hair out of her eyes and walked to his side. "Why do people say that? Of course I don't need to do it, but if I say I'm going to, then that's it. Decision made. Trying to give me a way out of it just slows things down."

He had no response to that. She busied herself unwrapping a small loaf of bread that smelled like the bakery he'd passed each morning last winter on his way to mucking out the local livery stable. His stomach growled, suddenly unsatisfied with the slice of cheese and half an apple he'd eaten at dawn. He'd have to eat the bread or risk offending her. Somehow he didn't think it was going to be a hardship.

"Cranberry orange bread with a cinnamon-sugar crust." She broke it in half and handed him a piece as big as his hand. "I baked it myself. It's better than Mama Eleni's, but don't tell her that."

"Who is Mama Eleni?" he asked as he took a bite and savored the softness of the bread and the warm sugared-fruit flavor that tasted exactly as he'd always imagined something like this would taste.

"You know . . . Mama Eleni. The cook." She shook her head. "You really should pay more attention to the name of the woman who cooks for you every day. She's a good ally to have. You never know when you're going to need an extra snack."

He shrugged. "I don't eat in the palace kitchen, so I've never met her." He raised the bread to his mouth again, but stopped at the expression on her face.

"If you don't eat the servants' meals, what do you eat?"

"Bread, apples, and cheese."

"That's *it*?" She was staring at him with a mixture of horror and pity.

"That's enough to get me through each day. Speaking of which, we should get started on your—"

"Food isn't about getting through the day, Sebastian." She waved her bread under his nose as if he didn't already have his own piece just begging to be finished. "It's about stopping and appreciating the moment. It's about exploring new tastes and textures. It's about giving yourself a little piece of comfort or joy and sharing that with others."

"And here I thought it was simply to keep one's body going," he said, and finished off the rest of his bread quickly. Talking with the princess was easy—far easier than it should've been—and he was in danger of forgetting that he had a job to do, a job that didn't include letting her think they were going to be friends. It was time to get started on her lesson and remember his place at the bottom of the society that she held in the palm of her hand.

"Come to the kitchens tonight. It's dessert baking day, so there will be something special on the table."

He dusted crumbs from his hands. "I'm fine. I don't like the kitchens."

She threw her hands into the air. "Why not?"

"Because there are people there."

"Yes, but there's also *pie*."

His lips twitched upward. "I can live without pie."

She grinned, but then froze as she looked past him to the arena's doorway. A frown etched itself between her brows, and she clenched her hands into fists.

"What? What's wrong?" He spun on his heel, but could see nothing in the darkness beyond the distant faint shadows of the trees that lined the drive. When he turned back to face the princess, she'd grabbed his cudgel from the table of weapons beside them and was running for the door.

"Wait! Princess!"

"He's here!" She was nearly to the doorway. "The man from the market. The one who was in charge of all Teague's men. He's *here*, and he must be coming for Cleo."

She disappeared into the night, and Sebastian swore as he snatched up a mace and a dagger and went after her at a dead run.

THIRTEEN

SHE WASN'T GOING to be too late. She refused to be too late.

Her feet flew across the lawn and onto the palace road. It was hard to run and hang on to Sebastian's stupidly heavy cudgel at the same time, but she did it.

She couldn't see Teague's man anymore, but she didn't need to. She knew where Cleo was. Now she just had to get there in time.

Please let her get there in time.

Her breath was searing her lungs by the time she reached the garden's entrance, but she didn't slow down.

What had she done since Teague's visit to bring this on Cleo? She hadn't been to Kosim Thalas. Hadn't asked any questions. She'd spent her time sparring with Sebastian, cooking with Cleo, and reading every book on contract law and Llorenyae in the palace library.

She hadn't done anything to put Cleo in danger.

Cleo was in danger anyway.

Her calves ached as she reached the curved drive in front of the palace. Maybe there was a spy in the palace. Someone who'd reported on Ari's activities. Maybe Teague had decided Ari was still a threat.

It didn't matter why Teague had sent his man. It only mattered that Ari reach Cleo in time. Cleo would be in the kitchen. It would be faster to cut through the garden than to go into the palace itself.

She dragged in a deep breath, trying to quiet the stitch in her side. The cudgel clutched in her hands was slick with sweat. Somewhere behind her, footsteps pounded against the ground. Sebastian, probably.

She launched herself into the garden, her feet sliding against the path, and then froze as voices cut through the night.

"—no right to come here." Thad's voice was raised in anger. Thad?

Where was Cleo?

Ari missed whatever response the stranger made because she was too busy trying to silently hurry down the path toward the sound.

"His Royal Highness commanded you to leave." Thad's guard Ajax raised his voice.

Ari turned to the left, leaving the path in favor of cutting a direct line toward the voices and nearly tripped over a small bush.

"Daka!" she swore as her toe connected with a thorn. Hastily, she moved around the bush and climbed into a flower bed. Her shoes crushed blossoms into the dirt as she ran.

"You signed a contract." The stranger's voice reminded Ari of the thick, weighted calm that covered the kingdom right before a storm unleashed itself on the land. "You don't try to break a contract with my employer without suffering the consequences."

She had the sudden, sick feeling that Ajax hadn't been as discreet as he should've been while making plans to find and kill Teague.

Maybe this wasn't about Cleo after all.

Maybe Ari was in danger of losing Thad.

Would Teague hold Ajax's actions against her brother?

The nearly healed bruise on her neck throbbed in time with her pulse, a vivid reminder that Teague would do as he pleased.

Ari slid over a patch of rocky soil and nearly dropped the cudgel. She was almost there. A handful of trees was all that separated her from her brother.

The fact that she didn't know what she was going to do when she got there didn't matter. She'd figure it out.

"Who said anything about breaking the contract?" Ajax asked.

Ari moved into the trees.

"This is insulting." Thad sounded furious. "I've done nothing to warrant this. I've held back the city guard and turned a blind eye to Teague's business. I've upheld my end of our bargain. You have no right—"

"Your man here has a reputation for killing lesser fae than my boss. Now we hear rumors that he's got his sights set on Teague himself. That was a mistake."

"Rumors and lies." Ajax sounded angry, but Ari could hear the thread of fear beneath it.

The stranger laughed, though he didn't sound amused. "You

boys are in so far over your heads, you don't even have the sense to know you're drowning."

The dull thud of a fist smacking flesh sent Ari hurtling forward. She skidded around a tree and stopped as she took in the scene.

Thad was on his knees, holding his rib cage, while terrified rage lit his face. His guard rushed for the stranger, and the man pivoted and slammed his fists into the side of Ajax's face as he passed. Ajax fell to the ground, and then a knife was in the stranger's hand, driving into Ajax's side.

Turning, the stranger stood over Thad with his back to Ari and said grimly, "My employer has a message for you."

His fist crashed into Thad's nose, and blood flowed.

Ari wrapped her hands around the cudgel and lifted it above her head.

"You cannot get out of the contract you signed." He kicked Thad in the stomach.

Ari crept forward as her brother moaned and retched.

"You cannot protect yourself from him." The knife flashed, and Thad cried out as it sliced into his arm.

Ari judged the remaining paces between herself and the stranger and prayed she wouldn't miss.

"You should've enjoyed your last nine years of freedom so that you would never have to see my face." The man raised the knife.

Ari lunged forward, closed the distance between them, and swung the cudgel at the stranger's head like she was hammering a nail.

The weapon hit the man with a terrible wet crunch. He

dropped to the ground and lay motionless.

Thad fell back, moaning in pain, and Ari raised the cudgel, her body trembling as she waited to see if the man would get up and threaten her brother again.

"Princess!"

She looked up the path, and then Sebastian was there.

"He was hurting my brother." Ari's voice shook, and her teeth began to chatter uncontrollably as the man lay silent and still, blood pouring from his head to form a viscous ring around him. "I had to stop him."

Sebastian crouched beside the man and pressed two fingers against his neck. "You can put the weapon down, Princess. He's dead."

"Oh, stars." Ari dropped the weapon and backed away from the body.

Carefully, Sebastian rolled the man onto his back, and then went still.

"You were right, Princess. This is Daan, Teague's collector. His top employee." His voice was hard. "If Teague finds out his collector died here, you'll be in more trouble than you can possibly imagine."

FOURTEEN

SEBASTIAN'S MIND RACED as he stared at the dead body of Alistair Teague's collector. Footsteps crashed through the garden, and he whirled, fists raised, but it was only Cleo, a sack of cookies in her hands.

"Cleo!" The princess stumbled toward her friend. "What are you doing here? Never mind, don't answer that. Just go."

"I was bringing a snack to the new boy who works in the stables and I heard a commotion." Cleo clutched the cookies to her chest, her eyes wide as she stared at the king, still doubled over on the ground, at Ajax with blood spreading across his uniform, and finally at the body of Teague's collector.

"Is he—"

"Yes," Sebastian said quietly.

"Cleo, go inside." The princess's voice shook.

"You clearly need help, so stop ordering me to leave," Cleo said, though her voice was just as shaky as the princess's. "Should we call the palace guard?"

"No," the king said, crawling to Ajax and pressing his hands against the knife wound in the man's side. "No guards."

"We keep this to ourselves," Sebastian said as he calculated the odds of somehow handling this without Teague learning the truth.

If Teague discovered that the princess had killed his most valuable employee, he'd make her pay for it, and she probably wouldn't survive. And, of course, Teague would know that his man had been at the palace. His collector didn't visit anyone unless he'd been sent.

Which meant Teague was expecting Daan to return with an update on his conversation with the king. How long did Sebastian have to protect the princess from the wrath of the most dangerous man in Súndraille?

He looked up. The moon was halfway between the eastern horizon and the midpoint in the sky.

Still early evening. Teague had no way of knowing how long it would take Daan to find a way to confront the king. Surely that bought Sebastian at least until midnight, if not longer.

He'd have to use the time to get the body as far from the palace as possible.

"We have to hide the body," the princess said as if she could read his mind.

Sebastian met her gaze. Her eyes were wide with the residue of panic and she still trembled with shock, but she wore the tiny frown she got when she was thinking hard.

"Yes," he agreed. "But not here. Not on the palace grounds. Teague has to think his man delivered his message and left without coming to harm."

"We could toss him into the sea," Cleo said. "Just drag him to the south field. It ends in a cliff."

"If we dump him off the palace cliffs, the body could wash ashore on our beach." The princess rubbed her arms as if she thought she'd never get warm. "But first, Thad and his guard need medical attention."

"There are places in the deserts of Akram where he'd never be found," Ajax said. His left eye was swelling shut, and his speech was slurred.

Sebastian considered his suggestion.

"If we do that, his boss will assume that the last place he was seen was the palace," the princess said as she stepped closer to Sebastian and looked down at the sprawled figure of the collector. She made a noise of distress in the back of her throat and tipped her head back to drag in a deep breath.

"He can assume all he wants. That's not the same as proof," Cleo said as she joined the king to help Ajax up off the ground. The king swayed and breathed in sharp little coughs. Both of them needed the palace physician. Quickly.

"Alistair Teague doesn't need proof to decide he's justified in punishing the princess for killing his collector." Sebastian picked up the fallen cudgel, strapped it to his chest, and tried to put his body between the princess and the sight of the man with the crushed skull lying silently on the dirt.

How was the king mixed up with Alistair Teague? The only kind of business anyone did with Teague was criminal—buying apodrasi, selling it, smuggling stolen goods across kingdom borders, or hurting those foolish enough to try to cheat Teague out of what he was owed.

Unless the king was one of the poor fools who'd made a wish.

Sebastian's chest ached with tension, and he forced himself

to breathe steadily. What the king was doing wasn't his concern. Sebastian had a job to do. And he had to do it before Teague realized his collector wasn't coming home.

He bent toward the body again, gauging the best way to transport it.

The princess stepped forward and addressed the king and Ajax.

"You both need medical attention. For now, we have to assume that Teague has a way of knowing whether the message was delivered. Cleo, please get them into the palace and then call for the physician to see to the two of them. Make sure the staff knows that a man attacked them in the garden and then ran off when you showed up. If Teague hears that story, and the physician's records document their injuries, we have a chance to make Teague believe his man delivered his message and left here safely."

"What about you?" Cleo asked as she began helping Ajax walk toward the palace.

"You need to return to the palace too, Ari." The king's voice was pained, and coughs racked his body. Probably a broken rib.

"Not until I've helped Sebastian with the bo—" The princess choked on the word *body* and cleared her throat. "With him. Go to the palace and be convincing when you tell the story. Give Sebastian and me forty minutes and then send guards out to patrol the grounds as if you believe the man could come back."

As Cleo, Ajax, and the king made their way out of the garden, the princess rejoined Sebastian, who was crouched beside the body. The air was thick with the metallic sweetness of blood.

125

"We can't drag him off the palace grounds without leaving a trail," Sebastian said. "Plus, he'll be heavy and cumbersome. We need a—"

The princess jerked away from the man, stumbled to the grass, and fell to her knees retching.

Sebastian stood and moved toward her, his hands hovering in the air above her bent head.

What was he supposed to do? Pat her on the back? Hold her hair away from her face?

Pretend he couldn't see her?

"I'm sorry," she whispered as she huddled on the ground, her shoulders suddenly shaking with sobs.

Panic laced through Sebastian, hot and bright. This was worse than the vomiting. A pat on the back wouldn't fix this. Nor would pretending he couldn't hear her. He should go to the palace and get Cleo.

He didn't have time for that. The palace guards would be patrolling soon, and he had no idea how much time was left before Teague realized there was a problem.

He was all the comfort the princess had.

With that daunting thought in mind, he leaned down, took her shoulders, and gently moved her away from the mess on the grass.

"I'm sorry," she gasped again, her body trembling as if she were caught in a gale.

His mother had cried sometimes. When his father turned on her instead of on his sons. When she had a rare moment of realizing that the life she'd dreamed of was never going to be within her reach. But when his mother cried, she didn't want soft words of comfort. She wanted pipe weed and a stiff mug of ale.

The princess would want words and—stars help him—a steadying touch to help her see that everything was going to be all right.

Slowly he lowered himself to the ground beside her, his heart aching in an unfamiliar way when she carefully leaned away to give him space while she cried.

"I'm sorry," she whispered again, her voice catching on sobs. "I thought I could keep myself together long enough to get this done, but . . . he's dead. And I did it. And the worst part?"

She tipped her head up to look at him, her tears glittering in the starlight. "I'd do it again. Without hesitation. Even knowing that I would hit him hard enough to kill him. I'd do it again if it meant stopping him from hurting my brother."

"I know," he said, and wished he had other words. Better words. Words that would wipe the horror from her face and give her peace instead.

Her breath shuddered, and she wiped at her cheeks with her palms. "And I'm about to get up and haul his body somewhere else in order to protect myself. To protect my brother. What kind of person does that make me?"

"The kind of person who doesn't flinch from doing what needs to be done to protect those you love, even when it costs you a piece of yourself," he said quietly. "And the kind of person who knows how to stay in control of your emotions long enough to make decisions and give orders."

"I'm not sure that sounds like a very good person."

He met her gaze. "I'm sure."

She swayed toward him, her arm brushing his, and then

straightened again. They sat in silence for a moment, and every second that ticked by felt like an eternity.

"Your Highness, I'm sorry about this, but we need to move. If you'd rather not help with—"

"Ari." Her voice was husky with the residue of tears.

"I can't call you that." He stood and offered her his hand.

Her fingers were cold and trembling. He wrapped the warmth of his hand around hers and pulled her gently to her feet. The moment she was standing, he let her go, but his skin didn't crawl at the memory of her touch, and his blood didn't boil with the awful need to flee or get ready for a fight.

"Please," she said as they turned toward the body. "I can't be friends with someone who only calls me 'Your Highness.' And I really need a friend right now."

It was impossible. Her reputation would be harmed. He would lose his job and any hope of saving up enough money to relocate his mother and himself before his father returned from Balavata. He couldn't bear to tell the princess any of that. Instead, he said, "I'd be comfortable with calling you Princess Arianna."

"That's not much of an improvement, but I'll take it." She smiled wearily at him, though it slipped from her face the moment she looked at Daan's body. "Thank you for letting me fall apart and then helping me put myself back together." She squared her shoulders. "Carrying him is out of the question. What should we haul him in?"

He was grateful to retreat from the dangerous ground of courting a friendship with the princess and focus on the details of making it look like Teague's man had left the palace after delivering his message.

"We need a wagon and some blankets. Something that doesn't look like it came from the palace," he said.

"I know just the thing. Follow me."

Moments later, they had tossed fresh dirt over the bloody ground, wrapped the collector in two coarse gray blankets the princess had taken from the grooms' quarters, and were driving a nondescript horse and a wagon that was covered in dirt from hauling rocks and soil out of the south meadow. The princess had also wrapped herself in another blanket, throwing part of it over her head like a hood to keep from being recognized by anyone who might still be out on the streets.

As the palace disappeared in the distance, and Kosim Thalas spread before them with its pastel clay buildings stacked close together and its network of canals gleaming beneath the moonlight, Sebastian focused on the task in front of him—find a convincing place to dump Daan's body and keep the princess from landing on the list of those Alistair Teague wanted dead.

FIFTEEN

SHE HADN'T MEANT to kill him.

Ari gripped the edges of the wagon bench as the vehicle creaked and swayed and tried to stop remembering the heft of the cudgel. The sickening crunch as it slammed into the man's head and the smell that thickened in the air as he died.

She *tried* to stop, but the sounds were a splinter in her thoughts that she couldn't help touching.

As Sebastian guided the wagon through the quieter side streets of Kosim Thalas, the body in the back jostled against the side of the wagon with every bump in the cobblestoned road, and the memory of the cudgel's impact on the man's skull played over and over in Ari's mind.

She was going to be sick again if she didn't stop.

Hastily scrambling for something else to think about, she said, "You seem to know a lot more about Alistair Teague's business structure than I do."

"What do you know about it?"

"Nothing except that he sends thugs to the market on Thursdays," she said, and he raised a brow at her. "All right, yes. I can see how it would be easy to know more than I do, but still. You recognized his employee by sight and knew his name."

"Where I come from, everyone knows who works for Teague."

"Where do you come from?" she asked and wished for some water or mint to swish around in her mouth because, stars knew, revisiting her dinner the hard way had left a terrible taste on her tongue.

He was silent for a moment as mist shrouded the beach to the south and gulls swooped across the sky, their bodies lithe bits of shadow that fleetingly blocked the stars. She was getting used to the rhythm of Sebastian's conversation. If he thought she was expecting something from him as the princess, he would answer promptly. If she was asking something personal, he would take his time—sometimes answering, sometimes not.

Finally, in a voice as emotionless as the road beneath them, he said, "I grew up in east Kosim Thalas."

She was also learning to listen for the things he didn't say, because usually that was where the real Sebastian hid. And she was learning that when he sounded like nothing mattered to him, whatever he was saying meant a great deal.

"Was that difficult?" she asked and then wanted to smack herself on the forehead. What a stupid question. Everyone knew that east Kosim Thalas was the holding ground for the destitute or the despicable. That it would be difficult to grow up there was obvious.

He was quiet, and she couldn't bear to force him to think about the answer.

"Of course it was difficult. That was careless of me to ask. Let's talk about Teague. What does he do in east Kosim Thalas?"

They turned onto a narrow road that hugged a gentle swell of land as it headed east.

"Teague runs a criminal empire throughout Súndraille that is headquartered in Kosim Thalas. Crime doesn't happen in this city without his permission, though he has enough underlings in place that it's rare to actually see the man himself," Sebastian said. "He's been in business for decades. Maybe for a century. He has his hand in a lot of things, but for the past six months he's mostly been manufacturing a drug called apodrasi and selling it here and in Balavata. There were rumors once that he might be selling in Llorenyae as well, but I doubt it. He won't have anything to do with that place."

"Llorenyae." Ari sat straighter. "I wonder why he doesn't live there anymore. Something must have happened if he won't even do business with them. Maybe it's something Thad can use against him."

The street curved, wrapping around the hill. The homes and shops that were clustered together inside the city limits spread out here, and there wasn't any torchlight to be seen.

Sebastian's voice was quiet. "The king isn't the first person to try desperate measures to get out of paying Teague. Somehow, Teague always wins."

"Not this time," Ari said grimly. "I'm going to get to the bottom of this, and I'm going to find a way to stop him from coming after my brother."

"If you poke a snake with a stick, it will bite you, Your— Princess Arianna."

"Then I'll have to be very careful." Especially since Cleo would pay the price if Ari got caught.

Sebastian made a humming noise in his throat, and twitched the reins against the horse's back to make him move faster as the wagon crested the hill. A rock-strewn pasture met the left side of the road, and a large block of a building was on the right about two hundred paces ahead. There were torches lit beside the building's door and all along its perimeter, and Ari caught movement along its roof.

"Where are we?" she whispered.

"One of Teague's warehouses. Stolen goods, drugs, and sometimes people he's taken as slaves to be sold in Balavata are kept here." Sebastian's voice was barely audible. "Few know where it is. It could make sense for Daan to have gone here after visiting the palace. If his body is found nearby, it will deflect suspicion from you and your brother because you'd have no idea how to find this place."

It was on the tip of her tongue to ask how *he* knew where to find it when a shadow detached itself from the wall of the building and became the figure of a man, sword out, walking briskly toward the road as if to intercept them.

Ari's palms grew slick. The last thing they needed was an armed man finding Teague's dead collector in the wagon bed. "What do we do?" she breathed.

"Act normal," Sebastian whispered. "We're just two ordinary people driving home after a day of selling goods in the markets."

Ari scooted closer to Sebastian. His body was coiled with tension, his jaw locked tight. He looked like a fighter about to launch himself into a fray.

Which, to be fair, was probably his version of acting normal, but to an onlooker was going to be a glaring clue that something wasn't right. They had to do more than act normal. They had to hide their faces so that when Daan's body was found, no one could give an accurate description of the couple who'd passed by in a wagon.

She had to fix this before they reached the man with the sword.

She could pretend to be sick and draw all the man's attention to herself. It wouldn't take much to put on a convincing show. But then she and Sebastian would be far more memorable than they wanted to be.

She could pretend they were arguing, which would explain the tension that radiated off Sebastian, but that would give the man a chance to memorize what their voices sounded like. Plus, she doubted Sebastian's ability to argue. He'd probably sit there like a rock while she caused a (far too memorable) scene.

That left option number three. Her stomach pitched at the thought of it, but this time instead of feeling nauseous, she felt like the time she'd (accidentally on purpose) drunk fizzy wine at the winter ball while hiding in the servants' hall watching the guests dance. Which was a foolish way to feel because this was an act.

"Follow my lead," she whispered as she leaned into Sebastian's space.

He jerked the reins, and the horse shied.

"We have to act normal, but you look like you're about to start a fight, and I probably look like the princess wrapped in a stable blanket." She breathed the words as her thigh pressed against his, and her head tipped toward his shoulder. "We need to hide our faces and make him believe there's nothing to see here."

"What are you doing?" There was a note of panic in his voice.

Not exactly how Ari had thought her first kiss would go, but she couldn't think of another way to handle the situation.

"Kissing you," she said. "Please play along. We're going to be discovered in a minute."

The wagon was eighty paces from the man. Ari angled her entire body toward Sebastian and tipped her head back. His eyes glinted dark and mysterious in the starlight.

All right, fine, they weren't mysterious. They were full of panic and dismay, but mysterious sounded much better for a first kiss.

She couldn't force him to do this. Not even when it seemed like the only option. She waited and hoped he'd see that hiding their faces and appearing to be just another couple returning home after a long day of work was the best way to deflect any suspicion.

He wasn't going to do it. His body was rigid, his breathing rapid. She'd asked for too much. The man with the sword was going to see that something was wrong and was going to stop them and find the dead man, and then Sebastian would get into a fight, and Ari was going to probably have to hit the man with a rock, and then they were going to have *two* dead bodies to bury and—

He covered her lips with his, and every racing thought in her head dissolved into bubbly, skin-tingling surprise.

The wagon creaked, the body thumped, and at some point

they passed the man with the sword and left him and the building he guarded behind, but Ari wasn't aware of any of it.

Her world was the gentle roughness of Sebastian's lips and the warmth of his body chasing shivers across her skin.

Her heart pounded, and she tilted her head to get a better angle.

This was much more fun than the practice kissing she'd tried on her bedpost when she was twelve. Sebastian made a tiny noise in the back of his throat, and Ari grabbed the front of his tunic as a delicious tingling swirled through her belly.

Sebastian pulled back, his breathing unsteady. "Your Highness—"

"Ari," she said, still leaning toward his lips.

He winced at the same moment that Ari realized with absolute mortification that her mouth still tasted vaguely of vomit.

She scooted away from him. "Oh, stars."

"Princess Arianna—"

"I am so—"

"That was—"

"Awful. I know."

He stiffened and fell silent.

She buried her face in her hands. "I'm so sorry. There are no words for how sorry I am."

"It worked. That's all that matters." He was using his formal, reserved, I'm-dealing-with-nobility voice.

"I forgot," she said quietly, still hiding her face.

"Forgot what?"

"That I'd recently been sick and hadn't had any mint. I don't think I can ever look you in the eye again."

Which was definitely going to put a crimp in their developing friendship.

Well . . . *more* of a crimp than kissing him with vomit breath had already accomplished.

He was silent for an agonizingly long time. Ari contemplated jumping out of the wagon. Changing her name and moving to Ravenspire. Hiding in her room for the next five years.

Finally, he spoke. "I wasn't going to say it was awful." He sounded friendly and amused. "I was going to say it was smart. I would never have thought of it. And it's okay that you hadn't had mint. We weren't kissing for real. It was an act. No need to be embarrassed."

She was pretty sure she was going to be embarrassed for the rest of her life.

The wagon swayed to a stop.

"Princess Arianna, you don't have to cover your face anymore."

Slowly she peeled her fingers away from her eyes and risked a glance at his face.

His eyes crinkled.

If he could smile about this, then so could she. She made herself give him a wobbly grin, which disappeared the instant she looked around and realized they were at the edge of a ditch that had been dug across the back of an empty field. The road was at least three hundred paces behind them.

"What is this?" Ari looked over her shoulder, half expecting the man with the sword to have followed them up the road, but no one was there.

"This is where Alistair Teague dumps the bodies of those

who die in his warehouse. Leaving Daan here will make it seem like only someone with intimate knowledge of Teague's business could have killed him. He'll look hard at his suppliers, his employees, and his competitors in Balavata. Hopefully, he won't be looking at you or the king."

"How do you know so much about Teague's business?" she asked because it suddenly occurred to her that she was trusting him—with her life and with her brother's—on the basis of a friendship that had been in existence for a week. And while her instincts about people were rarely wrong, this time being wrong could cost her everything.

Sebastian was quiet for a long moment. Finally he said with quiet intensity, "My father works for Teague. So did my brother before he died." He met her gaze and something fierce burned in his eyes. "You don't have to worry, Princess Arianna. I'd rather die than follow in my father's footsteps. You're safe with me."

Ari nodded and ordered her traitorous stomach to stay right where it was as she turned toward the body. "I believe you. And this is a brilliant plan, Sebastian."

"I have my moments."

He jumped down from the wagon and offered her his hand. "Ready?"

"Ready." She took his hand and climbed down, and together they moved to haul the body out of the wagon bed and throw it in the ditch.

SIXTEEN

"WE NEED TO talk." Ari closed the door to Thad's bedroom suite, locked it, and then pulled his writing chair over to the side of the bed and took a seat. Her brother was ensconced in a mound of pillows, a tiny bottle of willow bark and poppy leaves resting on his nightstand for when he needed help controlling the pain of his broken ribs and lacerated arm. It had been three days since his beating at the hands of the now dead collector, and the palace physician was still unwilling to allow the king to leave his bed.

Three days since Ari had kissed Sebastian with vomit breath and then subsequently skipped going to the arena for lessons because, stars knew, she had no idea what to say to him after that.

Three days and Ari had only checked on Thad from afar. Partially because she wasn't sure how to approach the problem of Alistair Teague and hadn't wanted to discuss it with Thad until she had a plan, and partially because it had taken three days for her to stop losing her lunch every time she remembered the sickening crunch of the cudgel hitting the collector's head.

Especially when that memory was always followed instantly by her mother's gruesome last moments, leaving Ari shaking and longing to curl up alone in her mother's old bedroom and cry until she had nothing left.

She needed to be calm and in control for this conversation, because Thad wasn't going to like what he was about to hear.

"It's about time you stopped avoiding me." Thad struggled to sit up, hissing in a breath as he moved his torso. "Cleo tells me that the two of you went to the market without Mama Eleni and asked merchants about Teague. And that Teague's men accosted you."

"Why would she tell you that? Is nothing sacred?" Ari glared.

"Because her loyalty to keeping your secrets means less to her than her desire to keep you safe." He leaned forward and winced. "What were you thinking, asking questions about Teague in Kosim Thalas?"

"I was thinking that I was going to protect my brother." She held his gaze.

"Ari, this isn't something you can fix for me." His tone begged her to believe him.

"Better me than your guard," she snapped. "It was his carelessness that earned you a visit from Teague's collector. Ajax is recovering well, by the way, and he sends his regards. Also, he's still using his contacts on Llorenyae to bring some fae guard beasts for the palace—an idea that will either work brilliantly or will get all of us killed. And he's still working on a plan to assassinate Teague, but since Teague already seems to know what

Ajax is up to, I doubt he's going to be successful, which is why we need a backup plan."

His eyes narrowed. "This backup plan had better not put you at risk."

Ari snorted.

Thad closed his eyes and tipped his head back. "Princesses don't snort."

"Princesses don't kill criminals either, but there you have it." Her voice was firm. "We have bigger problems than trying to curb all my unprincessy habits."

"*I* have bigger problems. Not you. And I'm working to solve it—"

"With your guard, yes. And I hope he really can kill Teague, and that the beasts he's ordering really can keep you safe. But if that plan fails, we have to be ready because your soul will come due, and I'm not going to stand by and let that happen."

"That's better than losing you to Alistair Teague!" Thad's voice cut through the room. "Please, Ari. I got myself into this mess. I will either get myself out, or I will lose my soul to the Wish Granter. But you . . . you're going to be safe. You're going to grow old and happy, and if that means you have to rule Súndraille, then that's what you'll do. You and I both know that if you wanted to, you would make an excellent queen. You're smart, you're brave, you're compassionate, and you don't let anyone intimidate you."

Ari leaned forward, her hands shaking as she wrapped them around her brother's. "I'm not going to grow old and happy without you."

"Ari, listen—"

"No, you listen. We're a team. We always have been. You and me against the world, remember?"

He opened his mouth to argue.

"You're the one who plays politics and knows how to be diplomatic. You're the one who understand the ins and outs of the Assembly and what Súndraille needs to thrive. But me? I'm the one who plans. I'm the one who sees a wrong and relentlessly works behind the scenes to make it right. I'm the one who says what you can't say because you're the king. I'm the one who doesn't pull her punches."

He squeezed her hands. "This is different from figuring out how to stop boys from bullying me, or how to find the quickest way for me to accomplish a task Father set out to test me."

She shook her head. "The stakes are higher, yes. But this is a problem, and, like all problems, it can be solved once we have the right information. Maybe we should just pay Ajax and call off the assassination attempt. We have nine and a half years to figure this out if we're careful. I won't haphazardly question everyone I know about the Wish Granter—I have no desire to have him sneak up on me in the garden again. And you won't—"

"He did *what*?" Thad's voice shook.

Oops.

"He was upset that Cleo and I were asking about him at the market. He made it very clear that if I didn't stop, he'd hurt her to punish me." She swallowed hard against the memory of his hand around her throat and drew in a deep breath to assure herself that she could.

"Then stop. Let me handle it. You spend your energy learning how to be queen, and if I'm able to stop Teague—"

"Lady Tassi told me that iron and bloodflower poison can hurt the fae, but I had an iron dagger with me when Teague accosted me. He grabbed it, and it blistered his hand, but the blisters disappeared in seconds. I don't think regular iron weapons are going to work. He's too old and too powerful. We have to gather every bit of information we can so that we can make a plan that works."

He sighed, his breath catching on a cough at the end of it. "I'm not going to be able to stop you, am I?"

"When have you ever been able to stop me?"

He rolled his eyes.

"Now, let's see what we know." Ari got up and began to pace as she ticked off the items on her fingers. "First, Teague left Llorenyae, and rumors say he'll have nothing to do with the isle. There has to be a reason for that. Maybe it's something that can help us. We should develop some contacts on Llorenyae."

"We'll soon know the hunters who are bringing Ajax's beasts."

"Yes, we will, though I think it's a bad idea to let those beasts onto the palace grounds. It just puts everyone around you in danger."

"We have the barn with iron cages being built in the south pasture. Ajax says the hunters will train us how to control them. Plus he says they will be a deterrent to Teague."

Ari tapped her finger against her lips as she thought. "We need to make sure we talk to these bounty hunters without anyone else around to see if the fae have any weaknesses besides iron and bloodflower poison. We can combine whatever knowledge we get from them with the history in the *Book of the Fae* once I have my hands on that. And we can keep looking into weapons.

Sebastian has a few ideas on that front." Ari turned toward the window that overlooked Kosim Thalas. The midday sun had settled across the city in a haze of gold that glinted against the white domed roofs like shards of ice.

"Who is Sebastian?"

Ari turned from the window. "Honestly, Thad, don't you know your own staff? He's your new weapons master. The boy who helped me hide the collector's body. He's also the one who rescued Cleo and me at the market. He's my friend, and he's been teaching me self-defense."

"A princess—"

Ari whipped her hand into the air. "If you're about to say that a proper princess doesn't make friends with a servant, we are going to have serious problems. Are you going to tell me I can't be friends with Cleo either?"

"Of course not. But this is a boy, and you need to think of your reputation if you're spending time alone with him—"

"Learning how to put out a man's eye or take him down at the knees. Very romantic stuff, Thad. Very romantic. Oh, and we also hid a dead body together, so we're practically engaged. Now, let's talk about what else we know about Teague."

She raised her fingers again and continued. "He used to live on Llorenyae but won't have anything to do with it now. He lives somewhere in Kosim Thalas, though it's hard to find anyone who knows exactly where. That might be useful knowledge for Ajax. I wonder if there are property records at the city magistrate's office."

"I can check. I have a meeting scheduled with the top city officials tomorrow. I'll order an audit of all property owners and ask to see the records so that it doesn't look like I'm singling him out."

Ari nodded. "Good. And I'll write to the considerable amount of men who danced with me at your coronation and discreetly ask what they know about the Wish Granter and the fae."

"I told you it was worthwhile to dance with everyone who asked."

"A proper king doesn't say I told you so. It's unbecoming. Now we need time to get all this information—the *Book of the Fae*, contacts on Llorenyae, Teague's home address, and information from our allies. We have to stall Ajax. We can't risk a failed assassination until we know another proven method to either kill or control Teague. Tell him that you think it's wise to slow down preparations since Teague is suspicious enough to send his collector to give you a warning. Get him to agree to wait at least a few months—"

"Do you really think we'll have a solution in a few months?"

Ari held Thad's gaze. "If we don't, then we'll stall him again. There's a solution out there. We just have to find it."

Thad smiled, though sadness lingered in his eyes. "You're the bravest, most stubborn person I know. I want you to add 'careful' to your list of attributes. This had better work, Ari, because if my stupid decision costs me my sister, I'll never forgive myself."

"It will work." Ari's voice was firm. "I won't accept anything less." She sat at the edge of his bed and took his hand. "You and me against the world, right?"

His eyes were full of regret. "Always."

SEVENTEEN

ALISTAIR TEAGUE STOOD across the street from Edwin's spice shop, his pipe in his hands, and watched a cluster of shoppers enter the building. Beside him, a messenger stood ready, parchment in hand, to complete the list of tasks Teague was delegating to his head street boss, Felman.

"Raise the quota for art and jewelry procurement. I don't care if they have to break into homes in the dead of night and kill the people inside, I want my warehouses full."

The messenger scribbled on the parchment with a quill dipped in the tiny pot of ink strapped to her belt.

"And get someone to survey the merchant district for a shop we can use. We'll be selling some of those stolen goods right here. If the shop we want is occupied, get rid of the owners."

More scribbling. Teague lifted his face to the breeze and stared at the shop across from him.

"Finally, send a message to Jacob in Balavata. Tell him I want him back here immediately. We can't let the position of head collector in Kosim Thalas remain open for long."

The messenger finished her list and left for Felman's headquarters in east Kosim Thalas, and Teague turned his attention to the matter at hand.

The sun blazed in the sky overhead. The streets were packed with people.

And the few city guards he'd seen had turned away the moment they laid eyes on him.

It was the perfect setting for an object lesson in what happened to those who defied him.

He took a puff of his pipe, turned it upside down, and gently tapped the bowl to discard the remaining tobacco. Then he pocketed the pipe and strode across the street.

The shop's door creaked and a tiny bell rang as Teague stepped into the room. The place smelled of dried herbs, wild roots, and sharp spices. The shopkeeper was bent over an open jar of candied ginger with a pair of tongs in one hand and a small burlap sack in the other.

This man—this plain, unassuming man—had spent time alone with the princess and her friend. According to the employees who'd been visiting this shop to collect Teague's weekly protection fee, he'd told Arianna and Cleo not to let anyone know they'd visited his shop, which meant he'd done something he didn't want Teague to know about.

Teague was going to enjoy prying the secret out of him.

The shopkeeper finished bagging the candied ginger. Handing it to the woman who'd ordered it, he reached for her coin and his eyes met Teague's.

The coins clattered to the floor as the shopkeeper dropped his hand and took a step back.

Teague smiled.

"Going somewhere, Edwin?" he asked.

The man shook his head, though his eyes darted toward the shop's back exit.

Teague's smile grew sharp. "Oh, do try to run from me. I enjoy chasing down my prey."

Edwin swallowed hard, and sweat beaded his brow. "I'm not . . . What are you doing here?"

The two customers closest to the front door tried to brush past Teague and leave. He glanced at the door and said, "*Glas.*"

The door refused to open, no matter how hard the men pulled on the handle. The rest of the customers stared at him in wide-eyed fear. So easy to terrify humans. A simple bit of magic, a command any fae worth their weight could accomplish, and everyone in the room was transfixed.

And he was just getting started.

Walking toward Edwin, Teague said, "You know why I'm here."

The shopkeeper shook his head vehemently. "I paid! I paid my fee on time!"

Teague's eyes narrowed. "You met with the princess."

Edwin shrugged as if that fact meant nothing, but his voice shook. "She shops here often."

Teague stopped five paces from the man. The other customers backed away, pressing against the front window or the racks of spices that lined the far wall.

"If the princess shops here often, and her visit wasn't unusual, then why tell her to keep it a secret?" Teague ran a finger over a shelf of delicate amber jars with blue wax seals for stoppers.

"I didn't." Edwin glanced around the room as if looking for

help. "There were collectors. She didn't know about them, and they didn't know about her. I wanted her away from here while that was going on. I didn't want her to get hurt."

"I'm confused." Teague stepped closer, and the smell of the man's fear sweat hit his nose. "You didn't tell her to keep it a secret? Or you did because you thought it would keep her safe from my collectors? Which is it?"

"I . . . it was just to keep her safe."

"Yet you were in the act of making her leave your shop and go back out to the street. The street that was full of my employees, some of whom, I will admit, are a bit enthusiastic when it comes to taking unprotected members of the noble class into custody." Teague raised a brow and waited for Edwin's response.

The man swallowed and twisted his hands in the apron he wore at his waist. "She was going out the back way where it was safer —"

"You sent her out the back of the shop, on collection day, while her guards were standing at the front, unaware of her location, and begged her not to tell anyone she'd visited you. Is this correct?" Teague's voice was dangerously calm.

Edwin remained silent, his expression miserable.

Teague lunged forward and shoved the man against the wall. His voice was a clap of thunder that shook the shelves and sent the jars of spices careening against one another. "You will answer me!"

"Yes!" Edwin raised trembling hands as if begging for mercy, but Teague wasn't interested. He'd shown mercy to a human once, and look what it had cost him.

Mercy was for the weak. For the fools too ignorant to know they were being exploited.

Mercy was for those who didn't have the stomach to destroy their foes.

Leaning close, Teague said softly, "Tell me why the princess was here."

"She bought spices." Edwin's words were rushed. "I swear it. She bought spices."

"Which spices?"

"Monkshood, basil, and cinnamon." The man's eyes darted toward the back door and then fixed on Teague again.

He was hiding something.

"And what else?"

Edwin frowned. "That's all."

"She didn't ask questions about me?"

Edwin hesitated a split second before saying, "No."

Teague smiled, slow and terrible. "Liar."

"I promise, she only bought spices. That's all—"

Teague wrapped his hand around Edwin's throat and throttled him until he choked on his words and gurgled for air, his hands beating ineffectually at Teague. When Teague released him, Edwin slid down the wall, gasping.

Teague crouched beside him and said, "I already know she was in the market asking questions about me. Her own guards, who are now my loyal employees, told me that. And I know that she specifically intended to come to your shop. So either she thought you knew something useful about me, or she wanted to buy something from you that you shouldn't have sold her. Which is it?"

Edwin shook his head, his hands rubbing at his throat.

It didn't matter what the shopkeeper had told the princess.

He didn't know much about Teague's business, and even if he did, what was the princess going to do about it? One wrong move, and he'd kill her friend Cleo.

Slightly more worrisome was the idea that Edwin could have sold her something to use against Teague, but even then, Teague was centuries old. It would take an enormous amount of poison to incapacitate him, much less kill him. And to even try it, the princess would have to get close enough for Teague to see her coming.

And then, of course, Cleo would die.

No, he was safe from whatever Edwin had told the princess, and it was time to make sure no one else in Kosim Thalas considered defying his absolute rule of the city streets.

Turning to face the others in the room, Teague said, "One of you will be my messenger. Which of you wants the job?"

The people glanced uncertainly at one another, and then the man closest to the door tentatively raised his hand.

Teague clapped his hands once. "Excellent. That leaves"—he turned in a slow circle and made a show of counting the rest—"one man, three women, and two adorable little children. And of course Edwin, on whose head all your deaths will be blamed."

It took a second for his words to sink in, but when they did, two of the women grabbed their children and rushed for the back door. Teague snapped his fingers. "*Glas.*"

"Unlock the door!"

"Let us out!"

"Please, we had nothing to do with this."

Teague looked at Edwin. "Betraying me has consequences."

"No. Please. Please!" Edwin's voice rose to a scream as Teague bent down, snapped his fingers, and brought a flame to life in midair. With a flick of his wrist, he sent the flame onto Edwin's apron. It caught fire instantly, and in seconds the flames had spread along his body until he resembled a human torch.

Teague wrinkled his nose as he turned away. Few things smelled worse than burning humans, though he supposed sending the spice shop up in flames might help mitigate that.

A few more snaps and flicks of his wrist, and his fae fire coated the floor, the shelves, and the people he'd marked for death.

His messenger was pressed against the front door while flames licked the doorframe, watching the horror unfold with wide, glassy eyes.

"Nobody defies me and lives," Teague said coldly. "Spread the word."

Another snap of his fingers, a whispered "*saor*," and the front door flew open. The messenger stumbled out, retching, while the screams of those condemned to burn alive followed him into the street.

Teague straightened his jacket, retrieved his pipe, and left the burning ruins of the spice shop behind him.

EIGHTEEN

IT HAD BEEN five days since Sebastian had seen the princess. She hadn't come to the arena for her lessons. She hadn't been in the kitchen the three times Sebastian had finally scraped up the courage to eat meals with the rest of the staff in the hope that the princess would be there—an experience he had no desire to repeat. Who could stand eating while being surrounded by so many people? He'd been trapped into constantly scanning the room for threats while those who sat closest to him expected him to find things to talk about. It had been a nightmare, even if the pie was excellent.

By day four, he'd taken to walking the grounds. He told himself it was because he needed to make sure none of Teague's employees were sniffing around the palace. If he happened to see the princess while he was checking the stables, the garden, and the stone barn that was quickly being built in the south field, that would be a happy coincidence.

But that morning, five days after he and the princess had

left Daan's body in the ditch and returned to the palace in near silence, he finally admitted the terrifying truth.

He missed her.

It was ridiculous. Dangerous. Completely foolish. He was a servant. He couldn't risk losing his job and his chance to save his coin until he could buy a life of solitude and freedom. He hadn't signed on to get mixed up with a princess who refused to treat him as anything less than her equal.

But as ridiculous and foolish as it was, he couldn't escape the fact that he wanted to hear her confidently proclaiming that the two of them were friends. He wanted to watch the way her emotions played across her face and marvel at the fact that she was careful not to make him feel threatened. He wanted to be amused at the way her eyes lit with mischief when she laughed.

He wanted to make sure she was safe.

When the time for her lesson on the fifth day came and went with no sign of the princess, he abandoned all pretense and headed straight for the palace.

Maybe she was done wanting to learn self-defense—unlikely considering the threat of Teague's discovering her role in the collector's death, but possible. Maybe she'd decided she had more important things to deal with than spending time with the weapons master.

Or maybe the mortification in her voice after they'd kissed had kept her from resuming their normal relationship. If he'd been a betting man, that's the option he'd choose.

It was strange to find a chink in the princess's confidence, but it had been a traumatic night for her. And he could've handled it better. He could've told her that until she'd pulled back and spoken to him after the kiss, he hadn't thought about her bout of sickness. All he'd been able to focus on was the way everything inside him crashed and tumbled as it always did when anyone touched him. The way some primal part of him had braced for the first bright slash of pain that had always come hand in hand with touch while he was a child trapped beneath his father's rule.

He made himself walk through the side entrance to the kitchen without hesitating, and admitted that even if he could've found the words to share that with the princess, he would have remained silent.

"Sebastian!" Cleo looked up from the rack of game hens she was basting, her eyes glowing with relief. "Just the person I was hoping to see."

He eyed her warily. "Why?"

She brushed olive oil over the last game hen, sprinkled it with freshly chopped herbs, and slid the entire rack into the brick oven. Then she came toward him, wiping her hands on her apron. She was a full head shorter than the princess, who stood nearly eye to eye with him, and he had to tip his head down to meet Cleo's gaze as she stood in front of him.

She glanced around the kitchen, noted her mother's preoccupation with inventorying a fresh shipment of vegetables and the quiet movements of two maids who sat in a corner shelling almonds, and then motioned for him to follow her into the pantry—a room twice the size of Sebastian's quarters—shutting the door behind them.

"You have to get Ari out of the palace." She turned to scan the pantry's contents.

Sebastian's pulse kicked up a notch. "Why? What's wrong?"

"It's her obsession with Teague." Cleo took a few steps forward and pointed toward a woven basket high on a shelf above her head. "Can you get that for me?"

He removed the basket and handed it to her. "I haven't seen her in five days."

Cleo set the basket on a table that rested in the middle of the room and began pulling food from the shelves. "Most haven't. She's either in the library, reading up on contract law or on the history of Llorenyae, or she's writing to her contacts in other kingdoms to ask them if they know anything about the Wish Granter, or she's arguing with Ajax about the way he wants to handle Teague."

"I don't envy Thad's guard."

"The point is, Ari's exhausted. She barely sleeps. She barely eats. She won't quit looking for a way to stop Teague, and it's wearing her down. Plus, there have been a few odd visitors to the palace. Always to the servants' entrance, always asking about something benign, but always finding a way to work in a question about the king's condition and whether there have been any strange happenings here."

"Teague's employees."

"Has to be. They haven't mentioned Ari."

He breathed in the relief. Teague knew Daan was dead, but he didn't yet know that the palace had been his place of demise. "You're a good friend, Cleo. I'm glad she has you."

"She has us both." She scooped up two oranges, some dates, and a hunk of cheese wrapped in cloth.

"Oh, I'm not . . . we're just . . ." He took a step back and bumped against the shelf behind him. "I work for her."

Cleo broke a loaf of bread in half and slipped it into the basket. "You're her friend. She told me. And besides, I'm not an idiot. I saw your concern for her that night in the garden. You didn't have to step in and help her take care of things, but you didn't hesitate. And then you kissed her, so—"

"She told you about that?" He stared at Cleo in horror.

Cleo laughed. "Best friends, remember? Anyway, you did what you had to to protect her because she's your friend."

"She can't be my friend. She's the *princess*."

Cleo shut the basket and pushed it into Sebastian's hands. "She's *Ari*. There really isn't another label that fits. And she needs us. Someone has to make sure she breathes fresh air and doesn't lose her mind chasing after the faint hope that she can fix this for Thad. I'll go get her."

"What am I supposed to do with this?" He lifted the now full basket.

"Take her on a picnic," Cleo said as she disappeared out of the pantry and headed into the palace proper.

He'd come here only to check on the princess. To see with his own eyes that she was all right. And maybe to show her that nothing between them had changed, and she could feel comfortable resuming her lessons if she wanted to.

He'd just let her know that he still had lesson time available. He'd give her the basket and tell her Cleo had made lunch for her and that she should eat it. And then he'd leave, and it would be up to her to show up at the arena or stay away.

With this plan firmly in place, he walked out of the pantry just as Cleo and Ari stepped into the kitchen. He stopped in his tracks, taking in the princess's appearance with a swift glance.

Her shoulders were bowed as if she carried an enormous weight. There were faint smudges of exhaustion beneath her eyes, and her hair was carelessly thrown into a haphazard bun on top of her head. She blinked wearily at him and mustered a tiny smile.

His heart twisted as he locked eyes with Cleo. She raised a brow and glared pointedly at the basket in his hands.

And, stars help him, he opened his mouth and said, "There's something I need you to see."

The princess frowned. "What is it?"

Cleo gave an exasperated huff. "Go with him and find out. Now. Before Mama puts you to work in the kitchen. You know you're too tired to bake. Stars know, we don't need you confusing paprika for cinnamon again. I still get heartburn just thinking about those cookies."

Before the princess could argue further, Cleo gave her a little push in Sebastian's direction. He looped the basket's handle over one arm and used the other to open the door for her. She blinked in the brilliant sunshine and shivered a little as the sea breeze gusted over them.

"What do I need to see?" she asked.

He panicked, scrambling for an answer that would keep her outside long enough for the break to do her any good. The barn that was nearly complete in the south field? The arena and the weapons he'd thought they might try after she mastered the throwing star?

She wouldn't come with him for either of those things. He needed something different. Something that held enough meaning to keep her attention on him rather than on the problems her brother faced with Teague.

He opened his mouth to tell her stars knew what and was

shocked to hear himself say, "I need you to see something that means a great deal to me."

Mortification was a hot flush of shame that rolled over his skin and left him wanting to take every single word back, but then she gave him a weary smile—a real one—and said, "As long as it isn't a shield specifically designed to protect you from my throwing star or a patch of mint to protect you from my kisses, I'd love to."

His lips twitched. "No shield. No mint. I don't need protection from you."

"I'm not sure that's entirely true, but lead on."

They walked south, past the arena, over the long expanse of pasture that was sometimes used for the palace horses, and into the south field where the stone barn was nearly finished. Color returned to her cheeks as they hiked, and her shoulders straightened.

"You wanted me to see the barn?" she asked.

"No."

She looked around as they walked beyond the barn and down to where the field dipped into a sparse forest of aspen and cypress trees interspersed with enormous white boulders that were scattered about like the remnants of a giant's broken toy.

"The trees?" she asked.

"Not quite."

He led her through the trees, the band of tension that always squeezed his chest easing as the breeze fluttered through the leaves above him and the sound of the Chrysós came closer. When they reached the point where the land broke off into a jagged cliff, he set the basket on a slab of white stone and faced the glittering gold of the sea.

She was quiet as she stood beside him. Her hair tumbled out of its bun to stream in the wind, and she closed her eyes as seabirds swooped overhead, and the trees rustled softly behind them.

"It's perfect," she said quietly.

"I'm going to live in a place like this one day."

"It suits you."

"Does it?" He turned from watching the waves thunder against the shore to study her instead.

She opened her eyes, and there was a spark of confidence and compassion there that had been buried by exhaustion earlier. "It's solitary and unknowable on some level, no matter how long you stand here. There's a restless, pent-up power in the sea, and you know if it ever decided to stop respecting its boundaries, it could destroy you. But it *does* respect its boundaries. It stays where it should, so its power feels safe. When you stand here, surrounded by mystery and beauty and power, you feel safe."

"And you think I need to feel safe?" he asked, though he didn't want to. Her words had stripped him bare in places that he'd fought for years to hide. He didn't know which was worse—that she saw him so clearly, or that he wanted her to.

"We all do." Her voice was gentle. "But when I said this suits you, I meant that its restrained power and mystery remind me of you."

He didn't know what to do with her words, so he sat, letting the cold from the rock seep into his clothing. She sat beside him, and he opened the picnic basket.

"Cleo packed this. She was pretty determined to get you out of the palace for a while."

The princess laughed, though she sounded tired. "She usually just follows along with my ideas, but when she gets fixed on one of her own, there's no stopping her."

She took an orange and peeled it. The bite of citrus in the air made his stomach rumble. He reached for the other orange as she said, "I heard you ate with the other staff recently."

"Word travels fast."

She grinned. "Faster than you'd think. I'm told that you're particularly fond of potatoes and pie—I *told* you the pie was good—but that your conversational skills are somewhat lacking."

He gave her a pained look. "People kept talking to me."

"They tend to do that."

"And they expected me to talk back."

She laughed and bumped his shoulder with hers before pulling away to give him space. "If it makes you feel better, they've decided you're mysterious instead of rude."

"Maybe we should talk about what you've been doing instead of coming to lessons or sleeping or eating."

Her smile disappeared, and her shoulders slumped. She watched the waves toss themselves relentlessly against the shore for a long moment, and then in a quiet voice, she said, "Thad made a wish."

Sebastian's stomach sank. He'd suspected it, of course. But there were other ways the king could've become mixed up with Teague. Knowing now that the stakes were the king's soul, and that the princess wasn't the kind of person who would stop trying to save her brother, filled him with dread.

"It was before the royal family died. We were running for our lives. Mother had just been killed in front of us because she took a blow that was meant for Thad. Teague found him when Thad was thinking about jumping off a cliff and into the sea so that I would be safe from the queen's hunters. Thad tried to just wish for my safety, but Teague would accept nothing less than a wish for Thad to be king."

"He owes Teague his soul, doesn't he?" Sebastian asked.

She nodded, tears glimmering in her eyes. "That's why the barn is being built. Ajax has contacts with hunters on Llorenyae, and he's killed rogue fae with them before. He's ordering some beasts to protect the palace grounds, and he's working on a plan to assassinate Teague, but he wasn't discreet enough, and that's why Daan was sent to visit Thad. Ajax seems to think he can kill Teague as easily as he's killed other fae."

"Teague isn't just any fae. He's the Wish Granter, and he has to be at least a century old."

"I know." She wiped at her tears and sat up straighter. "I'm working on a better plan. I just need time to get all the information on Teague. To see the picture clearly. He might be powerful, but he isn't immortal. He can die, and somebody out there has to know how to kill him."

He couldn't bear to see her be crushed beneath the weight she was carrying, even if he did think that there was no way her brother was going to get out of losing his soul when the contract came due.

"Tell me everything you've learned. Maybe talking it out will help you see a solution," he said. And then he listened as the sun slowly moved across the sky, and the sea hurled itself against the cliff while the princess talked herself hoarse before falling asleep against his shoulder.

NINETEEN

ARI'S LIFE FELL into an exhausting rhythm. She'd get up early to help with breakfast—overriding Mama Eleni's objections because if she was going to be required to attend every Assembly meeting, then, by the stars, she was going to have the joy of making pastries in the morning first. Besides, in the past two months she'd lost her mother and her anonymity, learned that the Wish Granter was real and was going to take her brother's soul, and killed a man. She desperately needed the small sense of normalcy that shrugging on an apron and burying her hands in butter and flour provided.

After breakfast, she'd head to the library for a few hours of research on Llorenyae and contract law in Súndraille. Stars knew, they owned a lot of books, and so far not a single one of them had given her the key to getting Thad out of his bargain with Teague, although it would help significantly if she had a copy of the actual contract. Not that she believed the law would be binding over a magical contract, but she had to try every option that came to mind.

When she'd finished with the library, she'd spend an hour or two sparring with Sebastian, talking through what she'd learned, and convincing him to share her lunch. Afternoons were reserved for Assembly meetings and sitting in on Thad's discussions with city officials who told harrowing tales about outbreaks of violence in the merchant quarter and grew increasingly frustrated and resentful of the king's reluctance to send in the city guard. Knowing that Thad couldn't use the guard without violating his contract, Ari tried to suggest other solutions, but it was hard to think of anything effective that wouldn't incite Teague.

Sometimes she'd receive a letter from one of her contacts in another kingdom, but so far none of them had any insight into the Wish Granter beyond vague recollections of hearing the story as a child. Most nights she stayed up researching and taking notes long past when the rest of the palace had gone to bed.

She'd kept up this routine for nearly three weeks when something happened to bring everything in the palace to a halt.

"They're here!" Cleo ran into the library, her eyes wide with excitement.

Ari yawned. "Who's here?"

"The bounty hunters from Llorenyae. They just got off a ship an hour ago, and they brought two big crates with them."

Ari shot out of her chair. "Who saw them arrive? Did they use the palace dock?"

If Teague got wind of this, he could easily decide that Thad hadn't paid attention to his first warning and send another. Of course, if these beasts really could kill Teague, as Ajax promised, then the man himself was welcome to come calling.

"Yes, they used the palace dock." Cleo grabbed Ari's arm and pulled her out of the library. "And I don't know who saw them arrive, but everyone is paying attention now."

Ari's stomach dropped. "Everyone?"

"Trust me. Nobody could possibly look away from this. Come on."

Together they hurried out of the library and down a long hallway lined with pictures of previous kings and queens, cut through the east parlor, and reached the entrance hall just as Thad and his guard finished descending the stairs from the royal suites.

"Thad, wait a minute," Ari said as he started toward the open front door. The hum of excited conversation drifted in from the courtyard.

He paused to let her catch up.

She reached his side and asked, "What if those beasts escape their handlers? What if they *eat* their handlers? What if they aren't capable of killing Teague, but he decides to take their presence here as a threat? Maybe we should just put them back on the boat."

"If Teague hears about it, then he'll know better than to send another messenger to the palace," Ajax said.

She glared at him. "Teague could ignore this, or he could decide it's a precursor to Thad's trying to keep Teague from collecting on his contract."

"Teague is constrained by the rules of his magic, as are all fae," Ajax said.

"But we don't know the rules of his magic! We only have assumptions and folklore. Before we tempt him to retaliate against Thad for a perceived act of aggression, we need to know exactly what we're dealing with."

Thad leaned down to whisper in Ari's ear. "We need the hunters as allies. They might know how to defeat Teague. We have to accept the beasts for now." Straightening, he moved to the door. Ajax followed.

Cleo slung an arm around Ari's shoulders. "Ready?"

Ari nodded, but inside she had a terrible, gut-wrenching fear that her brother was hurtling toward disaster and there was nothing she could do to save him.

She followed Cleo out of the palace and into the front courtyard, where staff and nobility were packed side by side along the perimeter. Thad and Ajax were cutting a swift path through the onlookers, and Ari hurried to follow.

When she reached the courtyard proper, she stopped and stared at the frightening spectacle in front of her.

Two enormous iron crates rested on the pale stone floor, each covered with a black cloth embroidered with silver runes around the edges. Vicious snarls filled the air, and the occasional scrape of a talon against the bottom of the crate sent a chill down Ari's spine.

What kind of (terrifying, probably ravenous) monsters were hidden beneath those cloths?

Beside the crate closest to Ari stood a girl about her age with the lithe, muscular frame of someone whose body was a sharply honed weapon. Her dark red hair was worn long, and a brilliant strip of shocking white that started at her left temple was braided and tied with tiny silver chains. She wore all black, and several of the runes that were embroidered on the cloths were inked into her forearms. In her hands, she slowly twirled a black whip studded with iron spikes.

Ari suddenly felt tremendously underdressed for the task of helping Thad take ownership of the caged beasts.

The girl's ice-blue eyes landed on Ari and then flicked away to study the rest of the crowd. Something in the way she held herself reminded Ari of Sebastian—always searching for a threat.

One of the beasts screamed—a bloodcurdling howl that had the crowd stumbling back to the tree-lined edges of the courtyard, as if that would somehow keep them safe.

A boy who looked nearly identical to the girl, down to the runes on his skin and the streak of white in his dark red hair, leaped on top of one of the crates, a thick iron chain with a wicked-looking spiked ball at the end of it in his hands.

"Your Highness and assembled guests, there is no need to fear."

The girl's eyes narrowed.

Ari guessed that meant the boy was telling them a big, fat, you're-probably-going-to-be-eaten-by-a-monster lie.

"I'm Hansel, and this beautiful but surly girl is my sister, Gretel. Watch out, she bites."

Gretel bared her teeth.

"We bring you two of the finest specimens from our latest hunt on the isle of Llorenyae." His voice rose and he threw his arms out to the sides as if to draw all the onlookers toward him. "Of the *Felinaes sapiaena* species, pure-blood young adults in their prime!"

Felinaes sapiaena. Ari's mouth went dry. Panther shapeshifters. There was no way Teague, and everyone else in Kosim

Thalas, wasn't going to hear about this.

Hansel warmed to his subject. "Fiercely territorial and unrepentantly carnivorous, *Felinaes sapiaena* make the perfect guard beast when properly restrained."

"And how do we make sure they are properly restrained?" Thad asked.

Ari scanned the crowd and found Sebastian standing at the far edge, just outside the courtyard. Their eyes met, and she could practically feel the tension vibrating from him.

Finally, someone else who understood that bringing panther shape-shifters onto the palace grounds was a terrible idea.

"An excellent question, Your Highness." Hansel leaped lightly from the crate. "As with all creatures who have fae blood, iron causes weakness. The younger the beast, the greater the effect of the iron. When you carve certain runes into the iron, you exert additional control."

He whipped the cloth from the crate beside him, and a ripple of screams and gasps swept the crowd. Ari clenched her fists and fought to remain calm and poised on the outside while she stared at the pair of monsters crouched on two feet inside the crate. Their limbs were long and catlike, but the beasts stood on two legs. Ari estimated that at full height they would tower over Sebastian. They were covered in black fur, their lips were pulled back in vicious snarls, and glowing amber eyes glared at the onlookers. Gretel pulled the cloth from her crate to reveal a matching pair. Iron collars with runes hammered into the surface circled the creatures' necks.

What happened if the beasts managed to get their collars off?

A tremor swept Ari, and she clenched her muscles in an effort to hold steady.

"The collars allow you to control the beasts. Certain commands activate different runes, and the iron keeps the creatures from shifting to another form," Hansel said.

"What other form would they take?" Thad asked.

Hansel shrugged. "Usually a rather monstrous sort of human, though some are capable of becoming venomous snakes. Not to worry, though! Our collars will keep them safely in panther form."

Ari didn't find his words comforting.

"Would the handlers for these fine specimens please step forward?" Hansel called.

Ari pitied the four grooms who stumbled toward Hansel, their faces taut with fear.

She listened closely to Hansel explain that one pair would patrol the grounds during the day, and the other would patrol at night. He detailed how to move the beasts from the stalls where they would sleep to the areas of the palace grounds that needed protecting, what to feed them, and how to teach them that the palace was their territory.

When he paused for a breath, his sister said quietly, "Better give them the scent of everyone who lives and works here, so the creatures understand not to harm them. No wandering outside the protected areas. No wandering at night. Visitors should stay within their carriages until escorted into the palace by the staff. We wouldn't want the wrong person disemboweled."

The handlers shuddered, and Thad asked, "How do we get them back into their stalls each morning?"

Hansel smiled grandly and said, "*Ar ais*."

Instantly, the beasts dropped to the floors of their cages, covered their ears, and howled.

"*Nach*," he said, and they slowly quieted, shaking their heads and shivering. "Once you've shown that you can hurt them, and that you are in control of their pain, they'll obey."

Ari stepped forward. "So these beasts are vicious guard creatures unless the intruder knows the fae commands to make them obey?" She shot a look at her brother and willed him to remember that Teague was fae, which meant he might know these commands too.

"Never fear." Hansel pressed his hands together. "We trained these creatures especially for you. They have their own set of commands. We never give the same commands to creatures heading for different locations. It's a security measure we pride ourselves on."

He bowed low at the waist before Thad. His sister barely inclined her head. Thad nodded.

"These are acceptable. Grooms, take them on a tour and show them their territory." Thad turned toward the bounty hunters. "You've had a three-day journey by ship and must be tired. Please, be my guests for the night. We have a feast prepared in your honor."

Ari sidled away from the cages and headed for Sebastian.

"This is a disaster," she said as she reached him.

"Teague is going to hear of it," he said.

"Everyone is going to hear of it, but I can't talk Thad out of this. We need a relationship with the hunters."

Sebastian made a rude noise.

"Exactly." Ari turned to face the spectacle in the courtyard as the staff rushed back inside the palace, anxious to have four solid walls protecting them before the crates were opened.

"If Teague is still connected to Llorenyae, the hunters might have a relationship with him. They could tell him that you're asking questions." Sebastian sounded worried, which warmed something inside Ari that felt suspiciously like the tingling she'd felt when they'd kissed.

Not that she wanted to remember that piece of abject (still completely mortifying) humiliation.

"Then I'll have to be subtle about it. They're my best chance to get something solid to go on. I have to take it."

He leaned toward her for a second before pulling away. "Be careful."

"Always."

He raised a brow.

"Fine. Usually."

His eyes crinkled, but the worry didn't leave his face. Ari knew how he felt. Teague was circling, the contract was still intact, she didn't have a solid plan, and now they had panther shape-shifter monsters roaming the palace grounds, which was sure to draw Teague straight to them.

It was hard to imagine things getting much worse.

TWENTY

"UGH, REALLY?" ARI set her breakfast plate on the table and stared at Thad.

"I can't go back on my word. Holding the ball in your honor officially launches you into society and presents you as heir to the throne."

"Well, I figured it was canceled, what with an angry fae Wish Granter after you and some relentlessly carnivorous monsters roaming the palace grounds." Ari sank into the chair beside Thad. "You can't guarantee the safety of your guests, and Teague—"

"The guests can stay in the palace overnight, and Teague can see that I am going about my life as usual, which might deflect suspicion from our efforts to get rid of him."

"But to hold a ball when there's so much unrest in Kosim Thalas and so much—"

"You have to be seen as the heir. The kingdom has to be kept safe, and that's *our* responsibility, Ari. If that means we hold a ball so that I can make sure you are launched properly, then that's what I'm going to do."

"Thad." She wrapped her arm around his shoulders, and he leaned against her the way he had throughout their childhood when she was his only source of comfort in the face of a father who expected perfection, peers who treated him like a pariah, and a mother too overworked and overtired to know what to do with a son who was being groomed for a life so far above her own.

"I'm sorry I ever saw Teague. Sorry I made that stupid wish. I just wanted to protect you, but now I can't even protect anyone in my entire kingdom. Teague is ravaging the streets. He burned down a merchant's shop. Killed a woman on the docks and took her children. Sent his employees to rob any shop whose owner refused to pay Teague a tax on each item sold. Crime is growing. And I sit here impotent because to lift a finger against him would make my contract instantly due." He turned to her. "You aren't going to like hearing this, but I can't keep standing idly by while Teague ruins Súndraille. I've given permission for the assassination plan to move forward whenever Ajax can find the right moment. I'm going to present you as the heir, make sure the alliances I've been building with you in the Assembly and with key officials are secure, and then I'm going to set the city guard against Teague's men. If he's still alive, he'll come for me, and you will become queen."

Panic flared, bright and jagged. "I just need more time, Thad. Just give me a little more time. Don't do anything rash."

"It isn't rash, Ari. Over the last weeks, our people have begun to suffer because of Teague. If I don't take action to protect them, I don't deserve to wear the crown."

Quick footsteps sounded outside the dining room door, and Thad instantly straightened and shoved his last bite of muffin into his mouth. The bounty hunters entered the room, moving with a controlled grace and speed that Ari would never be able to manage even on her best day.

Thad's countenance transformed into the beaming, genial expression he wore for welcoming honored visitors from other kingdoms. "Hansel. Gretel. I hope you slept well."

"Like a changeling," Hansel said.

Gretel just flicked her gaze over Ari and Thad and then turned to get some food from the sideboard.

"I was just telling my sister that the palace is hosting a ball three nights from now. I would be honored to have you in attendance."

"What would I do at a ball?" Gretel asked, her voice as controlled as her movements.

"You would dance, you absolute infidel." Hansel laughed, but there was something forced about it. He flashed a grin at Thad and Ari. "She's spent so much time tracking down beasties, she hardly knows how to do anything else."

"If you haven't brought proper attire, I'm sure our seamstress could make something to suit you," Thad said.

Gretel set her plate on the table across from Ari and said, "We're leaving in an hour."

"Oh." Thad sat back, and Ari understood his disappointment. They'd hoped to have several days to build an alliance with the hunters to get more information about Teague's history on Llorenyae.

"Business calls." Hansel sat down beside his sister and took a huge bite of sausage.

"Where will you go next?" Ari asked.

Hansel swallowed. "On to the port in Balavata, and from there a truly wearying camel ride into Akram with the majority of our cargo."

"Akram?" Thad asked.

Hansel smiled. "Our best customers. Maqbara prison can't seem to keep their beasties alive for long."

A page stepped into the room. "If I could have a moment, Your Highness."

"Of course." Thad stood and then turned to the bounty hunters. "A pleasure to make your acquaintance. You are always welcome here when you come through Kosim Thalas. Now, if you'll excuse me."

They stood and bowed—Hansel with a flourish and Gretel with the barest show of respect—and then resumed their seats as Thad left the room.

Ari tapped her fork against the tablecloth. She needed information about Llorenyae, about the fae, that only someone with an intimate knowledge of the place would have. If she could build the beginnings of an alliance on the ballroom floor in the space of time it took to dance a *contradanse*, she could do the same over a plate of breakfast food.

"These muffins are delicious," Hansel said.

Ari nodded and glanced at the open door. Staff bustled by on errands and chores, but for the moment, she was alone with the bounty hunters. It was an opportunity she couldn't pass by.

She looked up and found Gretel watching her with her eerily

pale blue eyes. "I've always wondered about the fae."

Gretel's gaze didn't waver, but Hansel shifted in his chair. "They're best left alone, Princess," he said.

"Yes," Gretel said softly. "Stay in your safe little palace and leave them alone. You don't want anything to do with the fae."

"How did you two end up on Llorenyae? Isn't it mostly fae?"

"There are human cities scattered throughout, each with its own leader, but all humans acknowledge the royalty of their respective fae court as the ultimate ruler of their half of the isle," Hansel said.

Ari frowned. "You mean the Summer and Winter courts?"

Hansel nodded. "Half the isle belongs to the Summer Queen and half to the Winter King."

"How did you become bounty hunters?" Ari asked.

Hansel's eyes darkened, and Gretel went still.

"It's a long story," Hansel said, his tone implying that he wasn't inclined to share any of it with her.

"Why do you want to know?" Gretel asked.

Ari tapped her finger against her plate for a moment, and then said, "I'd like to understand how one gets the courage to fight monsters and terrible fae creatures who have magic."

"Do you need that kind of courage?" Gretel asked.

Ari held her gaze. "Yes."

The girl nodded at Hansel, who sighed and said, "I wasn't kidding when I said it was a long story, so here are the highlights. We were abandoned in the woods far from our home when we were little, a fae enchantress bespelled her home to look like it was made out of candy, and she kept a veritable flock of orphans locked away for things I'm not going to discuss. Gretel and I were there for years until one day she got careless. And then we killed her."

"And once she was dead, we hunted down the other fae who'd bought orphans from her, and we killed them too," Gretel said quietly.

"Turns out, we had a knack for it." Hansel smiled grimly. "Before long, the Summer and Winter courts were hiring us to catch rogue fae, and the humans were hiring us to keep beasties out of their cities."

"Rogue fae." Ari considered her words for a moment, and then said, "We have a legend here. A bit of folklore about a creature called the Wish Granter. He's supposed to be fae."

Gretel cocked her head. "If I were you, I wouldn't make a wish."

Ari's heart pounded hard against her chest. Was Gretel simply warning her to stay away from all fae? Or from Teague in particular? Time was running out. Soon the hunters would leave, Teague would feel threatened by the beasts or by Ajax, and Ari would lose her brother. She leaned toward Gretel and took a gamble. "There's a man in Kosim Thalas who is rumored to be the Wish Granter. He does terrible things."

Hansel put the rest of his muffin back on his plate. "We should go."

Gretel remained unmoving, her eyes locked on Ari.

Ari had one more question that had to be answered. She drew in a deep breath as Hansel got to his feet and put his hand on his sister's arm.

"Regular iron weapons don't work against him. We need to know how to stop him. Would you have any ideas about that?"

she asked, and then waited, stomach in knots, palms sweaty as she prayed that Gretel would give her something—one tiny scrap of a clue that could send Ari in the right direction.

"No, we haven't. Gretel, let's go."

Gretel stood, and Ari sank against the back of her chair. She'd gambled, and she'd lost. Either they didn't know of Teague, or they were too scared of him to tell her.

Or they knew him all too well, and Ari had just condemned both Cleo and her brother to a visit from Teague.

Hansel nodded briskly to Ari and then walked toward the door. Gretel met her eyes again, hesitated, and then said softly, "I've always enjoyed reading *Magic in the Moonlight: A Nursery Primer*."

Ari sat up straight, question spilling across her tongue, but Gretel left the dining room.

It didn't matter. Ari had information she could use now. A glow of triumph spread through her as she hurried to the library, slid the book off the shelf, and grabbed a sheaf of parchments. Sharpening a quill with shaking fingers (which, in retrospect, turned out to be unwise as she cut herself twice), she dipped the nib into a pot of ink and went through the primer, taking notes on anything interesting.

Nothing stood out to her. There were rhymes about tree nymphs and water sprites with pictures of ethereal fae with branches or waterweed for hair. Warnings about dancing with faeries beneath a full moon. A brief poem about a tall woman with a wolf's head, bird's talons for hands, and goat hooves for feet who left the secret of her power behind at birth and another about a witch who made pies out of children. Both were accompanied by illustrations that had made Ari shudder as a child. There were catchy poems about changelings and salt lines and iron hanging from one's windows. Ballads about the Summer and Winter courts. Even a ballad about wish granters, because apparently on Llorenyae there was more than one. Ari studied the wish granter ballad for nearly an hour, but if it contained a secret she hadn't yet learned, she couldn't find it.

Turning to a fresh sheet of parchment, she began listing everything she'd learned about Teague.

The bulk of Teague's business and employees operated out of east Kosim Thalas.

No one seemed to know exactly where Teague lived. Some said to the east of the city. Some said to the south, just above the sea. Nobody seemed to know any useful details about his house, which in and of itself was a useful detail. Maybe Teague kept his home a secret because he'd made so many enemies on the streets of Kosim Thalas. Maybe he was vulnerable there, though Ari had no idea where to even begin looking for his home, much less how to exploit it for weaknesses.

She went back to listing the things she'd learned.

He manufactured a powerfully addictive drug called apodrasi.

He sold pipe weed, apodrasi, stolen valuables, forged artwork, and people he either bought from other places or tricked into slavery. Many of these sales happened through the brokers in Balavata.

He was the Wish Granter.

He was fae.

He'd left Llorenyae and never returned.

Ari looked over her list and added another column—"Things I Know About the Fae."

What did she know? Iron harmed them, but lost its power the older the fae got. Runes were effective when used with iron and spoken commands in the fae's tongue, but she didn't know any runes or any commands other than the two she'd overheard Hansel teaching the beasts' handlers. She knew that Gretel believed an answer to her problems was hidden somewhere in the nursery primer.

She also knew that Gretel had warned her not to become involved with the fae.

It was too late for that. She'd been involved with a fae from the moment he decided to take advantage of her brother. And she planned to stop him, once and for all; but to do that, she needed to fill in the gaps in his history. Find out where he lived. Learn how to take him down.

And to do *that*, she had to start with the place where he apparently spent most of his time and energy.

She had to go into east Kosim Thalas.

TWENTY-ONE

"OUT OF THE question." Sebastian slapped a shield onto the table in the middle of the armory and faced the princess.

"It's the next logical step."

"Sure it is, if your goal is to be dead by morning." His voice shook. His entire *body* shook, and it took more effort than it should have to rein it in.

He'd stopped trying to argue himself out of being friends with the princess two weeks ago because when she'd said she could be relentless, she'd been telling the truth. They'd become close before he truly realized he'd forgotten to keep his guard up. But here was the cost of that friendship punching him in the stomach and sending waves of panic crashing through his body.

She wanted to go into east Kosim Thalas.

No, not *wanted*. That implied that she sometimes announced plans she had no intention of implementing. She was *going* into east Kosim Thalas.

Worse, she was going in looking for information about Teague.

It was a death sentence, and he had to make her see it.

"Princess Arianna, you have no idea what going into east Kosim Thalas means for someone like you." He made a conscious effort to keep his hands from becoming fists. "You'll be instantly pegged as an outsider, as nobility or merchant, and several things will happen. You'll be robbed, beaten into submission, and then either sold to Teague as a slave or . . ."

He couldn't finish. He couldn't put into words the horrors unsuspecting youth from the nicer parts of the city experienced at the hands of those in east Kosim Thalas who'd spent years without enough food to feed their bellies but with plenty of injustice and pain to feed the rage that fueled them now.

She drew in a deep breath. "I know I'm risking another run-in like I had with Teague's men in the market. And I have to be very careful that I don't ask the wrong person a question, because it can't get back to Teague. I have to do this, but I don't want Cleo to pay the price. That's why I was hoping you might come with me."

He stared at her. "If you go through with this, then of course I'm coming with you. Did you really think there was a chance I wouldn't?"

She gave him a relieved smile, and he took a step toward her.

"You don't understand, Princess. All those things I just listed that would happen to you? They'll happen to me too, if I'm not ready. If I'm not on guard. And even then . . . even then things happen there. It only takes a split second to lose focus and then lose your coin and possibly your life."

"I don't want to put you in danger." Her thinking frown took up residence between her brows. "Maybe if I dress like I've always lived there, I could go in unnoticed on my own, and then—"

"No."

"But—"

"I'm not discussing that option. Ever."

Stars, his knees weren't going to hold him if he couldn't control his panic. He closed his eyes and fought to keep his mind from showing him the street runners' faces if they recognized the princess. From seeing people pouring out of the buildings to surround them, everyone desperate for a piece of the princess's wealth, and when that was gone, for a piece of *her* as punishment for being born outside east Kosim Thalas.

One mistake. That's all it would take. One single mistake, and she would suffer horribly before she died or was sold to a broker.

"Sebastian?" Her voice was gentle. "If it's too much to ask you to go back there, I can find someone else to go with me."

"There is no one else." He opened his eyes and found her standing right in front of him, her hand hovering in the air as if wanting to comfort him with a touch when they both knew there was no comfort for him there. "Unless you know of someone else who was raised there and who has a reputation for winning every fight—"

"I'm sorry." She let her hand fall without touching him, and he told himself he wasn't disappointed. Of course he wasn't disappointed. That was a foolish thought distracting him from the real problem at hand. "I don't know what else to do. I have to know where Teague lives—"

"Please tell me you aren't planning to break into his home."

"The thought crossed my mind, though it's probably pretty

hard to break into a fae's house."

"Argh." He turned from her and began pacing through the armory, gathering weapons as he went. If he was going to escort the princess, stars help him, into east Kosim Thalas, he was going to do it armed to the teeth.

"I need to know if he's hiding anything. If he has any weaknesses." The princess grabbed a dagger and strapped its sheath to her ankle. "There has to be a way to bring him down."

She slid a throwing star into her handbag, and he began praying that there'd be no need for her to throw it.

Squaring her shoulders, she moved toward the stairs that led from the armory to the arena.

He followed her into the arena and then outside. He was about to continue their argument when she stiffened and took a step back, nearly running into him. He peered past her and froze, his heart racing, as one of Ajax's beasts, half crouching, half running on its hind legs, came straight for them.

"Daka," the princess whispered.

Sebastian wrapped a hand around her arm and pulled her behind him as the creature thudded to a halt in front of Sebastian and locked its amber eyes on him. A deep growl grew in its chest as it thrust its face toward Sebastian and sniffed.

His knees were shaking, and every instinct screamed that he needed to grab one of the weapons he carried, but he knew he wouldn't have time. If the beast decided Sebastian wasn't allowed on the palace grounds, he would be dead before he finished reaching for a blade.

The beast pushed past Sebastian, its claws digging into his shoulder as it shoved him away from the princess.

He reached for his sword as it sniffed her, but then its growl softened into a whine, and it turned and loped away.

"I can't wait to be rid of those things," the princess whispered as the creature disappeared in the direction of the garden. Rubbing her arms briskly, she turned to Sebastian. "Ready?"

"If we're going to go into east Kosim Thalas, then we do it my way. Agreed?" He waited.

"Agreed."

"You let me take the lead. You do what I say. And if trouble happens, I will get you free of it"—please, please let him be able to get her free of it—"and you run. You run out of east Kosim Thalas, and you don't stop until you are as far away as you can get."

She glanced down at her generous curves. "I'm not much of a runner."

He leaned toward her. "You and I both know you are not to be underestimated. If I say run, you *run*. You can do anything you set your mind to."

"I like your confidence." She smiled at him. "Now, what should I wear?"

Two hours later, Sebastian's pulse was thunder in his ears and every muscle was coiled and ready for a fight as he walked beneath the crumbling gateway to east Kosim Thalas with the princess by his side.

Granted, she no longer resembled the princess. Her hair was done in a simple peasant's braid. Her clothing was patched and dirty—she'd had to rip and mend a dress and then drag it through the garden to achieve the look—and she'd wrapped an equally tattered and dirty scarf over her head and covered most of her face with it as if trying to avoid a sunburn.

His cudgel was a solid weight in his hand, and he slung a bag of food for his mother over his shoulder as they approached the first line of buildings. Tension hummed through his muscles, and he focused on every movement, every sound that whispered toward him.

They walked rapidly. He tore his gaze from the people sitting on their front steps or smoking on balconies long enough to check that the princess looked anything but royal. She was walking with slumped shoulders, her head bowed, and her feet shuffling as if she were too exhausted to walk properly.

Movement caught his eye, and he snapped his gaze to the runners who hovered on the street corner. They knew him, but they weren't used to seeing him with anyone. Their eyes were locked on the princess, and he could practically hear them making calculations as she moved.

Nobility? Not with those clothes. Merchant? Too dirty. And Sebastian wouldn't be with someone from either class. That left a servant or a peasant from the countryside. Were there signs that she worked for a family who might pay for her safe return?

There weren't. He'd made sure of it. He'd double-checked every detail. Still, he gripped his cudgel as they walked past the runners and turned up the hill toward his mother's place.

Dread curled through Sebastian's stomach, oily and slick. When he'd looked at everything the princess hoped to accomplish in east Kosim Thalas, there'd only been one obvious solution.

His mother.

She used apodrasi. Thanks to his father's line of work, she

knew something about Teague's employees and system of business. And she spent a lot of time doing favors for those employees in exchange for . . . whatever it was she wanted in exchange. Probably more drugs. He'd learned early on not to ask questions that he didn't truly want answered.

If there was anyone in this part of the city who'd be willing to talk to him about Teague without disclosing that he'd been asking questions, it was his mother.

Unfortunately, there was also the possibility that she'd refuse to talk. That she'd scream and curse and beg for coin he wouldn't give.

He had to force himself not to slow down as they came abreast of his mother's building. Behind them, people had detached themselves from walls and doorsteps, just as he'd feared, but no one had attacked. Yet.

He figured they were waiting for the runners to come back with orders from the street bosses. He could only hope the fact that his father was one of Teague's most valued collectors would give Sebastian and the princess a degree of protection.

The irony that his father might finally be protecting him by virtue of being a criminal wasn't lost on Sebastian.

He climbed the rickety stairs, the princess following silently, and then stood outside his mother's door, listening as always for a hint that his father had returned.

It was worse—so much worse—to listen and panic and fight to control his emotions when he had the princess depending on him. He didn't want to show her this side of himself. The fear and poverty. The bitter, shifting moods of his mother.

Stepping across the threshold into his former home was like

stripping away the bandage that hid his deepest wound.

"It's okay," the princess whispered. "We can ask someone else if you don't want to go inside. I saw quite a few people on the street."

"You saw people who are waiting to hear from the street bosses whether they should leave us alone or rob us and sell us to Balavata."

It hurt to breathe, and the scars on his back prickled and ached. Before he could second-guess himself, he turned the doorknob and went inside. The princess followed him.

His mother was alone, sitting in a chair at her flimsy kitchen table, picking at a plum with her dirty fingernails. "Who's there?" his mother asked.

He moved into her line of sight, and she sat up straighter.

"Come to rob me again?"

He sighed. "I never rob you."

She spat a bit of plum onto the floor.

He held up the sack. "I brought food for the week."

"Did you bring coin too?"

"No."

His mother looked at him, her eyes bright with desperate need. "I'm out, Sebastian."

Before she could say another word, he stepped aside to let her see he hadn't come alone.

"Who's that? A girl? Thinks she can snatch you up and take over my house?"

He gritted his teeth. "She doesn't want your house."

"Too good for me, is she?"

Sebastian didn't look at the princess as he crossed the room to unload the food into the cupboard, his face burning with humiliation.

He heard the soft swish of the princess's dress as she followed him into the kitchen, and then she was crouching beside his mother and looking up into the older woman's face.

"Your son is a good person. A great person, actually. I'm sure you're proud of him."

Sebastian's chest ached at the look of surprise on his mother's face. "Proud of what? For leaving me here just like his father? Just like his brother?"

"Children grow up and leave, but he takes care of you. He brought you food."

"I don't need food." She looked at Sebastian, and his gut twisted. "I need coin. I haven't had any for days. Your father is supposed to send what I need. Teague is supposed to send what I need."

The princess latched on to the mention of Teague. "How does Teague send it to you?"

His mother glared at the princess. "He sends Daan, of course. Can't trust an expensive product like apodrasi to just anyone. But everyone says the collector is dead, and Teague is busy trying to figure out who killed him, who's coming after his business, and now I'm out."

Sebastian glanced out the window and saw a crowd gathering below. His chest tightened until it hurt to breathe. He needed to hurry this along. The sun would set in little more than an hour, and he needed to have the princess long gone from this part of the city before then. It was much harder for the street bosses to control people when no one could see what they were doing.

"Mother, do you know where Teague lives?"

She straightened. "Wouldn't tell you if I did, now would I? I know how to be loyal. Learned that from your father. It's a lesson that didn't ever seem to take with you."

The princess patted his mother's hand gently. "Maybe I could go to Teague's home and get what you need. Would that help?"

His mother turned her hand over and grasped Ari, palm to palm. "You do that. You go there and bring me a vial of apodrasi."

"I will," the princess said solemnly. "Tell me where to go, and I'll do it."

His mother's lip curled. "I can't tell you where to go, stupid girl. Only the collectors know where he lives. Give me coin. I'll buy it myself."

Sebastian stepped forward and disentangled the princess's hand from his mother's. "I'll send more food next week, Mother. Don't forget to eat."

He hurried the princess from the room as his mother hurled invectives at their backs. The crowd parted sluggishly for them, but Sebastian moved with purpose, flexing his shoulders and glaring at everyone who would meet his gaze.

He didn't realize he was shaking until they walked out of east Kosim Thalas without injury.

The princess said, "Now we know that Teague is distracted by the loss of his collector and that only collectors know where he lives," and then stayed quiet while they wound their way through the merchant district and toward the hill that led to the palace.

Sebastian was in agony. Was she disgusted by the truth of his upbringing? Did she pity him? Would she look at him and see him through the bitter lens of his mother's eyes?

They reached the bottom of the hill, the only two people left climbing toward the palace this close to sunset. The princess stopped and turned to him.

He ordered himself to meet her eyes without flinching. To shove his fears and shame into a box and show her nothing while he waited for her judgment.

She tilted her head back and studied him for a moment. He couldn't find any hint of pity on her face, but he braced to hear it in her voice.

Finally, she said, "There's a ball at the palace tomorrow night."

He frowned. "I . . . What?"

What did that have to do with east Kosim Thalas and the miserable hovel he'd called a home?

"Dancing. Fancy dresses. And really excellent snacks."

"Oh."

She leaned closer and locked eyes with him. "I'd like you to go with me."

He opened his mouth, but found he had absolutely nothing to say.

"Sebastian Vaughn, my loyal, strong, faithful friend, I would be honored to go to the ball with you."

She waited, but he still couldn't find a single response.

He couldn't go to a ball. Out of the question. That was for nobility. What would he wear? What would he do? Her reputation would be in tatters. He would make a fool of himself and probably lose his job.

It was preposterous.

And yet, her words wrapped around the tightness in his chest and loosened the knot until he could breathe again.

She'd be honored to go with him. She'd seen where he'd come from. She'd heard his mother's hate. And still she'd be honored to be seen by everyone.

With him.

His lips twitched upward, and warmth spread through him as he said, "I can't dance."

"Dancing is for people who don't truly appreciate the buffet."

"I have nothing to wear."

"I'll find something for you."

"The nobility will gossip about you until the day you die," he said. One last attempt to talk sense into her even though he knew it was a lost cause.

"They needed a new hobby anyway." She smiled at him. "What do you say? Will you go with me?"

Stars help him. "Yes."

TWENTY-TWO

SEBASTIAN HAD LOST his mind.

There was no other explanation why a boy from east Kosim Thalas would be standing just inside the servants' entrance to the kitchen, wearing a fancy silk-blend dress coat, pants, shirt, and pocket handkerchief.

A *pocket handkerchief.*

Until this morning, when Princess Arianna had brought him a stack of borrowed clothes, he hadn't even known such a thing existed.

His stomach felt as though he'd swallowed rocks. He kept pulling at the buttoned collar of his shirt and fidgeting with the strap he'd used to secure his cudgel beneath his long-tailed coat. Staring out the large window above the sinks, he watched carriage after carriage roll to a stop in front of the palace, disgorging another group of well-dressed nobility before making room for the next vehicle, and a band of anxiety wrapped around his chest and tightened until it hurt.

He couldn't do this. Not even for the princess. He couldn't go into a crowded ballroom. He couldn't bear to brush up against so many people. His pulse thundered, his blood raced through his veins like fire, and he retreated until his back was against the door.

He'd tell the princess he was sorry. She'd understand.

He'd tell her he appreciated the gesture, but that he was better off in his servant's quarters. She'd understand that too.

He groaned and dropped his face into his hands.

"Sebastian?"

He looked up, and the fear racking his body boiled into something far more dangerous.

She was beautiful.

He'd known that, of course. Stars knew, they'd spent enough hours together every day for the past month that he was familiar with the way the sun glistened against her golden skin and the way it lightened strands of her thick brown hair. He had her smiles memorized, and he could read her every emotion in her dark eyes.

But *this*.

This stole his breath and doubled his pulse. This made him want to dance with her even though it meant touching her— maybe *because* it meant touching her.

Her dress, a deep green edged with silver, lingered over every curve of her body. He stared at her plunging neckline, tore his gaze away, and then found himself looking at way the fabric curved over her hips before finally widening out into a skirt fit for dancing.

"Are you all right?" she asked as she moved toward him, her

hips swaying with every step.

He was never going to be all right again. He was staring at the *princess*—like he wanted something he had no right to want.

"Sebastian?" She stood in front of him, smelling like cinnamon and oranges, and he forced himself not to look at anything but her face.

Worry filled her eyes, and she leaned closer to him. He tensed but it wasn't because he thought she might touch him.

It was because for the first time, he desperately wanted her to.

He was in so much trouble.

"You don't have to do this," she said softly. "It will be all right. You can—"

"I'm not leaving you."

Pink blossomed in her cheeks, and her chest—which he was *not* supposed to be looking at—rose and fell a little faster. "Are you sure? Because if you need—"

"I'm sure."

She smiled—shy and pleased. He'd thought he had her smiles memorized, but this was something new. His lips twitched upward in response, and her smile grew.

He should say something. Compliment her. Ask her to accompany him to the ballroom. Anything but stand here staring at her like he was seeing her for the first time.

"You look . . . that dress is very . . . it's nice," he said, and groaned inwardly. She was going to think he was an imbecile.

She looked down at her dress, and he fought to keep his eyes from following hers. "Well, I was going for something a little better than nice, but—"

"You succeeded." He breathed the words, and the faint pink in her cheeks bloomed brighter.

He really, really needed to not be alone with her in this kitchen for another second, or he might do something he could never take back.

"I believe you said something about excellent snacks," he said, relieved that his voice didn't reveal the way his heart raced and his stomach spun in lazy circles.

She stepped back and swept an arm toward the door that led to the main palace. "I'm a girl of my word. Come with me."

The ballroom—an ornate space with arched windows, marble pillars, and gilt practically dripping from every available surface—was nearly two-thirds full. Servants carrying trays of sparkling wine or cheese or pastries lined the outskirts, and musicians sat on a stage at the north end of the room playing a swift, lilting melody. A fiery sunset spread across the sky and lit the western windows with gold and orange.

Guests were scattered throughout the room. The older ones, dressed in the kind of sweeping sheaths that the princess usually wore, were seated in clusters, wine and cheese in their hands. The younger ones were wearing brilliant jewel-toned dresses or long-tailed jackets and were already dancing. Sebastian swept his gaze over the room, noting the two open doorways in the western wall that led out to the garden where torches had been lit, though a servant stood at each door to warn guests not to step past the veranda that hugged the outside wall.

Nobody wanted to give the beasts cause to attack.

"You won't want to go back to the arena tonight," the princess said, turning toward him with dismay on her face. "Not with those beasts stalking you in the dark, even if they do know your scent. I didn't think of that. I'll find a place for you to stay in the palace."

He shrugged. "I'll manage. I can always sleep in the kitchen."

She rolled her eyes. "You aren't sleeping in the kitchen. I think all the guest rooms are taken, but if I can't find anything else, you can always have the couch in my sitting room."

Stars no, he wasn't going to sleep in the princess's rooms. Not when simply standing next to her was making everything inside him tumble like he was caught in a hurricane.

"I see we've invited the riffraff to the ball." Makario, the nobleman who liked to taunt Sebastian in the arena, sneered at him as he approached. "Really, Your Highness, have a care for your reputation."

The princess snorted. "If you haven't figured out by now that I don't care what you think of me, let this be the lesson that sticks."

Anger lit Makario's eyes. "If you won't have a care for your own reputation, then consider the reputation of Súndraille. Imagine what would happen if the nobility from other kingdoms saw a sewer rat from east Kosim Thalas attending a royal ball as a *guest*."

"If you are disrespectful toward Sebastian one more time, I will permanently ban you from the palace," the princess said, wrapping her arm through Sebastian's and pulling him against her hip. "Sebastian is my invited guest. He will be treated as such."

Makario's lips thinned. "I mean no disrespect, but he is beneath your new status, Your Highness."

Sebastian flexed his shoulders and rolled to the balls of his feet.

The princess's voice was cold. "The only ones beneath my status are those who treat others like chattel."

Makario lowered his voice and took a step closer, crowding the princess against Sebastian. "Do you think we don't know why you brought your little toy with you?" He flicked a glance at Sebastian. "You think that now that you're the acknowledged princess, you can make up your own rules. Do as you please with no consequences. That's not how life works, Your Highness. You're a bastard princess, a half blood. You need to think very carefully about your next move." Makario's voice rose, and those closest to them turned to stare.

Sebastian's pulse roared, and his breath quickened.

The princess gripped Sebastian's arm tightly and lifted her other hand to stab her finger at Makario's face. "My next move is going to be to remove you from the palace."

Blind rage flashed in Makario's eyes. "You fat, ungrateful—"

Sebastian tore free of the princess's grip and plowed his fist into Makario's face.

Screams rose from the crowd as Makario stumbled back; and for one second, Sebastian thought they were screaming because a servant had just broken a nobleman's nose.

"Sebastian!" The princess's voice was bright with panic. She grabbed his hand and spun him to face the western wall. A bone-chilling cry echoed across the ballroom as the monsters from Llorenyae stood upright in the open doorways that led to the garden, their amber eyes feral and vicious, their snouts dripping saliva as they snarled at the crowd.

Behind the tallest beast, Teague stood illuminated by the garden's torchlight, an ivory pipe in his mouth. He smiled, cold and cruel, and said, "*Ithe.*"

With bloodcurdling screams, the beasts launched themselves into the ballroom.

TWENTY-THREE

"GET TO THE cellar!" Ari yelled to those around her. When they stared at her in confusion, she grabbed the closest servant. "Lead the way to the cellar and get as many inside as you can. Shut the door and lock it behind you, and don't open it again unless you're sure it's a person knocking and not those monsters."

The maid dropped her tray of pastries and ran for the east exit.

"Follow her." Ari pushed those closest to her in the right direction, while terrible screams of pain rose from the western side of the room. "Go!"

Sebastian shoved past a knot of panicked nobility to reach her side. "What was the command to stop those creatures?"

"I can't remember." Her hands shook as she snatched at the tunics of a pair of older women who were huddled on the floor sobbing and pulled them to their feet. "Get out of here. See where the crowd is going? Follow them. You'll be safe in the cellar."

She hoped she was telling the truth. Surely those monsters

couldn't break down a stone door that weighed as much as two horses.

A man cried out—a terrible, wet sound of agony that ended abruptly—and the crowd fleeing from the western side of the ballroom slammed into Ari and tore Sebastian from her side. She went down hard, and someone kicked her in the back, sending her sprawling.

"Daka!" She tried to get to her hands and knees. Her (gorgeous, but ill-suited for crawling) dress made it hard to gain any leverage. Especially when she was having to cover her head with her arms to keep from being crushed.

Another kick hit her in the chest, and the air rushed out of her. She panicked, clawing for breath, trying to curl up in a ball to protect herself, but there was no protection. She was simply an obstacle lying between the crowd and safety.

She was going to die. Trampled, suffocated, and then torn limb from limb by those terrifying beasts. Tears pricked her eyes as she struggled to draw in a full breath.

And then Sebastian was there, shoving people away from her with one hand while he reached for her with the other.

She took his hand and struggled to her feet, her breath whistling in her lungs. Another wave of panicked people struck them, and Sebastian braced his feet, wrapped his arms around her, and hauled her against his chest.

"Where's Thad? And Cleo? Were they on the west side of the ballroom? I have to find them." Her teeth chattered, and her hands were ice.

"Think," Sebastian murmured against her ear, his body swaying as the next wave of panicked guests jostled him on their way to the eastern exit. "You can remember. Close out everything that's going on around you, and think back to the courtyard. Hansel. What command did he tell the handlers to use to stop the beasts?"

She closed her eyes, latched on to the sound of his voice, and buried her face in the front of his shirt while she replayed the scene from the courtyard.

Hansel, with his chain and his easy smile. The handlers trembling with fear. The beasts howling with misery in their crates until Hansel said—

"*Nach*!" She pulled away from Sebastian's chest, and was nearly thrown to the floor as a man used her shoulder for leverage to pull himself over another man who'd been trampled and lay unmoving on the floor beside them. Sebastian grabbed her arms and pulled her against his body.

"Good." His voice was calm, but he was breathing quickly, and his body was tensed for a fight. "*Nach*!" he yelled, but the panicked screams of the crowd swallowed his voice.

"We have to get closer," she said, though everything in her wanted to run in the opposite direction.

They pushed against the crowd, many of whom were injured and were trying desperately to crawl toward the eastern doorway. Ari let go of Sebastian as they sidestepped a group of nobility who were stumbling toward the exit, and her horrified gaze took in the carnage that spread across the western side of the ballroom.

Blood and bodies littered the floor and splattered the gilt-covered walls. The two beasts hunched over mangled bodies, snarling and snapping at each other.

"*Nach*," she said, but her lungs still ached, still refused to take a full breath, and her voice was too weak to reach them. Sebastian tried as well, but they still weren't close enough to be heard.

In the doorway leading out to the garden, Teague stood, watching it all with a wicked smile on his face.

Another wave of screams rose, and Ari tore her gaze from Teague just in time to see one of the beasts lunge across the ballroom heading toward the eastern doorway, its long arms reaching for the fleeing crowd.

The other beast was coming straight for Sebastian.

He was facing her, keeping her safe from being trampled by the crowd. He wouldn't be able to move in time.

"No!" she screamed as she launched herself in front of him.

The beast collided with her, sending them both tumbling to the floor. It was like being hit with a boulder. Her chest ached in sharp bursts. She couldn't breathe. And terror was a fire blazing through her, obliterating everything in its path.

The beast's talons sank into her arms as it peeled back its lips in a vicious snarl.

Sebastian struck the beast with a cudgel, and its thick fur rippled as it shuddered, but it didn't take its eyes off Ari. Saliva dripped onto her face, and she struggled for the air to speak.

"*Nach*!" Sebastian yelled, and the creature shook its head and whined, though it kept Ari pinned.

Sebastian grabbed the beast around its neck. "I said *nach*."

The creature shivered and sank onto its haunches, and Sebastian tore it off Ari and sent it scuttling into the buffet table. The other beast was cowering beneath Sebastian's command in the center of the room.

Teague walked into the ballroom, clapping his hands slowly as he carefully stepped over bodies and puddles of blood. "*Bas*," he said, and the two monsters shuddered, their eyes rolling back in their heads and their mouths foaming as they fell to the ground, twitching until they lay still.

"I find it best to destroy a weapon that proves itself unpredictable," he said in his cold, elegant voice.

Teague was *here*. He'd come for Thad's soul, and Ari had to stop him. The alternative was unthinkable.

She gulped for air, reached for Sebastian, and forced a single word past her lips. "Help."

He crouched beside her, his cudgel raised as he kept his eyes on the closest beast, and took her hand. He remained steady as a rock while she slowly pulled herself to a sitting position.

"Hmm," Teague said as he studied Sebastian. "There's something familiar about you." He tapped his ivory pipe against his lips. "Not nobility. Not carrying a weapon like that. You remind me of an employee of mine—Jacob Vaughn."

"He's my father." Sebastian's voice reminded Ari of the bleakness of a frozen, snow-covered lake. Any emotion was buried so deep, it was impossible to find.

"Then you must be Sebastian, as I remember ordering the death of Jacob's other son for failing to follow orders. Interesting to find you rubbing shoulders with royalty at a ball."

Sebastian gave a one-shouldered shrug and let go of Ari. "I do what I'm paid to do."

He was lying. He'd done so much more than what he'd been paid to do, but if he needed Teague to believe he was simply her employee, Ari wasn't going to argue.

Teague smiled. "Like father, like son."

Sebastian's body tensed, but he remained silent.

Movement caught Ari's eye, and she turned to see her brother slowly climbing out from behind a table that had flipped to its side during the struggle. There was blood pouring from a wound in his head, and he could barely keep his balance, but he was still alive, and Ari's throat thickened with tears as she looked at him.

Teague turned to face Thad and pocketed his pipe. Withdrawing two arrows from an inner coat pocket, he held them up. Candlelight reflected dully against the arrows' metal surface.

Iron.

"Tsk, tsk, it seems our dear king has been injured." He glanced at Ari, who was still trying to breathe past the pain. "As has our resourceful princess. Such a shame, though I did warn you to leave me alone. Imagine my surprise when a pair of creatures much like the two I just destroyed were sent to attack me as I traveled to one of my warehouses this afternoon." He looked back at Thad, his eyes glowing with malice. "When they failed to kill me, a man sent two arrows into my back. Obviously, he also failed to kill me. It didn't take much of an interrogation to learn he was working for you. You really should hire people with higher pain tolerance."

Ari's heart sank. Ajax had failed, and Ari still didn't have a viable backup plan.

She had no way to save Thad.

Teague tossed the arrows to the floor and stepped over them. His tone was cut glass. "A lesser fae would've died, but you aren't dealing with a lesser fae. You're dealing with Alistair Teague."

The walls shook, candlelight flickering as his voice rose. "I am ancient. I have survived battles in wars long lost to history. I have survived assassination attempts from those much more learned in fae lore than you." He closed in on Thad. "I have survived betrayal, exile, and the miserable pretense of obeying human law, and you can be sure I will survive *you*."

He reached into another pocket and withdrew a scroll of parchment and a vial that glittered as if it were made from diamonds. "Do you know what this is?"

He held up the parchment, and Thad nodded miserably.

The contract. Ari lurched to her feet. Sebastian stood as well, though he didn't touch her. Maybe she could grab it. Burn it. Chew it up and swallow it if she had to.

Teague unrolled it with a flick of his wrist. "It's the contract you signed. The one where you gave me your soul and the right to run my business in your kingdom without your interference."

Ari took a step forward, wincing in pain.

Teague's voice became a whiplash of cold fury. "I warned you not to try to break the terms of our bargain." He raised the parchment and read from the bottom of the page. "It says here that if the undersigned, which is *you*, attempts to harm me, renegotiate terms, or break your vow in any way, the debt you owe comes due." He looked up and met Thad's desperate gaze. "Immediately."

Thad's knees buckled, and he slid to the floor as his gaze locked on Ari. She could read the fear, the regret, and, most of all, the desperate plea for her to do what he'd been preparing her to do all along: take the crown and rule in his place.

The wound in Ari's heart that had opened the night her mother died ached fiercely, and tears blurred her vision.

She was going to lose Thad if she didn't *do* something.

"Get to your feet, you worthless boy." Teague stalked toward him, and Ari started moving, Sebastian on her heels. "You didn't care what the price was as long as your sister was safe. I held up my end of the deal, and what have you done? Sent your sister into the market to ask questions about me and to buy poison for the monster killer you hired to assassinate me. Purchased beasts from Llorenyae to fend off my just attempts to get you to honor your debt. I'll bet you didn't expect me to be able to control them, did you? You see, I speak fae, and I read runes. I am nearly immune to iron, and you'd have to fill me with bloodflower poison for it to kill me. And I am out of patience with you."

"You're making a mistake." Thad's words were slurred, and he seemed to be having trouble focusing his eyes. He needed medical attention, but if Ari didn't find a way to stop Teague from ripping out her brother's soul, none of that would matter.

"No, *you* made the mistake! We had a bargain. A mutually beneficial relationship that was supposed to last for ten years. I offered you the desire of your heart." Teague's voice rose, shaking the floor. "And you took it. You *took* it, and now I will take what is owed me."

Ari's chest throbbed, and desperate fear drove her forward as Teague put the contract into his coat pocket and unstoppered the glittering vial.

She was never going to see him again. Never going to hear him laugh at her crazy plans or list all the things a proper princess didn't do.

He would be gone, and she would be left wearing a crown she'd never wanted.

Alone.

The pain in her heart stabbed deep, a fierce ache that felt as if she was already grieving him.

She was going to lose her brother, and Teague would get away with it because Ari didn't know how to stop him. Thad would die, and she would be left alone in the palace to pick up the pieces of a life she didn't want to live without knowing that her brother was safe.

Her mind skipped from one desperate idea to the next. She knew a myriad of details about his business. His life. There had to be something she could use.

He hadn't just wanted Thad's soul. He'd wanted unimpeded access to the city.

He'd wanted immunity from the consequences of his actions.

He'd wanted to be the unrivaled power behind a puppet king.

He wanted *power,* but if he took Thad's soul, he'd be giving that up.

In a voice that shook the room, Teague said, "*Ghlacadh anam de* Thaddeus Glavan *agus*—"

"Wait!" Ari threw herself at Teague, an idea born of furious, desperate love taking shape inside her head. He wanted power. He wanted immunity from his actions. He wanted puppet kings on paper thrones dancing to his whims.

If she could give Teague that long enough to buy herself time to uncover the key to stopping him, maybe she could save Thad and free him to be the just, fair ruler he wanted to be.

"If you take Thad's soul, you'll be squandering the opportunity of a lifetime," she said as she held Teague's gaze.

He glared. "I think not."

"His soul isn't what you're really after. You want freedom to run your business as you please." Her words were rushed and desperate, her fingers knotting together as if in supplication. "You want power. And a man like you—an ancient, powerful fae—wouldn't be satisfied with the kind of power that keeps Kosim Thalas under your thumb. That's just one city out of thousands. You're the *Wish Granter*. You deserve to have entire kingdoms to answer to you, and Thad can make that happen."

"Ari," Thad mumbled. She ignored him. So did Teague.

"He's a seventeen-year-old who's only been on the throne for a few weeks," Teague said. "He can't deliver kingdoms to me."

"It doesn't matter how long he's had the throne." Her voice shook. "It only matters how many powerful allies he has in other kingdoms."

Teague paused to study her expression for a long moment, and then said, "Go on."

"I've been looking into your affairs," she said to Teague.

His golden eyes narrowed, and pressure built in her chest. She rushed to get the words out.

"You're highly reliant on your brokers in Balavata to move all the product you don't sell in Súndraille. That means you have to raise your price to pay their commission and still make the profit you need to pay your employees and keep supplies coming in."

"A necessary inconvenience."

"Not if Thad can get you a direct distributor in the kingdoms where he has strong allies. If he can introduce you to the most powerful and influential royals and nobles he knows." She could barely stand to hold Teague's feral gaze. Her teeth chattered, and she clasped her hands together tightly to keep them from trembling. "Imagine if you promised each of them the desire of their hearts in return for absolute immunity within their kingdoms. Or in return for consulting with you on every decision. You wouldn't just be the power behind Súndraille's throne. You'd be the power behind the thrones in seven of the ten kingdoms."

And, stars, she hoped she really could learn how to stop him soon because otherwise, she'd have just sacrificed most of the known world for the sake of her brother and the hope that she could stop Teague from ruining Kosim Thalas.

She wasn't sure this made her a very good person, but now wasn't the time for moral contemplation.

Teague's eyes narrowed. "Seven of the kingdoms?"

"We have strong alliances with Akram, Balavata, Ravenspire, Loch Talam, Morcant, and Eldr. Add those to Súndraille, and you have seven kingdoms that could all answer to you."

He watched her in unblinking silence. Ari shuddered as fear chased ice through her bones. He was going to finish taking Thad's soul. And then he'd kill Cleo. Maybe kill Ari too. And there would be no one left to rule Súndraille.

No one but Teague.

Her mouth went dry, and the air felt too thick to breathe as that horrible thought took root and grew.

He'd already proven to the people of Kosim Thalas that he could do as he pleased. That the king couldn't or wouldn't protect them. Stars only knew how many members of the Assembly were indebted to Teague for a wish or a piece of his criminal empire. If Thad and Ari were gone, who would stand between Teague and the crown?

Who would dare?

Teague smiled slowly, and Ari felt sick.

What if this was what he'd been after all along? Unimpeded access to Súndraille's throne after ten years of proving that he was the only power that mattered in the kingdom, and then eventually access to every other throne as well, one wish at a time.

And she'd just offered him a shortcut to all of it on the faint hope that she could somehow find the key to destroying him before he did any more harm.

"You're suggesting I forgo taking the boy's soul and use him as a royal puppet instead." Teague's smile grew.

Ari couldn't speak past the lump in her throat.

Teague looked past Ari to Thad, still on his knees, blood pouring from his wounds while he swayed. "Becoming the real power behind the throne in Súndraille and exerting influence and control over other kingdoms as well is a very tempting offer."

How fast could Teague ruin Súndraille? How fast could he infiltrate and then ruin other kingdoms? Ari had a terrible fear that he could move a lot faster than she could find out how to stop him. It was time to stop hiding in the palace library doing research. She'd start with a trip to Llorenyae, and she wouldn't leave until she learned who had exiled Teague and, more important, *how*.

Sebastian met her eyes, and she was afraid the worry that filled his was written on her face as well.

"What happens if the boy decides not to play along? What if he sabotages my business interests or keeps trying to ruin me? The potential has to outweigh the risks, my dear." Teague stepped closer, and Ari flinched. "I will let your brother continue to live on two conditions."

"No," Thad whispered as he leaned forward to rest his palms on the floor for support.

"I'm no longer doing business with you, dear boy," Teague said. "Here are my conditions. First, Thaddeus will grant me the status of royal adviser and immediately begin introducing me to his contacts in other kingdoms with the understanding that I speak for him." He locked gazes with Ari. "And second, as an insurance policy against any potential betrayal on his part, I will take you as my prisoner. You will remain alive with your soul intact for as long as your brother is obedient to me."

A chill slid over her skin as Thad said, "No. I forbid it."

Sebastian gave her a look she couldn't decipher, his hands fisted at his sides.

"I'd have to go live with you?" she asked, wrapping her arms around herself in a vain attempt to ward off the chill that seemed to be sinking into her bones.

His smile was cruel. "Indeed."

"Ari, no!" Thad's voice was forceful.

Ari stared at Teague. If she refused, he'd take Thad's soul, kill Cleo, and probably kill Ari and anyone who tried to defend her. And then he'd either take the throne or run the kingdom through his network of thugs regardless of who the Assembly found to sit on the throne.

If she agreed to become his prisoner, she'd have access to his home. A chance to watch him for weaknesses she could use against him. Most of all, she'd buy all of them the time they needed to come up with a plan to stop Teague, and Thad and Cleo would still be alive.

"Only if you tear up Thad's contract," she whispered, her

heart pounding painfully in her chest.

"Princess!" Sebastian moved toward her, but stopped at the look she gave him.

A look that begged him to trust that she had a plan—which she did. Mostly. If you called choosing the best of two terrible choices a plan.

"Ari," Thad whispered. "You can't do this."

"I'm taking your place." She lifted her eyes to Teague's and glimpsed Sebastian's stricken face behind him.

"No!" Thad said. "It was my mistake. My wish. Punish me, but don't take my sister."

"Oh, I think this will punish you nicely." Teague reached for the contract, whispered a few words, and the ink on the parchment scurried to rearrange itself until Thad's name was gone and Ari's was in its place. "I'm confident she means enough to you that you'll do whatever I require just to keep her safe. Make a wish, my dear."

Ari tried desperately to keep her voice firm. "I wish to take my brother's place."

Sebastian moved toward Ari as Teague leaned down, snatched her hand, dragged it through the bloody cuts on her other arm, and pressed a crimson fingerprint to the contract.

"I'll find you," Sebastian mouthed as Ari met his gaze and held it while Teague chanted.

"*Ghlacadh anam de* Arianna Glavan *agus mianach a . . .*" His smile was cold and cruel. "Shall I continue? One word left in the incantation. One word, and your soul belongs to me."

Ari's stomach pitched, and she shook her head. Teague stepped closer, and she smelled pipe smoke and something vibrant and wild. Something that reminded her of misty meadows and over-grown forests and the stories whispered about fae creatures who would snatch you in the middle of the night if you were foolish enough to fall into one of their traps.

"Be very, very sure that you do not cross me," Teague said in his cold, polished voice. "If I ever suspect treachery on your part, or on the part of your brother, I will finish the incantation, and you will cease to exist."

Her voice shook, and it felt impossible to draw a full breath. "I understand."

"Excellent." He put the stopper back in the vial. "We're leaving."

"Ari!" Thad's voice broke, and Sebastian reached a hand toward her as Teague grabbed her arm and pulled her from the palace.

TWENTY-FOUR

SEBASTIAN HELD HIMSELF in check until Teague and the princess had disappeared, and then he crossed the distance between himself and the king in five long strides.

"Call the guards," the king said as he gripped the edge of a table and pulled himself to his feet. Blood still seeped from the wound in his head, and his skin looked ashen. "Send them after her. We have to find out where Teague lives and keep an eye on her so that we know she's safe."

"Guards would be too obvious. We can't risk Teague deciding to take Ari's soul. I'll handle this."

The king met Sebastian's eyes. "Don't lose her."

"I won't."

Leaving the king standing in the midst of the ballroom's wreckage, Sebastian raced for the garden. He knew Teague's carriage. He'd seen the glossy black vehicle with the golden spinning wheel painted on the door several times. He couldn't keep up with the carriage on foot. Stars help him, he was going to have to figure out how to ride a horse.

Ducking under low-hanging branches and hurtling over bushes, Sebastian ignored the gleaming rock path that wound through the garden and cut a path straight for the stables. When he ran out of the garden's south entrance, he found the road leading from the palace choked with carriages as the nobility who hadn't heard to lock themselves in the cellar scrambled to get away from the danger.

Praying that Teague was stuck in the line of carriages, Sebastian sprinted for the stables. He burst through the door, nearly running into a groom who was holding the bridle of a brown horse wearing a carriage harness.

"I need a horse," he said, his breath coming in hard pants. "Quickly."

"Listen, we've got a line of people who want their carriage horses harnessed, even though those beasts are out there—"

"The beasts are dead, and the princess has been taken by a very dangerous man. I have to follow her." Sebastian leaned closer to the groom, his temper fraying. "I need a horse. *Now*."

"The princess is in danger?" The groom dropped the bridle of the brown horse. "Follow me."

Moments later, Sebastian was perched on top of a huge black horse—one he'd been assured was the fastest stallion from the latest shipment of Akram's finest.

"Don't let me fall," he breathed as he nudged his heels into the horse's flanks and gripped the reins with white-knuckled fists. The horse moved briskly away from the stable, and Sebastian held its sides tightly with his knees. When he still swayed precariously to one side, he let go of the reins with his left hand

and grabbed the front of the saddle instead.

The horse jogged toward the packed palace drive, and Sebastian leaned forward to study the carriages.

There. Five carriages back from the turn onto the road that led down the hill to Kosim Thalas. Curtains were drawn over the carriage windows, and the driver was focused on edging the carriage closer to the one in front of it.

Sebastian had no intention of being the lone horseback rider on a road full of fancy carriages. If Teague decided to open the curtains and check his surroundings, he'd know at once what Sebastian was doing.

Instead, Sebastian decided to cut down the side of the hill, enter the city itself, and wait in an inconspicuous place for Teague's carriage to pass. Sebastian urged the horse away from the road and aimed its head down the hill. One good nudge with his heels, and the horse started running.

Sebastian bounced wildly in the saddle, and cursed as his flailing feet hit the horse's sides and made it move faster.

How did one ride a horse down a hill in the dark without dying? Was he supposed to lean forward? Lean back?

He leaned forward and hung on with everything he had while the horse thundered down the hill. When they reached the bottom, Sebastian's fingers were numb from gripping the reins, and his body felt like he'd fallen down the hill instead of riding.

Flexing his hands, he gently pulled back on the reins, relieved when the horse instantly slowed to a walk. Another ten minutes of walking through a sparse grove of date trees, with the road at the edge of his vision, and they'd reached Kosim Thalas. He cut over to the road and slipped between two carriages. Torches lit the city, throwing their golden glow across the cobblestones in wide circles. He urged the horse toward the first intersection, and then pulled his mount to the side to wait in the shadow of a shop with bolts of cloth, beaded belts, and feathered headbands on display.

The carriages from the palace rolled past with agonizing slowness. Left with nothing to do but wait for Teague, the full weight of the princess's situation hit Sebastian, and a stomach-churning punch of panic started as a ball of ice in his chest and then spread to every part of him until he was trembling from head to toe.

She was under contract to the most ruthless man in Súndraille.

She was one tiny word away from having her soul ripped from her body. From being *gone*.

And there was nothing Sebastian could do to stop it.

His breath came in sharp gasps, and he leaned his face against his horse's warm neck while he fought for control.

He'd felt fear like this before. When he heard the sound of a whip cracking through the air. When Parrish had died, and he was the only one left to absorb his mother's bitterness and his father's rage. When he'd first decided to flee east Kosim Thalas because starving to death in the merchant district seemed like a better fate than the life laid out before him.

But that fear had been for himself. For the pain he knew was coming, or the future he was terrified to pursue.

This was so much worse.

This was his closest friend—his *only* friend.

This was Ari, a name he could only bring himself to call her in the safety of his thoughts.

He had no way to rescue her from the danger she was in. No way to take the risk on his own shoulders instead. He didn't kid himself. The princess, with her skills, her connections, and her confidence, was worth five of Sebastian to a businessman like Teague. There would be no more trades. No more negotiations.

He closed his eyes and focused on taking slow, deep breaths. On counting to one hundred and then counting again while he waited for his heart rate to slow. For his muscles to stop shaking.

He couldn't rescue her, but the princess was remarkably capable of rescuing herself. He had no doubt she could prove it if put to the test.

But she wasn't going into Teague's home to find a way to rescue herself. He knew his princess. She was going to search for the key to destroying Teague.

And what would happen to her if she got caught?

Sebastian swallowed hard and straightened in the saddle. He might not be able to rescue her, but he could help her with her search. He could be another set of eyes and ears. He could protect her from getting caught.

All he needed was a way to earn Teague's trust and gain entrance to his home.

Teague trusted only those who proved themselves absolutely loyal to him. Who didn't hesitate to do every unspeakable thing he required.

Sebastian's skin crawled at the plan that was taking shape inside his head. It would mean becoming everything he hated. It would mean diving headfirst into the squalid underbelly of east Kosim Thalas.

It would mean following in his father's footsteps.

The band of tension around his chest felt like it was crushing him and his scars burned, but he ignored them as Teague's carriage entered the street and moved toward the intersection.

He shoved the rest of his fear into the dark, shadowy corner of his mind where the memories of his childhood lived. He'd put his plan into motion. He was doing this for the princess. It didn't matter what it cost him as long as she was safe.

Holding on to that thin comfort, he urged his horse onto the road several carriages behind Teague's and began to follow it.

TWENTY-FIVE

ARI WOKE, BRUISED and sore, to find the sun streaming through the windows of her room on the second floor of Alistair Teague's villa. She hadn't been able to see much of the property when she'd arrived the night before, but even with the sparse torchlight provided at the gates and the porch, she'd been able to tell that the place was nothing like the rest of the homes in Súndraille. Instead of gently domed rooftops and gracious arched windows, Teague's house squatted in the center of a wide, tree-filled lawn. The roof was flat, the walls were dark, and the windows resembled narrow cat's eyes glaring suspiciously at the world. She'd gone to sleep feeling trapped and terrified.

This morning, the shutters on her narrow window were thrown wide, and a crisp sea breeze tangled gently with the sheer drapes. She closed her eyes as the scent of brine and sun-warmed grass drifted in and imagined she was standing on the south cliff with Sebastian, reveling in the power and mystery of the sea.

Tears burned her eyelids, and she blinked rapidly. She wasn't on the south cliff. She wasn't with Sebastian. She was trapped in a monster's lair, one simple word away from losing her soul.

She was alone.

All her life, she'd been surrounded by people she cared about and who cared for her. Her mother. Thad. Cleo. Mama Eleni. Sebastian.

Now her mother was gone. Her brother and her friends were out of reach. And Ari had foolishly thought she could bargain with the Wish Granter and win. She'd thought he'd choose not to take Thad's soul in exchange for a chance at unlimited power and the promise of safety that power brought, but that he'd leave her out of the bargain.

Leave her free to find how to destroy him.

Instead she was trapped in his villa, cut off from everyone she knew and every resource she had, and Teague was poised to exploit Thad at the cost of entire kingdoms.

Grief swelled in her throat, and tears spilled onto her cheeks.

What if she never saw Thad, Sebastian, and Cleo again?

What if she couldn't find anything that would show her how to stop Teague?

A knock sounded at her door, and she quickly wiped tears from her face as the door opened and a tiny woman old enough to be Ari's grandmother shuffled in carrying a tray.

"Breakfast," she said matter-of-factly, as if finding the princess here was business as usual.

Ari sat up slowly. Her arms had long slashes from the beast's talons. Her back ached where she'd been kicked. And something in her chest sent a sharp pain through her whenever she moved.

The woman's eyes, nearly buried in mounds of wrinkles,

watched shrewdly as Ari struggled to get from the bed to the slim wooden chair that rested beside the open window. The woman put the tray, with its covered plate and mug of tea, on a table beside the chair.

"I'm Ari," the princess said, her breath catching on the pain in her chest.

"I know who you are," the woman said in the dry, papery voice of old age. She lifted the lid off the plate, revealing a dish of yogurt with honey drizzled on top and a slice of dry toast.

It was barely enough food to qualify as a snack, much less breakfast, but Ari found she couldn't stomach the thought of putting a single bite into her mouth. Not with the pain that lit her on fire from the inside every time she moved.

She looked away from the food and found that her window faced the sea. Last night, hearing the crash of the waves against the shore had comforted her. Now it somehow made her life at the palace seem unbearably distant.

"Eat," the woman said. "You'll need your strength. The boss won't tolerate someone who doesn't pull her weight." She sounded smug. Like she'd already decided Ari would be a liability Teague would soon cut loose.

"I'm not hungry." Ari reached for the mug of tea, which smelled like lemons and cream and something dark and exotic that she couldn't quite place. She took a sip. It was just as delicious as it smelled.

The woman smiled grimly. "That will fix what ails you. I'm Maarit. I do the washing up, the ironing, the dusting, the sweeping, and the shopping. Don't expect to be taking any of those from me."

Ari took another sip. "Am I going to be doing housework?"

Maarit sniffed, though she watched the princess closely. "What else would you be doing?"

Ending Teague, she hoped.

"I don't know. I'm good at bargaining, sums, and baking," Ari said. And snooping. There were definite advantages to having been raised by a servant mother who'd taught her how to move unseen through the palace so as not to disturb the royal family.

She took two more swallows of tea and looked out the window again. The sun danced over the water, golden diamonds glittering against the sea, and thick, pillowy clouds wandered across the sky. Her throat closed on tears that she refused to shed in front of Maarit. She wanted to go home. She wanted to see Cleo and eat Mama Eleni's raspberry scones. She wanted to see if Thad was recovering from his head wound.

She wanted Sebastian.

Stars, how she wanted Sebastian. She wanted his quiet strength and his confidence that she could do anything she set her mind to. She wanted his crinkle-eyed smile and the deep stillness of his body when he mentioned his past. Missing him was a bittersweet ache that sank into her bones like it never meant to leave.

"Thinking of running away?" There was a tiny spark of curiosity in Maarit's voice for the first time. "You wouldn't be the first."

Ari turned away from the window, surprised that the movement didn't hurt as much as it had a moment ago. "I don't run from my promises."

Especially when she was one word away from having her soul ripped out of her body. She'd always been a loyalty-or-death kind of girl, but this was taking it to an extreme.

There was a glimmer of approval in Maarit's eyes as she said, "Finish your tea. You'll feel better soon."

Ari took the last swallow of tea and then blinked. The room grew blurry at the edges and spun in slow, sickening circles. She had the unsettling sensation that the walls were breathing—in and out, a slow gentle rhythm that sent a chill skittering down Ari's spine.

Setting the cup down, she rubbed her eyes, but nothing changed.

"What's in this tea?" she asked, her tongue feeling too clumsy to properly form the words.

"Little bit of fae herbs blessed with magic. Good for knitting broken bones and cleansing the body of bruises." Maarit lifted the cup out of her hands, and Ari caught a whiff of something that smelled of wild, overgrown forests and dark, loamy soil.

Teague had smelled like that. Or maybe it was the open vial he'd held. It was unsettling to think that she'd just ingested something that smelled like the man she desperately wanted to destroy.

She tried to sit up straighter, but it was hard to feel her legs. The walls seemed to breathe a little faster.

"Back to bed," Maarit said as she wrapped a wiry arm around the princess's back. She was stronger than she looked, and Ari leaned heavily on her as they made their way back to the bed.

Once Ari was settled, Maarit said, "When you wake, all will be healed. You have clothes in the wardrobe. The boss will meet you in the library on the main floor. You may go in any room on that floor except his study, and you are never to go to the third floor. That's the boss's private living quarters. I take care of it for him."

Ari tried to nod, but the bed was soft and welcoming, and little dancing lights were frolicking at the edge of her vision. She drew in a deep, pain-free breath, closed her eyes, and heard the walls sigh.

Distantly, she was aware of Maarit taking the tray of uneaten food from the room, leaving Ari to listen to the sea and wish for Sebastian as she slowly fell into a deep sleep.

TWENTY-SIX

THE CRUSHING NOOSE of fear that had wrapped around Sebastian refused to ease. He'd followed Teague's carriage to a sprawling, gated villa on the southern edge of the wealthy side of Kosim Thalas, and then had made his way to the streets he used to call home. He'd sold the horse to the liveryman—probably for half of what it was truly worth, but he was still flush with coin because of it. And then he'd entered east Kosim Thalas, heading for his mother's building, weapon out, coin hidden, wearing the rage he usually kept locked away on his face for all the world to see.

He was going to need it if he wanted to help the princess.

He'd have to be ruthless. Lethal. Unflinching.

He'd have to be like his father.

Before that thought could eat away at him, he shrugged into his coat and got to his feet as the sun blazed through the morning fog and the streets came to life. The princess needed him. It was time to get started.

A haze of pipe weed hung over the streets and the stench of rotten garbage baked beneath the morning sun. Apodrasi users dotted the street corners, their bodies thin, their eyes desperate as they begged for money to buy their next dose. A crowd had already gathered in front of the building as Sebastian stepped away from the front door.

"Look who got thrown back where he belongs."

"Still think you're better than us?"

"Gone soft now, look at him. We could take him."

The calls followed Sebastian as he left his mother's building.

Last night he'd made sure that the runners and plenty of others made note of his arrival. He'd taken his time walking to his mother's place and had informed one of the children who was clinging to the doorstep of the building to spread the word that Sebastian Vaughn was looking for a job. And then he'd gone upstairs and slept against the wall outside his mother's door. When he'd left after Parrish's burial, he'd promised himself he'd never spend another night in that apartment again.

It was a promise he planned on keeping.

Judging by the crowd waiting for him on the street, everyone knew that Sebastian had moved back. It wouldn't be long before a runner would come looking for him, sent by a street boss who would expect Sebastian to take whatever job he planned to offer.

His face grim, Sebastian faced the crowd of onlookers. Whichever street boss took the bait first was going to regret it.

The youths surrounding him fell silent as he stared them down one by one, letting the desperate fury that drove him cool into the kind of dangerous calm that made it hard to meet his gaze.

"Who wants to see if I've gone soft?" he asked quietly. "Take your best shot. I dare you to."

A few murmurs swept the crowd, and a pair of boys, both younger than Sebastian, pushed forward.

"Bet you've got coin from your job at the palace," the shorter one said, raising his fists and rocking forward onto the balls of his feet.

"You can give it to us, or we can take it from you." The other boy flicked his wrist and a homemade knife slid out from under his sleeve and into his palm.

Sebastian rolled his head from side to side and flexed his shoulders. "No one is taking anything from me."

The reputation for winning every fight that he'd built before he'd left the district had protected him when he was just returning for the occasional brief visit. The news that he'd come back to stay was another matter entirely. Now he was a threat to the established pecking order. He didn't know how many challenges he'd have to face to climb back to the top, but he was more than ready.

The two boys lunged for him at the same time. Sebastian pivoted, letting the shorter one stumble past him. Stepping into the taller one's charge, he turned his body to the side, slammed the flat of his palm into the arm that held the knife, and then jerked his elbow up to smash it into the boy's face. Stepping between the boy's feet, Sebastian held the assailant's knife arm and twisted the boy sharply to block the shorter one's renewed attack. Three punches and one well-aimed kick later, and both boys were on the ground, bleeding and cursing him.

"Anyone else?" Sebastian turned slowly, staring down the motley collection of boys who had the hard, weary eyes of old men, girls with weapons in their hands and defiance on their faces, and the occasional young child tagging along with an older sibling because their parents were either working, using apodrasi, or dead.

A few met his gaze and held it. Most found something else to look at. Sebastian set a course toward the northern end of the district where two of Teague's bosses lived, and started walking. The crowd parted to let him through.

He'd gone three blocks and won two more fights when a runner found him.

"Sebastian Vaughn?" the girl asked, taking a dagger out of the small arsenal of weapons she wore around her waist and aiming it at him. "Felman wants to see you."

For one sickening moment, the truth of what he was about to do sent a dizzying wave of fear and loathing through him, but he swallowed it down and kept his expression blank as he followed the girl through the warren of streets and alleys that led to Felman's headquarters.

He was doing what he had to do to gain Teague's trust and protect Ari.

If that meant he had to walk a few steps in his father's shadow, he'd endure it.

Felman, a thick-necked, thick-bellied man who was at least ten years older than Sebastian, ran his corner of east Kosim Thalas from the sagging remains of a building that decades ago had been a respectable mercantile. Guards stood at the doorway, swords drawn, as they scanned the streets. Sebastian clenched his jaw and rode out the wild urge to strike as the guards roughly ran their hands over him, searching for weapons. They found his cudgel immediately, and set it aside for him to pick up as he left.

It didn't matter. He was the true weapon, and they wouldn't see him coming until it was too late.

It was time to play the role that would get him close to the princess. He gathered up his memories of the last month—the way Ari smiled at him, the way he could stand close to her without his instincts screaming at him to fight or flee, the peace he'd known when he'd sat beside her for hours staring at the sea—and locked them away where they wouldn't be touched by the filth of the life he was stepping into. In their place, he focused on one single thought: get close enough to destroy Teague.

He was ready.

When one of the guards found his bag of coin and tried to remove it from Sebastian's boot, he leaned down and said softly, "If you take a single coin from me, there won't be enough of you left to bury."

The man started to laugh, caught sight of Sebastian's expression, and fell silent as he backed away to let Sebastian and the runner through.

"You're going to make enemies, talking to people like that," the girl said as they entered a long hallway lined with doors that led to rooms full of whatever stolen goods Felman's network of thieves had scooped up within the last week.

"I'm not here to make friends."

She shrugged and knocked at the last door on the right. When it swung open, she motioned him inside, but didn't follow.

He let the door shut behind him while he swept his gaze over the room, taking stock. A box of an office, one desk in the center, three chairs against the west wall, one chair behind the desk.

Two men standing slightly behind Sebastian on either side of the door. One woman standing on the far side of the desk swinging a mace back and forth like a pendulum. Felman in the desk chair, studying Sebastian with a smug little smile on his face.

Four to one. All of them armed.

They weren't the best odds, but he hadn't survived east Kosim Thalas—hadn't survived his father—without knowing how to take a beating and still reach his goal.

"The prodigal returns," Felman said. "Couldn't hold on to your fancy palace job, eh?"

Sebastian pivoted, drove his fist into the man to his right, and then hung on him for balance as he snapped a kick into the face of the man on his left. The man on the left went down hard and rolled on the floor, holding his face, but the man in front of Sebastian came up swinging.

His first blow landed on Sebastian's jaw. The second grazed his stomach. Behind them, Felman was shouting for his guards to beat the boy to a bloody pulp, and Sebastian heard the woman with the mace run toward them.

The mace struck his back, and the pain lit a blinding inferno of rage inside Sebastian.

He was six, huddled on the kitchen floor beneath the pounding of his father's fists, screaming for help that wasn't coming. He was nine, trying desperately not to cry as his father hit him with a stick while his mother turned her back. He was sixteen, jaw clenched, eyes dry, as the whip flayed strips of flesh from his back and the rage boiled inside him, the only antidote he had to the unending pain.

The woman struck again, and something inside him broke.

With a primal roar, he spun toward her, grabbed the mace midair, and twisted it from her grasp. As the man behind him attacked, Sebastian whirled, smashing the mace into the man's throat and then spinning back toward the woman as the man fell.

She launched herself at him, a dagger glinting in her hand. He lowered his shoulder and met her halfway, sending both of them to the floor. The blade scraped his arm, but he barely felt it. Using the mace to block her next blow, he gripped the pressure point in her neck. Her eyes rolled back in her head, and he was on his feet and moving toward Felman before she'd finished losing consciousness.

"Do you have any idea what you've done?" Felman's face was red as he came around the desk for Sebastian. "You've declared war. You're going to rue the day—"

Sebastian swung the mace and knocked Felman onto the desk. The man kicked, catching Sebastian in the thigh, but the fire burning inside him swallowed the pain and fed him rage instead. He kept coming. Taking the blows. Boxing Felman in. Absorbing the beating like he'd absorbed so many before.

Felman made one final lunge, and Sebastian ducked the blow, shoved the handle of the mace beneath Felman's chin, and slammed him, back first, onto the desk.

Leaning over the man, Sebastian said, "Where is the list?"

Felman's face turned red and he gasped for air, but Sebastian didn't let up. "I know you have it. With Daan dead, every street boss will have a list so debts don't go unpaid. Where is it?"

Felman spat in Sebastian's face.

Sebastian leaned closer, holding Felman's gaze. "You know

what my father is capable of doing. There's a reason he's the collector for the most dangerous city in Balavata. What do you think he'd do to you if he wanted that list and you refused to give it to him?"

Felman blanched. Sebastian swallowed hard and forced himself to say with conviction, "Like father, like son. Give me the list."

Felman's eyes darted toward the right corner of the desk. Sebastian eased off the man's neck but kept the mace handy as Felman doubled over, coughing and gasping for air.

Walking around to the far side of the desk, Sebastian tried the drawer. It was locked. "Open it."

Felman's hands shook as he fished a key out of his vest pocket and threw it toward Sebastian. The lock opened with a faint snick, and then Sebastian was holding a roll of parchment in his hands with the names, addresses, and debts owed of everyone who'd been foolish enough to do business with Teague. Sebastian glanced at the parchment to be sure Felman had given him the real thing. He was sure Teague's soul debts weren't on this list, but that didn't matter. There were enough uncollected debts coming due to give Sebastian the leverage he needed to get close to the princess.

Taking a handful of coin from his boot, he tossed it onto the desk. "Take your family and get out of the city. Once Teague learns that you gave up the list, there won't be anywhere in Kosim Thalas that is safe for you."

Felman gave Sebastian a hard stare and said between coughs, "Your father would've killed me once he had what he wanted, not paid for my freedom. You said you were just like him."

Sebastian pocketed the list, his scars burning as he forced his rage back under control and headed for the door. "I lied."

Wishing he could leave the bitter residue of his actions behind as easily as Felman's headquarters, Sebastian headed toward the first person on the list.

TWENTY-SEVEN

BY THE TIME Ari woke from her tea-induced sleep, the sunlight was disintegrating across the horizon in spools of crimson and gold, and the breeze that still rushed through her open window chased a chill across her skin. She'd been too exhausted and hurt when she'd arrived to pay attention to anything but the bed and, later, the chair and table where Maarit had given her tea. Blinking away the last bleary dregs of sleep, Ari craned her neck to look around the room.

The furnishings were plain—an armoire, a small sink with a hand pump, the bed, and the chair and table by the open window—but the rest of the room made up for it. The ceiling was painted to look like Ari was lying on her back in a forest, looking up at the sky through a lattice of tree branches. The sky on her ceiling matched the sky outside her window.

The walls looked like a collection of tree trunks lashed together with strips of leather. The texture of the bark—complete with whorls, twigs, and even a few spare leaves—made the trunks look real. A mirror hung over the sink, and a framed picture of a tall, thin man too impossibly beautiful and wild to be human adorned the wall beside the door.

Ari stretched carefully, expecting the bite of pain in her chest and in the lacerations on her arm, but there was nothing. Pressing her hands against her rib cage, she drew in a deep breath. No pain. She ran her fingers over the places where the beast had dug its talons into her, but her skin was smooth and unbroken.

Apparently the tea that Maarit had given her really did heal injuries as promised.

But it was still creepy to remember drinking something that smelled as wild and strange as Teague.

Her stomach growled, and a wave of dizziness hit. She hadn't eaten since the previous afternoon. Her eyes were gritty from sleep and tears, and loneliness felt like a blanket made of stone pinning her to the bed.

She wanted to curl up beneath the covers and hide from Teague and Maarit.

From the truth that she was stranded in the home of a monster who would destroy everyone she loved if she couldn't figure out how to stop him.

For one long moment, she gave in to the loneliness and let the ache of missing Thad, Cleo, and Sebastian fill her from the tips of her toes to the top of her head. She breathed in the pain, allowed it to linger for the space of a few heartbeats, and then gently pushed it to the back of her mind.

She couldn't hide. If she didn't find a way to stop Teague, he'd destroy Súndraille with violence, which would destroy Thad. And if he moved on to ruin other kingdoms as well, that would be on Ari's shoulders. She had to get up despite the loneliness and grief that felt like they were woven into her very bones. Had to take the next step and then another step after that.

It was the only way she could try to undo the terrible bargain she'd made with Teague.

The first step she'd take would be to get herself something to eat. Once she'd restored her strength and cleared her head, she'd learn what she could about Teague's routine and figure out where to start looking for the key to stopping him.

And, stars, she hoped there *was* a key to stopping him because the alternative was too horrifying to contemplate.

Frowning, she tossed off the covers and stood. The dusty wooden floor creaked, and something soft and damp swept over the bottoms of her feet—something that felt suspiciously like a tongue.

Ari shrieked and jumped onto the bed again, her heart pounding wildly as she stared at the floor.

It was empty of everything but the pair of sandals she'd been wearing the night before.

She huddled in the center of the bed for a moment longer, but nothing seemed out of the ordinary. Tentatively, she scooted to the edge of the bed and carefully touched one toe to the floor.

Nothing happened.

Maybe she was still suffering the aftereffects of the tea. She'd seen the walls breathing right before she fell asleep, so clearly ingesting fae magic caused hallucinations.

Telling herself this made sense, she slowly put both feet over the edge of the bed and stood.

The floor rippled with a soft shush that sounded like the

whisper of the wind through a tree's leaves and the same damp *thing* swept over her feet.

Ari leaped for the bed again, her body shuddering. She tucked her feet beneath her, wrapped her arms around her stomach, and rocked back and forth.

Maybe she was hallucinating. Maybe not. Regardless, she had no intention of getting out of bed until either the floor stopped doing whatever it was doing or Maarit came to check on her and explained what was going on.

She huddled on the bed, shivering in the damp sea breeze and staring at the motionless floor, until she gradually became aware of a whisper behind her.

Her heart thudded heavily against her ribs as she turned her head.

The wall was breathing.

In.

Out.

In.

Out.

Gentle swells lifted and fell, and Ari's eyes widened in horror as a twig peeled away from the trunk closest to the center of the headboard and stretched toward her.

It chuffed, the two leaves that clung to it flaring like nostrils.

It was *sniffing* her.

Ari scrambled back until she was at the far edge of the bed. Panic, bright and jagged, raced through her, leaving her trembling in its wake.

Hallucination or not, she needed out of this room before she started screaming.

Without giving herself time to second-guess it, Ari leaped out of bed, skidded across the floor, and shoved her feet into her sandals as the (completely creepy) floor rippled and shuddered beneath her. Then she raced for the door, hauled it open, and hurried into the hall.

Her room was on the second floor, close to the landing on the stairs that connected all three levels of the villa. The hall was covered with a thick green rug, and thankfully the floor remained still as she grabbed the wooden bannister and started down the stairs.

Halfway down, a twig curled out of the underside of the bannister and brushed the back of her hand. She yanked her hand to her chest and stumbled down the rest of the stairs, bracing herself in case something else that shouldn't be alive reached for her.

Lanterns already burned in the main level of the house as the gloom of twilight filled the sky outside the windows. Ari stood in the parlor at the base of the stairs, trying to figure out where to find the kitchen, even as she watched the walls, floors, and anything else made of wood with a close eye. Plush chairs covered in evergreen velvet flanked bookcases that stretched from the floor to the ceiling along one wall. The other wall held curio shelves full of fairy statuettes dancing in grotesquely beautiful poses, carved ivory instruments, and sculptures of beasts that looked at once familiar and terrifyingly strange. Everything was covered with a thick layer of dust, but still the effect of the green rug and chairs, the wood-covered walls, and the pale yellow ceiling made her feel like she was trapped inside a fae forest.

Her pulse jerked unsteadily as one of the statuettes slowly pivoted until it could look Ari in the eyes.

The princess hugged herself and scanned the room for a way out. From the north side of the parlor, a hall bisected the back of the villa with doors leading to rooms on either side. In the other direction, the parlor's doorway led to what looked like a formal dining room, which meant the kitchen would be close by.

Ari started in that direction, but froze when Teague's polished marble voice echoed from the hallway behind her.

"Princess Arianna, I've been expecting you for some time. I'm told you woke nearly an hour ago."

She turned, and the room seemed to quiver and stretch wider than it had been a moment earlier. Her voice sounded small as she asked, "Who told you that?"

He stepped into the parlor, his immaculate clothing pressed to perfection, his alabaster skin glowing in the lantern light, and smiled coldly. "The house, of course. It's been months since it woke up. I never know what will set it off, but it seems to find humans interesting."

Ari wanted to deliver a fabulously sarcastic reply, but the fairy statuette was slowly spinning, its face split with a maniacal smile, and several of the monstrous sculptures were blinking as they watched her.

Teague beckoned her toward him, and she moved forward on feet that felt as though she'd kept them in the frigid winter waters of the Chrysós for too long. Another twig unfurled from the closest wall and hovered over her head. She flinched and stepped aside before it could sniff her.

Teague's laugh was cruel. "Best to let the fae wood get acquainted with you, or it will never leave you alone."

"Fae wood?" She shuddered as the twig dipped down and

swept its leaves over her cheek. Tiny little puffs of air tickled her skin, and she was swamped with the scent of damp forest floors and sunlit treetops.

"The house is built entirely out of trees I had chopped down on Llorenyae and then shipped here. It wakes when it wants to, sleeps when it wants to, and can be tricky if it decides it doesn't like you." He sounded sure the house was going to despise her.

Ari decided the feeling was mutual.

Working to make her voice sound as normal as possible, she said, "If my bed swallows me in the middle of the night, Thad won't introduce you to any of his allies."

Teague's smile disappeared. "Foolish girl. Only the house is fae wood—floors, ceilings, walls. Everything else is from Súndraille."

Ari eyed the curio shelves as another statuette smiled, sending a crack through its plaster face. "And those?"

"Keepsakes from my homeland. Come along, Princess. You're needed in the library."

Without giving her a chance to respond, he gripped her arm firmly and guided her along the hallway to the second door on the left. The library was lit by lanterns resting along the middle of an enormous table that stretched down the center of half the room. Floor-to-ceiling bookshelves crowded every wall, though some of the shelves had been used to store weapons in glass cases, decanters of wine, or more creepy relics from Llorenyae.

Teague turned Ari away from the table, and she found a sitting area in the other half of the library with six upholstered green chairs surrounding a plain wooden spinning wheel that sat beside a basket of hay. A man huddled in one of the chairs, his wrists bound by rope. Another thick rope was lodged between his teeth and tied behind his head, making it impossible for him to clearly speak.

"Have a seat, Princess." Teague motioned toward the chair beside the bound man.

"Why?" she whispered as the man's eyes sought hers and begged for something—for help? for mercy? Whatever he needed, she had no power to give it.

"Because you're here to ensure that I expand my business interests across the kingdoms." His feral golden eyes held hers. "And I'd like you to see what happens to someone who gets in my way instead. Object lessons are so much more effective when they're delivered face-to-face."

She shook her head, but the look on Teague's face turned her knees to jelly, and she collapsed in the chair beside the captive man. He made a noise in the back of his throat, but Ari couldn't bear to look at him. Instead, she stared at Teague as he sat at the spinning wheel and picked up a few long pieces of straw. Pressing the straw against the leader yarn, which was already threaded and attached to the bobbin, he adjusted the tension knobs and began treadling. The flyer spun quickly, and the straw twisted. Ari's mouth dropped open as instead of straw, the bobbin began collecting a spool of glittering gold thread as thick as a candle-wick.

When the last bit of straw had been turned into gold thread, Teague stood, removed the bobbin, and looked at the man. "I didn't ask for much, did I?"

The man made a strangled noise and jerked against the ropes that bound his wrists.

Teague circled the man's chair and began unspooling the thread.

"It was a very simple transaction, Peder. I offered fair market value for your shop, didn't I?"

Ari's pulse raced as the man shook his head and tried to speak around the thick rope in his mouth.

"Oh, I know," Teague said softly as he stretched the length of golden thread taut between his hands, his eyes on the back of Peder's head. "You didn't want to sell. It's been in your family for generations. Very touching, except that I wanted it."

In one quick movement, Teague dropped his hands in front of Peder's neck and pulled the thread back against the man's throat. Peder bucked and screamed around his rope gag, but Teague yanked the thread like he was hauling on a horse's reins and it bit deep into the man's skin.

Ari's stomach heaved, and she lurched out of the chair and toward the library's door as Peder made an awful wet gurgling noise, and Teague said in his cold, elegant voice, "No one defies me and lives."

She escaped the library and rushed down the hall, through the parlor and dining room, and finally into the kitchen, where, thank the stars, the walls weren't breathing and there weren't any creepy fae relics to stare at her. Bile burned the back of her throat, and she scooped water from the sink into her mouth with shaking hands.

Teague had promised an object lesson for those who got in his way. Those who defied him.

He'd delivered.

Terror blazed through her, stark and unrelenting, and she

clung to the sink to keep from collapsing onto the floor.

Teague would kill her if she tried to stop his plans.

But even as fear shuddered through her, she thought of Thad, sitting on a throne bought with blood. She thought of Peder dying because he didn't want to sell his shop. She thought of the seven kingdoms she'd offered up to Teague as leverage to save her brother's soul, and she knew.

Teague would destroy her if he caught her trying to ruin him.

She had to do it anyway.

TWENTY-EIGHT

IT HAD BEEN five days since Ari had arrived at Teague's villa. Five days of jumping at shadows because she never knew which part of the house might come alive next. Five days of eating the tiny, plain meals that Maarit cooked and then searching Teague's extensive collection of books for anything that might give her a clue about who had exiled him from Llorenyae and how they'd accomplished it.

Five days of aching for the life she'd had before, as Teague gave her ledgers and contracts to peruse with the unyielding expectation that she'd find places for him to improve his margins in Balavata even as he began collecting debtors from the Súndraillian nobility in residence at the palace where Teague spent every morning.

And she *did* ache for her former life. The fae magic in the tea Maarit had given her had healed Ari's injuries, but nothing could heal the loneliness that hurt with every breath she took.

She looked warily at her bedroom walls as she pulled on a long yellow dress and draped a delicate gold chain around her waist. The room had seemed uninterested in her since her first day there, but she couldn't relax. Couldn't stop listening for the whisper of breathing or the damp scrape of a fae tree's tongue on the soles of her shoes.

Five days, and she was no closer to figuring out how to destroy Teague, save Thad, and get back to the palace and her loved ones. The answer wasn't just going to fall into her lap. She had to work for it.

She washed her face in the basin and quickly pulled her hair into a bun, securing it with a trio of hairpins. Her shutters were thrown open as they were every morning—it was unsettling to think that Maarit must come into the room before Ari awakened—but today's sea breeze was a slap of damp, chilly air that heralded the approach of a storm.

Ari moved to the window and shivered as she gazed at the choppy gold waters and the purple-gray clouds that pressed low against the horizon. A pair of Teague's guards patrolled the edges of the property, but Ari ignored them. There would be another pair on patrol during the day and the watch would double at night, but they never approached the villa itself. As the first raindrops splashed against the ground, she hugged her arms around herself and let herself wonder where Sebastian was.

Five days, and she hadn't seen a single sign that he'd followed her. That he was watching over her.

She'd been sure that he would—that when he'd held her gaze in the midst of the ballroom's carnage and mouthed "I'll find you," he'd do it. Sebastian didn't say things he didn't mean. She'd catch herself looking out of windows in hope of seeing him coming toward the villa entrance. Each time the road was empty, and each time her hope sank a little lower. She didn't realize she was crying until the first tear traced a scalding path along the coolness of her cheek.

Something whispered along her arm, and she jerked back as a branch unfurled from the windowsill and chuffed against her skin as if it could smell her. Another branch whipped out from the wall beside her, wrapped around her waist, and firmly pushed her back toward the windowsill again.

Ari held her breath, her heart pounding, as the first branch sniffed her cheek and then slithered toward her mouth. She pressed her lips in a thin, hard line and drew in a long, shuddering breath as the rough bark brushed her mouth and then scraped over her cheek, a wooden tongue licking up her tears.

It was over just as suddenly as it had begun, and in seconds the branches had become one with the wall and windowsill again. She wrapped her arms around her chest, her knees shaking, but she didn't move away.

The house hadn't hurt her. It was creepy, yes, but maybe it was more benign than Teague had led her to believe. She needed to talk it over with Sebastian. She hadn't realized how much she'd depended on his friendship until it was out of reach. She wanted to tell him about the house. About the straw that Teague had turned into a weapon of gold thread. About the nightmares that flooded her sleep until she woke with her own screams ringing in her ears. She wanted to sit beside his comforting stillness and spill every thought until she'd been cleansed of the terror and the loneliness. Until she could see clearly what to do next.

The rain swept down in curtains of misty gray that blurred the landscape, a barrier that seemed to cut Ari off from the rest of the world. She closed her shutters and turned away.

There was no point in dwelling on how alone she felt without Sebastian. She had a monster to destroy, and she couldn't wait around for help that might never come.

She'd gained Teague's permission to borrow some books from his library to pass time in the evenings, and had been delighted to find *Magic in the Moonlight: A Nursery Primer* on the shelves, though she'd been careful to take other books as well so it wouldn't look like she was focused on tales of the fae. So far, nothing had come of it, though she'd studied it every night. If there was information about Teague's weaknesses somewhere in the villa, Ari hadn't found it.

The problem was that Ari was never truly alone. On her second day at the villa, Teague had given her a small office beside the library so she could look over his ledgers and assess how well his current contracts might perform in other kingdoms. She'd taken her time with it, working meticulously while she waited for a chance to be alone, but the chance never came.

She didn't care about the guards who patrolled the property, but Maarit and Teague were a different issue. One of them was nearly always underfoot. Teague left the villa early for business each day, but Maarit spent her mornings popping into Ari's office regularly to "check on her," which Ari figured was a euphemism for "report problems to Teague." The housekeeper took an hours-long nap after lunch and ate dinner in her rooms, but it didn't matter because Teague was often home in the afternoons and evenings, watching Ari like a cat toying with a mouse.

To uncover whatever Teague was hiding about his past on Llorenyae, Ari was going to have to find a way to get Maarit out of the house during the morning.

Leaving her room, Ari walked briskly to the back staircase that led down to the kitchen, careful to avoid touching the bannister in case it woke. If she was going to start aggressively going after Teague, she was going to need a decent breakfast. None of that yogurt and dry toast nonsense. This required meat and at least two pastries.

She entered the kitchen, and there was a flash of movement at the corner of her eye. Turning, she found Maarit standing by the sink, a plate and cup in her withered hands.

"What are you doing in here?" Maarit demanded. "I always bring your breakfast."

"Not anymore." Ari moved toward the pantry and began assembling ingredients. "I'll cook for myself. I'll cook for you and for Teague too, if you'd like."

"You can't just decide to— What are you doing with those plum preserves? Those are for holidays only!"

"Not anymore." Ari hugged the preserves close to her chest in case Maarit decided to try taking them from her and hauled out a sack of flour, a clay jar of butter, and some salt.

Maarit reached her side much faster than Ari thought a woman her age ought to be able to move and blocked her progress toward the counter. "The boss likes those preserves."

"Then I'll make him some more. It's not hard. But I'm done eating yogurt and dry toast. Seriously, what is the point of having all this butter if you aren't going to use it?" She stepped around Maarit and placed the ingredients on the counter except the preserves. She was hanging on to those. "Now, please tell me you have bacon or sausage."

Maarit shook her head.

"Then let me go to the market to get some," Ari said as she opened cupboards searching for a bowl and a rolling pin.

"So that's what this is about." Maarit's voice was cold.

"Excuse me?" Ari blinked at her.

"You think I'm going to fall for your tricks and let you out so you can run away." Her eyes flashed with anger. "I had a feeling you'd try something like this soon enough."

Ari dumped the bowl and rolling pin onto the counter beside the flour and turned on Maarit. "Where am I going to run? You tell me that, because I'd love to hear it. Teague is fae, and the stars only know what kind of magic he's capable of. All he has to do is say one more word, and he ends my very existence. I'm stuck here, and I'm going to make the best of it. And that means I'm going to bake some pastries with Teague's favorite plum preserves, and, by all that's sacred, it means I am going to eat some *meat*."

Maarit stared at her for a long moment. Ari was getting used to the older woman's shrewd, calculating looks, but that didn't mean she had to stand there and take it on an empty stomach. Turning away, Ari measured flour, butter, salt, and water into her bowl and began making dough.

Finally, Maarit said, "I'll go to the market and get sausage."

"And bacon."

"Anything else?" Maarit's voice was loaded with sarcasm, but Ari didn't care.

"Yes. I want the ingredients to make chocolate cake."

An hour later, Maarit wrapped a scarf over her head and braved the storm to head to market. Not that taking one of Teague's carriages was a hardship, but still. The older woman had kept her word, and Ari was grateful. Not just because sausage and bacon were (finally!) going to be a part of her morning routine again, but because Ari now had the opportunity to start looking for anything she could use against Teague.

Fortified with plum tarts and a slice of melon, Ari started exploring, careful to check each room to see if the walls were breathing or the knickknacks were watching her before she did anything that could look like snooping. The door to Teague's personal quarters on the third floor was locked, and she was terrified that if she managed to pick the lock, the rooms inside would be awake and waiting to either alert Teague to her presence or pin her to a wall until he returned.

The second floor was a collection of ordinary rooms—Ari's and Maarit's among them. None of them seemed to hide any secrets, although Maarit's had a sweet, musty scent that reminded Ari of Cleo's grandmother.

That left the main floor of the villa. The rooms were all decorated in Teague's preferred shades of misty green and gold. With its dark wood floors and pale yellow ceilings, moving through the main level felt like walking through a forest. There were more strange dust-covered knickknacks scattered about every room—painted vases with fairy dancers who appeared to change positions depending on which side of the vase you were on, opaque squares of glass with runes of gold melted onto their surface, and wax sculptures of fantastical creatures that both intrigued and repelled Ari. In the hallway that bisected the back half of the villa, behind a thick tapestry that depicted some sort of fairy feast, Ari found a long, narrow box set back into a hole in the wall, but when she opened the box, there was nothing but the velvet-lined outline of a pipe inside.

Before long, Ari had thoroughly searched every room but Teague's study, which was also locked. Other than the empty pipe box in the wall and another yellowed copy of *Magic in the Moonlight: A Nursery Primer* on a small shelf in the back parlor, the only remarkable thing she'd found was that Maarit was a complete failure at housekeeping.

There was dust on every surface. Candle wax had dripped from sconces and hardened on the floor. And Ari was positive the rugs hadn't been taken outside for a good beating in at least a year.

This is what came of hiring a housekeeper old enough to have seen the birth of Súndraille itself.

Ari used her finger to draw a line through the dust on the mantel in the front parlor and wondered how much time she had left before Maarit returned. A quick glance at the curio shelves showed her that all the fae relics seemed to be asleep. If she was going to risk snooping where it really mattered, now was the time.

She'd start by seeing if she could pick the lock to Teague's study. Unlike the enormous lock on the door to Teague's personal quarters, the lock to his study looked relatively simple. Ari had learned the skill of opening simple locks with a hairpin when she was eleven and Thad took to locking himself away after he'd endured yet another bout of Father telling him he had to work extra hard, be extra perfect to make up for his bastard birth.

For a moment, the pain of missing Thad and the pain of

missing her mother flared into something unbearable. Something that stung her eyes with tears and filled her limbs with heaviness.

She blinked away the tears and made herself move away from the mantel before she could collapse in front of it and cry. Missing her family wasn't going to get her any closer to Teague's secrets.

Dusting the house, however, was.

Minutes later, Ari had collected a soft cloth and some lemon oil from the broom closet and a hairpin from her hair. To really sell her story in case she got caught, she started dusting in the back parlor. The lemon oil was nearly impossible to open—further proof that Maarit hadn't properly cleaned in ages and should probably retire—but soon Ari had the parlor gleaming and smelling like a citrus orchard. The next logical room to clean was the room beside it, which just happened to be Teague's study.

Far be it from Ari to be illogical.

Pausing outside the locked door, Ari held her breath and listened. Rain fell in soft waves against the windows. The house creaked and settled, but there was no sound of breathing. No faint hiss as one of the relics turned to look for her.

She was alone.

Telling herself that that fact should make her happy instead of miserable, she straightened the hairpin and slid it into the lock. In seconds, the door was open. Bending the hairpin back into shape, she slid it into her hair and entered the study.

It was depressingly normal.

An enormous desk dominated the room. Neat rows of quills

and inkpots lined the top of the desk while equally neat stacks of parchment were centered on its surface. An entire wall was lined with bookshelves and an enormous floor-to-ceiling cabinet whose doors were nearly as big as the door to Ari's bedroom, and there were a few knickknacks here and there, but nothing that said, "Look at me, for I am the key to Teague's undoing."

She rounded the desk, polish in hand, and studied its contents. The top desk drawer contained pots of ink, a few spare quills, and a dagger for sharpening them. The bottom drawer held ledgers whose cracked leather bindings looked at least one hundred years old.

She turned her attention to the stacks of parchment on the desktop. One stack was blank. One looked like shipping orders and bills to be delivered to out-of-town customers. And one was a stack of contracts like the one Thad had signed, except that on these the spaces for the debtor's name, the price of the debt, and the bloody thumbprint were blank. Teague's signature was already in place, however. The thought that he needed to be prepared for granting dozens of wishes in a short space of time made Ari feel sick.

Still, this could work to her advantage. She could take the contract and read the stupid thing as many times as it took to find a loophole. She grabbed the top sheet, folded it quickly, and then turned her back to the door so she could stuff it down her bodice and into her chemise. The parchment smelled faintly like the woodsy scent of the fae tea Maarit had given her on her first morning at the villa.

She'd just finished adjusting herself when something in the far corner of the room caught her eye. Frowning, she took a few steps forward so she could see by the dim light of the closest window.

A bronze statue, nearly tall enough to reach Ari's waist, showed a woman with a wolf's head, bird's talons for hands, and goat hooves for feet. Dust clung to it, but there was something familiar about it. Something Ari had seen recently.

She took another step toward it, dust cloth raised, and it hit her.

This was the woman whose picture was in *Magic in the Moonlight: A Nursery Primer* beside the poem about the monster whose source of power was a secret she'd buried at her birth.

If this statue was in Teague's study, locked away from prying eyes, then it meant something to him. Maybe it was a gift from someone he cared about, and he thought keeping it in here was safest. Or maybe it was piece of the puzzle Ari needed to solve. She needed to study the poem again.

She took another step toward the statue, and its eyes flew open. Ari froze beneath its blank, white gaze just as a voice behind her said, "What are you doing in here?"

Ari spun around to find Maarit standing in the doorway, glaring.

TWENTY-NINE

"I ASKED YOU what you were doing in here." Maarit crossed the threshold, and Ari's pulse roared in her ears. Behind her, the wall began breathing in quick, shuddering gasps. Ari shivered and refused to look at it.

This was a disaster. If Maarit thought Ari was spying on Teague, she'd tell him, and then Ari would lose everything. Desperately hoping her story would hold up, Ari started talking.

"I'm cleaning," Ari said in the most matter-of-fact voice she could summon with her heart pounding and her knees shaking. Marching back to the desk, she picked up the rag and lemon oil to prove her point, trying hard to move without making the parchment hidden in her chemise rustle.

Maarit's eyes narrowed. "I do the cleaning."

That was debatable.

Ari gave her a little smile. "I know you do. But you were nice enough to go to the market for me. I wanted to do something nice in return."

"This door was locked."

Ari frowned. "It opened right up." It really had. Teague should invest in better locks.

Maarit furrowed her brow and turned to examine the door-knob. "It was locked. I'm sure of it."

Ari shrugged. The parchment in her undergarments rustled, and she quickly reached to straighten a stack on the desk, making plenty of noise as she did so. Maarit looked up. "Get away from those! You aren't supposed to be here."

Ari took the rag and the lemon oil and stepped away from the desk. "I'm sorry. I started in the back parlor and thought I'd dust the entire main level, one room at a time. The door opened for me, so I thought it would be all right."

"Empty your pockets."

Ari blinked. "I'm wearing a dress. I don't have pockets."

She just had her chemise and a desperate hope that Maarit wouldn't think to check it.

Maarit went toward her—the woman could move quickly when she was angry—and said, "You were told never to come in here uninvited."

"I was?" Ari tried for her best I-am-so-confused expression. Maarit didn't look convinced.

"Your first morning here. I told you the rules. I was very clear." Anger lent strength to her papery voice.

Thank the stars Maarit had given Ari the lecture about off-limits areas *after* she'd nearly knocked her unconscious with the magic fae tea. It was the only scenario that would lend credibility to the princess's story now.

Ari shook her head, her pulse pounding. "All I remember is drinking that tea and everything getting hazy, and then I fell asleep. When did you tell me any rules?"

Maarit stared at her for a long moment and then mumbled, "After you drank the tea."

Ari bit her lip. "I'm sorry if I wasn't supposed to come in here. It won't happen again. Do you want me to finish dusting since I already started?"

The older woman glared. "I want you to get out."

Ari complied, and Maarit locked the door behind them.

"Are you going to tell Teague?" the princess asked, her voice trembling.

"Why shouldn't I?" Maarit snapped as she brushed past the princess. The faint scent of overgrown forests and sun-warmed soil followed her.

Ari had a sudden, sickening fear that Maarit was fae too. Either that or the woman needed a drink of magic fae tea now and then just to keep her (seriously old) self alive.

Choosing her next words with care, Ari said, "Because I'd like to tell him myself. I have nothing to hide, but I have plenty to lose. I want a chance to explain myself before he decides to just end my life over a misguided attempt to help you with housework."

Maarit shrugged and walked away. "Dust if you want to. Come bake a cake if you want to. Might as well do it now since you'll most likely be dead before morning."

"That's not very reassuring," Ari muttered.

Whatever reply Maarit might have made was cut off by the sound of someone pounding on the villa's front door.

Maarit stiffened, and Ari glanced out the nearest window as if that would tell her why, after five days of absolutely no one but Teague, Maarit, and the villa guards coming and going from the house, someone would be on the porch.

"Where are the guards?" Maarit whispered, flexing her wrinkled hands as though she could somehow stop someone from getting into the villa.

"Are we expecting someone?" Ari asked, as wild hope tangled with fear within her.

Maybe Sebastian had finally found her.

Maybe it was an enemy of Teague's.

Maybe it was—

"No, we aren't." Maarit's voice shook as whoever was on the other side of the door pounded on it again. "Curse this body. I can't fight, but—"

"Stay here," Ari said as she pushed in front of the housekeeper and ran down the long hallway. "Or better yet, hide."

"Don't open that! No one was invited. We wait until the boss returns, and then—"

Boom, boom, boom. The pounding reverberated throughout the main level.

Sebastian would be subtle. Careful.

That meant whomever was at the door wasn't a friend to Ari and wasn't a friend to Teague.

The irony of having to defend the home of the monster she wanted to kill wasn't lost on Ari.

"I'm not going to open it." Ari rushed down the hall and skidded around a doorway into the library. "I'm getting a weapon. We have to assume the guards are out of commission. We also have to assume that whoever wants in badly enough to batter down the door won't hesitate to rip off a shutter and come through a window."

260

"What are you going to do with a weapon?" Maarit demanded as Ari snatched up a thin, delicately wrought sword that rested in a dusty glass box.

"I'm going to use it." Ari met the older woman's eyes. "Go hide, Maarit. I'll do what I can to protect you until Teague gets home."

The housekeeper glared. "Why would you protect me? I don't like you."

"Because it's the right thing to do. And I don't like you either. Now go hide."

Without waiting to see if Maarit was going to comply, Ari crept back down the hall and into the front parlor. Rain still fell in thick, misty sheets. It was impossible to see anything out of the parlor windows except indistinct blurs.

Would the person on the other side of the door try to come in through the parlor windows? Or the sitting room on the other side of the entrance?

Maybe she should just shut the doors to both and shove a heavy piece of furniture in front of the doorways to block them. She glanced around for anything that could make that plan work—the claw-footed chair with the ugly floral fabric? She doubted she could wrestle it through the doorway in time to use it from the outside of the room.

She'd have to go into the entrance hall and find something there.

Creeping out of the parlor, Ari scanned the entrance. There was an umbrella stand, a coatrack, and lanterns hanging from brackets on the wall.

"Teague!" someone yelled on the other side of the door, and

Ari's breath caught in utter surprise.

She knew that voice. She'd thought when he came for her that he'd be subtle. Careful. Never in her wildest dreams did she imagine she'd hear Sebastian pounding down Teague's door.

The sword clattered to the marble floor as she ran for the door. Her shaking fingers fumbled with the lock twice before she managed to unbolt it. She threw open the door.

Sebastian stood on the porch, his hair plastered to his head, his clothes dripping wet. There were bruises and cuts on his face. His dark eyes found hers and held.

For a heartbeat or two, they stared at each other, and then he said quietly, "Princess Arianna."

She launched herself against his chest and wrapped her arms around him. Damp from his clothing soaked the front of her dress as she clung to him, her body trembling from head to toe.

His arms slowly came around her, and he gathered her so close that she could feel the steady rhythm of his heartbeat beneath her ear. She wanted to tell him that she'd missed him. That she was so grateful to not be alone any longer. But there were no words to describe the way the hollow loneliness within her filled with warmth at his touch. She held on to him with desperate strength and cried.

He rested his cheek on the crown of her head and said softly, "I told you I'd find you."

She gulped for breath and pulled back to look into his eyes. "How did you do it?"

"I followed Teague's carriage the night you were taken." He was staring at her as if he was trying to memorize her face even as he let his arms drop to his sides.

"That was five days ago."

He looked miserable. "I had to do some things before I could come here."

"What things?"

He shook his head. "Things that would make Teague trust me enough to let me stay here at the villa with you."

"You're *staying*?" Her knees threatened to give out as she stepped back to give him the space he needed. She'd thought Sebastian had come to see if she was all right. It hadn't occurred to her that he would find a way to stay.

"If Teague will have me. I think I'll make a pretty convincing case."

Hope was a desperate, painful thing fluttering in her chest, but it was followed swiftly by the harsh slap of reality.

Sebastian wasn't contracted to Teague. He hadn't made promises that would cost him his life to break.

It wasn't fair to expect him to stay with her just because he . . . Wait.

"*Why* would you want to stay here?" Every word hurt to say, but she said them anyway. Convincing Sebastian that he wasn't obligated to her was in his best interest, but already the hollow space in her chest was starting to hurt again.

"Because you're here," he said simply.

Three simple words, but Ari felt as if he'd lit a torch inside her heart.

"But your job at the palace—"

"I quit."

"This is dangerous," she said.

"I'll risk it."

"Teague might get mad and kill you the moment he sets eyes on you."

"I'm betting he won't."

She swayed toward him, and stopped herself before she touched him again without his permission. "What if he expects you to sign a contract?"

Sebastian closed the distance between them in a single step and held her gaze. "Then I'll sign it."

"Sebastian," she breathed as he hesitantly raised a hand to gently wipe away her tears.

"Yes?"

Her lit-torch heart spread heat along her veins until she thought she must be glowing with the wonder of it. "You're touching me."

"Yes."

"On purpose."

Worry filled his eyes, and his fingers tensed against her cheek. "Should I stop?"

For the first time in five days, Ari smiled. "No."

He gave her his crinkle-eyed smile in return, and for one glorious moment, nothing existed but the steady patter of the rain and the boy who'd followed her to the lair of a monster and who was willing to risk everything to stay.

Then from behind Ari, Maarit said, "The boss is going to want an explanation for this."

THIRTY

SEBASTIAN DROPPED HIS hand from the princess's cheek as a woman old enough to be his great-grandmother shuffled toward them, her wrinkles folded into a fierce glare. He'd been so relieved to see the princess unharmed, so caught up in the wonder of being able to quiet the panic as she touched him, that he'd temporarily lost track of his surroundings.

He was in the heart of his enemy's kingdom. Every word, every gesture he made mattered. Instantly, his expression hardened into the face he showed on the streets of east Kosim Thalas.

The princess spun to face the woman and said, "If you sneak up on me one more time, I swear by all the stars that I won't give you a single piece of chocolate cake. And, trust me, Maarit, missing out on that would be a big mistake. Unlike you, I know how to use butter to my advantage."

"Keeping watch over you is my job." The woman's eyes flicked to Sebastian, shrewd and calculating, and his body tensed as he moved to stand beside the princess.

The princess tossed her hands into the air, her voice rising. "What is there to see? I sleep, I eat—if you call consuming plain, tasteless food eating—I check ledgers and make expansion plans for Teague, and then I sleep some more."

"And you sneak into private studies—"

"I was dusting. Something you might want to try once in a while, since you're so insistent that the housekeeping is your job."

"Were you *dusting* when you somehow got a message to your special friend here telling him to come rescue you?"

"Don't be ridiculous. How is he supposed to rescue me? One word, Maarit. That's all it takes, and I'm gone. Forever."

Sebastian watched the back-and-forth between them closely. It seemed impossible that anyone could be in danger from the old woman, but he could sense the tension that vibrated through the princess's body. He could hear the way her breath caught between her words.

She was afraid.

The woman came toward them, and suddenly Sebastian understood why.

How did a woman that old move so fast? Just seconds ago, she'd been shuffling along like she could barely move one foot in front of the other. Now, she was practically gliding over the marble floor, her eyes full of rage.

In one smooth step, Sebastian put himself between the princess and Maarit and then reached for the sack of coin he had chained to his belt.

"I'm not here to rescue her," he said in a quiet, controlled voice that belied the way his muscles wanted to tense so he could meet the incoming threat with force. "I'm here to offer my services to Teague."

The old woman pulled up short and stood five paces away, watching him warily. "The boss isn't going to exchange the girl for you."

"My services have nothing to do with her. I need a job. I think Teague is going to want me as an employee."

She sniffed and looked at the bag in his hand. "What's that?"

"That's between me and Teague. Where is he?"

"Out on business." The woman glared at him and then at the princess for good measure. "Don't just stand there with the door open. You'll let in all the rain."

The princess moved past him, and Sebastian quickly entered the villa, shutting the door behind him.

"Teague leaves before dawn and doesn't come home until after lunch," the princess said, giving Maarit a wide berth as she moved through the entrance hall.

Sebastian kept his expression neutral.

He'd spent five days shaking Teague's empire down to its very core. He'd moved through the list he'd taken from Felman, collecting debts where he could and secretly paying them with his own coin when he found people too destitute to honor their contracts. He'd survived confrontations with the other three street bosses. He'd beaten back a steady stream of runners and other low-level players who didn't approve of him skipping ranks and going straight for the top.

Everyone on the street knew that Sebastian Vaughn was collecting in Teague's name and that crossing him resulted in nothing but pain and misery. It had to be enough to get himself hired to replace Teague's Kosim Thalas collector, Daan. If it wasn't, Sebastian was out of ideas.

Holding himself poised and ready in case the woman became

a threat again, Sebastian raised a brow as the princess picked up a sword that was lying on the floor and muttered, "So glad I risked my life to protect yours." She aimed the words at Maarit.

"I didn't ask you to protect me," the old woman snapped.

"Honestly, Maarit. You are *this close* to no cake." The princess met his gaze, and something shifted in her expression. Something that told him she needed him to hear what she wasn't saying. "I'm going to go put this away in the library and then change out of my wet dress. Since it's almost lunchtime, I'll meet the two of you in the kitchen and save you from her cooking. You're welcome."

She stalked out of the room, but not before he'd given the barest hint of a nod. She'd delivered her words rapidly, but lingered for a second on the word *two*.

He needed to keep Maarit with him and give the princess a few minutes alone.

"What did she protect you from?" he asked before Maarit could follow the princess.

"From you." She pointed one gnarled finger at his chest. "Pounding at the door. Scared us both. Where are the guards?"

"They'll be waking up any minute now." Sebastian took a step closer to Maarit, crowding into her space even though it sent waves of panic crashing through him and set his teeth on edge. "So the princess heard what you both thought was someone dangerous at the door, and she grabbed a sword and ran toward the sound. To protect *you*."

And didn't that sound exactly like Ari.

"I didn't ask her to do that," Maarit snapped, but her frown softened.

"You didn't have to," he said quietly. "Now, where's the kitchen?"

Maarit led the way past a sitting room and into the kitchen, a generous space with large, rain-streaked windows, enough knives and heavy pots to use as decent weapons in a pinch, and two separate exits. She motioned for him to sit at a long rectangular table lined with benches on either side. He sat with his back to the wall and watched her.

The older woman said nothing while she tossed a hunk of bread and a handful of seasoned olives on a plate and put it in front of him. Her eyes wandered to the coin bag he'd unchained and placed on the table at his elbow. He leaned forward to block her view.

"That is for Teague alone."

She sniffed and turned away. There was a whisper of sound from the north doorway that led to the dining room, and Sebastian turned to see the princess walking into the kitchen. She'd changed out of her damp dress and braided her hair. Taking one glance at his plate, she said, "Don't eat that."

He leaned back and watched as she checked the firebox beneath the stove and then put a skillet onto one of the raised cooking surfaces.

"I made him lunch." Maarit sounded offended.

"No, you put something barely edible on a plate." The princess grabbed bacon, eggs, and a slab of cheese from the icebox. "Don't worry, I'll make you one too."

"I'm not hungry. I had the marketing today and then all this extra excitement. It's enough to wear a body out." Maarit yawned and looked at the door that led to the dining room and from there to the rest of the villa.

Sebastian watched the tiny smile playing at the corners of the princess's mouth with interest. What was she thinking about? When he realized his interest had wandered to the way the fabric of her dress draped across her hips, he made himself stare down at the plate Maarit had given him while the smell of frying bacon filled the air and his thoughts sent heat spiraling through his body.

She was still the princess. And after what he'd done in east Kosim Thalas to earn Teague's trust in the last five days, he was something worse than a servant.

But even though he could come up with one hundred reasons why he shouldn't notice her skin or her hips or the secret smiles she tried to hide, all he really wanted to think about was the fact that he'd stood close to her. He'd touched her. And he'd forgotten to brace for pain.

"Are you sure you don't want one?" the princess asked Maarit as she set a plate in front of Sebastian. A fried egg and several slices of bacon were layered over a thick piece of toasted bread and topped with melted cheese. His stomach instantly reminded him that he'd barely eaten in the last day and a half. He hadn't been able to afford it. Every spare coin he'd gained from selling the palace's horse had gone to relocating Felman or to helping pay out contracts owed to Teague.

"That bacon was for breakfast," Maarit grumbled.

"There's no wrong time to eat bacon." The princess set another plate beside Sebastian's, her secret smile back in place.

Maarit turned for the door. "The boss will be home shortly. If I were you, I wouldn't do anything stupid."

Sebastian waited until the woman left the kitchen before asking, "Where is she going?"

"She naps all afternoon. On days when she's gone to the market, she naps even earlier. She's really old." The princess swept around to Sebastian's side of the table, settled onto the edge of the bench, and then scooted until she was beside him.

He was acutely aware of the slim space between them. Of the warmth of her body against his rain-chilled skin. He took a bite of his food before he said something that could ruin everything.

"Why were you pounding on the door?" she asked softly, her eyes darting toward the doorway where Maarit had disappeared to go upstairs. "I was sure it wasn't you because I thought you'd be more subtle."

"I got tired of waiting for Teague to come to me. And I couldn't stand not knowing if you were all right."

She smiled down at her food, and her cheeks turned pink.

What did that mean? That he amused her? That she was embarrassed by his actions?

A second later, she twisted to look at him. "Wait. Why would Teague come to you?"

"Because I have something that belongs to him."

Her eyes widened. "Please tell me you didn't steal from him."

"Says the girl who planned to do just that." He nudged her gently with his elbow. "No, I didn't steal from him. You'd have to be a fool to do that."

She suddenly found something fascinating to study on the ceiling. "Well . . . I wouldn't necessarily go that far."

He froze in the act of putting another bite in his mouth. Slowly setting his fork down, he said, "You didn't."

Her eyes found his again, and there was equal parts terror and exhilaration on her face.

"Princess—"

Swiftly she leaned forward and whispered against his ear, "I broke into his study and stole a blank contract. Maybe I can find a weakness in the wording. Something we can use."

He closed his eyes at the thought of her breaking into Teague's study alone. "Thank the stars you weren't caught."

"Well, actually . . . Maarit found me in there, but I'd hidden the contract, so . . ."

She kept her lips next to his ear, and he realized that he'd stopped listening because her body was pressed against his arm, and soft tendrils of her hair were tickling his face, and she smelled like plums and rainwater, and he couldn't think.

Why hadn't he ever noticed that before? He'd spent hours moving her into the correct position for daggers or throwing stars. Hours sparring with her, their bodies touching briefly every time she struck or blocked. And his thoughts had been perfectly clear. Perfectly sane.

Now he sat here like an idiot, wishing he knew how to finish closing the distance between them and knowing he never would.

"Are you listening to me?" she asked, pulling back so she could look him in the eye.

"I . . . What were you . . . I got distracted." Was his face on fire? It felt like it was on fire.

"By what?" She glanced around the room and then met his eyes again. Her expression softened, and that shy, secret smile played across her lips.

His words were rushed. "You said you took a contract."

"That's why I needed to go to my room and change without Maarit deciding to tag along. I'd folded it up and stuffed it down my"—she gestured toward the low scoop of a neckline on her dress—"you know."

Yes, his face was *definitely* on fire.

He shrugged like he had no idea what she meant, and her smile widened. The silence between them became a thing of tension and anticipation that made his heart thud against his chest while his stomach felt as if he'd jumped from a cliff.

He cast about for something—anything—to say that would break the tension, but then they heard the front door to the villa open. Footsteps moved briskly down the main hallway and into the back of the house. A moment later, the footsteps returned, rapidly crossing into the dining room and toward the kitchen.

She grabbed his hand and squeezed. "Don't do anything dangerous for me."

He squeezed back and then let her go as Teague, his pipe in his mouth and his golden eyes ablaze, entered the room.

THIRTY-ONE

TEAGUE STALKED ACROSS the kitchen and stood in front of Ari and Sebastian on the opposite side of the table, his exquisitely tailored clothing still unwrinkled and mostly dry. Ari guessed even the rain didn't dare upset the Wish Granter.

The rain didn't, but Sebastian apparently did. Ignoring the way Teague's eyes glowed with fury, the way his lips clamped around the stem of his pipe in a hard, white line, Sebastian rose to his feet, picked up the sack he'd brought with him, and tossed it onto Teague's side of the table. It hit with a thud and the jingle of coins.

Teague yanked his pipe from his mouth and said in his polished marble voice, "How did you find this place?"

"I'm resourceful." Sebastian's voice was the kind of dangerous quiet that meant he had himself under tight control, but if you pushed him too hard, he would come off his chain with a vengeance. Ari had only ever heard him use that voice once—when he was escorting her through east Kosim Thalas and the boys, who were gathered on doorsteps and street corners, called out creative suggestions for things Ari could do with her body.

At the time, she'd felt comforted that Sebastian clearly wouldn't tolerate anyone abusing her honor. Now she took one look at Teague's feral golden eyes and scrambled to her feet, panic closing her throat.

Sebastian wasn't messing with a mouthy boy now. He was facing down a fae monster, and Ari didn't have any bargaining capital left if he got in over his head.

"She's under contract to me." Teague's eyes flicked over her, and even though her skin was flushed with heat, Ari shivered. "There's nothing you can do to rescue her. And now you've invaded my home, assaulted my guards—"

"I've done far more than that."

"Sebastian," Ari whispered, but he didn't look at her.

"Oh, I've heard." Teague cocked his head to study Sebastian the way someone might study an ant before grinding it to death beneath his boot. "Robbing me, beating my employees, making sure I know that you know where all my business holdings are."

Sebastian ignored him and pulled a folded piece of parchment from an inner pocket of his vest.

"Did you expect me to find you? To stop you?" Teague's smile was cruel. "No doubt that was your plan. Distract me by making me believe one boy poses a threat to my empire so that I fail to pay attention to the true prize you're trying to take from me."

The food she'd eaten was a rock resting in her stomach as Ari said, "I'm not a prize."

"Don't sell yourself short, my dear." Teague's cold voice filled the room. "You are intelligent, intuitive, and are showing signs of being good at finding ways to trim the fat off my business and make me a far richer man. Plus, with you as my prisoner, the king has no choice but to advance my interests in the other kingdoms however I instruct him to. I'm pleased with my choice to spare you, but now I must weigh that choice with this boy's actions."

Sebastian unfolded the parchment he held and cleared his throat.

"How much has he taken from me? How much work has he cost me by incapacitating my employees?" Teague stared at Ari, and she tried hard not to tremble beneath the icy rage on his face. "Is it more than what you bring to the table? An investment is only worth keeping if it continues to pay dividends."

He was going to take her soul. She could practically see the plan forming in his mind, the intent spilling out of the icy, unreachable part of him that showed its face whenever he thought she might try to cross him.

Her knees shook, and there was a strange ringing in her ears as he locked eyes with her and opened his mouth. She grabbed for the table with shaking hands and dropped to the bench as her legs refused to hold her.

"Aegeus Pappos. Pipe weed shipment. Thirty kepas." Sebastian's voice was steady.

Teague frowned.

"Nico Alferis. Weekly protection fee for his smithy. One hundred kepas."

Teague broke Ari's gaze and looked at Sebastian instead. Ari wrapped her arms around her stomach.

"Zenia Demataki. Four drams of lily root to treat her daughter's illness. Two hundred seventy-five kepas."

"What is this?" Teague rubbed his thumb and forefinger over his ivory pipe and reached for the bag of coin with his free hand while Ari struggled to breathe past the noose of panic that had wrapped itself around her throat.

"That is the payment due from everyone on your collection list." Sebastian met the fae's eyes.

"And how did you get that list?" Teague's voice was far too quiet for Ari's comfort.

"I stole it." Sebastian seemed to take up more space than he had before. Maybe it was the grim confidence in his voice or the way he flexed his (still unfairly distracting) shoulders. "I beat my way through Felman and his guards, took the list, and then beat anyone who tried to take it from me. I've spent the last five days collecting every debt owed to you. It's all in the sack."

"And you think this is going to buy the girl's freedom?"

Sebastian shook his head. "I think this is going to get me a job. I no longer work at the palace. I'm not interested in being a runner or in guarding a street boss. I want to be your new Kosim Thalas collector."

Ari pressed her hands together to keep them from shaking as she stared at Sebastian. He'd stepped back into the world he hated. The world he'd escaped from.

For her.

The panic around her throat eased, though the expression on Teague's face kept her heart racing in fear.

Teague leaned back on his heels, his thumb feverishly rubbing the pipe as he contemplated Sebastian. "You did all this to apply for a job?"

"Not just any job. The top job. You don't get a position like that without proving that you're capable." Sebastian threw the list onto the table and gestured toward the sack of coins. "I'm capable."

Teague took a long moment to count the coins and study the list. "It's all here." He sounded surprised.

"I'm not interested in double-crossing you."

"Then you're a different breed from your brother." Teague flicked a glance at Sebastian's face. Sebastian's expression remained unreadable, though his body took on the wary stillness that said Teague had probed too close to something that mattered deeply.

Ari frowned. What did Sebastian's brother have to do with Teague?

"I need a job that matches my skill set. Who else is going to hire a boy from east Kosim Thalas who managed to lose his job at the palace?"

"And the fact that this job would put you in close contact with the princess is simply a nice bonus?" Teague asked.

A muscle along Sebastian's jaw tightened, and Ari heaved a dramatic sigh, grateful and terrified when Teague's attention immediately swung to her.

"You and Maarit, I swear. Always so suspicious. Why shouldn't we have the bonus of being with each other? You hold all the power. One word and you end me. What are you afraid we'll do to you when we know you have that sword hanging over my head?"

Teague smiled slowly. "You really are quite the negotiator."

"I'm just using logic. It doesn't hurt you to give Sebastian the job. He's already done most of it for you, by the looks of it. It strengthens your business."

"Especially when I now know that if he does something that displeases me, I can punish you, and that will be sufficient punishment for him as well." Teague's voice was chilling. "Very well, Sebastian, you are my new Kosim Thalas collector. We will sign an employment contract. You collect every debt that comes due and give me the full amount. If you fail even once, the fast-talking princess will pay the price."

Sebastian glanced at her, his eyes haunted, and she knew he was feeling the terrible weight of being responsible for her fate. Ari understood all too well how it felt to have the fate of others rest on your decisions, but there was no backing down now. For either of them.

"Agreed," Sebastian said.

"Excellent." Teague sat at the table and began packing tobacco into his pipe, his pale fingers working quickly while he stared at Ari. "Now, you and I have some matters to discuss."

"Do we?" She blinked at him, pressing her trembling hands together beneath the table.

He raised a brow at her, and Ari's heart thudded heavily against her chest.

Oh, stars, did he already know about Maarit catching her in his study? The creepy monster statue must have told him somehow. She'd have to warn Sebastian about the house the first chance she got. If she survived the conversation with Teague long enough to do so.

Whatever she did, she had to convince him that she wasn't standing in his way. That she wasn't trying to keep him from what he wanted. She desperately didn't want to end up like poor Peder with her throat slit by golden thread magically made from straw.

When she didn't say anything, Teague snapped his fingers and a thin wisp of flame leaped to life in midair. He leaned forward, put the bowl of his pipe beneath the flame, and puffed a few times until the tobacco caught.

She'd seen him do the same thing a dozen times, and it never got any less creepy.

He took a deep drag and blew a cloud of smoke toward the ceiling. She felt like she had when she'd been the one to accidentally set the gardener's shed on fire as a girl, and her mother had simply waited her out until the silence became too much for Ari, and she confessed. Her leg bounced up and down, her fingers twisted together and then came apart, and her mouth went dry. She could feel the words swelling in her chest, ready to spill out in a torrent of hasty excuses and desperate explanations.

Sebastian pressed his thigh against hers until her leg stopped moving.

"What have you been doing with yourself while you've been here?" Teague asked with implacable expectation in his voice.

Somehow he knew about the study. Maybe Maarit really was fae, and they had some sort of magical mind connection.

Ari needed to spin the situation back to her favor as fast as possible. Keeping her leg pressed against Sebastian's, she met Teague's eyes and said, "Most days I've been going over your accounts, finding places you can cut out the middlemen and streamline things, or I've been borrowing books from your library." Though all she'd read was the nursery primer, still hoping that somehow Gretel's hint would pay off with information Ari could actually use against Teague.

"And today?" Teague's eyes glowed with fury, and Ari's stomach dropped.

"But today I got sick of Maarit's awful excuse for cooking. She was kind enough to go to the market to get some things I requested, so I decided I would help her with the housekeeping."

Warming to the story she was selling, Ari leaned forward and lowered her voice as if worried Maarit, who slept like the dead, would overhear. "I'm sure you've noticed that she's not very capable of keeping up with the housework anymore. The amount of dust on the main level is absurd. It's like she hasn't cleaned in a year. It's nice that you feel a sense of loyalty toward her and want to keep her on staff, but maybe you could put her in charge of a few maids? And also a cook, because, stars know, the stuff she serves is barely edible."

"So you helped with the housework today?" Teague puffed on his pipe, his gaze unwavering.

Ari met his eyes, her heart pounding, and tried to work a note of contrition into her voice. "I thought I'd at least take care of the dust. I started in the back parlor, and then moved to your study, and then—"

"My study is off-limits."

She nodded. "I know that now." Quickly she gave him the same story she'd given Maarit about the tea and the haziness and her inability to remember anything that was said to her after she'd finished the drink.

There was a long silence once Ari finished talking. Teague studied her—it was unbelievably disturbing that he didn't blink for minutes at a time—his pipe burning unnoticed in his fingers.

Ari couldn't swallow. Couldn't look away. Could barely breathe as she waited to see if he believed her or if he was going to kill her the way he'd killed Peder.

Finally, he stood, and even though he was barely tall enough to reach Ari's shoulder, he seemed larger than life as he leaned toward her, wrapped his cold, pale fingers around her wrist, and smiled as he felt the proof that her heart was racing.

His voice was little more than a whisper. "I have ways of knowing a person's weakness. Your weakness, Princess Arianna, is that you think you still have secrets, when the truth is that the only one in this room with any secrets left is me."

His grip tightened until little sparks of pain shot up her arm.

She gritted her teeth to keep from crying out.

"Get up, Princess," he said. "We're going to go see if you are telling the truth."

THIRTY-TWO

HUMANS WERE LIARS—weak and feckless to the very marrow of their bones. The princess was no exception.

He glared at her as he pulled her away from the kitchen table.

She'd been in his locked study. Even if she hadn't heard the rules Maarit gave her on her first morning at the villa, she knew that a locked door meant stay out.

She was lying about the door being unlocked. Lying about having no reason to go into his study except to dust. The princess was a smart, resourceful girl, and she didn't do things without an ulterior motive.

She was hunting for something.

Ice filled his veins, and he tightened his grasp around the princess's wrist until she gasped with pain.

She was hunting, but she was looking in the wrong place. There was nothing in the villa she could use against him. Any humans who knew his secret had long since been buried. He'd made sure of that. And the few fae left on Llorenyae who were old enough to remember his birth would never speak of it to a human.

Death was the only way out of a bargain with Teague, and as soon as he was finished using the king to put himself in a position of unassailable power, he would personally destroy the meddling princess.

But first, he had to expose her deceit and punish her for it.

The princess hesitated as they neared the doorway, and Teague yanked her forward, his fingers gripping her wrist like a shackle. Sebastian moved to follow them, and Teague snapped, "Stay."

The boy wanted to disobey. Teague could see it in the way his jaw tensed while his eyes followed the princess's every move. But then he met Teague's gaze, and his expression became a blank, unreadable mask. His fists relaxed, and he leaned a hip against the table as if to say, "Go ahead. I'll just wait here."

Teague smiled. "I didn't think either of Jacob's sons had it in them to live up to their father's reputation for vicious self-preservation, but you may prove me wrong."

He pulled the princess into the hall and headed toward his study. The boy was smart and ruthless, but the princess was still his weakness. Now that Sebastian was Teague's top Kosim Thalas employee, he'd be staying in the villa as his predecessor had done. If Teague couldn't trust him to obey, regardless of his personal feelings for the princess, then the boy would have to be disposed of.

It would be a shame to lose someone with his potential.

"What are you doing?" the princess asked as they reached the study. Her voice was breathless from pain and panic.

"Proving you a liar," he said softly, and waited for her to flinch.

She didn't. Instead, her golden cheeks flushed with color, and her voice rose. "I've never met anyone more suspicious than you and Maarit. I was dusting. Haven't you noticed how terrible the place looks? I was *helping* you."

"Helping yourself to something of mine is more like it," he said, letting go of her wrist to unlock the door.

She glared at him and stomped across the threshold. Gesturing wildly, she said, "What could I possibly want out of here? A book written in a language I can't read? Sounds fascinating. Or maybe I was hoping to decorate my walls with sheets of parchment? I've heard it's all the rage."

She stalked past his desk, and he couldn't tell if her voice was shaking from fear or fury. "Oh, I know. I decided to move that creepy statue to my room because it's not enough that my walls and floor are alive. I'd like to be watched by a monster as well."

"*Stop.*" He snarled he word.

She took one look at his face and stumbled back a step.

"Don't move." Ignoring her, he moved through the study, counting books, rifling through the stacks of parchment on his desk, and opening drawers with sharp, vicious jerks so he could examine their contents.

Nothing seemed to be missing.

It didn't make sense. Slowly he approached her and leaned in close to study her face. She held herself still—prey sensing that a predator was waiting for one wrong move to attack.

His voice was dangerously quiet. "This room is always locked."

She lifted one shoulder in a tiny shrug and whispered, "The door opened right up."

His eyes narrowed. "You stole from me."

She shook her head, her dark eyes filled with trepidation and anger.

It was the anger that threw him off.

She should be quaking in terror, her knees refusing to hold her. She should be begging for mercy, confessions of her wrongdoing spilling from her like blood from a mortal wound.

He gave her a slow, cruel smile. "Shall we search your rooms, then?"

"Fine." She lifted her chin to stare him down, but her hands were twisted together in a knot.

He took her elbow, fingers digging into her skin, and said, "Your friend Cleo isn't the only one who will pay the price for your actions, my dear. I saw the way you looked at my new collector. It would be a shame to lose him, but the wonderful thing about you humans is that you just keep breeding. Anyone can be replaced."

She remained silent as he escorted her up the back stairs, down the hall past Maarit's closed door, and into the princess's room.

"Stay put." He pointed at a spot in the center of the room and then began his search.

Ten minutes later, he'd upended every drawer, tested every floorboard, and checked over, under, and inside every conceivable surface.

He'd found nothing but the books he'd already said she could borrow.

Her arms were folded across her chest, and she glared at him as he tossed the contents of her last drawer aside. "I suppose you expect me to clean up this mess?"

He cocked his head and watched her in silence.

He'd been locking his study door since the princess took up residence. Maybe he didn't have anything inside that could jeopardize him, but he hadn't wanted her anywhere near his contracts.

He'd locked the door before leaving that morning. Hadn't he?

He couldn't remember. It was a new routine for him, and he'd been distracted with the heady news that Thaddeus was hosting a trade summit and powerful members of the nobility from across the kingdoms would be present.

It was possible he'd left the door open. It was possible the princess really had been simply dusting. He'd peeked at the back parlor as they'd headed toward the stairs, and it gleamed.

It was possible the princess was truly cowed by the knowledge that he could end her with a single word.

"Never enter my study again," he said.

She nodded, and he turned on his heel and left her with the mess.

Perhaps the princess, afraid for her life and the lives of those she loved, was trustworthy. Perhaps his new collector, hungry for the recognition that came with the title and interested in staying near the princess, was prepared to put Teague's interests above his own.

Or perhaps the two of them were the most accomplished liars Teague had met since he'd had the terrible misfortune to care about a wretched girl sitting at a spinning wheel, surrounded by straw.

He couldn't afford to be distracted from what really mattered.

He had wishes to grant, nobility to break, and kingdoms to infiltrate. He needed another trusted employee to watch the girl and keep Sebastian in line—at least until Teague's business with Thaddeus was concluded and he could kill the royal family, take the throne, and be done with it. He needed someone who could match Sebastian's ruthlessness and who couldn't be intimidated by the princess's quick wit. Someone who would punish both of them without a second's hesitation.

He needed Jacob Vaughn.

Thankfully, he'd had the foresight to instruct Felman to recall Jacob from Balavata the moment he'd realized that Daan was dead. He'd thought to install Jacob as his new Kosim Thalas collector, but Sebastian had already proven his worth, and Teague couldn't possibly trust the boy to watch the princess's moves and report back.

Jacob, however, wouldn't just report on the princess. He'd hurt her if she stepped out of line. Kill her if necessary. He'd even kill his own son if that's what Teague wanted. He'd proven that once, and Teague had no doubt he would prove it again if asked.

Jacob would be back in Kosim Thalas any day now, and that would free Teague to focus all of his energy on the young king and the throne that would soon be Teague's.

THIRTY-THREE

ARI WOKE THE next morning to the smell of frying sausage. Flying out of bed, she snatched the first dress she found and shoved her feet into her sandals. Splashing water on her face, and brushing her teeth with mint at lightning speed, she skipped braiding her hair in favor of running for the stairs.

Maarit was going to cook that sausage until it no longer resembled anything that might safely be called food. Ari was still shaken from yesterday's terrifying confrontation with Teague, especially because he had decided she needed to stay in her room for the rest of the day with nothing but the occasional visit from Maarit for company, when all Ari really needed was to see Sebastian and feel safe again. Still, she'd counted it a victory. He hadn't found the stolen contract. He'd unwittingly given her time to study the poem in the nursery primer, though it hadn't helped. What she really needed was to find a way to get the *Book of the Fae* from Rahel's shop. It should have arrived by now. And there was finally meat in the house because she'd convinced

Maarit to buy some at the market. She hadn't gone through all that just to go back to eating yogurt and dry toast for breakfast because the (ancient, holy stars, *why*-haven't-you-retired-yet) housekeeper ruined the sausage.

She skidded into the kitchen and yelled, "Maarit, get away from that stove before you— Sebastian?"

He turned, his tunic straining over his shoulders, a pair of tongs in his hand. "Princess Arianna." His voice held a wealth of relief and something darker. Something that sounded like regret. He tossed the tongs onto the counter and strode toward her.

Her stomach tingled like she'd had fizzy wine for breakfast.

"I'm sorry," he said when he reached her. Her heart ached at the guilt in his eyes.

"For what?"

"For not following you when Teague took you to the study. I should have. I know that. I just thought—"

"You thought that if you disobeyed Teague, he'd hurt me to get at you, and then take your job away and kick you out of the villa," she finished for him. "And if you get kicked out of the villa, I'll be completely alone."

He nodded, but misery was etched on his face.

"It was a smart decision." She stepped closer to him, and willed him to listen to her. "It was the *right* decision. You have nothing to apologize for. If you'd acted rashly, we could've lost everything."

He lowered his voice and glanced behind him at the open doorway that led out to the dining room. It was empty. "We could've lost everything anyway. He could've found the contract. You could've been hurt. I had to take his word for it that you weren't because I didn't see you again yesterday." He pressed his lips together and then blurted, "I barely slept. I kept thinking that I made a terrible mistake, and that you were alone and afraid, and I should have—"

"No." She moved closer to him, and he didn't flinch. She checked the hall. Still empty. Checked the walls. Not breathing. Her voice barely more than a whisper, she said, "I was alone and afraid, but I can survive that. Especially knowing that you did what you had to do to stay here with me. And now he trusts me a little more. He didn't find where I'd hidden the contract."

Sebastian glanced at her chest, and Ari's face heated. "No, it wasn't . . . That's not where . . . I hid it in a dusty vase just inside Maarit's room. Last place he'd ever look."

Sebastian jerked his eyes back up to hers and took a small step back. "I'm sorry. That was . . . I'm sorry. I didn't mean to notice anything."

The misery disappeared from his face, replaced by mortification, but there was something warm in his eyes that hadn't been there before.

Ari smiled as the fizzy tingling in her stomach spread to her veins, a welcome relief from the loneliness and tension of the past week.

His eyes swept over her with a faint hint of desperation. "I mean I was, um, noticing that I like your hair down."

She patted her hair as if just now discovering that she hadn't braided it—which was a stupid reaction, but somehow his words made her feel like whatever she'd done right with her hair this morning needed to be repeated every morning for the rest of her life.

The scent of scorched bread brought her up short. "Are you making toast?" She craned to see the stove behind him.

"Burning it, more likely." He hurried to the stove, grabbed the tongs, and scooped the blackened bread out of its pan.

Ari glanced around the empty kitchen. "Where's Maarit? It's not like her to allow a decent breakfast to hit the table."

"Teague said she isn't feeling well this morning and is staying in bed." He turned the sausage and poured a bowlful of beaten eggs into another skillet.

She joined him at the stove and sniffed appreciatively at the chives he'd sprinkled into the eggs as he put butter and two new slices of toast into a pan. "Mmm, compliments *and* a full breakfast. You sure do know the way to a girl's heart, don't you?"

"I know yours," he said quietly without looking at her.

The heat from the stove had nothing on the warmth that rushed through Ari, rekindling the torch in her heart and igniting something deep within her.

Her breath caught, and Sebastian's shoulders braced as if he expected a blow.

Longing spread through her. Somewhere along the way, between sparring sessions and long talks about everything and nothing, Sebastian had become something far more precious to her than a weapons master turned friend. She wanted him to look at her the way he had when he'd seen her in her ball gown. She wanted his fingers on her cheek and his arms around her waist. She wanted his smiles, his silences, and his kisses.

Stars help her, how she wanted his kisses.

It was lunacy. She was trapped in Teague's villa, one word away from dying, and the choices she was making would either ruin her keeper or destroy herself. She had no right to want more than friendship with Sebastian when she wasn't sure she'd live to see the next morning.

"That was . . . I'm sorry. Again," Sebastian said into the silence, and the reserve in his voice galvanized Ari into action.

"Only apologize if you didn't mean it," she said, and waited, hardly daring to wish for him to turn toward her. To show her his face so she could know if he longed for her too.

He was silent for an agonizingly long time, his body held perfectly still the way he did when he was looking for threats in a new environment. She willed him to trust her. To trust himself.

To want her.

Finally, he said, "I shouldn't say things like that to you."

"Were you telling the truth?" She reached past him to flip the toast before it burned, and then stirred the eggs.

"It doesn't matter."

Forget waiting for him to turn toward her. Ari wiggled between him and the stove, prayed her hair wouldn't catch on fire, and looked up to meet his gaze.

His brown eyes widened, and he started to step back.

"Please," she said, "stay."

He stayed—separated from her by a breath of space, his chest rising and falling rapidly, his lips parting as he stared at hers.

Every part of her strained toward him, but she held still. Waiting. Letting him get comfortable with almost touching. With staying.

Her heart was thunder, her blood lightning, and the rest of the kitchen fell away as he slowly bent his head toward hers.

She swayed toward him and pressed her palms to his chest. "Sebastian," she breathed.

"Princess Arianna," he whispered.

She closed her eyes.

"I do hope I'm not interrupting anything." Teague's cold, polished voice spoke from the doorway.

Sebastian jerked back from her, his body instantly tense as he spun to face Teague. Ari glared at the fae.

"Just for that, you don't get any sausage." She turned toward the stove and plated the food while she waited for her skin to cool and her heartbeat to return to normal.

Under no circumstances was she going to deal with Teague while her body still wanted Sebastian.

"We have errands to run. Eat quickly," Teague said as he took an apple from a bowl in the center of the table, sat down, and took a bite.

Ari grabbed her plate and then risked a quick glance at Sebastian, her cheeks warming at the (absolutely delicious) memory of almost kissing him.

He gave her his crinkle-eyed smile.

So much for not wanting Sebastian while she had to deal with Teague. Thank the stars she had a real breakfast on her plate. She was going to need it.

Her search for the secret to stopping Teague was at a standstill. She had the empty contract, and she planned to read through it at her first opportunity, but it wasn't like he would've carelessly included an addendum with instructions on how to kill him.

She needed information she couldn't find inside the villa. She needed a contact on Llorenyae to research Teague's past, she needed her vial of bloodflower poison she'd unfortunately left behind in her suite the night of the ball, and she needed the *Book of the Fae.*

None of those were going to be easy to come by while she was trapped in the villa beneath Maarit's and Teague's watchful eyes. She put a bite of egg into her mouth and met Sebastian's gaze.

She might be trapped in the villa, but he wasn't. The next time Teague and Maarit left them alone, she'd ask Sebastian to go out and gather what she needed.

Sebastian crinkled his eyes at her, and she gave him a quick little smile, even though eating near Teague was nearly enough to kill her enjoyment of the sausage.

Teague stayed in the kitchen with them for the entire meal—an act that made Ari wish a pox upon him and anyone unfortunate enough to be related to him. When breakfast was finished, Teague said, "Sebastian, see to the shipments at the dock this morning. There's a horse saddled and waiting for you in my stables. Princess, you'll accompany me."

"Where?" Ari asked, her hands trembling at the thought of being stuck alone with Teague for hours on end.

He smiled. "I have a special debt to collect at the market today."

She frowned. "Why do you want me to come along?"

His smile grew. "Maarit is unwell, and I think we both know I'd be a fool to leave you unsupervised."

Ari's heart pounded painfully and her palms were slick with sweat as Teague escorted her out of the villa and into his waiting carriage. A golden spinning wheel was painted on the door.

Maybe yesterday hadn't been the victory she'd assumed it was if Teague was still suspicious of her.

But Teague didn't have proof of her actions yet. And he was taking her to the one place where she might finally get some useful answers about him.

She just had to find a way to get to Rahel's bookshop and hope that the *Book of the Fae* was there waiting for her. And that she could sneak it back into the villa under Teague's nose.

Matching Teague's malicious little smile with one of her own, she settled back against the carriage seat, looked out the window, and began to plan.

THIRTY-FOUR

THE MARKET WAS teeming with people, and Ari realized with a start that it was Mama Eleni's usual market day. Housekeepers and cooks tromped through the streets with groups of maids, grooms, or personal guards carrying wide baskets loaded with goods for the household. She recognized a face here and there, and fisted her hands in her lap to subdue the sharp edge of bitter jealousy that they could walk the sunny streets freely, doing whatever they wished without worrying that one wrong move would cost them everything.

She had no right to be jealous. She'd chosen to intervene, to negotiate with Teague, to save her brother. She'd do it again in a heartbeat.

The air inside Teague's carriage smelled of leather seats and his wild, woodsy fae scent. The combination set her teeth on edge. She wanted to be in the streets smelling the tang of brine, the sweetness of window box flowers, and the yeasty goodness of baking bread.

As the carriage slowly bumped its way past the bakery where Ari and Cleo always stopped for a pastry, the princess caught sight of a bright blue scarf wrapped around black curly hair, and pressed her face against the window.

Cleo sat at one of the bakery's delicate iron tables, a mostly untouched pastry in front of her. Ari's throat ached and tears burned her eyes, turning her friend into a blurred smudge against the pastel backdrop of the bakery.

She missed Cleo. Missed getting up at the crack of dawn to cook breakfast with her and their late-night talks after both girls were absolutely sure their mothers were asleep. Missed the inside jokes, the pranks played on Thad and the few stableboys they deemed worthy of the effort, and missed the confidence that no matter what she did, Cleo would be there to defend her.

Except this time. This time getting Cleo involved could cost her friend her life.

Ari blinked away the tears just as Cleo looked up at the passing carriage. They locked gazes and stared at each other for a long moment. Then Cleo jumped to her feet as if to run to the carriage, but Ari shook her head, hoping that Cleo would just accept what couldn't be changed and leave it be. There was no way Ari could allow Cleo to be anywhere near Teague. She had no bargaining power left, and he was already far too interested in the ways he might hurt Cleo and use her pain against the princess.

The carriage bumped and jostled over the road and then turned onto the street that held Edwin's spice shop, leaving the bakery and Cleo behind.

Ari's heart ached, and loneliness was a deep, dark well inside her. It was too easy to add up her losses—her mother, Thad, Cleo, her home—and feel like she'd never be whole again.

Except she hadn't really lost Thad or Cleo. They were still alive. They might be distant from her, but they were still alive, and if she was careful, if she was smart, they would stay that way.

The carriage wound up the hill, and Teague shifted in his seat, leaning forward so he could look out Ari's window.

No, not out her window. He was looking at *her* with that cold smile playing about his lips.

"What?" she asked, her voice sharper than she'd intended. "Do I have sausage in my teeth?"

"Shall we make a stop?" he asked.

She shrugged, though the intensity of his gaze and the fact that they were close to Edwin's spice shop sent prickles of unease over her skin.

Did he somehow know about the bloodflower poison the way he'd known she'd been in his study?

She turned to look at Edwin's shop and froze, dread pooling in her stomach.

The shop was a charred skeleton of blackened lumber, the roof caved in and drooping toward the buckled floor. Shards of the pretty glass bottles that had held Edwin's spices were scattered among the ashes.

Something else lay among the ashes too. Something shriveled and curled in on itself.

Teague's driver opened the door, and the faint stench of burned spices and scorched flesh drifted in. Ari's stomach heaved, and she fought to keep her breakfast down.

"Let's visit your friend Edwin," Teague said in his polished voice. As if they weren't staring at wreckage. As if the shriveled, curled thing in the ashes hadn't once been a person.

None of it mattered to him. None of it touched that cold, remote place inside Teague that made him see people as expendable tools he could use to build the life he wanted for himself.

Her hands shook as she held on to the carriage door and slowly climbed down.

She'd come to the market on a collection day. She'd sought out Edwin because she wanted bloodflower poison. She'd been caught at his shop.

She'd brought this disaster on his head.

"Why?" She choked on the word, forcing it past the horror that clogged her throat.

"He defied me." Teague brushed a crease from his jacket and took out his pipe. "It's important to make a punishment truly horrible. Teaches others not to make the same mistake."

"He didn't—he just wanted to sell spices and be left in peace!"

Teague turned on her, his golden eyes filled with unblinking malice. "He answered your questions while you were here with your friend Cleo. He told you something or gave you something that he didn't want me to know about. And when I questioned him, he refused to tell me the truth. So I punished him and nearly everyone who was in his shop."

She stared at him, sickness crawling up the back of her throat. "You burned his customers too?"

He smiled. "All but one. An object lesson is useless if you don't have a witness ready to spread the tale. Now the entire city knows the cost of discussing me in secret. Now they know that lying to me results in unimaginable pain." Leaning closer to her, he said quietly, "It's a lesson you needed to witness as well."

"I haven't lied to you." She put as much conviction into her voice as she could muster, but she couldn't look away from Edwin. Why hadn't his family collected him? Why hadn't he had the decency of a proper burial? She'd bet Teague had something to do with that as well.

"I hope that's true, because if it isn't, you and everyone you love will be the next object lesson."

Teague said something else, but Ari wasn't listening. Stumbling forward, she stood at the entrance to the shop and let the truth of it sear itself into her heart.

Let the memories cut deep and draw blood.

The reports that a woman had been killed at the docks and her children taken by Teague while the city guard stayed away on Thad's orders. The merchant district living in fear of collection day. The crumbling streets of east Kosim Thalas where so many were wasting away on apodrasi, and so many more were doing unthinkable things on Teague's behalf because to refuse him would be to die.

Like Peder had died, a golden thread slicing into his neck for the crime of refusing Teague.

Like Edwin had died, burned to death for remaining loyal to his princess—a sacrifice that rested heavy on Ari's shoulders and even heavier on her heart.

She may have led Teague to Edwin, but none of them would be in this position without Teague's greed for power. He'd backed Thad into a corner, used his weakness for his sister's safety against him, and then tricked him into a blood contract that forbade him from interfering with anything Teague wanted to do in Súndraille.

Ari owed it to Edwin, to Peder, and to everyone else who'd

been hurt by Teague not to look away.

She'd decided to fight Teague because she couldn't stand the thought of losing her brother. She'd started using stealth because she didn't want to lose Cleo.

But this was bigger than Thad and Cleo. Bigger than keeping her own soul in her body.

This was her kingdom. Her people. Until she'd started attending Assembly meetings and seeing the long list of needs her people had, she'd always seen them as Thad's responsibility—he was the one who'd been raised to rule, after all.

But they needed protection now, and Thad couldn't do it. It was up to Ari. She was the princess of Súndraille and it was time she stepped up to the mantle of responsibility that came with that.

She was going to *ruin* Teague, no matter what it cost her. She'd enlist Sebastian to get what she needed. She'd poison Teague's food every day with iron and bloodflower. She'd study the contract she'd stolen and find something she could use as a loophole. She'd get her hands on the *Book of the Fae* and read every single page. She'd unlock the meaning behind the poem in *Magic in the Moonlight*. And she'd find an ally on Llorenyae who could uncover the reason behind Teague's exile.

He had a weakness. He had secrets. And he'd done enough damage to her people.

By the time she was finished with him, Teague was going to regret ever setting foot in her kingdom.

THIRTY-FIVE

LIVING UNDER THE same roof as the princess and Teague was an exhausting balancing act. Sebastian was caught between being the ruthless, violent person who collected debts for Teague, the messenger who brought news of Ari's well-being to Thad's trusted palace guards and gave them information Thad might find helpful as he worked to find a way to rescue his sister, and the boy who longed to just sit beside Ari and memorize her smiles.

Two months ago, all he'd wanted was enough coin to buy a solitary life far from Kosim Thalas and the memories it held.

Two months ago, he'd been willing to break his promise to his brother for a chance to avoid another confrontation with his father. To avoid discovering just how like his father he really was inside.

He still wanted his cottage on a sea cliff. He still wanted to avoid his father.

But now he wanted Ari's safety more.

Figuring out how to protect her kept him up at night, tossing and turning in his little room in the far corner of Teague's villa while he ran various scenarios that always ended with the same conclusion.

If Teague wanted her dead, there was nothing Sebastian could do to stop him.

He didn't have magic. He didn't have weapons that could work against the fae. He had brute strength and fighting skills, but none of that mattered when your enemy had only to speak a single word to tear your world apart.

What Sebastian did have, however, was the princess herself. She was smart, resourceful, courageous, and determined—not to mention sneaky when she had to be. Maybe Sebastian couldn't stop Teague the way he could stop challengers in east Kosim Thalas, but the princess didn't rely on traditional weapons and situational awareness. She didn't approach problems as if the right fighting stance would decide the outcome.

Ari gathered information from every source she could find and trusted herself to reach the right conclusions. She made multiple plans of attack. She acted decisively, but could brazen it out if a plan went sideways. And it never occurred to her that failure might be an option.

She'd warned him when they first met that she was relentless.

She'd been telling the truth.

Sebastian had no idea how they were going to ruin Teague; but he had confidence in his princess, and when she needed his strength and his skills, he'd give them to her.

Rising after another night of restless sleep and half-remembered nightmares, Sebastian washed, dressed, and followed the scent of cinnamon bread and frying bacon to the kitchen. Maarit was sitting at the table, slicing an apple into thin pieces, her fingers fumbling to hold the fruit steady. The princess hovered over a skillet of bacon on the stove, and Sebastian paused in the doorway just to look at her.

She wore a plain blue dress today, and the way it traced her curves did strange, dizzying things to his head. Her cheeks were flushed from the heat on the stove, and her hair was piled on top of her head in a messy bun that looked in danger of coming undone.

He wanted it to come undone.

He wanted her thick, gorgeous hair to fall down her back. He wanted her to give him that shy, secret smile she got when he stood close to her. And, stars help him, he wanted to touch her.

He wanted to see if he could hold her without bracing for pain. If the scars on his back would ache, or if the crashing sea of panic inside him that seemed to gentle when she was near would subside completely. But mostly he wanted to touch her because being with her felt like finding the answer to a question he'd been asking all his life.

"Well, look who finally decided to join us," Maarit said as she clumsily popped an apple slice into her mouth.

Ari turned, her face lighting up in welcome when her eyes met his. His heart beat faster, and he ignored Maarit as he joined the princess.

"Are you hungry?" she asked as she flipped the bacon and then turned to cut thick slices off a loaf of bread with a cinnamon-sugar crust.

"Very," he said, looking at the tendrils of hair that had escaped the bun and were clinging to the back of her neck.

"I've made bacon, poached eggs, and cinnamon bread, but I can whip up something else if you'd rather." She turned to face him, her cheeks still flushed. "What would you like?"

His gaze slid from her eyes to her lips, and he was in danger of saying something incredibly stupid like *you*, but Maarit snapped, "Just put food on a plate and eat it already. The boss has a list of things for you to do today, boy."

"Your mood would greatly improve if you'd eat some of this bread," Ari said, pointing the bread knife at Maarit before turning back to dish up the food.

Maarit ignored her. "The trade summit starts tomorrow. The boss will be gone all day. Maybe into the night if some of the new debtors he gains tomorrow want to take a look at the goods he can ship to their kingdoms. He's out checking the warehouse inventory now. He wants you"—she pointed one shaky finger at Sebastian—"to collect everything the street bosses have in storage from this week and bring it to the south warehouse."

Sebastian took the plate Ari offered, his fingers brushing hers. She smiled at him, but there was something underneath it—a sadness that hadn't been there when he'd seen her yesterday before she went to the market with Teague.

Leaning down to grab a fork, he whispered, "Are you all right?"

She gave a barely imperceptible shake of her head, and Sebastian frowned at Maarit. He didn't want to leave the villa until he knew what was wrong with the princess—beyond the fact that she was trapped here with the threat of losing her soul while Teague prepared to make puppets out of the high-ranking nobility in kingdoms across the land—but she wasn't going to tell him anything with the housekeeper in the room.

"You said Teague left a list?" he asked as he set his plate on the table and sat facing Maarit.

"Already told it to you." She fumbled with another apple slice, dropped it, and then struggled to pick it up with her trembling hands. Ari set her plate beside his and reached across the table to retrieve the apple slice for Maarit.

"Are you feeling well?" she asked the older woman. "You seem off today. Maybe you need to drink some of that magic fae tea."

Maarit snapped her head up to glare at the princess. "Why would I do that?"

"Because it helps heal us, and you don't seem to be feeling like yourself."

"Want to make me too sleepy to watch over you, is that it?"

Ari sighed. "Seriously, Maarit, a slice of bread would do wonders. If it didn't put you in a better mood, it would at least give you something to do besides snap at me for being concerned about you."

Maarit was silent for a moment, and then she said quietly, "You're right. I'm not feeling well. I'll call some of the guards inside to watch you and take the tea to my room. Don't disturb me."

"I wouldn't dream of it," Ari said as the old woman shuffled from the room, her remaining apple slices lying forgotten on the table.

The moment she was out of earshot, Sebastian said, "What's wrong?"

Ari pushed her full plate of food away and turned to face him. "I need your help."

"Anything."

She smiled, though her eyes were full of sadness. "Yesterday Teague took me to the market to show me that he'd burned down my favorite spice shop, along with the merchant and some of his customers."

Sebastian's stomach coiled with tension. Cautiously, he said, "That's the kind of thing Teague does, though up until your brother's coronation, he did those things in secret."

"He burned Edwin and left him lying on the floor of his ruined shop." Her voice was thick with tears. "He called it an object lesson."

"I'm sorry." Should he reach for her? Hold her hand or brush the tears from her face?

Once upon a time, he'd known exactly where the boundaries in their relationship stood. Now, he was in unfamiliar territory without a map.

She wiped her own tears and said with vicious force, "I'm going to stop him, Sebastian. And not just to free my brother and myself. He can't be allowed to terrorize my people any longer. I'm going to *stop* him."

"*We're* going to stop him." He bumped his shoulder against hers because it seemed safer than taking her hand. "What's the plan?"

She tapped her fingers on the table and lowered her voice to a breathy whisper as they heard Maarit and some of the villa guards tromp through the front door. "The plan is to weaken him with poison, research his origins in the *Book of the Fae*, examine the blank contract to find a loophole if one exists, figure out why Gretel wanted me to read *Magic in the Moonlight*, and hire someone to go to Llorenyae and get answers on who exiled Teague and how they did it."

"That's a good plan. How can I help?"

Outside the kitchen, Maarit was giving instructions to the guards to keep a close eye on Ari until either Teague got home or Maarit felt well enough to leave her room again.

Ari leaned close to him, her arm brushing against his as she whispered in his ear, "There's a bottle of bloodflower poison in my suite at the palace, Thad would know who to send to Llorenyae, and the *Book of the Fae* is waiting for me at Rahel's bookshop."

The guards entered the kitchen, and Sebastian whispered, "Consider it done."

Moments later, he was riding away from the villa on the horse Teague had set aside for his use, his saddlebag full of parchment, ink, and quills—the tools he'd need to mark down the inventory from each street boss's establishment.

He couldn't go directly to the palace. If Teague heard of it, he'd be instantly suspicious. He could, however, send someone in his place, if he was careful.

Directing his horse west toward the market and the distant palace, Sebastian scanned the streets until he found what he was looking for. A flower girl, her basket overflowing with roses in lush colors, stood on her usual corner, hawking her wares to the early morning passersby. Pulling his horse to a stop, Sebastian dismounted and scanned the area before approaching her.

No street runners. No thieves. No one who belonged to Teague's organization anywhere in sight.

"Good morning." Sebastian made himself smile at the girl, even though his scars tingled as he turned his back to the rest of the street. She looked half his age, though the weariness in her eyes made her seem older. "I'd like to buy some flowers."

"How many, sir?"

"All of them, but only if you're able to deliver them for me. I'll pay extra."

She flashed him a quick grin. "If you buy the whole lot, I'll take them anywhere in Kosim Thalas."

Sebastian reached into the saddlebag, wrote a quick note on a bit of parchment, folded it up, and handed it to her, along with a generous amount of coin. "Take the flowers and this note to the servant's entrance of the palace kitchen. Ask for Cleo. There's extra coin in it for you if you get there within the hour."

Sebastian mounted the horse and watched the girl practically run down the street toward the main thoroughfare that would lead her to the palace's hill. Then he turned his mount east. While the girl delivered his message and Cleo figured out how to respond, Sebastian had work to do if he wanted to keep his job with Teague.

THIRTY-SIX

SEBASTIAN WORKED HARD to finish inventorying each street boss's establishment by noon. The note he'd sent to Cleo had said he'd meet her at the pauper's cemetery an hour past the palace's scheduled lunchtime. He'd figured she'd need some time to make excuses for her absence to Mama Eleni, and he'd needed time to get the latest round of stolen goods entered into his ledger and then sent to the south warehouse.

Plus he needed time to make sure none of Teague's people were watching the cemetery.

He rode past the thin iron gates that marked the entrance to the cemetery and scanned the street carefully.

Nothing.

He circled the hill, taking his time as he watched for a hint of Teague's spies. Never mind that in all the months Sebastian had been visiting his brother's grave he'd never once seen any of Teague's people here.

Being cautious was the only way to keep Cleo out of danger.

When he was satisfied that the cemetery was safe, he tied his horse to the fence and began climbing the hill.

Five hundred fifty-nine stairs. Ninety-eight gravestones to the right, just past the olive tree. Sebastian climbed quickly, his scars itching at the way his back was exposed to the road.

There were a few visitors scattered throughout the rows of graves, but no one who gave Sebastian cause for worry.

Reaching Parrish's grave, he crouched beside it and brushed grit from its surface. The summer sun warmed his back, and seabirds shrieked overhead as he sat in silence beside his brother.

The last time he'd visited, he'd been proud of his new job at the palace. Full of plans to save up his coin and get away from Kosim Thalas. Away from Father.

Now, he was working for the man who'd ordered Parrish's death, and some days he could no longer tell the difference between how he did his job and how his father would've done it. He'd accessed the ruthless, rage-driven part of himself because it was the only way to survive the streets he walked. The only way to keep hunting down debtors while fending off attack after attack from those who hoped to kill him and convince Teague to give them the job instead.

He wasn't sure Parrish would understand any of those choices.

The branches of the olive tree beside him creaked in the sea breeze, and Sebastian turned to scan the hillside.

No sign of Cleo yet. No sign of threats, either.

His brother's gravestone sat beside him, silently accusing him of becoming someone he no longer recognized. Someone who would break a promise to his brother to save himself from having to confront their father—to keep himself safe from the darkness of the life he'd left behind—but who would then dive back into that darkness because of a girl.

Not just a girl. Because of Ari and the way she smiled when he entered a room. The way she'd insisted on treating him like an equal until he was dangerously close to believing it. Because she was comfortable with his silences and careful to give him the space to breathe.

Because Sebastian didn't want to live in a world without Ari in it.

He traced his brother's name and said quietly, "I'm in over my head, Parrish. You're going to think it's stupid, and maybe you're going to be mad because things have changed. I've changed."

Sitting back on his haunches, he watched a carriage pull to a stop beside the cemetery's entrance. A petite girl with dark curly hair and a tall boy wrapped in a plain gray stableboy's cloak with its hood up disembarked and entered the gate. The boy carried a sack in his hands.

Dread coiled in Sebastian's chest. He'd told Cleo to come alone. He had no way of knowing which of the king's new employees were loyal to Teague, and it was imperative that Teague never learn of Cleo's involvement. Now here she was, about to meet with Teague's top collector and hand over the only poison known to affect the fae, and she was walking up the steps with a stableboy.

No, not a stableboy. Sebastian's eyes narrowed as he took in the way the boy moved up the steps with the sort of confident sense of ownership that comes to those who are born knowing they have more privileges than the rest of the world.

Stars help him, Cleo hadn't brought a stableboy. She'd brought the king. The one other person who absolutely couldn't be seen talking to Sebastian.

A headache throbbed behind his eyes, and he pressed his fingers to his forehead for a moment.

There were only four other people on the hillside, all over the age of sixty. None of them were paying attention to the pair climbing the stairs. It was going to be all right. It had to be.

As Cleo and the king reached the terrace that held Parrish's grave, Sebastian stood and moved to the olive tree. When the pair reached him, he motioned toward the windswept grass.

"Let's sit. Draws less attention from the road and makes us look like we're mourners here to visit a grave."

They sat, and Sebastian took a moment to study the king. His eyes were weary, and his cheekbones stood out in sharp relief. Exhaustion had left dark smudges beneath his eyes. His fingers clutched the sack he carried as if it contained the most important thing in the world to him, but Sebastian knew the truth. The most important thing in the world to the king was trapped in Teague's villa, and living with the strain of that was destroying him.

"I told you to come alone," Sebastian said—though he couldn't find any anger to fuel his words.

"I insisted." The king's voice was a shadow of its former self—muted by grief and guilt.

"If either of you are caught talking to me, it could mean your deaths. It could mean Ari's death, so we'll make this quick," Sebastian said. "You brought the poison?"

Cleo nodded toward the sack. "It's in there, along with the *Book of the Fae*."

Sebastian's brows rose. "I didn't ask you to pick up the book. I was going to go get it right after this."

"Well, now you don't have to." Cleo stared him down. "Besides, Rahel knows me. She didn't hesitate to give me the book because she sees me with Ari all the time. How would you have explained your request to her without risking that either she wouldn't give you the book or that she'd report your actions to Teague to try to gain his favor?"

He'd been wrestling with that problem himself all morning, but that didn't stop the worry from spreading through him and sharpening his voice. "Never mind how I would've done it. I was trying to keep you from being seen by any of Teague's employees."

She sniffed. "I go to the market every week. So what if they see me doing some more shopping?"

"Do you always go shopping with the king dressed like a stableboy? Do you always ask for a book that we both know Teague would be furious about?"

"The king stayed in the carriage—"

"Did you go to other shops as well?"

"We didn't have time," Cleo said. "We were only there for a minute—"

"Exactly!" Sebastian's voice frayed at the edges, and he fought to stay quiet. He couldn't afford for his words to echo across the hillside. "You went into the market on a day when you usually wouldn't, and instead of stopping at various shops like you usually do, you went to one specific shop, retrieved a package, and then left the market. If any of Teague's employees noted that behavior, the shopkeeper is probably already on the way to

Teague's holding facility for questioning, and you are in deep trouble."

He scanned the road below, taking his time, noting every shadow, every shape.

No threats.

"How is Ari?" the king asked, his expression a naked plea for reassurance.

Sebastian met his gaze as he reached for the sack that held the poison and the book. "She's safe. She's managed to take over the kitchen."

Cleo laughed, and Thad's lips quirked as if he wanted to smile but just didn't have the energy.

"What else can we do?" the king asked.

Sebastian glanced once more at the road. Still empty.

He wasn't reassured.

It was time to end this meeting and dive back into his life as Teague's collector before the wrong person saw him meeting with Cleo and the king.

"You can hire someone—someone you absolutely trust—to go to Llorenyae and get the true story of Teague's exile."

"That's all?" the king asked, his disappointment evident.

"That's important," Sebastian said. "If Ari—I mean, if Princess Arianna knows how someone gained control of Teague before, she can figure out how to do it again. In the meantime, she can search for his origins in the *Book of the Fae* and use the poison if necessary."

His scars tingled, and he swept the street again. A wagon drove past the cemetery, but from this height, Sebastian couldn't tell who was in it.

"It's time to leave. You go down first. I'll watch you leave and make sure no one follows you or tries to harm you," he said.

"Sebastian." The king leaned forward and gripped his arm like it was a lifeline. "Thank you for being there for Ari."

Sebastian met the king's eyes and nodded. Holding the sack that contained what he hoped would be the key to ruining Teague, he watched them climb down the hill, get into their carriage, and drive away.

No one followed.

It was time to push this part of himself into the corner of his mind and become Teague's top collector again. He stood. Throwing his shoulders back and hardening his expression, he strode down the steps of the pauper's cemetery and back into the streets of Kosim Thalas.

THIRTY-SEVEN

IT HAD BEEN four days since Ari had gone to the market with
Teague and witnessed the remains of Edwin and his shop. Since
then, Sebastian had brought her the little jar of bloodflower poison and the *Book of the Fae*, both courtesy of Cleo—a fact that
still made Ari's stomach hurt with anxiety—and had told her
that Thad had promised to send a spy to Llorenyae to unearth
the story of Teague's exile so many years ago.

It was progress, but Ari was no closer to an answer.

Teague had been gone every day to the trade summit Thad
was hosting at the palace. Sebastian had been gone all day as
well, working from dawn to dusk on a list of tasks for Teague.
Ari suspected Teague was simply finding a way to keep Sebastian and Ari apart in his absence. Even Maarit had been gone.
Teague had sent a carriage for her each morning so that the palace physician could care for her since she'd been feeling poorly.

Ari figured the physician would diagnose her with old age
and grumpiness.

In Maarit's absence, a pair of villa guards had been sent indoors to keep an eye on Ari. She'd spent the days baking—chocolate cake, plum torte, butter twists, apple puffs, and fig crepes—while she left the *Book of the Fae* lying open beneath a cookbook so she could read without raising the guards' suspicions.

The pages were filled with small, precise handwriting. Reading about the first fairy war—the one that had divided them into Summer and Winter courts—was fascinating, as was the list of royal births and fae gifts bestowed upon favored humans, but she'd yet to find a passage about the birth of a short, pale Wish Granter with a taste for violent power.

In between baking and sneaking a peek at the *Book of the Fae*, she'd been busy listing her options and trying to come up with a workable plan for stopping Teague.

She had a copy of one of his wish granter contracts ready to study at her first opportunity. With Maarit gone during the day, Ari had sneaked into the old woman's bedroom, lifted the stolen contract from its hiding place inside the vase, and folded it back into her chemise. She had the *Book of the Fae*, which she hid inside a soup pot when she wasn't baking. She had the jar of bloodflower poison that she'd hidden on the spice shelf—one place she was absolutely sure Maarit didn't even know existed. She had her brother's spy looking for the truth about Teague's exile. And she'd memorized the nursery primer poem about the wolf-headed woman who'd left the secret to her monstrous power behind at birth.

Now she needed to see if bloodflower poison actually worked on Teague, or if she was stuck reading the rest of the *Book of the*

Fae while she waited for results from Thad's spy.

Popping a bite of fig crepe in her mouth, she glanced at the guards, who were sampling the plum torte while a branch from the wall behind them chuffed, alternating between sniffing the torte and the guards. With the guards distracted by the creepy branch, Ari retrieved the jar of bloodflower. She poked holes in the left side of the chocolate cake and poured a small dose of the poison over it. Then, whipping butter and sugar together until she had a bowl of fluffy frosting, she decorated the cake with delicate roses, vines, and thorns, making sure to put the biggest rose over the area that had absorbed the dram of poison.

She didn't want to eat that piece by mistake.

Pulling out the ingredients for cherry tarts, she checked that the guards were still eating the torte and that the house was still curious about them instead of her, and then she surreptitiously turned the page to read the next section in the *Book of the Fae*, but it was hard to concentrate. Something about the poem in the nursery primer—the one about the woman with the wolf's head, bird's talons, and goat's hooves—was niggling at her thoughts. She closed her eyes and ran through the rhyme, hoping something would jump out at her. When that failed, she examined her memory of the statue.

Teague kept it in his locked study. It matched a poem in the book Gretel had said she should read if she wanted to unlock the secret of the fae. It had to be connected, but she couldn't figure out how.

She was deeply engrossed in her thoughts when the wall behind the counter shuddered, and a pair of branches whipped into the air, their nostrils flared as they hovered over the book.

Her mouth went dry as she slowly slid the cookbook back

into place and reached for another mixing bowl.

Maybe they hadn't seen anything—she didn't even know if they could see.

But if they had, and they had a way of telling Teague, she was going to be in trouble.

One of the branches curled around the mixing bowl, tugging it out of her hands until it hung suspended in midair. The other wrapped around her wrist and pulled her toward the wall. She leaned against the counter, the wall breathing in front of her while the branches dumped the bowl and slithered over the books instead.

She had to assume the house had seen the *Book of the Fae*. There was only one solution.

Pushing a plate of cherry tarts toward the branches as a momentary distraction, she whipped a dish linen around the *Book of the Fae* and shoved it into the burlap sack of eggshells and discarded food she'd been planning to bury in the garden for compost.

"Off to bury the rotting food. Who wants to help?" she asked. Her voice was too loud, too bright, but the guards didn't seem to notice. They escorted her out of the villa, across the back lawn, and into the garden. Without looking at them, she swiftly dumped the contents of the burlap sack into the compost ditch and then turned to hurry back inside.

If the house told Teague about the book, he wouldn't find it in the kitchen. Of course, he might still find it in the garden, but this was as close to safety as she was going to get.

She'd just have to feed him a slice of poisoned cake before he ever started looking.

THIRTY-EIGHT

THE SUN HUNG low in the sky by the time Maarit returned to drag herself wearily up the stairs and into bed, waving off all attempts at conversation and offers of fresh-baked pastries.

Ari tossed lamb shanks with olive oil and garlic cloves and put them into a skillet while she waited for Teague to return.

Giving him poisoned cake might be a terrible idea. If he realized what she'd done, he would surely take her soul.

But she'd only used a little. At the ball, when he'd confronted Thad about sending an assassin, he'd said it would take an enormous amount of poison to kill him. He might be right. But she wanted to see if it would affect him, and how fast it would wear off, because any weakness on Teague's part was an advantage to her. If he complained of not feeling well after eating the cake, she would blame it on bad eggs or rancid butter.

When Teague finally entered the villa, the lamb shanks were cold, and the guards were yawning. Sebastian still hadn't returned, and Ari's fingers trembled as the guards left her alone with Teague. He stared at the baked goods that were spread across the counter.

"You've been a busy girl."

"I thought I'd try some new recipes." She nodded toward the cookbook and tried to keep her hands from shaking when his gaze slid over the kitchen. Did she imagine him lingering over the burlap sack she'd used to discard the *Book of the Fae* with the food scraps?

"I've been busy as well." His eyes gleamed. "Eight new contracts signed today. All with nobility from Akram, Ravenspire, and Morcant."

A chill spread over her skin at the thought of Teague gaining a foothold in those kingdoms—and all because she'd wanted to save her brother and had been so confident she could quickly uncover the secret to Teague's undoing.

Time to go on the attack.

"That sounds like something we should celebrate," she said, pulling the chocolate cake toward her and grabbing a knife. "Cake?"

"I don't eat cake. Besides, our bargain is paying off, and that calls for a proper celebration." Teague's eyes were feral as he smiled. "Come with me."

Who didn't eat *cake*? A pox upon this miserable man with his creepy smile and non-cake-eating ways. Now how was she supposed to poison him?

Heart pounding, Ari followed him as he entered the long hall that led to the back of the villa. Being alone with Teague was not how she'd hoped the night would go.

For a moment, she thought he was taking her to his study,

but he stopped at the library instead. Teague lit the lanterns on the table and moved toward the shelf that held the wine. Removing two delicate fluted drinking glasses and a pale blue decanter, Teague turned to her.

"Here." He handed her the glasses and pulled the stopper from the decanter. The liquid that splashed into the glasses was a rosy gold whose scent reminded Ari of sun-drenched meadows and wild spiced honey. Teague replaced the decanter and took one of the glasses. Raising it, he said, "To a successful venture."

Ari obediently clinked her glass to his and then pretended to take a sip.

She wasn't a fool. If it smelled like it was steeped in fae magic, it probably was, and there was no way she could risk becoming intoxicated in front of Teague.

Teague drained his glass in one long swallow and poured himself another. Ari sank onto the far corner of the sofa and surreptitiously poured half of her glass into the space between the cushion and the side. Her hand shook as she raised her glass and pretended to take a tiny sip.

Teague leaned back against the couch, brushed at a speck of imaginary lint on his trousers, and said, "I don't like humans."

Ari made a noncommittal noise.

"They're weak." His elegant voice began to slur, and Ari shivered. "Always grasping for what they don't have. Always desperate for someone to give them what they haven't earned. They'll promise anything, but their promises are false."

He drained the rest of his glass and set it on the floor. Pulling out his pipe, he began packing the bowl with tobacco. "I value loyalty."

"Is that why you've kept Maarit employed long past her usefulness?" she asked.

"Should I throw her on the street? She's served me well for years." He looked at her as if truly interested in her reply.

"Of course not," she said. "But maybe get her some help with the chores. And, for stars' sake, stop allowing her to use the kitchen."

He smiled. She *really* wished he would stop doing that. Being on the receiving end of his smiles felt like being a mouse trapped beneath the paw of a bobcat.

"You don't care for Maarit." He snapped a flame to life in midair and lit his pipe.

"She's rude and generally unlikable, but I don't wish her ill." Ari took a tiny sip of her drink because Teague was frowning at her glass. The wine hit her tongue, a rush of spices and honey that tapered into an intoxicating flavor Ari couldn't identify. Dewy meadows. Frost-kissed trees. Flowers that grew in secret places far from the prying eyes of humans. Her head spun as she swallowed.

Teague took a long puff of his pipe. "Humans protect themselves. They sacrifice others for their own needs. But you volunteered to protect Maarit when you thought an intruder was trying to break into the villa."

Maybe it was the fae wine going to her head—all right, definitely it was the fae wine going to her head—but Ari was tired of hearing how awful humans were from a monster who ripped the souls out of people's bodies.

"You're wrong," she said. He paused, his pipe halfway to his mouth, and slowly turned the full weight of his gaze on her.

Oops.

She started talking. Fast. "About humans, I mean. You're wrong about us. We protect each other. We sacrifice for those we love. That's what got Thad and me into our bargains with you in the first place. We step up and do the right thing because it needs to be done. Yes, we have moments of terrible weakness, but we balance that with moments of incredible courage and strength. If all you ever do is look for a person's moments of weakness, you'll miss out on the best they have to offer."

"I knew someone like you once." He puffed his pipe, his eyes still holding hers. "She was an idealist. She believed, as you do, that people were basically good. That *she* was basically good. And that she would always keep her promises."

Something dark and dangerous flared to life in his eyes, and Ari shrank against the back of the couch.

"She convinced me to believe it too." He rubbed the carved stem of his pipe, and for the first time since she'd arrived at the villa, he was sitting close enough to her that she could study the design.

Long wisps of thread were carved into the ivory stem, and a spinning wheel was carved into the bowl.

Just like the spinning wheel on the other side of the library. The one with straw being turned into a bobbin full of golden thread.

Thread that sliced through the necks of those Teague thought needed a lesson.

He followed her gaze and held the pipe out to her. "Take it." His tone was the deadly calm of frozen tundra, ice hiding the dangers that lurked below.

She didn't dare refuse him. The pipe was warm from stem to

bowl. The ivory was smooth as satin at the top end of the stem, but the carvings formed a rough texture beneath her fingertips.

"Samara," Teague said in his quiet, cold voice.

"Who?"

"That was her name. The human girl who became my friend and used my wishes far beyond her ability to pay until the day she betrayed me." There was a hint of grief in his voice. His words were still slurred. "She was ordinary. Just a miller's daughter in my city. But she had the ability to make everyone around her want to be her friend. Even me. You remind me of her."

What was she supposed to say to that? Thank you for noticing a resemblance between me and the girl who betrayed you? Besides, she was still trying to adjust to the idea of Teague having a friend.

Teague had lapsed into silence, and showed no desire to take the pipe back, so Ari finally said, "I'm sorry she hurt you."

He smiled, slow and awful, and Ari's pulse sped up.

"Her father was a fool. He was less than ordinary. An untalented, unremarkable little nothing of a man who wanted to be so much more." Disdain coated his words, but there were jagged teeth of rage just beneath it. "He bragged about Samara—her beauty, her grace. He wanted her to fetch a high bride price, but, as I told you, she was ordinary. The daughter of a miller who could barely keep his mill running. No one wanted to pay to marry her."

"It's barbaric that anyone would try to gain money by selling his daughter's hand in marriage."

Teague laughed, but there was no mirth in it. "This was well over one hundred years ago, my dear. Things have changed."

She found herself running her thumb over the spinning wheel carving. "Just how old are you?"

"What an impertinent question. Now, as I was saying, Samara's father, realizing that touting his daughter's beauty and grace wasn't getting him anywhere, decided to make up stories. Wild, fantastic stories that would surely catch the attention of someone who could afford the kind of bride price he hoped to receive. He said Samara could make herbs grow overnight. He said she could turn a barren cow into a breeder. And then one day, full of ale and foolishness, he said that she could spin straw into gold."

Ari's skin went cold, and she stopped rubbing the spinning wheel carving.

"The king heard the rumor and visited the miller, demanding to know if it was true. The man couldn't admit to lying, not to the king, so he said that it was true, but that Samara didn't always choose to do as she was told. The king announced that Samara would spend the night in a room full of straw, and that if she didn't choose to turn it into gold by morning, she would die."

"That's terrible."

"Samara cried out for me, because in those times, everyone knew how to summon a Wish Granter—"

"There's more than one Wish Granter?" Ari asked even though she knew the answer from the poem in the nursery primer. She extended the pipe to him, but he ignored her outstretched hand.

"Of course. The seventh child of a seventh child of pureblood fae descent is always a Wish Granter. There were four of us working at that time. I primarily contracted with the fairy queen of the Summer Court to grant wishes to her subjects in exchange for goods and favors. A very prestigious position, and one that Samara put in danger."

"How?"

He rose to refill his glass again. "I helped her the first night simply because we were friends. The wish magic only works if there's an exchange. I took a ring she'd once found in the riverbed, and then I spun a room full of straw into gold." He took a sip and glared at Ari. "Instead of being satisfied, the king demanded that she do it again, this time with a much larger room. I helped in exchange for the locket she wore—a gift from her grandmother, but what could I do? She had to pay for the wish, and she had nothing else of value."

Ari nodded because he seemed to expect it and raised her glass to her mouth, letting the liquid splash against her lips without passing her teeth.

"The king was insatiable. More rooms. More nights. More straw into gold. Always threatening to kill Samara in the morning if it wasn't done. I couldn't let my friend pay the price of her father's foolishness, so I kept helping. Taking a loaf of bread, a patch of cloth, whatever she could spare as payment."

"Why didn't she just wish for the king to stop asking for gold?" Ari set her glass on the floor and looked for a safe place to set the pipe.

"That's not how wishes work." Teague sounded impatient. "I can't modify someone else's choices. I can only get them out of the way."

"You can only kill them, you mean." Ari shuddered.

"I can take a life, or I can spare a life, but a wish like that costs a tremendous price, as you are now aware."

"It costs a soul." Her voice caught on the words, and she swallowed hard.

He lifted his glass in salute. "As is proper. If you take a life, you should have to give yours up as well. I couldn't do that to my friend. But my reputation was failing. Word had gone out that I was so busy helping a miller's daughter, I was neglecting my duties at the Summer Court. It was obvious that Samara wasn't paying my usual prices. My competitors were moving in on my territory. I had to do something. And so when the king announced that if Samara would turn one last enormous room full of straw into gold, he would marry her, I agreed to help but only in exchange for something worth the cost of the wish."

He stared at the pipe in Ari's hands. "She offered her first-born child. Neither of us thought it would come to that. She hated the king. If he married her, she planned to drink a tea each month that would keep her from becoming pregnant."

Ari's heart sank. "He married her, didn't he? And despite her precautions, she became pregnant."

Teague's smile twisted something inside Ari that felt like grief. "She did. And when the baby was born, our blood-signed contract brought me to her bedside. She was heartbroken at the idea of giving up her daughter. I didn't want to make her go through with it, but we were both bound by the contract."

Ari's skin tingled, and the hair on the back of her neck rose. "She found a way to break the contract."

The polished marble of Teague's voice cracked, and rage bubbled out. "I *told* her how. I trusted that she would use it to spare her daughter and set us both free of the contract. Instead, she used the power I'd given her to banish me from Llorenyae forever."

Ari pressed her spine into the back of the couch as Teague stalked toward her, but there was nowhere for her to go. Crouching in front of her, he blinked, and the rage that had filled his face was gone, banked behind the ice he wore like a second skin.

"I'm sorry that happened to you," Ari said, her voice shaking as badly as the hand that still held the pipe he'd carved to remind him of the friend who'd betrayed him.

"I'm not," he said softly, his eyes on hers. "It reminded me not to get involved in the affairs of humans unless they could pay my prices. And in case I ever feel myself softening because someone comes along who looks like she keeps her promises"—he smiled at Ari, cruel and cold, and her throat closed until it felt impossible to breathe—"I simply pull out the pipe I had carved from Samara's bones after I had her taken from Llorenyae, brought to my new home in Súndraille, and killed in front of me, and I remember that humans are liars who can never be fully trusted."

The pipe fell from her fingers, and he caught it before it hit the floor. They watched each other in fraught silence for a long moment, and then he said, "It's late. You should get some sleep." He offered his hand to help her from the couch.

She flinched as she took it, cringing at the way his pale, smooth skin reminded her of the ivory stem of his pipe.

And then she left him holding his creepy pipe and staring after her as she climbed the stairs on shaking legs and wished desperately that she could lock her bedroom door.

THIRTY-NINE

TEAGUE TOOK A long puff on his pipe and stared out the library window at the night sky. Things were coming along nicely. Sebastian had made excellent progress on the tasks set before him, and now Teague had a newly organized workforce with the most obedient, most ruthless employees at the top, and five warehouses full of goods marked for shipment to various kingdoms. He'd offered to toast Sebastian's accomplishments, but the boy, upon seeing that the princess was already in her rooms for the night, had opted to go to bed.

Not that it mattered. One bout of drinking with a human was enough. He'd had a bit too much wine, shared a bit more with the princess than he'd wanted to, but the fear on her face when she'd left him made it all worthwhile.

Yet another object lesson to keep her obediently under his thumb until his plan was finished.

Teague took another puff on his pipe and considered the excellent progress he'd made at the trade summit. He'd moved freely among the most powerful echelons of society, granting wishes and signing contracts that all promised to benefit him greatly. He'd whispered suggestions in the right ears and planted the seeds for a harvest of wishes he could collect in the very near future.

And he'd done it all with the silent blessing of young Thaddeus, who was frankly looking the worse for wear these days. Not that it mattered. Teague had Súndraille well in hand. His reputation for vicious public retribution and unrivaled power that even the king wouldn't challenge had spread far and wide. And now he had influential nobility in three other kingdoms who owed him debts that required them to allow him to do in their cities what he was already doing in Kosim Thalas.

Tomorrow, he'd approach a few from Loch Talam and Balavata—those he'd identified today as weak enough and greedy enough to make a wish for their heart's deepest desire without looking too hard at the consequences. And on the final day of the summit, he'd—

A brisk knock at the villa's door interrupted his thoughts.

He tamped out his pipe and moved quickly toward the door.

Very few people knew where he lived. Even fewer would dare disturb him without his permission. Either this was a matter of dire importance, or someone was about to die.

He threw open the villa's front door and stared at the man who stood on his porch, his large hand firmly wrapped around the arm of a petite girl with black curly hair.

Raising a brow, he met the man's hard, calculating brown eyes—so like his son Sebastian's except that they never softened. Never hinted at anything beyond the wide streak of viciousness that was the hallmark of Jacob Vaughn's life.

"Jacob, I've been expecting your arrival for some time now." He stepped onto the porch and closed the door behind him.

"I wanted to come as soon as you sent word that Daan had been killed. But there was a situation with one of our brokers that had to be dealt with personally before I left Balavata. Some things you just can't trust to an underling." His voice was just as hard and calculating as his eyes.

"Indeed. And it seems you've brought me a present." Teague turned from Jacob to smile slowly at the terrified expression on the girl's face. "Cleo, isn't it?"

"Stopped at home on my way here, and the runners saw me. They knew I was heading here, so they gave me the girl to deliver to you. Said you'd asked everyone to keep an eye on her activities. Apparently, she was seen in the market on a day she doesn't usually go, and she only went to the bookshop. One of our men applied some pressure to Rahel and learned that the princess had ordered a copy of the *Book of the Fae* weeks ago. This girl was picking it up for her today."

"And did you deliver it to her?" Teague asked Cleo, his voice deadly calm even while anger boiled within.

"No," she said with conviction, but her voice shook.

Teague wrapped his hand around her throat, feeling the rapid-bird flutter of her pulse against his skin. All births were recorded in the *Leabhar na Fae*. Its spelled pages automatically added births, deaths, marriages, and binding magical contracts to its pages as they happened. Only the Summer Queen and the Winter King were supposed to have copies—a safeguard to keep their subjects both loyal and safe—but there'd been talk of a third book. One that had been illegally made to magically update the births and deaths of the fae just like the original pair and had then been smuggled off Llorenyae.

The chances of the princess finding a way to use the book against him were slim, but that did nothing to stem his fury.

Leaning close, he bit off his words and spat them at Cleo. *"Did you deliver it to her?"*

She swallowed hard and shook her head, but it didn't matter. She'd seen the book. She knew it was a tool to be used against him. She had to be disposed of.

And so did the princess.

His hands shook with rage as he threw Cleo to the ground. "Make her suffer," he said to Jacob as he turned on his heel to go fetch the traitorous princess from her bed.

He'd warned her to do as she was told.

He'd break the princess, finish using her brother, take the throne, and then kill them both with such spectacular cruelty their demise would be the legend he built his kingship upon.

FORTY

ARI WOKE WITH a start, her ears straining to capture the whisper of sound that had torn her from her slumber. She was lying on her side facing her window. Clear, cold starlight drifted in past the sheer drapes and bathed the floor in silver.

She shivered and pulled the covers up around her shoulders. She was still jumpy from her conversation with Teague earlier. From the knowledge that he'd carved his pipe from the bone of the friend who'd betrayed him.

The one who'd learned how to get out of her contract.

The whisper came again, and Ari froze, her heart thundering painfully in her chest.

That wasn't a whisper.

That was her wall *breathing*.

She rolled to face the doorway, certain she would find a twig reaching for her. Instead, Teague stood beside her bed, his golden eyes glaring, his lips peeled back in a terrible parody of a smile.

"What are you—"

He snatched her hair and yanked her out of bed.

"You're hurting me!"

He leaned close. "I'm trying to."

Her throat closed at the wild light of rage in his eyes. What had happened to put him in such a dangerous mood? Was he still drunk on fae wine? Had Thad decided he could no longer stand back and allow Teague to behave as he pleased without the interference of the city guard?

Her stomach pitched—a slow, sickening roll. Stars, he'd found the book or the bloodflower poison, and he was going to take her soul.

"What's going on?" Her voice was tight with pain as he pulled mercilessly on her hair to guide her out of her bedroom. She stumbled at the top of the stairs, and he let go of her hair to grab her arm instead.

"I'm keeping my promises, Princess," he said, pushing her to take the stairs faster. "That's what I do."

"I don't understand," she said, though she was terrified she did.

Why hadn't he just said the final word to rip her soul out of her body? Maybe because he didn't want the hassle of cleaning up her dead body afterward. Maybe because he wanted her to see the evidence of her crimes against him—the fact that she hadn't stopped looking for a way to kill him even though he'd warned her of the consequences.

Or, stars, maybe he wanted to do it in front of Thad and Cleo. In front of Sebastian. Her entire body shook as they reached the hall and began moving toward the front door.

He wanted to kill her in front of those who would hurt the

most over her death. An object lesson to keep them in line. Isn't that what he'd promised?

"Go outside," he snapped when she hesitated in the entryway.

She risked a quick glance at his face and then reached for the doorknob as the sharp crack of a whip stung the air. A girl's voice cried out, and Ari's breath left her body in a little sob.

She knew that voice.

Her palms, slick with fear sweat, slid off the knob when she tried to turn it. She scrubbed trembling fingers against her nightdress, grabbed the knob, and wrenched the door open.

A man who looked like an older version of Sebastian stood on the steps, a whip in his hand. Cleo lay shuddering on the porch, her dress torn to ribbons, blood streaming from the lashes on her back. Her eyes were closed.

"Cleo!" Ari lunged forward and dropped to her knees beside her friend. "You're all right. You're all right." She wiped hair off Cleo's face and cursed as her fingers came away bloody from a gash that had sliced through Cleo's skin from her forehead to her jaw.

Teague laughed. "She's hardly all right, Princess." He crouched to look Ari in the face. "Didn't I promise you that if I caught you interfering with me again, she'd pay the price?"

Bright, hot panic blossomed in her chest and spilled into her veins. "I didn't interfere. You went to the trade summit. You signed contracts. You have—"

"I have a girl who fetched a copy of *Leabhar na Fae* for her good friend the princess." Rage cracked the polished marble of his voice. "And a princess who thought she could hide her treachery from me. Did you really believe you could get your brother and yourself out of what you owe me? I am as close to invincible as any fae who has ever lived, and you are a liar who is going to get what you deserve."

It was over. He knew about the book. Probably knew about the poison too. That's why he'd killed Edwin, only he hadn't been worried enough to track it down because he was too old for iron and bloodflower poison to kill him.

She couldn't save her brother, her kingdom, or herself.

All that was left was to save Cleo.

"She was only involved because of me," Ari said. Tears filled her eyes. "Please, you've hurt her enough. She doesn't deserve your anger. I do."

Teague gave the man a quick nod, and the whip whistled through the air and bit into Cleo's exposed back. Cleo moaned and whispered, "Help me, Ari."

Ari whirled to face the man and screamed, "Stop! You're killing her."

His lip curled into a sneer. "She deserves it."

"No." Ari turned back to Teague, her tone beseeching. "She doesn't deserve this. Please. You've made your point. I'll give you the book and the poison. You win. You don't have to kill her."

His eyes, full of unblinking malice, met hers. "Don't I?"

She shook her head, her teeth chattering. "You win. I have nothing left to use against you. Please."

He reached for Cleo, smoothing the bloody hair from her forehead, and then wrapped his hands around her neck and jerked her head sideways.

"No!" Ari wailed as Cleo's bones splintered and broke with a terrible sound. She threw herself on top of Cleo, punching and kicking at Teague to get him away from her friend.

"Jacob! Take her." Teague's voice snapped, but Ari wasn't listening.

"You're all right. You're all right." She said the words over and over again, pressing her face against Cleo's ear and willing her friend to hear her. To respond. "Please, Cleo. You're all right."

Strong arms grabbed her from behind as Jacob lifted her away from Cleo. Ari arched her back and reached for her friend, a wordless wail of agony ripping its way out of her as Jacob pulled her down the steps and into the yard.

"Throw her in the cage and keep her there." Teague's voice was once again cold and unreachable, his rage banked.

Ari elbowed Jacob in the stomach and wrenched to the side so she could slam her bare foot into his knee, but he was ready for her. Before she could even lift her foot, he'd locked his arm around her neck and was dragging her across the grass toward a small outbuilding she'd never looked twice at before.

Her lungs burned, begging for air. She clawed at his arm, but he only tightened his hold. Tiny sparks danced at the edge of her vision, and her head spun. Vaguely she heard the sound of a door opening, and then he was dragging her across a stone floor.

"Don't move," he barked as he tossed her onto a thin mattress and looped a chain around her ankle before fastening it to a hook embedded in the wall behind her. Pocketing the key, he returned to the door, slammed it shut, and then slid the room's single chair against the wall and sat down facing her.

Ari gulped in deep breaths of air, but it still felt like she was suffocating.

Cleo was gone.

Her best friend. Her sister in all the ways that counted.

Gone.

Somewhere inside the yawning pit of grief that was swallowing her, a spark of anger flickered, but she couldn't reach it. Her thoughts spun away from her, leaving her with only the terrible understanding that Teague had taken Cleo from her, and there was nothing Ari could do to change it.

Turning her back on Jacob, she curled into a ball on the thin mattress and cried until she was empty.

FORTY-ONE

FOR THE FIRST time in weeks, Sebastian woke without the smell of cooking breakfast in the air. Strange that Ari wasn't already downstairs, making pastries or bacon or whatever delicious thing she felt like eating this morning. Frowning, he swung out of bed, washed quickly, dressed, and headed to the kitchen. As he passed by the stairs that led to the princess's room, he glanced up.

Her door was open.

His heart thudded heavily in his chest, and he quickened his pace as the sense of quiet that shrouded the house pressed against him.

Where was Ari?

He rounded the corner, entered the kitchen, and pulled up short. Teague sat at the table, a sheet of parchment in front of him, his pipe clenched between his teeth.

Ari was nowhere to be seen.

"Busy day ahead," Teague said.

Sebastian's scars tingled at the malice in Teague's voice.

He glanced around the kitchen once more. No skillets on the stove. No mixing bowls with pastry dough clinging to their insides. No flour on the counter or the floor.

Ari hadn't been here.

"Where is the princess?" he asked, his steady voice belying the sudden rush of panic that churned through him.

Teague puffed on his pipe and regarded Sebastian for a long moment. Finally, he said, "Today is the day we see where your loyalties lie."

Fear was making it hard to breathe, but Sebastian slowly pulled out a chair opposite to Teague and sat down. He wasn't sure what game they were playing, but it was his move.

"I thought I'd proven my loyalty to you already. I proved it before you even asked for it." He reached for one of the apples Teague always kept in a bowl on the table and took a bite.

Teague regarded him in silence for another moment. "Did you prove your loyalty to me? Or did you prove that you'd do anything to stay by the princess's side?"

Sebastian swallowed the mouthful of apple and shrugged. "Since you own the princess for the rest of her life, the distinction is hardly important. I do what you ask, and I get to live here with her. I can be loyal to you both without a conflict."

Teague smiled. "I'm afraid that is no longer true."

The residue of apple on his tongue turned bitter as panic tumbled through Sebastian. "What do you mean?"

His fists were clenched, but he couldn't make himself uncurl them. Couldn't make himself take a deep breath around the vise that was squeezing his chest.

Where was Ari?

"Jacob wanted to kill her, you know." Teague folded up the

parchment and leaned across the table. "Very bloodthirsty sort, your father. But you already knew that, didn't you?"

He couldn't breathe. Couldn't think as his scars prickled and burned and the crashing sea of panic tore at him from the inside out.

It took every shred of self-control he possessed to keep his voice steady as he asked, "What does my father have to do with anything?"

Teague smiled. "Remarkable how alike you both are—so ruthless, so focused—and yet so different. You keep your temper, you think long-term, and you know how to organize and run a business without having to resort to using a whip to do it. That's why I've been happy with my choice to make you my Kosim Thalas collector, even though I'd originally planned to offer it to your father."

"He's in Balavata—"

"Hardly." Teague shoved the folded parchment into Sebastian's hand and stood. "I recalled him the moment we found Daan's body. It takes a while for word to travel between kingdoms, of course, but he's here now."

Sebastian looked wildly around the room as if his father was going to jump out of one of the cupboards, whip already lashing toward his son's back. "Where?" His voice was a breathless shadow of its former self, but it was the best he could push past the suffocating noose of panic that was closing in on him. His scars burned, sharp jolts of phantom pain searing his skin until he could hardly stand to have his tunic touching them.

Teague brushed his coat smooth and stepped toward the door. "He's out in the cage with the princess."

Sebastian's chest constricted. He shoved his chair away from the table and stood. His father—the monster who was so loyal to Teague that he'd beaten his oldest son to death on his boss's orders—was locked in a room with Ari.

If he'd touched one hair on her head, Sebastian was going to kill him.

Crushing the folded parchment into his fist, Sebastian shouldered his way past Teague, and took off running for the front door.

The cage was a small box of a building set apart from the main villa. Sebastian sprinted for it while his lungs burned and his scars sent prickles of pain through him.

His father was here.

His father had Ari.

His father only had Ari because Teague had ordered her taken to the cage. Teague had turned against her, and when Teague turned against someone, they never survived.

Somehow Sebastian had to handle the situation without getting the princess killed.

Without getting them *both* killed.

He had no idea how he was going to do it.

The door to the cage was unlocked and opened soundlessly when he pushed it. He entered the room and rolled to the balls of his feet, fists ready, as he took in the scene.

The princess lay on a sorry excuse for a mattress at the back of the room. Her ankle was chained to a hook in the wall, and she absently rubbed the chain with her fingers while she stared at the ceiling.

His father sat on a chair close to the entrance, his head tipped back against the wall as he slept.

Behind Sebastian, Teague entered the cage and closed the door behind him.

Sebastian was surrounded by threats, and he didn't know how to defeat them.

"Jacob!" Teague snapped.

The man's eyes jerked open, and he lumbered to his feet before catching sight of Sebastian. A flash of anger lit his face, and he placed his hand on the whip he kept hooked to his belt. "What are you doing in here? This is Teague's private villa. You don't belong here—"

"He works for me now," Teague said, stepping out from behind Sebastian so that Jacob could see him.

The air felt too thick to breathe, and the rage that Sebastian kept firmly locked away surged against its restraints. The princess still lay on the mattress staring at the ceiling. If she'd heard them, she gave no sign.

Jacob grunted. "I see you have him taking over the babysitting detail. You let me know if he isn't up to the task. I'll set him straight in a hurry."

"Like you set his brother straight?" Teague tsked. "I think not. Sebastian has great potential. Besides, all you have to do to bring Sebastian in line is hurt the princess. Isn't that right?" He smiled at Sebastian, and the rage clawed for freedom.

Keeping his voice as steady as he could, Sebastian said, "Why is she here?"

The hint of friendliness that had been on Teague's face vanished. "Because we learned her friend Cleo visited a bookshop and retrieved a very special book for the princess."

Sebastian's heart sank.

"I warned her." Anger warmed Teague's voice. "I told her to stop looking into my business and my past, but she defied me, and her friend paid the price."

"Cleo is dead?" Sebastian asked softly, as if by keeping his words from reaching Ari's ears he could somehow keep the truth from hurting her.

"She is. And she suffered horribly before she died, courtesy of your father." Teague beamed. "The two of you are quite a set. The blunt instrument"—he nodded toward Jacob—"and the precisely balanced sword." He looked at Sebastian and tapped a finger on the parchment still clutched in Sebastian's hands. "New debts came due today. Consider this your loyalty test. Collect them all by nightfall, and I'll keep you on as my collector here."

"You offered that job to me!" Jacob turned toward Teague, his fist wrapped around the handle of his whip.

"And yet young Sebastian proved himself so spectacularly suited to the position that I am loath to give him up." Teague's voice was hard.

"I don't understand how this is a test," Sebastian said to buy himself time. Time to figure out Teague's angle. Time to come up with a way to shield Ari from his father. "I collect for you all the time. How is this any different?"

Teague smiled. "Today is different because today there's a soul on the list."

It was difficult to swallow past the sudden dryness in his throat. He couldn't take someone's soul. Only a monster would do that, and he wasn't a monster.

"You never let anyone collect souls but you," Jacob scoffed.

"Times change," Teague said, his gaze locked on Sebastian. "Soul collecting isn't something a blunt instrument can do. And given the rash of interest in me—ordering poisons, looking up ancient fae texts—I don't think I'll risk collecting the soul debt myself."

He was afraid. Behind the marble voice there was a thread of fear.

That's why he'd killed Cleo. That's why Ari was chained to a wall.

But why was she still alive?

Sebastian held Teague's stare. Teague had already made connections at the trade summit. He now had high-ranking nobility in his debt across the kingdoms. He could easily use one of them to draw in other, desirable debtors. And his campaign of violence and terror across the streets of Kosim Thalas made it certain no one would oppose him if he chose to ascend the throne.

He didn't really need Thad anymore.

Which meant he didn't need Ari anymore.

So why was she still alive?

And why add a soul to Sebastian's collection list and call it a test of his loyalties?

He stared at Teague, keeping his father in his peripheral vision, and when the answer hit him, it came with a tiny spark of hope.

"This isn't a test of my loyalties," he said, bracing for a blow as his father cursed and stepped toward him. Teague lifted a hand in the air, and Jacob stopped.

"Isn't it?" Teague asked.

Sebastian pocketed the parchment, working hard to keep both the panic and the hope off his face. "No. It's a test to see if I'll break my contract with you."

He knew he was right even before Teague's eyes narrowed into furious slits.

Sebastian took a step back, keeping both his father and Teague in his line of sight. "According to our contract, bound by your magic and my blood, if I don't collect a debt you give to me, you can hurt the princess. The reverse then means that as long as I collect every debt, you can't harm her."

Teague's smile could cut a man to pieces, but Sebastian had grown up on a steady diet of cruelty and abuse. He was held together by scars and a stubborn refusal to quit, and he was impossible to break.

"I'm going to speak to the princess for a moment, and then I'll go collect every last debt." He met Teague's eyes. "I won't fail."

He moved to Ari's side and half turned so he could see any sudden moves the others made. Crouched beside her, his heart clenched at the misery on her face. "Princess Arianna?"

She turned her head slowly. "Sebastian?" Her lips trembled.

He brushed his fingertips across her cheek, catching a tear as it fell. Leaning down so his mouth was beside her ear, he whispered, "Don't lose heart. He can't hurt you as long as I keep my contract."

And, stars, he hoped that same principle extended to Teague ordering Sebastian's father to hurt the princess in his place.

"He killed Cleo."

"I know, and I'm so sorry." He held her gaze for a long

moment, letting her see his own grief. Letting her share the part of himself that made him feel naked and vulnerable to attack. Surprising himself with how easy it was to give her that piece of him. Teague cleared his throat, and Sebastian whispered, "I have to go to work now, but I'll be back, and we'll make a plan. You aren't alone, Princess . . . Ari."

She tried to smile again, but her heart wasn't in it. He brushed her cheek lightly once more and then turned, the raw, vulnerable part of him once more hidden behind the shield he'd built as his one defense against his father and the streets outside their front door.

"You'll need one or two bits of instruction before you can take the soul," Teague said, his eyes bright chips of malice. "You have until nightfall. If you fail to return with every debt by then, Jacob has my permission to do whatever he pleases to our dear princess."

His father pinned Sebastian with the look that used to turn his stomach to water and have him clenching his fists against the pain before the first blow struck.

Sebastian followed Teague out of the cage, his shoulders back and his head held high, while his scars burned as he left the girl he cared about more than anyone in the world with the monster who'd raised him.

FORTY-TWO

EVERYTHING HURT. ARI'S eyes burned from the tears she'd shed into the night and again this morning. Her muscles ached. And every heartbeat sent a shaft of grief through her veins.

She wasn't sure how long she'd lain on the mattress after Sebastian left—an hour? Three?—but her tears had dried now. She was a hollowed-out vessel, and the howling grief that had torn her to pieces in the night had become a weary kind of acceptance. She had no more tears. No more desperate pleas for Cleo to come back to life.

All that was left was a small flicker of anger whispering within her.

It was impossible that a few short months ago, she'd had her mother to smile at her with love and pride in her eyes and to scold her for chapping her hands when she was born to be a princess. She'd had Cleo by her side to break Mama Eleni's rules, to steal pastries and gossip about the nobility, and to fill a part of her that she hadn't know was incomplete until Cleo was gone.

She'd had Thad, unburdened by the weight of ruling a kingdom he couldn't protect. She'd had her anonymity and her ignorance of the true state of affairs on the streets of Kosim Thalas.

Now, her mother was dead. Her brother couldn't look at himself in the mirror. Her people were dying—*Cleo* had died.

And she could lay the blame for all but her mother at Teague's doorstep.

The flicker of anger that burned within her became a steady flame, consuming her despair and replacing it with furious purpose.

Teague, with his insatiable need for power at any cost, had laid waste to her life. Her family.

Her kingdom.

And now he was going to do the same to the rest of the kingdoms.

And she'd been the one to suggest it.

She wanted to be sick, but she had nothing in her stomach.

She wanted to cry, but she had no tears left. Besides, tears wouldn't change this. Wouldn't stop this.

She had no weapons, no *Book of the Fae*, no freedom, and no plan.

Despair dampened the edges of her anger, and she shoved it back.

She wasn't beaten. She *refused* to be beaten. This was a problem, and all problems had solutions. Instead of focusing on what she didn't have, she needed to look at what she did.

She had her memory of the poem in *Magic in the Moonlight*. The one that matched the statue in Teague's study.

Something about the poem had been tugging at her mind for days, but she'd been distracted by the house coming alive around her, and Maarit and Teague looking over her shoulder, and her research in the *Book of the Fae*. Now she had nothing but time and a stone cell, so she closed her eyes and examined the poem.

The story said that a werewolf had married a werehawk, and they were very much in love. But years passed without the wolf bearing a child, and she became more and more despondent until finally she refused to eat. On that day, the werehawk made a deal with a powerful devil who agreed to open the wolf's womb for a price. The wolf became pregnant, but when she delivered her child, both parents were shocked that the baby had the head of a wolf, the talons of a hawk, but the cloven hooves of a devil. In terror and dismay, the wolf tried to eat her child, but the baby possessed the power of all three of her parents, and she destroyed both the wolf and the hawk and left the secret given to her on the day of her birth behind with her parents. Henceforth, she was known as the Devil's Child, and no one was able to stand against her because no one could name her secret.

Ari picked up each piece of the story and examined it. The connection to Teague might be in the devil who granted the werehawk's wish, but Teague was a Wish Granter, not a devil. The book made a distinction between the two, so that meant the only logical connection was the secret that no one could name.

A secret, by definition, would be something no one else could name. Not helpful. Gritting her teeth in frustration, Ari slowly looked at every piece again.

A secret no one could name.

A secret given to her on the day of her birth.

What was given to a baby on the day of its birth? A blanket? A bracelet? Something specific to the fae?

A name?

Ari's skin tingled, and her eyes flew open.

No one could stand against the Devil's Child because no one knew her name.

Teague came from the isle of the fae. She'd heard the language he used when he spoke his commands over the beasts or his incantation to take her soul. The words were soft and lilting, rolling off the tongue like poetry.

They sounded nothing like the name Alistair Teague.

What if that wasn't his real name? What if the key to controlling Teague was to learn his true name?

Slowly, she sat up and brushed dirt from the front of her nightdress. Parchment rustled against her skin.

The contract. She'd taken it from Maarit's room the previous afternoon and hidden it in her chemise so she would have it at hand for her first opportunity to study it.

And because she couldn't think of a better hiding place after Teague had torn through her bedroom searching for anything that didn't belong, she'd decided to wear her undergarment beneath her nightdress and keep the contract with her.

"Don't look very royal to me," Jacob said from his chair by the door. He waited a beat and then said, "What are you, deaf? Or just stupid?"

Ari ignored him, her fingers still pressed to her chest as a whisper of hope flickered within.

She wasn't without options. Without plans.

She had a blank contract already signed by Teague.

She had Sebastian, hiding his grief and his fear so that he could be the kind of person he had to be to meet Teague's demands and keep her safe.

She had the contract, she had Sebastian, she had the idea that she needed Teague's true name, and she had herself.

She knew how to negotiate. She knew how to talk her way out of things.

And she knew how to solve problems.

Maybe she didn't have access to the secrets in the *Book of the Fae*, maybe iron and bloodflower didn't work on Teague, and maybe she was chained to the wall inside a room with the man who'd scarred Sebastian's back and left him afraid to be touched.

That wasn't going to stop her.

Nothing was going to stop her, because she had nothing left to lose. At some point, Teague would decide he was done with Thad's connections, and would kill her brother. At some point, he would push Sebastian too far—give him something even his devotion to Ari wouldn't allow him to do—and then with the contract broken, Teague would kill them both.

She was facing the most dangerous evil her kingdom had ever known, and she was going to be the weapon that brought him down.

She would be iron and bloodflower. She would be trickery and deceit.

She would uncover the secret he'd left behind at birth, and she would speak it.

And when she was finished with Teague, there would be nothing left.

FORTY-THREE

SEBASTIAN STOOD OUTSIDE a tiny clay house on the out-skirts of Kosim Thalas, his stomach in knots.

Until that morning, Sebastian hadn't been aware that anyone but Teague himself could collect a soul, but apparently, as with all of Teague's magic, it was a simple matter of blood contracts. A new contract had to be drawn up giving Sebastian the power to collect soul debts in Teague's stead. A short while later, Sebastian's bloody fingerprint was on another contract, and he was armed with a vial of fae magic, an incantation written out on piece of parchment, and a stern warning from Teague that the magic only worked on those who'd signed away their soul, so if Sebastian tried it on Teague himself, it would backfire and kill him instead.

Sebastian didn't dare fail to collect this debt. Not when he was contracted to collect on any debt owed to Teague. And not when a whiff of disobedience on his part would cause Teague to end the princess's life.

But even though Sebastian wanted to do anything to save Ari, he was having trouble scraping up the awful will to enter the house and take the soul that had come due. He'd been standing outside, watching the sun slowly chase shadows across the strip of grass that separated the house from the road for over an hour, and he was no closer to going inside.

Kora Mitros. He stared at the name on the contract Teague had given him. Kora, who ten years ago wished for a house of her own, paid in full.

How was that wish worth her life? Her soul?

And how was he supposed to look her in the face as he claimed what was owed?

He'd thought that only wishes that took a life cost a soul. When he'd said as much to Teague, the fae had laughed and said that some people were willing to pay anything for their wish, so why should he refuse them?

He closed his eyes as pressure expanded in his chest. His body tensed for a fight, though this was one enemy he didn't know how to defeat.

For weeks now, he'd waded through the filth of east Kosim Thalas, doing the bidding of the monster he loathed. It felt like he wore the stench of it beneath his skin where it would never come clean. There was blood on his hands, and he wasn't completely sure all of it belonged to the guilty.

Kora Mitros had made her bargain and signed it with her bloody fingerprint. There was no doubt about her complicity in the deal.

That didn't make it any easier for Sebastian to knock on her front door.

What finally galvanized him into action was the memory of the princess's face as he'd told her she wasn't facing this alone even while he was leaving her behind with his father.

The trust in her eyes. The connection between them that let him drop his guard, even with his father at his back. He couldn't bear to fail her.

He didn't know exactly how it had happened, but he couldn't escape the truth—he was so far past friendship with her that he had no idea how to find his way back.

He'd been careful since the moment a few weeks ago when he'd lost his mind and nearly kissed her at the stove before being interrupted by Teague. He'd tried to stay close enough to be her friend, but far enough away to keep himself from wanting the things that he could never ask her to give.

Turned out there was no distance far enough to keep him from wanting.

He couldn't be the one to push Teague into finishing the incantation that would kill Ari. If that meant he had to collect Kora Mitros's soul, even though it felt like losing part of his own, he had to do it.

Girded by this decision, Sebastian approached the house and knocked on the door. It was opened almost immediately by a short, softly rounded woman with graying black hair and skin just beginning to wrinkle.

Sebastian swallowed around the lump in his throat and said, "Kora Mitros?"

She nodded.

He tensed, rolling to the balls of his feet in case she decided to run. "I'm here on behalf of Alistair Teague."

Her face crumpled, and she slowly stood aside to allow him

in. The tears that slid down her cheeks felt like a knife in his chest.

"I've been expecting you," she said, her voice catching. "I've said my good-byes."

His stomach churned, and he had to grab the wall to stay on his feet as dizziness hit.

He couldn't do this.

He had to.

Kora had signed her life away for a house.

The princess had made a bargain in hopes that she could stop Teague and save both her brother and her kingdom.

"Why?" He forced the word out, desperate to hear something that would make her guilty of foolish greed. Something that would make his task a little bit easier. "Why did you sign the contract?"

Tears dripped from her face and plummeted to the floor, but her voice was steady enough as she said, "I had nothing. No shelter. No food. How was I going to take care of my babies?"

"Babies," he whispered.

"Six and eight at the time. Now they're grown enough to take care of themselves." She smiled, grief stricken and proud. "They have jobs in the market. They have this house. They'll be all right."

He couldn't speak. Couldn't see the incantation past the tears in his own eyes.

Here was a mother who'd done the unthinkable to buy herself enough time to raise her children in safety and security, and she would pay for it with her life, while his own mother had turned her back on her sons time and time again without a single consequence.

"I'm ready," Kora said quietly.

Sebastian shook his head and stared down at the parchment and vial he held. "I can't."

He didn't know how he would save the princess from the consequences of his failure, but he knew with absolute certainty that he couldn't take Kora's soul.

He also knew that the princess wouldn't want to be safe at the expense of this woman.

"What will the Wish Granter do to you if you don't complete my contract?" she asked.

He couldn't answer.

"I signed the contract. I understood the cost." She stepped closer, and he backed into the wall behind him. "This was my choice to do for my children."

Maybe he could find someone else—someone who no longer deserved to live—and take their soul instead. Maybe Teague couldn't tell the difference.

Even as he scrambled for other options, he knew the truth. The contract was in Kora's name, sealed with her blood. The magic would only work on her.

Kora gently put a hand on his arm. "What is a nice young man like yourself doing working for the Wish Granter?"

He clenched his jaw to keep from yanking his arm away from her touch and said quietly, "It was the only way I could help someone very close to me."

"I wish you could spare me," she said, tears spilling over again. "I wish I could let you. But you don't deserve to be punished for my sake. And neither do my children."

He frowned at her.

She tapped the contract he held. "I read the terms and conditions before signing. He said most don't, but I wanted to know exactly what I was getting into. It said if I tried to break my contract early, my soul would be due immediately. It also said that if at the end of ten years I failed to pay my debt for any reason, my daughters would pay instead."

Sebastian closed his eyes and fought to breathe past the noose of panic that wanted to suffocate him.

"I never dreamed there was a way to avoid paying, so I never thought my girls would be in danger." Her hand gripped his arm with fierce strength. "I have to pay this. I signed it. Not my girls. Not you. I'm ready."

He wasn't. He never would be.

But they were trapped by the terms of the contract. By the magic that wouldn't let Sebastian bend the rules and take someone who deserved it more.

He wanted to push his horror and regret into a box and lock it away where he couldn't be touched by it. He wanted the luxury of not caring when he looked into Kora's calm, tearstained eyes.

It wouldn't come.

Instead, his hands shook as he opened the vial. His voice caught on the words Teague had taught him to pronounce as he slowly whispered, "*Ghlacadh anam de* Kora Mitros *agus mianach a dhéanamh.*"

She stiffened, her mouth dropping open as if surprised. A brilliant light glowed beneath her skin, gathered in the center of her chest, and then slowly separated from her body. The life blinked out of her eyes, and her body hit the floor with a thud as the cloud of light hovered in the air above her for a moment, so achingly bright that Sebastian could hardly stand to look at it. He held up the vial, and the light streamed into it. When all of it was safely inside, Sebastian closed it and then sank to the floor beside Kora's body, his shoulders shaking.

There were no words for the way everything inside him churned and tumbled. The way he wanted to open his mouth wide and scream his horror, but couldn't unlock his jaw enough to make a single sound. There was nothing but a terrible, racking pain that scoured him from the inside out until he thought he'd promise anything just to make it stop.

The blood on his hands from the beatings he'd given in east Kosim Thalas was a tiny drop of water compared to the ocean of guilt he was drowning in now.

He needed to run, but there was nowhere to go that wouldn't cost the princess her life.

He needed to escape, but there was no escape from the storm raging beneath his skin.

He needed a way out.

He needed help.

He needed *Ari*.

He straightened Kora's body, closing her eyelids and folding her hands across her chest, and then he climbed to his feet, wrenched open the door, and began running toward the villa.

FORTY-FOUR

ARI STRETCHED, SLOWLY working each muscle from her neck to her toes. She'd been sitting with nothing but the thin mattress between her and the stone floor of the cage since the previous night, and it was now midafternoon. She was stiff, she was sore, and if she didn't get a chance to relieve herself soon, she was going to embarrass herself in front of Jacob Vaughn.

"I need to use the bathroom." She spoke into the silence that had stretched between them for hours. He'd tried to goad her into speaking a few times, but when she'd silently stared at her lap as if too depressed to talk—as if she wasn't sitting there planning how to hurt him and get away—he'd given up.

Now, he barked out a laugh. "I don't care what you need. Piss on yourself and sit in it."

She was dangerously close to having to do exactly that.

"I'm also hungry," she said, as if he'd already offered to meet her needs.

His lip curled. "So starve."

She lifted her eyes to his and gave him her best impersonation of Mama Eleni's you-are-unworthy-of-this-pie look, even though the thought of Mama Eleni and how frantic she must be to find Cleo sent a bright shaft of pain through Ari.

Fury followed hard on the heels of that pain. Jacob had Cleo's blood on his hands, just like Teague. Jacob had whipped her until she couldn't move. Couldn't do anything but lie there and bleed until Teague snapped her neck.

Ari wasn't going to cower in front of the man who'd helped kill Cleo.

"You don't fool me," she said with quiet intensity. "You don't have the power to decide if I starve. You don't have the power to decide anything at all. You're nothing but a babysitter for Teague. Less than one of the villa guards. Less than even a street runner."

His expression flattened, and he slowly climbed to his feet.

A tremble shook Ari as he stalked toward her.

She was hitting a venomous snake with a stick. She just had to pray she could talk fast enough to turn his venom toward Teague instead of her.

"Think you're pretty special, don't you?" His voice was rough.

"What I think doesn't matter." She kept her voice steady, but it was hard. He was closing fast, and the eager cruelty in his eyes made her want to shrink against the wall behind her.

"No, it doesn't." He was at her side in two more steps, and then he struck her face with the flat of his palm, sending her reeling.

Before she could recover, he grabbed her arms and gave her a quick, vicious shake. "You're my prisoner. I can do whatever I want to you as long as I leave you alive."

"I'm not your prisoner. I'm Teague's."

He grabbed her throat, dug his fingernails into her tender skin, and pulled her close enough that she could smell the staleness of his breath and feel the scratchiness of the rough tunic he wore.

There was nothing in his eyes but hatred. Nothing in his expression but rage.

How had Sebastian grown up with this much hate and cruelty aimed at him? How had he survived Jacob and found the strength to be the kind, protective boy she knew him to be?

It hurt to breathe. Hurt to swallow against the awful pressure of his palm. She did her best to make the pain a distant second to the purpose that burned within her, and met his gaze as he snarled, "I can hurt you. I can make you bleed. I can give you so much pain, you'll be begging for death instead. Sebastian knows all about that."

"I know." She pushed the words past the constriction of her throat.

"I have all the power here, and I'm happy to demonstrate that if you need reminding." His free hand reached for his whip, and Ari keep her eyes steadily on his. With a quick snap of his wrist, he flicked the whip beside her with a sharp crack that made her flinch. He leaned closer. "Still think you're too good for me?"

"No, but Teague does," she whispered.

His grip on her neck tightened, and she choked, but then he released her and stood. Before she could draw a shaky breath of relief, he moved behind her, the whip extended like a snake eager to sink its fangs into her skin.

"If Teague thought you were better than me, he'd have me

chained to a wall and not you." His voice shook with anger. "I'm going to enjoy teaching you to hold your tongue."

"If Teague values you so much, then why is Sebastian his collector here and not you?" She rushed the words, but, stars help her, he was raising the whip, and she was already braced for the terrible bite of agony it would bring.

There was a pause, and bitterness tinged his voice when he spoke. "Boy made a contract. Can't do anything about that. He'll fail at it sooner or later. That boy never did have his head where it should be. Me, though, I follow orders. Every time. Which means I can hurt you, Princess, as long as I don't kill you."

"You'll only prove to Teague that he was right to call you a blunt instrument and that Sebastian is the finely balanced sword. It's obvious Teague thinks the sword is what he needs. I think you should prove him wrong." And, stars, please let this work because if it didn't, Ari had nothing else to try against him.

He grunted, and then he was crouched behind her, his knee digging into her back. In seconds, he had the whip wrapped around her throat. She grabbed for it, pulling against his brute strength. The whip didn't loosen.

He spoke softly beside her ear. "Of course you want me to prove him wrong. You think I'm stupid? You just don't want the whipping you deserve for running your mouth."

Her voice was a harsh rasp as she struggled to speak around the slowly tightening leather cord. "I don't want Sebastian to be the collector anymore, and I know how to make Teague see that you're the better choice."

"Is that so?" He sounded mocking.

"Yes." Probably. As long as nobody had gone through the

parchment on the little desk she used in the study Teague had given her.

"And how would a chained-up princess know a thing about collecting for Teague?" He still sounded mocking, but the whip loosened around her throat.

"Because for the last month, I've been managing his accounts in Kosim Thalas, figuring out how to cut down his overhead in Balavata, and organizing connections for him with people in five other kingdoms. He's expanding his business, and that means he'll need to travel to those kingdoms to set up networks and put collectors in place."

"He already knows he can send me to another kingdom." The whip pulled, burning against her skin.

"But Kosim Thalas is the seat of his growing empire, and somebody has to rule over it in his absence. That someone will be Sebastian—"

Jacob cursed. "Taught that boy everything he knows, and he thinks he can just bypass me?"

"Sebastian doesn't think that." Stars, was he really this blind? "*Teague* thinks that. Change Teague's mind, and you will be the one to rule Kosim Thalas in his stead. Second in command over Teague's multikingdom empire."

"And why would you want to help me take that from Sebastian?"

Because Sebastian didn't want it in the first place. And because if Jacob thought she was helping him, he might help her. She'd love to be unchained from the wall and allowed to cook a whole raft of bacon, but at this point she'd settle for a privy bucket and a piece of dry toast.

"Sebastian can't further Teague's business interests much longer." He really couldn't. She'd seen it in his eyes before he'd set out to fulfill Teague's list that morning. "You can seize the opportunity to be a proactive leader, or you can keep behaving like the blunt instrument who follows orders but doesn't know how to give them."

The whip slithered off her throat, and she reached for the raw, tender skin as she said, "Right now, Sebastian is collecting today's debts, but I know what's coming due next week. Teague would be happy to have those collected early. And you know Teague's network of employees. You could handpick a team for him to take into each additional kingdom. Someone to handle theft—"

"Procurement."

"Whatever. Someone to handle enforcing—"

"I know what roles need to be filled." He stood and began pacing the floor beside her. "I just don't know if you should be trusted."

If *Ari* should be trusted? That was pretty hard to stomach coming from the man who'd abused his son and helped kill Cleo.

The anger within her flared, a hard, brilliant heat that filled her with visions of grabbing the whip from his hand and using it on him instead. When he turned to face her, she smoothed out her expression and tried to keep her fury out of her eyes.

"If the information I give you proves false, you'll know within the hour," she said, and hoped desperately that old, ailing Maarit hadn't taken it upon herself to do something totally out of character and clean Ari's study. "You'll need to avoid the housekeeper, though."

"That old woman?" He laughed unpleasantly. "Teague sent his carriage back to take her to the palace for the trade summit."

"More likely so the palace physician could try to coax a few more years out of her. Still, be careful. She's sneaky, and she has a way of showing up when you least expect her. Strange that a man like Teague is so devoted to a human, isn't it?" she asked because maybe Jacob knew something that could help her. She remembered the way Maarit sometimes smelled like the fae magic in the tea she'd given Ari. The way she sometimes seemed to move faster than she should be able to move. Maybe Maarit was fae. Maybe she was Teague's *mother*. Ari shuddered at the thought. Or if Maarit was human, she'd been the only one in Súndraille to gain his complete trust. Either way, she was adding "get Teague's secrets from Maarit" to her short list of ideas for how to take down Teague.

But first, she needed to relieve herself and eat whatever she could coax Jacob to bring her.

He crouched in front of her, his eyes boring into hers. "So what do you want in exchange for information about next week's debts? Be very careful what you ask for, Princess. If I don't like your answer, I'll just beat the information out of you instead."

"And then you'd only be proving to Teague that you're nothing but a blunt instrument." Her eyes widened as his raised a fist toward her face. "Besides, I don't want anything that would get you into trouble. I just want a privy bucket and some food."

And some privacy so she could look over the contract hidden in her chemise. She didn't kid herself. She wasn't going to be unshackled from the wall until Teague was ready to kill her. She needed time to think, time to plan, so that when Sebastian returned, she'd have a way for him to help her finish Teague.

There had to be a way to finish Teague.

Jacob held her gaze for a long moment, and her skin ran cold in anticipation of a blow from his fist, but then slowly he said, "I'll get you your bucket and something to eat. Where's the list of debts?"

"I'll tell you as soon as I have the bucket and the food. It would be stupid of me to give away my one bargaining chip before I get what I need in return. And you'll just whip me if the list isn't where I say it is, so you have nothing to lose but a little bit of your time."

He grunted and stood. "I'll be back in a few minutes. Don't try anything stupid while I'm gone."

"What could I possibly try?" She rattled the chain against the wall and raised her eyebrow at him.

He coiled the whip back onto the hook at his belt and strode from the cage. As soon as the door shut behind him, Ari snatched the parchment from her chemise, unfolded it with shaking fingers, and began to read.

FORTY-FIVE

THE SUN WAS drifting toward the west when Sebastian reached the edges of Teague's property. His father was disappearing into the villa, which meant either Teague was already back from the trade summit and was with Ari, or his father had left her alone while he got himself a meal.

Sebastian slowly opened the door to the cage. The princess was alone, standing with her back to him, hunched over something as if she was reading. A plate of mostly eaten toast sat at the edge of her mattress, and a privy bucket was set up in the corner.

Words didn't exist that could hold the depths of his agony and guilt. He held his body rigidly still, as if exerting that tiny bit of control would somehow stop the chaos that raged within. Panic cut him off from reason. His thoughts were fragmented and distant. All he could see was the light leaving Kora's body. All he could hear was the frantic thudding of his heart against his rib cage—a thudding that sounded so much like Kora's body hitting the floor that it made him sick.

He was coming apart at the seams, and there was no remedy. He'd been an island for so long, he no longer knew how to bridge the distance he'd put between himself and others.

He desperately needed Ari to be his bridge.

He must have made a noise, because her head whipped up, and she met his gaze.

"Sebastian, are you all right?" Worry puckered her brows as she quickly folded whatever she'd been reading and stuffed it down the front of her dress.

He wanted to tell her what he'd done. He wanted the painful exorcism of putting the horror into words. But when he opened his mouth, all that came out was *"Ari."*

Her eyes widened as he stumbled toward her.

She reached for him as he slid to his knees at the edge of her mattress. Falling to her knees in front of him, she gathered him in her arms and pulled his face against her shoulder. He wrapped his arms around her, fisted his hands in the back of her nightdress, and hung on like she was all that was keeping him from drowning.

"You're going to be all right. No matter what happened. I promise." She kept softly repeating the words as he shook. As he tried and failed to put words to what lived inside him. With one hand, she pressed firmly on the center of his back, on the scars that had slowly stripped him of any expectation of ever being loved. With the other, she cradled his head to her shoulder, her lips pressed against his ear as she filled his chaotic thoughts with the steady constant of her voice.

"Ari," he whispered, and then the words were there, terrible and stark. He told her about the things he'd had to do as

Teague's collector. How he worried that the line between himself and his father was blurring. And then he told her about Kora, and it was all he could do to speak past the awful pressure in his chest. All he could do to find the air to breathe as he let the truth tear its way out of him.

When he'd finished, spent and exhausted, she still held him. Her breathing was steady and calm, a lifeline he grabbed onto with desperate strength, though he still trembled. The warmth of her skin chased the chill from his, and when she spoke again, her lips hovering beside his ear, her words cut through the remaining panic and became a foundation he could stand on without fear.

"I'm sorry you've had to be hurt so many times, Sebastian. That's not fair to you. It makes me want to stand in front of you and fight everybody off, just to give you the space to see that you're worth so much more than you believe."

Gently, she lifted his head from her shoulder and framed his face in her hands. "You are nothing like your father. Nothing inside you makes you want to cause pain to others. You have more courage than anyone I've ever known. Sometimes having courage means the hardest tasks fall onto your shoulders, and those leave the biggest scars."

He held her gaze and made himself say, "I don't know my way back from this."

Her expression softened. "I do."

"How?" He breathed the word. Filled it with the pained hope that her words had given him and trusted her to somehow have the answer.

She smiled—the confident, knowing smile he loved best—and said, "Remember what you said to me when you cooked me breakfast and then almost kissed me?"

"What did I say?"

She leaned closer, and it was suddenly hard to steady his breathing. "You said you knew the way to my heart."

Her eyes warmed when he remained silent.

"Want to know a secret?" she asked, and he did. He really, really did.

"Yes," he whispered as her lips hovered above his, a mere breath away.

"I know the way to your heart too. I know your silences and your smiles. I understand you when you're still, and I hear the things you don't know how to say. You aren't facing any of this alone, Sebastian." She slid her hands into his hair, and all he could think about was the way she smelled like buttered toast, and things waiting to be discovered, and home.

He tilted his head back to look into her eyes. "I shouldn't say this to you."

"Oh, you definitely should."

He shouldn't. It was impossible. It was crazy.

It was also true, and he wanted truth with the princess.

With Ari.

He gathered his courage and said quietly, "I love you. I know that's inappropriate because you're the princess, and I'm—"

She covered his mouth with hers, and everything disappeared except the way she tasted and the incredible heat of her lips moving against his. He pulled her closer, desperate to erase any sliver of air between them. She wrapped her arms around the back of his neck and kissed him like he was the answer to every craving she'd ever had.

When she pulled back, he gazed at her face—at the flush of

pink on her golden skin and the disheveled tendrils of hair escaping her braid. At the vulnerable look in her dark eyes.

"Sebastian?"

"Yes?"

"I love you too."

He closed his eyes and pressed his forehead to hers. He was still horrified. Still grieving. So was she.

But they weren't facing any of it alone.

He'd told her the truth. She knew who he was and what he'd done, and she was still by his side. He drew in a deep, easy breath and kissed her again as the crashing, churning panic that had driven him into her arms subsided into something Sebastian hadn't experienced in years.

Peace.

FORTY-SIX

KISSING ARI WAS like following a map to the places inside himself that he'd given up on ever finding. It was peace and comfort and fire that warmed him in the best possible way. The stifling walls of the cage fell away, the stone beneath his knees disappeared, and all that existed was Ari. The way she leaned into him. The curve of her hips beneath his hands. The little breaths that caught in her throat as she pulled him closer.

"Is it strange to feel happy and sad and angry all at the same time?" she murmured against his lips. Whatever he would've answered was lost as she kissed him again.

When he finally broke the kiss, the walls of the cage closed in on him again, and he realized he was kneeling with his back to the door.

A door his father could reenter at any moment.

His scars tingled, and he glanced at the closed door before looking back at Ari again.

Ari caught his expression and said, "Jacob is making a copy

of the list of next week's debtors. He'll be in the villa for a little while."

"Why is he doing that?" He ran his fingers over her cheek and brushed tendrils of her thick hair behind her ear, even while panic began coiling inside him.

She was still a prisoner. He was still bound by his contract to do unspeakable things.

And his father—the man responsible for so much of Sebastian's pain, misery, and fear—could return at any moment.

Maybe he could just ignore his father like he'd done that morning.

His father was as likely to accept that as he was likely to let Ari go. Sebastian had two choices—he could leave the villa and escape the coming confrontation, or he could stay by Ari's side and face the man who'd haunted Sebastian's nightmares all his life.

"He's copying the list because I convinced him that Teague was going to leave someone in charge of Kosim Thalas while he expanded his business, and that if Jacob wanted the job instead of you, he needed to collect on next week's debts, among other things. I traded the information for a privy bucket and some toast, but really I traded it so I could have time to look over the copy of Teague's contract that I stole." Her voice was matter-of-fact, but there was something dark beneath it—anger and grief that he hadn't heard from her before.

He shook his head, half in admiration and half in disbelief, and tried to pretend he could keep the panic at bay. "Is there anything you can't talk your way out of?"

"The chain around my ankle." She turned her head to look

377

at the hook embedded into the wall behind her, and Sebastian sucked in a breath at the gouges in the tender skin on the side of her neck. Bruises the size of fingertips were gathering beneath her skin in purple and blue. It looked like someone with large hands had tried to strangle her.

Those bruises hadn't been there this morning.

The rage he kept deep within him flared.

She turned back to him. "Time to talk about my new plan. I could kiss you all afternoon, but that isn't going to stop Teague, and I think I know how to— Why are you looking at me like that?"

His heart thudded against his chest, and it took everything he had to speak calmly. "What happened to your neck?"

She held his gaze for a long moment, and he knew the truth before she said, "Jacob wanted to make sure I knew he was in charge."

His jaw clenched hard enough to hurt. "Jacob."

She nodded and then wrapped a hand around his arm. He looked down and realized he'd clenched his hands into fists.

"Jacob just works for Teague. If we stop Teague, we stop Jacob. We stop everything."

"Why do you call him Jacob?" he asked as the rage slithered from his belly and lit his chest on fire.

The taint of his father's cruelty had touched her. Left marks on her. Just like it had left marks on his mother. On his brother. On him.

Her eyes were fierce. "Because I'm not going to give him the honor of calling him your father. He's an abusive, violent monster—anyone who could hurt a child is—and he has nothing to do with the loyal, kind, protective, selfless person you became. He's Jacob, my babysitter, and as soon as we're finished with Teague, he's finished too."

"Is that so?" His father spoke from the doorway.

Instantly, Sebastian was on his feet, standing between his father and the princess. The rage that had lit a fire in his chest crashed against the surge of panic that hit at the expression in his father's eyes.

Sebastian knew that look.

The whip was coming.

"Wish I could say I'm surprised to hear you planning treachery, but you were always weak like your brother." His father reached for the whip and paced toward Sebastian like a cat circling its prey.

"Don't you dare speak of my brother." Sebastian's voice shook. His scars burned as he rolled to the balls of his feet.

His father's eyes narrowed into mean, angry slits, and he cracked the whip. It snapped through the air dangerously close to Sebastian's face, but he didn't flinch.

This time, Sebastian wasn't running. This time, he wasn't going to balk at discovering just how like his father he really was.

This time his father was the one who should be running.

"Your brother warned one of Teague's debtors in time for him to skip town before we could collect his children to be sold as payment on his defaulted loan. Parrish deserved what he—"

"He deserved to be beaten to death by his own father?" Sebastian's voice rose, and the fire in his chest spilled into his veins, chasing the panic into the corner of his mind.

His father's face was grim. "An example had to be made."

Sebastian took a small step forward, and his father stopped pacing to frown at him. "Is that the excuse you used when you beat me for not wanting to eat rotten apples when I was four?"

"Ungrateful for the food put in front of you—"

"Or the time you knocked out Parrish's front teeth because he'd shut the front door too loudly while you were sleeping off another bout of drinking?" Sebastian took another step forward, the words rushing out of him like they'd always been there. "Or when I didn't fetch you more ale fast enough to suit you? Or when Mother cooked carrots and you were in the mood for beets? What about the time you—"

"Enough!" his father yelled, eyes wild, and the whip snapped toward Sebastian.

Ari cried out a warning, but Sebastian was ready. Lashing out, he grabbed the end of the whip, wrapped it around his wrist twice, and yanked his father off balance.

The whip hung suspended between them as his father braced his feet, met his gaze, and pulled.

Sebastian hung on, the whip digging into his wrist. "You're done hurting people."

His father laughed and looked at Ari. "This the kind of man you want, Princess? All talk and no action? He ever show you his back? You ought to see it sometime. Proof that he's a coward. Proof he'll never erase."

Shame, slick and oily, pooled in Sebastian's stomach, but Ari snapped, "What a pack of lies. Sebastian is one of the bravest people I've ever known, and the scars on his back remind me that even though you tried so hard to break him, you failed."

His father's lip curled, and he raked his eyes over Ari's body.

"Mouthy and fat. Thought my boy would've had better taste in girls."

"Leave her alone." Sebastian's voice was quiet even as the fury within him rose up to choke him with its strength. "Leave *me* alone. In fact, just leave. Get out of Kosim Thalas and never come back."

His father jerked on the whip, but Sebastian held it steady.

"You don't order me around, boy." His eyes were wild, spittle flying as he yelled. "People tremble when I enter a room. Streets clear when I walk them. This is *my* town."

"Actually, it's Teague's. You're just his errand boy." Ari's voice was vicious, a first for her. "But that's all you have, isn't it? Pride in following a monster's orders even when it means killing an innocent girl. Even when it means killing your own son. When we stop Teague, and we will, I will personally lock you away in a dungeon so obscure that no one will bother to remember your name."

His father lunged toward Ari, aiming the butt of the whip at her face.

Fury roared through Sebastian, obliterating the panic and the shame and leaving nothing but a red haze in its wake. Launching himself into the air, he slammed into his father and sent them both skidding across the stone floor of the cage.

His father swore and landed a solid punch to Sebastian's chest, but he couldn't feel it. Couldn't hear the words spewing out of his father's mouth.

All he felt was the brilliant, hot purity of the rage that had broken free of its cage and filled him like an armor he wore beneath his skin.

Scrambling to his feet as his father rose, Sebastian absorbed the blows that struck him—one to the jaw that snapped his head to the side and sent blood running from his mouth, two to his shoulder, and another two to his chest—like he'd absorbed so many before. Only this time, he wasn't trying to escape the pain. This time, he wasn't trying to endure. This time, he was calculating his father's center of balance, his fighting style, and looking for a weakness.

He found it in the frenetic zeal of the man's punches—so concerned with breaking his son's body with his fists that he forgot to pay attention to the weapon they each still held in their hands.

Bracing himself against the strength of his father's blows, Sebastian snatched the middle of the whip that sagged between them. Pulling the leather taut, he ducked a roundhouse punch, held the section of whip in front of him like a horizontal pole, and lunged.

He thrust the taut leather against his father's throat, looped a foot behind his leg, and swept him off balance. Jacob stumbled, a tiny error that gave Sebastian everything he needed. Letting the whip slide through one of his hands, he wrapped the section he held around his father's neck and twisted until the man choked and clawed at the leather for relief.

"On your knees." Sebastian twisted the leather noose again and shoved his father to the floor.

The man abandoned his attempt to loosen the noose in favor of grabbing for a dagger strapped to his ankle. Sebastian stomped on the hand that was pulling the blade free and ground his father's fingers beneath his boot.

For one agonizing moment, he stared at the dagger and imagined picking it up. Burying it in his father's heart and whispering that he'd done it for Parrish. The rage that fueled him begged him to show no mercy.

But he was better than his anger. Better than his need for vengeance.

He was better than his father.

Releasing the noose, he let the man fall to the floor, gasping for air, and reached into Jacob's pocket for the key to Ari's chain. Sebastian's hands shook as he freed Ari's ankle, and for the first time he noticed blood dripping from his mouth onto his tunic.

Together, he and Ari dragged his father, who was still gasping, still holding his hands to the raw, abraded skin of his neck, onto the mattress, where Ari locked the chain around his ankle and then handed the key to Sebastian.

"You didn't kill him," she said.

"I wanted to." He backed away as his father let go of his neck to yank on the chain that held him.

Ari gave him a warm smile. "But you didn't, because you knew when you had him beaten, and that was enough for you."

It wasn't what he'd promised on Parrish's grave. It wasn't what he'd dreamed about when he'd first fashioned his cudgel from iron and wood.

But Ari was right. He'd beaten his father. He'd conquered his fear and his rage, and that was enough.

Glancing out the window, he noted the position of the sun as it began bleeding out across the distant horizon. "Teague will be back at nightfall. You sounded confident when you told my fath— Jacob that you could beat Teague."

Her smile grew fierce. "I think we can. And we're going to use his own magic to do it. All we need to do is steal another contract. Are you with me?"

"Always." He offered her his hand and together they left his father behind.

FORTY-SEVEN

SHE EXPLAINED THE plan to him as they crossed the lawn and hurried up the steps of the villa. The plan was simple, but the execution itself could be tricky. Thank the stars Maarit was still at the palace with Teague. Ari could tell the moment she walked into the house that it was empty.

Step one: break into Teague's study.

They stood outside the study door, and stared at each other for a moment.

This was it. Her last idea. The only plan they had left. Teague would be home within the next hour. If this failed, Teague would speak the remaining word to the incantation that would rip Ari's soul from her body. Sebastian would die. Thad would die. And Súndraille would be ruled by Teague.

"I'll watch out for you," Sebastian said as his lips brushed against the crown of her head and sent a delicious little shiver through her. "I promise."

She tipped her head back so she could look him in the eye. "Ready?"

"No." He closed the space between them and kissed her—a fierce touch full of longing that lit a fire beneath her skin. She clung to him, as much to keep her suddenly weak knees from buckling as to keep him close.

When he slowly pulled away, she pressed a hand to her racing heart. "I could get used to that."

"Then let's make sure you stay alive." There was a quiet agony in his voice that tugged at her heart.

"Exactly." She looked at the door. "Ready?"

"It's locked," Sebastian said softly as he tried the knob.

"It's an easy lock to pick. There are hairpins in my bedroom." She raced to her room, grabbed a hairpin, and returned breathless to find Sebastian glaring at the front of the villa, his entire body braced for trouble even though the house was quiet.

"Ready?" she whispered as she straightened the hairpin and inserted it into the lock. The lock turned with a satisfying snick.

He gave her a look that sent heat spiraling through her stomach, but all he said was, "Make it quick. I'll listen for trouble."

Step two: steal a blank contract.

She left him standing in the doorway, his back to the room while he watched the hall, and entered the study. Someone had recently polished the bookshelves and the doors to the enormous floor-to-ceiling cabinet, though the statue in the corner was still coated with dust. Ari rushed to the desk, where the stacks of parchment were still sitting. Quickly checking to make sure she was taking one that hadn't yet been filled out, but had the faint woodsy scent of fae magic to it, she folded it up and stuffed it down her dress.

"Ready!" she said as she spun back toward the hall in time to see Maarit step out of the enormous cabinet, her eyes livid with rage.

"Sebastian!" Ari scrambled back as the woman rushed toward her. The princess hit the desk and slapped her hand on its surface, looking for a pen, a letter opener, *something* that could protect her.

"Betrayer!" Maarit's paper-thin voice cracked as she raised her hands for Ari's throat.

Sebastian slammed into the older woman, wrapped his arms around her, and lifted her away from Ari. His lips were set in a thin, hard line, his expression fierce.

"How did you get in here?" Ari asked as she pushed herself away from the desk, the contract still safely folded up and stuffed in her chemise. "You spent the day with the palace physician."

"And you're so very sure you should trust Jacob's word, are you?" Maarit spat the words at Ari. "So very sure you understand everything?"

A chill crept over Ari's skin as Maarit smiled, cold and cruel.

"What are we going to do with her?" Sebastian asked.

"We can't keep her in the villa unless we find a way to make her stay quiet," Ari said, her mind racing, looking for options. "She'll tell on us the second Teague walks in."

"We can't keep her in Kosim Thalas. Teague has spies everywhere," Sebastian said.

Maarit's smile widened until it seemed like it would split her wrinkled, weathered face. "Yes, he does," she whispered.

Ari's mouth dropped in horror as Maarit's skin shimmered, a light spreading along her veins to gather in her chest.

"Sebastian, something's wrong with her," Ari said as Maarit

threw her head back, the cords on her neck standing out in sharp relief.

Ari's stomach pitched, and a yawning chasm of fear opened deep within her as the ball of light in Maarit's chest drifted out of her body and began spinning rapidly in place, a brilliant cyclone that hurt to look at.

Maarit slumped in Sebastian's arms, all vestiges of life drained out of her.

He let go and stumbled back as the woman's body hit the floor.

Ari met Sebastian's eyes for one heartsick second as the cyclone of light slowed to a stop and shimmered into the vague shape of a man.

"Run, Ari!" Sebastian yelled as the light shuddered, like a snake shedding its skin, and became Teague, standing there in the flesh, his golden eyes glaring, the glittering diamond vial clenched in his hand.

Ari lunged over Maarit's body, her hands reaching for Sebastian's outstretched arms as Teague's cold, polished voice said, "*Dhéanamh.*"

Pain, terrible and absolute, flooded her body—a thousand daggers slicing her to pieces from the inside out. Her veins glowed.

"No!" Sebastian screamed as he caught her and pulled her against his chest.

She met his gaze and tried to form the words "I love you" but the pain receded, the study faded, and then there was nothing.

FORTY-EIGHT

"ARI!" HER NAME ripped its way out of him, a jagged blade that scraped him raw and left unbearable grief in its wake.

He sank to his knees, clutching her to his chest as a hurricane careened through him, destroying the hope she'd given him, shredding the belief that with her love, he could become the man he wanted to be.

"Ari," he whispered as the hurricane's wreckage cut him to his core. Her head tipped back, and he looked at her eyes, begging her to let him see a spark, a hint of the princess who'd marched into the arena and turned his entire life upside down. Begging for hope he knew deep down was already gone.

Her eyes stared past him at nothing.

"She really was the most resourceful girl." Teague's voice was coldly furious as he stood over Sebastian, putting the stopper in the vial. "It would be a shame to let that mind of hers decay into dust."

He crouched and lifted a pale hand toward Ari's face.

"No." Sebastian hurled the word at him as he pulled the princess closer to his chest. "You don't get to touch her."

Teague laughed softly. "You foolish boy. Once I own their souls, I can do anything I want. Maarit's body has served me well for years." He lifted the vial as if to show Sebastian the trapped soul of Maarit caught somewhere inside. "But her limbs are weak, and her mind has nothing new to offer me."

"No," Sebastian said, but Teague continued as if he hadn't heard.

"Arianna's body, though, now that will be an excellent vessel. Intelligent, youthful, and very rarely sick." Teague smiled slowly.

Sebastian's chest burned with every breath he took. "You can't take her body. You can't just occupy something that isn't yours."

"Her body is an empty vessel." Teague twisted the vial so that it caught fragments of light from the window. "And I hold the key."

"She isn't *yours*."

Teague's golden eyes met his. "She is now."

Sebastian bent his head over Ari's chest and shook as the hurricane of grief that devastated him became a firestorm of bone-deep rage.

None of this would have happened if Teague hadn't orchestrated it.

If he didn't survive on preying on the innocent and the desperate.

Sebastian was one of the desperate now, and, by all the stars, Teague was going to make a bargain with him. He was going to give Sebastian the deepest desire of his heart, and that bargain was going to ruin the monster who'd killed Ari.

Sebastian had promised to protect her. He wasn't done keeping his promises.

Gently he lowered Ari to the floor, careful not to let any part of her touch Maarit. And then he stood, towering over Teague as he said with quiet vengeance, "I want to make a wish."

Teague laughed and stood as well. "No."

"I wish for you to return Ari's soul to her body and bring her back to life."

Teague shook his head, his laughter mocking Sebastian.

"In return, I will pay any price you name."

Teague stopped laughing. "If you think I'm going to play this little soul-swapping game with you after the princess betrayed me, you really don't know me at all."

"I know you." Sebastian stepped closer to Teague, his hands curled into fists, his body vibrating with the need to hurt him. "Have you forgotten? I've spent the last month and more running every part of your business. Collecting on your debts. Enforcing your punishments. Even taking a soul. There isn't a single task I haven't done for you. I know that power is what you truly crave and that you'll do anything to keep it. I'm offering you power over me, and through me, power over as many others as you'd like."

Teague cocked his head. "Explain."

"How many?" Sebastian asked quietly. "How many souls do you need to collect to secure your place as the most powerful man in the world? How many bodies waiting to be used by you? Spies in every kingdom at every level of authority and influence. An unlimited supply of apodrasi customers. And the unquestioning loyalty of everyone who hears of the Wish Granter, because they know that if they aren't loyal, I will come for them."

"And when you decide to betray me—"

Sebastian slammed his fist onto the desk. "You know me! You know me the way I know you. You know what to put in my contract to make sure I cannot be bribed, cannot be begged, cannot be moved to do anything other than your bidding."

Teague glanced down at the princess's body and smiled.

"Return her soul. Destroy her contract. Let her go and never have anything to do with her again, and I will be yours until the day I die. I will show no mercy on your behalf. I will tear kingdoms apart if that's what you ask of me. I will make sure no one ever gets close enough to you to betray you again." Sebastian's chest heaved as he struggled to contain his desperation. "Save her, Teague, and the world is yours."

Silence stretched between them, thick with tension. The tenuous calm that Sebastian was holding on to by sheer force of will began to unravel, and then Teague said, "How do you propose to get me these souls if I don't grant them a wish and make a contract with them?"

"Give me a stack of contracts with your fingerprint already on them. I'll get people to sign them."

"How?"

Sebastian's voice rose. "I'll trick them. I'll hurt them. I'll do whatever I have to do."

Teague met his gaze. "I believe you would. But how will you guarantee that the princess won't try to free you by coming after me?"

"Tell her that if she harms you, my soul is forfeit. She'll leave you alone."

Teague watched him closely. Sebastian held his gaze and willed him to take the bait.

Finally, Teague moved to the desk, lifted a contract, and quickly filled it out. Puncturing his finger on a dagger he kept in the top desk drawer, he pressed it to the debtee side of the parchment.

Sebastian reached for the dagger, but Teague held it just out of reach and said, "There's a limited window for returning a soul to a body. It's one thing to put myself into a vessel. A little touch of fae magic keeps a vessel in excellent shape for years. But returning an ordinary soul is tricky. If I wait too long, the body decays, and it can't be saved."

"Then *don't wait.*"

Teague's eyes glowed with vicious intensity. "Oh, I'm not going to restore the princess until I've seen proof that you're going to hold up your end of the bargain. I'm going to require a down payment on all of those souls you've promised me."

Sebastian's stomach plummeted, and panic wrapped around his chest, making every breath a struggle. "How many?"

"One hundred." Teague smiled. "By midnight."

One hundred innocent souls collected in the space of five hours. Sebastian held himself rigidly still while his heart thundered and his vision blurred.

He couldn't do it.

He couldn't refuse.

Teague had called him on his bluff, and it was either prove himself and trust that Teague would have to honor his side of the contract in time to save Ari, or walk away and lose her forever.

Forcing himself to cut through the chaotic panic that

screamed through his thoughts, he latched on to the plan.

Ari's plan.

The plan he still trusted was their best shot to destroy Teague, if only he did what it took to give her a chance to see it through.

"She's running out of time," Teague said softly.

Sebastian took a long look at the princess, lying so horribly still at his feet, and then he grabbed the dagger, pricked his finger, and sealed the contract with his fingerprint.

FORTY-NINE

"BETTER HURRY." TEAGUE finished pressing his bloody finger to the final parchment in a stack of one hundred and handed it to Sebastian. "You have about five hours left to deliver your down payment."

One hundred contracts waiting to be signed by those who had no idea what was coming for them.

One hundred souls collected in the glittering vial already stored in Sebastian's pocket.

The vial that now held the soul of the princess who'd insisted on being his friend and who had instead taken over his heart.

The thought of stealing one hundred souls for Teague sent sickness crawling up the back of Sebastian's throat and made his chest ache. He was going to do the unthinkable on the desperate hope that at the end of it, he could make everything all right again.

He could destroy Teague.

Rolling the stack of contracts into a thick scroll, he shoved them into his coat pocket, and then turned to face the princess's limp body lying at his feet.

"I'll keep watch over your precious Arianna while you're gone," Teague said as casually as if they were discussing the weather or the possibility of having an early dinner.

"I'm not leaving her with you."

"My dear boy, I own—"

Sebastian rounded on the shorter man and said with quiet vehemence, "I'm taking her with me. If you want to stop me and lose out on all the souls you're due to collect by midnight, then stop me. Drop me where I stand. If not, then get out of my way."

Teague arched a brow, though his eyes glinted with malice, but he didn't argue as Sebastian scooped up the princess and cradled her to his chest as he walked out of the study.

Her body felt strange—unwieldy and unaware—and he had to stop himself from straining to listen for a breath from her lips. From telling himself that maybe he'd felt her move on her own.

She was gone—locked inside the vial in his pocket. Hovering just out of his reach.

But not for long. He'd promised to protect her. He'd promised to help her destroy Teague. All that stood between him and keeping those promises was the terrible agony of collecting one hundred souls.

He laid her on his bed in the room he kept at the back of the villa and locked the door. The sight of her sun-streaked brown hair spilling around her body while her dark eyes stared at nothing nearly sent him to his knees with a fresh wave of grief.

He didn't have time to grieve. Not if he wanted to fix this. He had to put the next part of her plan into place and then go do his part to make sure she had the chance to finish it.

"Forgive me," he said as he carefully pulled free the blank contract she'd hidden in her chemise. Unfolding it at his desk, he dipped a quill into his pot of ink, took a moment to remember her exact wording, and began to write.

When he'd filled out the space reserved for the specific exchange of goods and services, he returned to the bed and pricked her finger with the blade he had strapped to his ankle. Pressing her fingerprint to the debtee's side of the contract, he refolded the parchment and carefully tucked it back into its hiding place.

Her plan was ready. All that was needed were the souls of one hundred people and an opportunity to turn the tide against Teague once and for all.

He bent and kissed the cool skin of her forehead, and then left the villa and headed into east Kosim Thalas.

He couldn't take the souls of one hundred innocent people. Not even for Ari. Not even to stop Teague.

Panic lanced his chest, bright and hot, and he clenched his fists.

There had to be a way to do this. To save the girl he loved without losing the rest of himself. His heart pounded painfully as he grasped for ideas that all seemed destined for failure.

Drawing in a deep breath, he willed his thoughts to settle and his heart to slow as one idea—one crazy, nightmarish idea—took hold.

He couldn't take the souls of innocents, but he could find the strength of will to dismantle Teague's entire criminal network, one employee at a time. He just had to trick them into thinking the contract they were signing was to renegotiate their terms with Teague. Or gain a promotion. Or stay on his good side. Whatever would motivate them into putting their mark on the contracts Sebastian held.

The runners assigned to night duty stood at attention when he stalked through the entrance of east Kosim Thalas. He swept them with a glance and barked, "Get your bosses and every single member of your teams to the north warehouse within the next hour. I will personally punish anyone who is late."

Without waiting for a reply, he headed through the warren of streets, glaring at anyone who dared to meet his gaze, until he reached the warehouse.

Two entrances. Skylights instead of windows.

It would do.

Ignoring the pounding of his heart and the sickness that kept creeping up the back of his throat, he chained the back door shut from the outside, lit a few torches along the inner walls, and stood by the front entrance as Teague's people began arriving.

In just under an hour, he had one hundred people gathered at the front of the warehouse. He'd turned away the extras, telling them simply that they'd been summoned by mistake. It was a flimsy lie, but they were in no position to question Kosim Thalas's collector. Not without displeasing Teague.

Now, he faced the crowd and felt his throat close as they grew silent beneath his gaze.

He was gambling with their lives. Betting on the princess and her plan, because if he didn't, Teague would win.

Still, it didn't matter how lofty he told himself his motives were. He was going to lie. Going to trick them into a bargain they'd pay for with their lives. The fact that if the princess's plan worked, he hoped to be able to put their souls back into their bodies didn't take away an ounce of his guilt.

He glanced through the skylight and tracked the position of the moon.

Three and a half hours left.

He cleared his throat and forced his guilt and fear into the darkest recess of his mind. This crowd expected to deal with Sebastian the collector—ruthless and unyielding.

"Teague is expanding his business," he said, his voice as hard as the floor beneath his boots. "He has inroads in Akram, Ravenspire, Morcant, and Loch Talam. He needs trusted employees with unquestionable loyalty to accept a promotion and an accompanying pay increase and prepare to go into those kingdoms to recruit and train new teams. You were all chosen"—he cleared his throat again and swallowed hard against the knot of guilt that lodged there—"because you arrived early. You left your homes, your families. You left everything behind the instant he asked you to, and that proves your loyalty."

He couldn't bear to see the mix of satisfaction and excitement on their faces. Instead, he pulled out the sheaf of contracts and unrolled them.

"A promotion requires a new employment contract with Teague. The terms of service list your new responsibilities and pay increase." It was sickening how easily the lies rolled off his tongue. He glanced at the moon again and reached for the dagger he'd strapped to his waist. "Form an orderly line and make your mark on your contract. Once all contracts have been marked, I will give you further instructions."

It took far longer than he wanted to prick each person's finger and push their bloody print onto the debtor's side of the contract.

He had just under three hours left, and the journey back to the villa was forty-five minutes.

When each person had marked a contract and stepped back, Sebastian drew out the glittering diamond vial and uncorked it. A murmur rippled through the crowd, but they stayed in place.

They didn't realize they needed to be afraid.

His hands shook as he smoothed out the bit of parchment with the incantation written on it. He'd have to make this quick. As soon as the crowd realized bodies were dropping, they'd rush for the exits. He was blocking the only one they could use, and he couldn't stop a mob from leaving. He'd start with the people closest to him and form row after row of bodies in hopes that it would slow the others down.

Taking a deep breath, he said, "Teague has instructed me to seal these contracts with a bit of magic in his old language. There's a small chance it will have an adverse effect on you, but don't worry. It will wear off."

Swallowing the bitterness of his lies and telling himself he was doing this to save not just Ari but the entire kingdom of Súndraille, he looked at the parchment and said, *"Ghlacadh anam de Elina Pappas agus mianach a dhéanamh."*

Before the light of Elina's soul could finish gathering in her chest, before her soul separated and sent her body plummeting to the floor, he'd spoken the incantation for Savas Andris, Athan Gretes, Vadik Palas, and five others.

Conversation erupted across the warehouse as the bodies fell and lay unnaturally still.

He read faster, whipping through the contracts and barking out the incantation as the frenzied bursts of conversation became screams of horror when the remaining people realized that those who had fallen were dead.

They rushed for the back exit first—fleeing the sound of his voice. He read faster, flinching each time a body hit the floor.

Each ball of light that arced its way from a body and into the vial he held left a mark on Sebastian's spirit. A scar deep beneath his skin that bore the name he'd whispered as he spoke the incantation that sealed their fate.

The bodies piled up. The contracts seemed to grow heavier as he moved through the stack. And the incantation, long-since memorized, became harder and harder to force out of his mouth.

By the time the remaining members of the crowd rushed for the front exit—for him—it was too late. He was down to eighteen names, and they were blocked by the enormous sea of bodies lying across the floor.

Eighteen more names to add to the scars that he carried inside. Eighteen steps closer to rescuing the princess and losing himself.

He'd told her after taking Kora's soul that he didn't know his way back from it.

She'd told him that he wasn't alone.

He was alone now, and every name he spoke, every ball of shimmering light he added to the vial, pushed him further away from any sort of help. He was an island of guilt, lighting torches to every bridge.

When he'd taken the final soul, he left the warehouse and locked the door behind him so that no one would disturb the bodies until he could restore their souls.

Stars, he hoped he could restore their souls.

He looked at the position of the moon, turned his steps

toward the villa and found it nearly impossible to move.

He'd done the unthinkable. If Teague didn't keep his word, or if Ari had been gone for too long, then every piece of himself that he'd just sacrificed had been in vain.

It didn't matter that he'd only gone after the guilty. It didn't matter that he was hoping that Ari's plan would succeed and that the vial full of souls would be freed to return to their bodies.

He had no actual proof that any of it was possible. He had nothing but desperate hope and faith in his princess.

His shoulders bowed, crushed beneath the weight of what he'd done. He'd become something worse than his father, and that knowledge was a razor blade to the part of him he'd tried so hard to extricate from the nightmare of his childhood.

There was no turning back now. He'd made his choices. All that remained was to see it through.

All that remained was to keep his promise to Ari.

Holding that thought close, he began running south through Kosim Thalas, the slowly drifting moon chasing his every step.

His breath tore through his lungs, and his sides ached when he finally reached the villa. He took the stairs three at a time and burst into his room. Ari was lying exactly as he'd left her. The contract hidden beneath the neckline of her nightdress rustled as he scooped her up and hurried down to the study.

Teague was standing at the window, his unlit pipe in his mouth and his back to the door. Maarit's body still lay crumpled where she'd fallen.

"I have them," Sebastian said, as he stalked across the room and gently placed the princess in the desk chair.

"Put her on the floor." Teague waved one elegant hand in the direction of Maarit's body.

"It's too late. We're almost out of time. Let's finish this," Sebastian said as he handed the contracts and the vial to Teague, making sure to bump the top desk drawer open just enough to see the glint of the dagger Ari had told him she'd seen on her first foray into the study.

Teague hefted the contracts and then set them down. Taking the stopper out of the vial, he sniffed at the mist that rose, and then smiled widely.

"Well done."

"Save her." Sebastian couldn't keep the desperation from his voice. "I held up my end of the bargain. Now you have to hold up yours. The magic binding our contract compels you."

Teague acknowledged this statement with a flash of his golden eyes. He swirled the contents of the vial, and then said, "*An anam* Arianna Glavan *filleadh ar a corp.*"

The mist swirling within the vial spun frantically, and then a single wisp of light rose out of the flask, gathered itself into a ball of brilliant white, and sped toward Ari.

Sebastian watched, heart pounding, fists clenched as the light sank beneath her skin and spread throughout her veins. When she remained still, her eyes closed, Sebastian felt himself sliding. Falling through the flimsy net of hope he'd managed to cling to and plunging into a pit of despair that felt endless.

But then the sallow skin on her face began returning to its golden sheen. A finger twitched, and her eyelashes fluttered. When she took her first shuddering breath, Sebastian had to grab the desk to steady himself.

She was alive.

She was safe.

Whether her plan worked or not, whether Sebastian was

freed or spent the rest of his life in servitude to Teague, for this moment, it was enough that she was here.

Slowly, she opened her eyes and found his. He was about to tell her that she was going to be all right, when he heard parchment being viciously crumpled behind him.

He whirled around and found Teague wadding up Sebastian's contract, his lips curled in malice as he threw the contract toward the wall.

As the parchment that promised safety for the princess in exchange for Sebastian's services hit the floor, Teague bared his teeth and said, "Thanks so much for the additional souls, my boy. That will give me the ability to manufacture enough apodrasi to quadruple my business. I'm afraid, however, that you and the princess are too much of a liability to keep around. Our contract forbids me to harm the princess as long as you uphold your end of the bargain, but it doesn't forbid me from killing you."

Sebastian barely had time to brace himself before Teague charged straight for him.

FIFTY

ARI BECAME AWARE of her body as if she was awakening from a long slumber. First, there was a sense of heaviness wrapping around her, anchoring her to the ground. Then her scalp tingled and her toes itched. She took a deep, shuddering breath and felt her rib cage expand and contract. Her nostrils flared and the scent of fae magic and blood swamped her.

Ari blinked, and the room swam into focus. She was sitting in Teague's chair in his study, her torso leaning against his desk. Her skin felt cold, her muscles sluggish. Just beyond the desk, the crumpled form of Maarit lay unmoving on the floor.

She stared at Maarit as her memories flooded back.

Stealing the contract. Teague somehow stepping out of Maarit's body and speaking the last word in Ari's incantation. Unbearable pain and her desperate attempt to reach Sebastian before everything disappeared into a vast sea of nothing.

Teague had taken Ari's soul.

And somehow, Sebastian must have found a way to make Teague give it back.

Something crashed into the bookshelves to her left. Slowly, Ari turned her head and saw Sebastian kick Teague off him and then lunge to his feet as the smaller man attacked.

Teague moved with incredible speed, landing punches that were a blur of motion Ari could barely track. Sebastian blocked some of the blows and took the rest, but he didn't seem to be paying attention to the fight the way Ari would have expected him to. Instead, he was steadily working his way toward the desk where Ari sat, flexing her fingers and marveling at the steady cadence of her heartbeat.

Sebastian rocked back on his heels as Teague's fist connected with his face, and blood began pouring from his nose.

A trickle of anger ran through Ari, igniting warmth in her chest. She pressed the palms of her hands flat against the desk and slowly sat back in the chair.

She had her soul again, but they were still in trouble.

Sebastian was in trouble.

Teague whirled and slammed his fists into Sebastian's stomach, sending him crashing onto the desk in front of Ari. She tried to reach for him, her movements disjointed and slow, but Teague got there first.

Landing on top of Sebastian, his face a mask of fury, Teague wrapped his hands around Sebastian's throat and squeezed.

Sebastian punched the fae, landing blow after blow, but Teague simply laughed while his fingers squeezed, and Sebastian's face began to darken.

Maybe Teague was stronger and faster because he was fae. Maybe Sebastian had already been injured to the point that he could no longer defend himself.

The reason didn't matter. All that mattered was that Sebastian was choking to death at the hands of a monster, and Ari, with her sluggish, uncoordinated movements, was his last defense.

Her legs shook as she tried to stand, and she gripped the edge of the desk as she swayed. Sebastian cut his eyes to hers and then stared at her chest.

Really? He was dying in front of her, and *now* he decided to stop being a gentleman about her neckline?

Teague laughed—a cold, cruel sound that sent anger flooding through her body, lending her strength.

She met Sebastian's eyes, trying to send him a silent promise that she would find a weapon and do her best to get Teague off him, but his gaze slid from hers and very deliberately looked at her chest again.

"I do enjoy killing a human with my own two hands." Teague's voice wrapped around the syllables with elegant rage.

Sebastian made an awful noise in the back of his throat and grabbed for Teague's hands, trying to pry them free, but his gaze on Ari's neckline was unwavering.

"The moment I kill you and nullify our contract, I will greatly enjoy killing your precious princess," Teague whispered as he leaned over Sebastian, his feral eyes wild, his hair in disarray for the first time in Ari's memory.

She cast around for a weapon, something easy to lift, and found nothing. Spilled inkpots, quills broken from the struggle, and a sea of parchment contracts scattered across the floor.

Contracts.

Holding desperately to the desk with one hand, she lifted the other and reached into her chemise.

The contract she'd taken before Teague had discovered her was still there, but this time when she pulled it out, there was a bloody fingerprint on the debtee's side. She examined her hands and found a cut on the index finger of her right hand.

She lifted her eyes to Sebastian's, and relief filled his face. He bucked beneath Teague, momentarily knocking the shorter man off balance, and slapped his hand against the side of the desk, shoving the top drawer open.

Teague attacked, a blur of motion that sent Sebastian flying off the desk to sprawl on the floor beside Maarit. He tried to get up, but Teague was already there, hands reaching for Sebastian's throat.

Ari unfolded the contract with shaking fingers and scanned Sebastian's cramped writing, while a vicious light of triumph ignited in her chest.

He'd done it. Somehow, he'd found a way to win back her soul and put her in a position to finish this.

To finish Teague.

Folding up the contract so that all that could be seen was the space reserved for the debtor's fingerprint, Ari shoved it into her chemise and looked for a way to pierce Teague's skin.

A blade glinted in the drawer Sebastian had opened. Ari snatched it and stumbled around the desk.

Sebastian bucked and twisted. Teague smiled and whispered something in fae as he crushed his hands around Sebastian's neck.

Ari steadied the blade in her hand and then launched herself toward them.

Teague saw her at the last moment and swung to face her,

momentarily letting go of Sebastian, but he was too late. Ari crashed into him and stabbed the dagger into his outstretched hand.

Teague snarled and yanked the dagger free. Blood poured from the wound, coating his fingers and dripping onto the floor.

"You're going to pay for that. You're going to pay for everything." Teague leaped from Sebastian, who coughed—wet, hacking sounds that shook his entire body—but still struggled to his knees.

"What are you going to do?" Ari asked with as much attitude as she could muster. "Make another pipe out of my bones? Another reminder of the second human girl to betray you?"

His eyes glowed with fury, and Ari took a step back, her hands fluttering to her chest as if terrified.

Which wasn't hard to do, because fear was a chest-crushing, breath-stealing monster living just beneath her skin.

"Taunt me again," Teague said softly, "and see what I do to you."

Ari's mouth went dry, and behind Teague, Sebastian tried and failed to get to his feet.

It was time. She would either save them both or die trying.

Her trembling fingers closed around the square of parchment beneath her neckline as she said, "You're nothing but a monster throwing a temper tantrum because a human got the best of you."

He came for her, closing the distance between them so fast she couldn't do anything but put her hands out as if to try to stop him as he collided with her and sent them both to the floor.

"Ari!" Sebastian's voice was hoarse as he began crawling toward them.

"Princess Arianna," Teague whispered, smiling his cold, awful smile. "You belong to me, now."

She closed her hand around his bloody fingers, the contract pressed between them, and a jolt of power wrapped the parchment in brilliant strands of light.

Matching his smile with one of her own, Ari said, "No, Teague. *You* belong to me."

FIFTY-ONE

ARI HELD TEAGUE'S gaze as strands of light danced over the folded-up piece of parchment lodged between their hands. He grabbed her shoulder, his fist raised.

"*Stop*," she said.

His fist, already moving toward her face, jerked as if he'd plowed it into a wall. Shaking with fury, he snarled, "What have you done, you miserable little human?"

Ari climbed to her feet, contract in hand. "That's no way to talk to your new master."

Teague's eyes glowed as he watched her walk past him and crouch beside Sebastian. "I have buried hundreds of your kind for lesser crimes against me, and I will bury hundreds more," he said.

Ari wrapped her arms around Sebastian, held him through another coughing fit, and then helped him to his feet. Sebastian laced his fingers through hers, and together they turned to face Teague.

His lips peeled back in a snarl. "You have no idea who you're dealing with."

"Then tell me," Ari said.

Teague froze.

Ari took a step forward, Sebastian right beside her. She held Teague's gaze and said, "Alistair Teague, tell me your birth name."

His eyes widened, and the cords of his neck stood out as he clamped his lips together. His pale cheeks reddened, and his chest heaved.

"You cannot refuse me," Ari said quietly. "I own your total obedience. Those are the terms of our contract."

His smile was slicked with desperation, and every word sounded as if he was forcing it past the name he refused to speak. "If those are the terms, then you have no need of my name."

"And if the contract burns or disintegrates in water? If you find a way to trick someone into destroying it or killing me?" Ari shook her head. "I want your birth name."

He gnashed his teeth and tore at his clothes, his pipe falling unheeded to the floor.

"Tell me your birth name." Her tone was hard and unforgiving. "Now."

His body shook, and he arched his back. Clamping his hands over his mouth, he tried to stop himself from speaking, but the terms of his contract were absolute.

The word seemed to swell in the back of his throat, a hum of noise that became a roar as it moved to the tip of his tongue. He threw back his head, and in a voice of wild forests and moonlit magic he cried, "Rumpelstiltskin!"

He shuddered and glared at her as his name echoed off the walls. After a long silence, he whispered, "I suppose you're going to banish me from Súndraille now."

Ari locked eyes with him. "Banishment is the least of your worries. Stand there, harm no one, and be quiet until I tell you that you can speak."

If hateful looks could drop a princess where she stood, Ari would've joined Maarit on the floor. Turning away from Teague (she couldn't quite think of him as Rumpelstiltskin), she stepped into Sebastian's embrace and held on tight.

"You saved me," she whispered.

"I just did what you would've done. I talked fast, made an offer he couldn't refuse, and then put your own plan into place," he said, but there was something dark and grief stricken in his voice.

She pulled back and framed his face with her hands, studying his eyes. He looked haunted—hollowed out and weary in a way that reminded her of Thad as he told her he couldn't bear to look at himself in the mirror.

"Tell me," she said, and he did.

She listened as he explained how Teague could possess a vessel once he owned the soul, and how the fae had planned to possess her. How Sebastian had argued until Teague agreed to restore Ari's soul before it was too late, but only if Sebastian brought him one hundred souls he had no right to take.

"I did it," Sebastian said, his shoulders bowed as if the weight of those one hundred souls was crushing him. "I tricked his employees into signing contracts and then took their souls because Teague had to be stopped, and your plan was our best chance."

He closed his eyes. "I couldn't see another way. I couldn't trick him into obeying me because I didn't have a contract filled out. The only way to sneak one out of the study was to demand that I get to take your body with me, but if I did that, the only guarantee that I would ever see Teague face-to-face again was if I offered something he couldn't possibly refuse."

"Sebastian," she said, and waited until he opened his eyes and looked at her. "Thank you."

She tried to put everything into those two little words. Her gratitude for a chance to grow old and try new foods and ride a dragon. Her respect for the courage it took to face down a monster alone and do the unspeakable because he could see that sacrificing one hundred people was the cost of saving the world from Teague. And her grief that he'd had to make that choice and walk that road alone.

He leaned into her, buried his fists in the back of her dress, and whispered, "Their blood is on my hands, Ari. We have to make Teague put their souls back."

"We will."

She turned toward Teague, who stood watching them with hate seeping from every pore.

"Do you have to be next to a body to return the soul? Or can you do it from here?"

Teague shrugged.

Sebastian reached him in three steps, wrapped his hands around Teague's throat, and lifted him off the ground. "You will answer clearly, or I will do things to you that would make even my father flinch."

"That's all right, Sebastian," Ari said softly. "If I order him to, Rumpelstiltskin will destroy his own body, one piece at a time."

Teague glared as Sebastian set him down, but there was fear lurking in his eyes now.

Ari moved in front of him. "Can you restore the souls from a distance? Answer me clearly, or I will have you break off your own fingers one at a time."

Which was a *disgusting* thought. Ari was half proud, half worried that she'd thought of it, but one look at Teague's face told her that her threat was effective.

"I can restore them from a distance," he said, his voice an ice storm of rage.

Sebastian pulled the glittering vial of souls from Teague's pocket and opened it. "Send them back," he said.

Teague spat at him.

"Send. Them. Back." Ari crossed her arms over her chest and glared at Teague.

His throat worked, but he couldn't disobey her. A stream of fae danced off his tongue, and wisps of light shot out of the vial to swirl through the air.

"They need a way out," Ari said, and Sebastian hurried to throw open the window. A gust of salty air rushed in, sending the wisps fluttering, but then they rushed for the opening. Ari joined Sebastian as they watched one hundred brilliant strands of light race for Kosim Thalas. He lifted the vial, which still had plenty of soul lights inside it.

"What do we do with these?" he asked softly. "The bodies are decayed. They can't return."

"Well they aren't going to spend eternity trapped in this vial either," she said, and turned to Teague. "Set these souls free."

"Free to do what?" he snapped.

"Free to find their way to what comes next. Do it now."

He spoke in fae again, and the rest of the shimmering wisps escaped the flask, danced through the air to the window, and then chased each other toward the canopy of stars above them.

"Good-bye, Kora," Sebastian whispered. Ari slid her arm behind his back and leaned her head against his shoulder as the wisps disappeared into the fabric of the brilliant night sky.

"One last thing," she said.

"Do you want me to do it?" he asked, his shoulders tense, but his tone steady.

Yes, she did, but that was unfair. He'd shown the courage to do the hardest things over and over again, and the scars he bore from it would last a lifetime. It was her turn to do the hardest thing. Her turn to bear the scar.

"Wait for me," she said, and left him standing with the sea breeze and the moonlight.

When she stood in front of Teague, his clothes ripped, his pipe forgotten on the floor, she held his gaze. "Do you have anything to say for yourself?"

Teague sneered at her. "If you're expecting an apology for Cleo or the merchant, you'll be disappointed. If you think I'm going to regret using your brother, you're wrong."

Anger burned within her, but it was fading into a weary, resolute purpose. She wanted to be done. She wanted all of Súndraille to be done.

"Let me guess," Teague said. "I'm your personal Wish Granter now. You want to expand the influence of Súndraille. You want riches. You want—"

"I want you to set your soul free," she said quietly. The words were heavy, cumbersome things that took all her strength to speak, but she could find no pity as his eyes widened and pleaded for mercy.

Mercy he had refused to show to Cleo. To Thad. To anyone who had dealings with him.

His mouth opened in a soundless howl of agony, and his skin shimmered with light that gathered in his chest and then poured out of him. She turned away as his body fell to the floor and joined Sebastian as they watched the soul of Rumpelstiltskin sway in the breeze, flutter over trees and through grasses, and then drift toward the open sea and the distant isle of Llorenyae.

For a long moment, they stood there, cocooned in silence and starlight. Ari leaned her head against Sebastian's shoulder, and he tangled his fingers with hers.

Finally, he looked at her, peace on his face and warmth in his eyes, and said, "Ready?"

She smiled. "Ready."

Hand in hand, they stepped into the windswept night and headed toward the palace.

FIVE MONTHS LATER

FIFTY-TWO

"I don't think I can do this." Sebastian tugged at the collar of his silk shirt and looked over his shoulder for the door that led from the palace library to the garden.

"Of course you can." Ari straightened his cravat and batted his hands away when he went for his collar again.

"There will be crowds of nobility in there."

"Yes, but there will also be pie."

He gave her a pained look. She smiled and leaned into him.

"So much has changed. Your father is in the dungeon for life. Your mother has a clean start in a new city. And you have the respect of everyone in Kosim Thalas."

"I wouldn't go that far."

She snorted. "You single-handedly dismantled Teague's criminal organization—"

"I had plenty of help from the city guard—"

"Who were following your orders. You cleaned up the streets of east Kosim Thalas—"

"Again with help from the guard." He looked at the exit.

"And then you started a school for children in the slums—"

"Actually I just found the teachers. They're the ones—"

"Who's giving this pep talk?" She glared at him.

His eyes crinkled. "I guess you are."

"If you can handle the renovation of east Kosim Thalas, you can handle a room full of nobility." She smoothed a hand over his hair and brushed a speck of lint from his shoulder. "Besides, I have a surprise for you afterward."

He ran his hands down her arms and tangled his fingers with hers. "It had better be a really amazing surprise."

She grinned, her heart feeling like it was expanding in her chest. It was an amazing surprise if she did say so herself. She couldn't wait to see the expression on his face when she showed him.

"Ready?" she asked as a page knocked on the library's door.

"No," he said, but he walked with her anyway. They left the library, moved down a short hall past windows closed to keep out the chillier winds of winter, and entered the ballroom.

"Sebastian Vaughn, our guest of honor!" Thad threw out his arms in welcome, a genuine smile on his face, and miracle of miracles, Sebastian managed to (awkwardly) smile back.

Ari walked confidently onto the platform and stood beside her brother. She was getting used to wearing a crown and to handling the responsibilities that came with it. And the people were getting used to Thad and Ari ruling Súndraille as a team.

"We should make this quick before Sebastian runs for the door," Ari said under her breath as her brother took her elbow and gently steered the two of them toward the stage that usually held the musicians for a ball.

"I heard that," Sebastian said.

"Is she wrong?" Thad asked.

Sebastian treated them both to a mock glare and then muttered, "No."

Moments later, the crowd of nobility was seated in the chairs that had been placed in rows before the stage, and Thad was listing all Sebastian's recent accomplishments while Sebastian looked like he wanted the floor to open up and swallow him.

Thad turned to Sebastian, his eyes gleaming with emotion, and said in a husky voice, "And finally, the throne recognizes your incredible act of selfless bravery, which saved the life of the princess and rid our kingdom of the threat of Alistair Teague."

Ari's throat swelled as Thad reached for the parchment that was lying on a table beside him. She still missed her mother and Cleo, and part of her always would. But there were things to be grateful for too. She had her brother back. The kingdom was on the mend. And Sebastian—the boy who'd sacrificed everything for her—was going to be recognized for the true hero that he was.

Thad held up the parchment and said in his most regal voice, "In reward for your acts of heroism, I, Thaddeus Glavan, do hereby promote you to the status of Lord Sebastian Vaughn, Duke of Kosim Thalas, and confer upon you all of the privileges that come with the title."

The crowd applauded. Thad smiled. And Sebastian, looking like he was three seconds from bolting, gave a little awkward bow to the king and then looked to Ari for rescue.

An hour later, when they'd greeted everyone in the room and sampled two pieces of pie each, Sebastian said, "How long do I have to stay?"

Ari grinned. "You're Lord Vaughn now. Unless specifically

ordered to by the king, you can come and go as you please."

He raised a brow at her. "Then I believe you mentioned something about a surprise?"

They ducked out of a side exit, and Ari shivered as the winter sea breeze whipped her hair.

"Where are we going?" Sebastian asked as he wrapped his coat around her shoulders.

"You'll see." She snuggled into his warmth and led him south, through the garden, past the arena and the stables, and then eventually to the south field, where the land ended and the sea began.

They walked past the empty stone barn and neared the cliff's edge when Ari pulled him into a circle of newly planted cypress trees. In the center of the circle were three white stones, each with a name carved into its surface.

RADA GLAVAN: PRECIOUS MOTHER
CLEO TOLES: CHERISHED DAUGHTER AND FRIEND
PARRISH VAUGHN: BELOVED BROTHER

He let go of her and moved to stand beside Parrish's grave, one hand reaching out to rest against the polished stone.

"The cypress trees symbolize sacrifice. I thought that was fitting. Rada is my mother—you probably figured that out—and I don't actually have her body, but this will give Thad and me a place to go when we want to remember her." She took a step closer to him, but he remained silently turned away.

A tiny thread of worry moved through her, and she said, "I kept the headstone that was on Parrish's grave in the pauper's cemetery. I'm sure it means something to you, and we can use it here if you'd rather. I can destroy this one. They don't have to match."

She was babbling, but he wasn't moving. Wasn't speaking. And for once, she had no idea what his silence meant.

"I . . . Sebastian, if I should've asked you before moving Parrish, I'm sorry. I thought . . . It doesn't matter what I thought. He's your brother. I should've—"

"Ari." He turned, took three long steps, and pulled her against his chest. Burying his face in her hair, he whispered, "Thank you."

She held him close, listening to the comforting rhythm of his heartbeat while the pale winter sun gleamed overhead and seabirds cawed over the sound of the Chrysós crashing against the shore.

After a long moment, he said, "This is a good surprise."

She smiled. "This is only part of the surprise."

He pulled back and arched a brow at her. "You really are remarkably sneaky when you want to be."

She grinned and turned him to face the western coastline. "See that cliff with the huge, solitary oak tree? The one just past the edge of the palace's property. Not there"—she reached up and adjusted the direction he was facing—"*there*."

"I see it. Did you bury someone there too?"

She snorted. "Not yet, but you should stay on my good side."

He leaned down and kissed her, gentle and sweet. Her stomach spun in warm, lazy circles, and she clung to him as he slowly broke the kiss. "Still on your good side?"

"Stop distracting me." She swept him with a look. "But hold that thought because you're going to want to kiss me again in a second."

"Am I?" He gave her the arched brow again.

"The property that contains the cliff with the oak tree was recently purchased. By Thad." She paused for effect, but he just frowned at her. She leaned closer and watched his face. "As a gift for the newest member of the nobility."

He froze, his body as still as a stone except for the wild beating of his heart, and then slowly he looked at the cliff again. "It's mine?"

"It's yours." She danced in place while he stared at the cliff. "You can build the cottage you always wanted. It's actually quite a distance from the main road, so you'll have plenty of privacy. Or if you don't want a cottage, you could build a—"

He covered her lips with his. She lost herself in the gentle roughness of his mouth. In the way he fisted his hands in the back of her gown and dragged her against him as if he couldn't stand to have a sliver of space between them.

When he finally came up for air, his eyes dark with emotion, she framed his face with her hands and said, "I'll visit you often. So often, you'll get sick of me."

"I could never get sick of you."

"I'll bring pie."

"I would expect no less."

The look on his face lit the torch in her heart and sent tingles through her veins. "I love you," she said softly.

He gave her his crinkle-eyed smile and whispered, "I love you too."

And then he kissed her until the sound of the waves disappeared, until the feel of the grass beneath her feet was gone, and all that was left was the taste of his lips and the steady beat of her heart.

ACKNOWLEDGMENTS

As always, thank you to Jesus for loving me unconditionally.

I couldn't write books without the support and encouragement of my family. Clint, thank you for being my other half and for always believing in me. Tyler, Jordan, Zach, Johanna, and Isabella, thank you for being proud that your mom writes books and for (mostly) letting me work in peace. Thanks, Mom and Dad, for helping with the kids and other details when I'm on tight deadlines and for supporting me. And thank you to my sister, Heather, and my BIL, Dave (aren't you glad I left out your nicknames?), for hanging with my kids, reading my books, and buying them for everyone you know. (And to Heather for being an awesome beta reader and an even better friend!)

Producing a book takes a village, and I have one of the best. I'm immensely grateful for my agent, Holly Root, who champions me, and for my editor, Kristin Rens, who always pushes me to deliver my best. I'm also grateful for the incredibly talented team at Balzer + Bray, including Caroline Sun and Nellie Kurtzman and their teams, Kelsey Murphy, Sarah Kaufman and Alison Donalty, and Kathryn Silsand, for being such rock stars.

Finally, even though I already dedicated the book to her, a big thank-you to my bestie, Melinda Doolittle, for beta reading every draft and for constant encouragement while I'm writing. I couldn't ask for a better friend in my corner.

Don't miss a book in this daring series

BOOK 1

BOOK 2

DIGITAL NOVELLA

BOOK 3

JOIN THE

Epic Reads

COMMUNITY

THE ULTIMATE YA DESTINATION

◄ **DISCOVER** ►

your next favorite read

◄ **MEET** ►

new authors to love

◄ **WIN** ►

free books

◄ **SHARE** ►

infographics, playlists, quizzes, and more

◄ **WATCH** ►

the latest videos